EARTH AND WIND

Legend of East Series • Book 2

CARRIE-ANN BARNES

For Bradley, my happy delay.

Table of Contents

* * * *

One

★ ★ ★ ★

"Do you mean it, Jeff?" Miranda East asked, hopeful, "You will break it off with your fiancée?"

Alex, playing Jeff, nodded, "Of course, Cara. I really like you."

Miranda smiled. She was about to deliver her next line when her brother yelled, "Cut!" Evan rubbed his face with a frustrated hand. It was the fifth time he had stopped the filming in the last 25 minutes, all during Miranda's parts. "I need five minutes," he continued and rose from his director's chair. He walked briskly out of the studio.

Miranda looked down at her hands. She was sitting in the studio, at a restaurant set with Alex. Evan didn't say it aloud but she knew he was frustrated with her. She could picture him pacing in the hallway, muttering to himself about how he wanted to yell at her, but couldn't due to recent events.

Miranda had delivered all her lines correctly, but they were emotionless. She tried hard to focus and was trying so hard to force her sadness away that her expressions showed nothing at all. The smile she thought she gave looked twisted and fake.

Miranda looked to Alex, who wasn't looking at her. He didn't even tell her off for her terrible acting, as he normally would. He

1

hadn't even really spoken to her since the funeral two weeks ago. It was their first day back to work. Alex took a sip out of the water glass in front of him and sighed, almost inaudibly. He looked like he was about to say something when Evan returned.

Her brother looked calmer than he did when he left. He came onto the set and walked towards Miranda. "Miranda," he said, cautiously, putting a hand on his twin sister's shoulder and kneeling beside her so they were on the same level, "If you need more time, I can postpone it again."

Miranda bit her lip, her eyes filled with the tears that came so easily now, much too easily. This was all her fault. She needed to be stronger. She should have tried harder. It was her fault *he* had died. She blinked back a few tears and forced a smile, her well-practiced fake smile, "No. I am ready."

Evan frowned deeply. Would she ever be really happy here? Her first two months in Utopia had been the worst in recent Utopian history and in her entire life. The deadly attacks by the mysterious evil group had grown increasingly frequent and she was nearly killed, twice. Since Jackson's funeral she had stayed in her room and become an expert on blocking her thoughts. Her family had no idea what she was thinking anymore. Evan and the rest of her family worried that she wanted to go home and he didn't blame her.

"I am fine, really," Miranda insisted.

"Do you want to stop for the day?" Evan asked.

She shook her head, "I'm sorry. I will try harder." She stared at Evan, giving him her most convincing look that she was fine, and he gave her shoulder another squeeze.

Once they had finished her scenes, Evan told her he would need her to stay a bit longer at the studio with Alex. He needed to review the outtakes and decide whether to re-do any of the scenes. It was possible the editing team could put something decent together, but he wanted to be sure.

Miranda stared at the bare pale yellow walls on her side of the dressing room and glanced over her shoulder at Britany's side. Britany had already left to go home and her side of the room was plastered in articles about herself and pictures of her posing with a different boyfriend or co-worker each time. Her walls seemed brighter and full of life. Miranda's wall should have two articles by now, but she couldn't bear to put the picture they published of her with Jackson up on the wall. The other had been with Alex and he looked so much like his cousin. She scrolled through the pictures she had taken on her phone, which were mostly of scenery. There were a few of her new Utopian friends which she had taken at the party several weeks ago and some from the night they all went to the club. There were some of her family on race night and a good one with Greta, her brother's fiancée, at the apartment. She had lost the photos of her Earth friends when the evil ones broke into her apartment and trashed her room just before the big attack at the school but she wouldn't be able to place those in the Utopian frames anyways since they were meant for digital pictures. Miranda decided she needed something up on her wall and chose some of her favourite pictures and beamed them into the empty frames which were scattered on her wall. They were all shapes and sizes but as with all Utopian technology, the frames could be stretched or shrunk despite the sturdy appearance. Miranda got up off her chair and went over to manipulate the frames. She made her favourite of her and Greta bigger and the shrunk the ones around it to make a neat pattern.

Miranda had lived on Earth for almost 17 years. Since the year was longer on Earth than it was on her home planet, she was almost

19 in Utopian years. She had been left on Earth by her birth mother for safety. Her life on Utopia was in grave danger and her birth mother was going to bring her back when she was old enough to face her destiny, but she had died several months ago and left a message for the remaining family members telling them of Miranda's existence. Her brother, Griffin, and his friend and neighbour Alex, located her on Earth and brought her back to her real home on Utopia. Her father and brothers seemed to have no idea why she had been hidden, but Miranda had figured it out with the help of a group who had banded together to uphold the Legend and protect the children of East and West to fight the lone source of evil that plagued the planet. Miranda had never met anyone from this group aside from Jackson's mother, Marcy, and Councilman Hope, who had been killed in the recent attacks. Miranda had to learn on her own that she had capabilities that regular Utopians did not, which were enhanced when combined with her protector, Jackson. When the evil chief attacked them at the senior school, Jackson had died. Now she wasn't sure she was strong enough without him. Jackson was her soulmate. How do you live without your soulmate? She had only known him for a month and it hadn't been enough time to fall in love. Do you even have to fall in love with a soulmate? She felt so guilty. She felt it should have come naturally and it didn't. And what if the evil came back? Miranda never felt more alone.

There had been no new attacks since the attack on the school two weeks ago. It had been devastating with 26 students and teachers killed. Utopian authorities believed it was over and that everyone evil had been killed in the attack on the school. Miranda didn't know what to believe. She had killed the chief but was unsure how many evil ones were still out there. Miranda was certain that they had not defeated all of them, though she hadn't had any of her nightmares since the night of the funeral.

After Miranda had arranged the pictures of her friends, she stared down at her phone of the few pictures she had of Jackson and the article they were published in together. She needed to be positive. That was the Utopian way of life. Pictures on her wall, even if they were of Jackson, should celebrate his life and she should be happy that he was in a better place and away from the evil. She selected her favourite picture of Jackson and beamed it to a frame, and then she selected the two articles, the one with Jackson and the one with Alex, and put them on the wall too. Finally, she beamed her favourites from her photo shoot with Alex onto the wall. Miranda looked back at Britany's wall then again at her own. That was a little better. It added some colour and life to her side of the room.

Miranda would have another article to add to the wall tomorrow. *Daytime Drama* magazine had delayed the printing of the photo shoot she had done with Alex since her debut episode wouldn't air until tomorrow. It felt like months rather than only a couple weeks since she had filmed that first episode of *Northern Shores,* the famous television show created by Evan, that she had landed a part in.

Miranda admired her own easy smile in the picture taken as she had walked out of the restaurant hand in hand with Alex. She thought Alex wanted to be with her. He had even asked her not to go out with Jackson. He promised he would protect her, but now she had heard he was dating someone. As much as she had wanted to be with him, could she after Jackson's death? It didn't seem a good way to honour his memory by dating the man she had already been infatuated with, his own cousin.

Miranda turned back to the wall wind her eye caught the article about her and Jackson. She wanted to keep at least one picture of him on the wall as a memorial, but the second one had to go. She couldn't bear to look at it all the time.

"How do I take these down?" Miranda asked no one. She tried pressing on the frame but nothing happened. Then she tried beaming another picture on top, but that just meshed the two pictures together and she could still see Jackson's face. The face that looked so in love. She felt her heart start to beat faster and her breathing quickened. She needed to get it off the wall.

Miranda tried a few buttons on her phone, getting more and more frustrated. She wanted to throw her phone. Instead, she grabbed the frame and tried to rip it off the wall. When it wouldn't come off, she let out a stream of curses and the tears erupted down her face.

Evan must have heard her outburst because he was at her side in a heartbeat.

"Evan, get it off the wall!" Miranda sobbed. She hugged him tight, "Please just take it down."

Evan rubbed her back, silently, and let her cry. When she had calmed enough for him to let go, he slipped the phone out of her hands and removed the picture. "Are you OK?" he asked carefully.

Miranda nodded and wiped her face with the back of her hand. "Sorry," she muttered, embarrassed at her outburst.

"You do not have to apologize," Evan replied and then looked at the wall. "Want me to remove that one too?"

"No. I need that to stay," Miranda said, not looking back at the wall, "Can we go home now?"

Evan nodded in reply and Miranda retrieved her purse, followed him out to the elevator and didn't look back.

As they waited for the elevator, Evan stood close by her, anxious. He was glad he had not been far away. She had not had an outburst like that since the day after the funeral. They were having dinner, trying to talk about happier subjects and she threw her water glass against the far wall for no reason at all except that she felt like she was breaking down and nothing was supposed to break in Utopia. It was supposed to be perfect.

"Why can't things just break here?" she screamed after she watched the glass bounce off the golden yellow wall and hit the floor where it bounced a few more times before it rolled under the table. Then she had gone to her room and cried. No one could comfort her, she just screamed at them to go away.

Evan bit his lip, wanting to ask her something, but paused. He didn't want to upset her. "We were thinking of going skating tonight," Evan said, finally, as they stepped onto the elevator to head to the top of building.

"Oh?" Miranda asked and Evan thought he saw a small spark of intrigue return to her eyes but she blinked and it was gone. He decided he had probably just imagined it. He didn't know what to say to her or how to talk to her now. Griffin and their dad didn't know either. When trying to get her to talk to them did not work, they had suggested several different outings over the past couple weeks, dinners, movies and even a hockey game, hoping something would get her to open up to them but Miranda politely declined each.

"Just Dad, you and I, if you would like to," Evan said, "Griffin and Greta are meeting with the wedding planner tonight."

Miranda shrugged and nodded as she followed Evan out of the elevator. "OK," she agreed. Her eldest brother, Griffin, and his fiancée, Greta, had set their wedding date for January 10th, just over two months away. Miranda had agreed to stand beside Greta at the ceremony and Evan would stand beside Griffin. She wasn't sure yet what the ceremony entailed but knew it would take place at City Hall. There were banquet centres available to use for weddings.

Evan pushed the 'call' button to get a bus pickup and they both sat on the bench, alone. Everyone else seemed to have left for the day. He studied his sister as she sat with her head down. She looked a lot thinner. She had been working out prior to the latest trauma, but now she had abruptly stopped and barely ate. She would push her food around her plate and they would have to reverse it and put it back into the bottles it had come from.

"Where is Alex?" she asked curiously, wondering why he was avoiding her. Perhaps it was for the best.

"He left already," Evan said, looking away. His lips formed a hard line.

Miranda went quiet till the bus showed up. She read Evan's mind clearly. Alex was out with some girl. He had left the minute Evan had told him the outtakes were fine and did not reply when Evan asked if he wanted to go skating that night. Evan assumed he was not coming. He barely saw him the last two weeks, as well. He seemed to be avoiding the whole family.

Evan tried to make small talk on the bus and Miranda offered very little to the conversation. Once they were home, she went to her room to practice her lines for the next day. Evan had prepared an eventful day tomorrow, and her scenes would be light and playful as she interacted with Alex. She watched herself in the mirror, trying to act natural, but it made her feel bad to be happy, especially when Jackson would never feel anything again.

Miranda skipped dinner with her family that night and lay on her bed, staring vacantly at her purple walls. She wondered how her father did it. He had recently lost her mother, his wife of 26 years. How did he cope? She wanted to talk to him about it, but wasn't sure if it would hurt him to talk about his wife. If he could cope with the loss of his soulmate, someone with whom he had been married happily for such a long time, then why couldn't she cope with the death of a man she had only known for just over a month? She finally came to the conclusion that she needed to get out of this room. Although she wasn't sure what her father had done when her mother died, she was sure it wasn't sit in his room and cry. Perhaps she should accept the offer to go skating after all.

When Evan knocked on her bedroom door at 26:25 to head to the arena, he was surprised to find her dressed and ready to go. He was so sure that she was going to decline again and give another lame excuse that he had not even gotten ready. Claiming he forgot something in his room, he went to quickly change. Their father had been more hopeful and was ready to go.

They went up to the parking garage and got into the family vehicle. Miranda sat quietly in the back and listened as her dad and Evan argued about the hockey game they had watched last night. She smiled a few times at them. Evan was so passionate about his team and it reminded Miranda of herself. She saw so much of herself in him. Their chocolate brown hair was the exact same shade, they shared the same bright blue eyes and even a love of acting and hockey. It was obvious they were twins even though they hadn't grown up in the same house, or even on the same planet.

Once they got to the arena, she got excited. Miranda drew in a deep breath. Although in Utopia everything tended to smell like flowers, the arena still had that fresh, cool scent tinged with sweat.

She followed her dad to the store inside the arena, where the skates were rented and sold.

"How about we just buy you a pair?" her dad suggested, "I am sure we will use them a lot."

Miranda nodded and sent him a fake smile.

The skates were custom made to fit her foot perfectly. They did not take long to make either. Miranda took a quick walk around the store in her new skates, surprised at the comfort. Her skates on Earth used to dig into her ankle bone. On her feet, they looked sleeker than her skates on Earth and they were all black, even the blade.

"What are they made of?" she asked, looking down at them.

"I do not believe you would know the alloy. It is similar to Earth steel but we call it dificiem," her father explained.

"Do I have to take them off?" Miranda asked as she sat down again, "Can I walk to the ice?" Her dad nodded as he finished paying for them with his card and led the way to the benches where he and Evan put on their skates.

Miranda anxiously waited for them, taking in the arena. The boards that normally surrounded the ice surface for the hockey games were removed for the public skate and there was a crowd of 50 or more on the ice already. There were dark grey rafters which looked a lot like the rinks on Earth, the difference being any banners or awards flying high. Instead, the local hockey team, the City 217 Arundinas (named after the flower emblem that adorned the city buses and school uniforms) had their awards displayed on the digital frames above the seating. The arena had a capacity of about 10,000 in the red seating that encircled the ice. Miranda turned her back on the rink and watched impatiently as they each tightened their laces.

Someone behind her came to an abrupt stop, sending a snow shower her way.

"What the..." she said, brushing the flakes of snow off of her, and turned to see who would do that to her.

Alex was there wearing a half smile and his usual baseball cap pulled low to hide his face, "Hi Maddie! What are you waiting for? Show me what you can do!" And he took off through the small crowd of people. Miranda saw a flash of the green Razorblades jersey that he had been wearing through the crowd. A lot of the people on the ice had their jerseys on. Even Evan had his Star Shooters jersey on. Miranda suddenly wanted one too. This time, Miranda sent a genuine smile to her dad and Evan and then turned back to the rink, excited and nervous to step out on the ice. She was nervous about the new skates and had not skated in at least half a year.

Miranda took a little step onto the ice, wishing the hockey boards were up so she could hold onto them for a minute for support. Alex was heading her way again and she covered her face, letting out a squeal of laughter before he snow showered her again.

He took off again, chuckling as he went. She hesitantly took a few test strides before she skated after him. When she had just about caught up to him, he stopped abruptly again.

Miranda swore under her breath and tried to stop. She had never been very good at it. She slowed a bit but couldn't stop her momentum. When she hit him, it felt like she had hit a parked truck and she bounced off, falling backwards. He reached out and encircled his arms around her, easing her gently down to the ice.

Alex chuckled as he straightened up, "Can you not stop, Maddie?" He put a hand out to help her up.

"No," she grumbled, taking his hand. She brushed the snow off her black cotton pants, "I was never really good at it."

"Well you almost had it. Just try to twist your hips more and put more weight on that left leg there," he coached and then demonstrated.

She copied him and smiled, "I can do it slow. I just get nervous when I am moving faster."

"Come with me then," Alex took her hand and picked up speed. When they had reached a good speed, Alex gave her a quick look, "You ready?" She shrugged and he counted down from three.

Alex stopped on a button. Miranda skidded a little and fell again. Without him to ease her down, she hit the ice hard.

He laughed and held a hand out to help her up again. She rubbed her sore backside and brushed the snow off again.

"You dug in too much," he explained, "Another try?"

They tried a few more times. Miranda got a little better but still couldn't stop as quickly as Alex could.

Evan skated up to them, their dad close behind. Mr. East was smiling at Miranda. Miranda could hear in his mind that he was so happy to see her laughing and smiling. He suffered just as much, she remembered again. He had lost his wife but that wasn't to say she shouldn't mourn for Jackson. She probably would have married him and she had lost that future.

Miranda sighed and stopped thinking altogether before she could get depressed again. She had only known Jackson a month. Who knows what would have happened?

Evan and her dad were staring at her, so she sent them a fake smile. They both shared a knowing look, understanding for a second that she had been happy and then they had somehow ruined it. Neither knew what she had been thinking.

"This is fun," Miranda said, and took a deep breath as she rearranged her face into a better smile. "Can we play hockey on Sunday?" she asked Evan, "Or maybe I can watch you guys play?"

"Yes, of course" Evan agreed and Alex nodded as well.

"Ok, then I will need to practice," Miranda said and turned away, not wanting to face their concerned looks anymore. The others followed and they spent the rest of the two hours racing around to see who was the fastest. Alex won each time. He looked so at ease on the ice. It made her jealous. Everything seemed to come easy to him.

Miranda hit the shower when they returned home, relishing in the heat of the water from the shower heads. She was severely disappointed again when they automatically shut off, missing the long showers she had on Earth, especially after being in the cold arena. She had a great time skating and she really needed to cheer up. Hiding and being miserable was not a great way to remember Jackson. Her brothers and father were dealing with the loss of their mother a lot better than she was dealing with Jackson's death. Even Alex dealt with his grief over the loss of his sister in a healthier way. Nevertheless, it didn't help her cope when she felt like she had lost the only person who understood what she was going through. On top of the grief and the guilt, she worried about evil and what she would do without Jackson if it returned. She imagined the ground trembling so often that sometimes she thought she was going insane. And on top of the grief, the guilt and the worry, she missed her Earth family and friends terribly. She was happy they weren't here though. Anyone who had been near her during her time on Utopia was in danger.

Miranda went out to the living room, something she hadn't done in the past two weeks. Her dad, Griffin and Greta were on the black leather couch, and Mr. East was talking about the skate.

Each masked their looks of shock as she joined them, taking a seat on the chair.

"Do you think we can watch today's episode of the show?" Miranda asked, "I would like to see how I look." She flashed them a smile, an authentic smile, not faking at all.

"Yes, of course," her dad smiled back, "Alpha, can you tune to today's episode of *Northern Shores*." Alpha was the apartment control unit. It controlled basically everything in the apartment from clothing, to lights, windows and, apparently, the television as well.

The television changed to the start of the episode.

Miranda gasped, "Oh! I thought you had to use the remote?"

Griffin chuckled, "Well, no. You can also use voice control but it is usually rude when other people are having a conversation."

"Cool!" Miranda exclaimed. She sat back as the episode started. "I won't be in till the very end at the party," she told them.

Evan joined them about halfway through. He also looked surprised to see Miranda there, but brushed it off quick as he took a seat on the floor by Miranda's feet.

"You should be coming up shortly," Evan said, looking up at her with a smile, "Are we all going to watch tomorrow's episode as soon as it is released?"

Mr. East nodded, "And then I think a celebration dinner is in order."

Miranda smiled, a little nervous for everyone to see her. She hadn't seen the finished product yet either.

"You did an amazing job. It looks great," Evan answered her thoughts, which she hadn't blocked, "I will have to get to the studio early tomorrow if I want to leave early so Alex can drive you there."

Miranda put up her mental block. It would be the first time she would be alone with Alex since before the funeral. A warm rush tickled her spine but she forced it away. She couldn't do that to Jackson, she thought as she frowned.

"Oh you look gorgeous!" Greta gushed, as Miranda made her first appearance on the television. Miranda looked up in time to see herself as the camera panned the room.

Mr. East agreed, "Absolutely beautiful." He reached over and squeezed her hand.

They all headed to bed after the episode finished. Miranda slept soundly, exhausted after the excitement on the ice.

Miranda knocked on Alex's door the next morning when he didn't show up at her apartment. They were going to be late. She had taken a long time to get ready since she had been nervously pacing in her room trying to convince herself that the episode was going to look great and that she deserved a part in the show. Although she knew they were going to dress her anyways for the scenes, she still wanted to look good. She ended up choosing her teal sundress. She also went for some light pink lip gloss and a bit of pink blush.

The door opened and a girl Miranda recognized stood there.

"Oh hi Miranda!" she exclaimed.

"Hello," Miranda returned with a frown, as she remembered where she recognized her from. She was wearing a tightly-fit button up black shirt and black pants, her work uniform. She was the waitress at the pasta restaurant that Alex had taken Miranda to. She was very pretty.

"Alex is just finishing up and we can go," she smiled, excitedly.

"Are you coming to the studio?" Miranda asked, curiously.

"Oh, no," she replied, "Alex agreed to drop me off at work on the way."

Miranda's mental wall went up as she chewed her bottom lip. Had she spent the entire night? She must have! Why would she take the bus here in the morning just to get dropped off at work?

Alex stepped out of his bathroom, ready to go in a yellow button down shirt and navy pants. "Hi," he smiled at her, "Are you ready?"

Miranda nodded, still chewing on her lip.

He put his shoes on and led the way to the airy parking garage. Alex's blue car was parked on pillars next to a blank spot which Mr. East's car normally occupied. Without saying anything, Miranda climbed into the backseat to let the girl have the front. Alex's car was always clean. He made sure to take care of it since it was also his race car, which he competed in anonymously most Saturday nights. Miranda erased the concern on her face and pasted a smile on. It shouldn't bother her that this girl was with him. Didn't she decide that she would never date Alex? She chatted politely with the girl on the way to her work while Alex silently drove across the town.

Alex let out a big sigh after the girl had gotten out of his car, "Come on, get in the front," he turned to Miranda. He didn't get out of the car to walk the girl into her work, nor did he kiss her goodbye, although it was obvious she wanted him to.

Miranda got out, said goodbye to the waitress, whose name she had never got, and slipped into the front seat.

"That was kind of rude," Miranda scolded after she shut the door.

Alex made a face, "She showed up at my apartment early this morning in hopes we could..." he paused and took a deep breath, "I just do not think I will be talking to her anymore."

"Oh," Miranda replied, a little shocked, "Sorry Alex. Did you like her?"

Alex shrugged, "She just liked me because of who I am. She got in the news like she wanted as my new girlfriend."

Miranda didn't know whether to believe that she hadn't spent the night.

"No," Alex snapped, "Do not even think that way again."

Miranda rolled her eyes. She couldn't help it. It sounded outrageous to her that someone would go to someone else's house in the morning, just for *that*. And the only way the news would report her as his girlfriend, would be if they had come right out and announced it.

Alex huffed and stepped on the gas. The car punched forward and Miranda grabbed the sides of her seat. If he was trying to scare her, it didn't work. She loved when he drove fast, though she was still afraid of the height they flew, and had to clutch the seat.

"Of course she announced it," Alex snapped, "They all do."

"Well, grow a pair and say no," Miranda retorted. She rolled her eyes. Alex was such a strong person, she had no idea why he would let girls walk all over him.

Alex barked out a laugh, his bad mood dissipated quickly and he sent her a small smile, "Grow a pair?"

Miranda blushed. She really didn't want to tell him that it meant grow a pair of balls, but he heard it in her mind and cracked up laughing. They didn't use a lot of Earth sayings in Utopia and Alex always found it amusing.

"Perhaps you should race," Alex said as his laughter faded. They neared the large windowed building of the studio in no time at all. "Since you seem to like the speed."

Miranda shrugged, "I don't even know how to drive. I had my beginner's license on Earth, but this looks complicated." She pointed to the buttons on the dashboard before putting her hand back. Sometimes she wished they had seatbelts on Utopia.

"I can teach you tonight. We can go to the track. They have it set up for the race tomorrow night."

"Sorry Alex," Miranda said, she turned to look at him, "We are going to dinner tonight after the episode airs. Are you coming as well?"

"Right, of course I am," Alex replied. He thought about it for a second and asked, "How about after work tomorrow before the race?"

Miranda nodded. It would be fun to learn how to drive.

"It is pretty simple."

"Hopefully you are a good driver and will not teach me any bad habits," Miranda teased with a small smile.

Alex glanced her way and smiled wide, "I am a great driver." He pushed a few buttons and skilfully parked in their work parking garage. Normally this was done on auto-pilot, but Alex loved to show-off his skills.

Miranda waited in her dressing room for Evan to be finished for the day. She was thought about waiting with Alex, but it still felt awkward to be with him. That morning had been fun, but she couldn't see the good mood between them lasting very long. It never did.

Alex entered her dressing room 10 minutes later, smiling. He tossed her his phone which she caught expertly and sent him a questioning look before she looked at it. It was their faces on the cover of *Daytime Drama* magazine! Her mouth dropped. She had almost forgotten it came out today. She swiped through the pages to the article and read.

The interview had been with her brother. He introduced her to the world and gave small indications about where the show was headed. Everyone would know now that she was likely going to break up Jeff and Janet. The pictures were proof. There was a full page picture of just her. It was a great picture. She had seen it before in the proofs but to see it available for all of Utopia was so exciting!

"Holy crap!" she exclaimed and jumped up off her studio chair.

She was so ecstatic that she hugged Alex tight, bouncing on her toes. "So cool! Look! I look awesome!" She showed him the picture of her.

He chuckled, "Yes, you do look great!" He took his phone back, "I read it already. You can set those frames to a slideshow of the whole article," he said, pointing to the frames. "I can see you learned how to send them to the frames."

He went over to her pictures on the wall and was quiet. His smile disappeared.

She went to stand beside him, her smile fading as well. She turned to him, "Can you show me how to do the slideshow?"

Alex looked down at his phone and selected the pages, then sent them to an empty frame beside the other picture of the both of them. The cover photo appeared in the frame. Shortly after, it changed to the first picture in the article of just herself, then to the article with other small pictures of her and Alex.

"I guess you have seen the magazine," Evan said from the door. He was a little anxious seeing her standing next to that wall of photos again, especially after yesterday.

Miranda pasted a smile on her face and turned from the frames, "Yes! Thanks Evan! Your interview was fantastic!"

Evan shrugged, "I had an easy subject, my dear twin." Miranda smiled up at him. "Are you ready to go watch your debut?" Evan asked.

"Yep! Let's go!" she said, her nervous excitement returning. She followed Evan and Alex trailed along behind.

When they got back to the East apartment, everyone was gathered in the living room. The show was about to start.

Miranda saw her smiling face staring back at her as her name flashed on the screen during the opening credits and everyone cheered. She had filmed that short piece just yesterday at the beach location. She was sitting on the sand, looking out over the water. All she had to do was look towards the camera and smile. Alex appeared right after her. He was filmed on the pier, also looking out over the water. He leaned back against the rail, and turned his head to the camera and his name flashed on the screen. He wore a button down shirt that was half open and Miranda stared at his well-formed chest before she shook her head. *No, do not look at Alex like that*, she coached herself. She couldn't like him, not anymore. As much as seeing him in that scene made her want to run her hands over his pecs, she convinced herself that it was wrong. It was not fair to Jackson to be this obsessed over his cousin.

Miranda pushed all thoughts out of her head and sat back on the couch to watch her debut episode. She smiled to herself as she watched the dance scene. She looked very elegant in her high heels as she swayed perfectly in time with Alex.

When it was over, they all congratulated her on how well she did and Greta gushed about how great the dress looked on her and praised her toned physique in the bikini. Miranda had to admit, she did look beautiful in that dress. "I don't know about the bikini though," Miranda went pink. Everyone who watched the show had now seen her in a bathing suit. She tried to remember the scene, if she had any fat sticking out anywhere. She would definitely have to watch it again later.

"You are gorgeous!" Greta said, "Do not be embarrassed."

"I have a surprise for you," Evan smiled.

"What is it?" Miranda asked, excited. They always had pretty awesome surprises.

"Well, that dress is now yours," he said, "I brought it home yesterday and Alpha has stored it with your other clothes."

"Are you serious?" she said jumping out of her seat. She hugged Evan, smiling, "Thank you so much for everything."

Evan shrugged, "We get all our clothes donated for free advertisement. Do you know how many girls are going to want that dress you wore? Sherry Mornington is going to be swamped with orders for it."

"So, where do you all want to eat tonight?" Mr. East asked.

"We should go to Vacca. I bet everyone will be excited to see Miranda. It will be expected," Alex suggested as he stood, "I am buying." Excitement radiated from him. He was so happy the episode looked good.

"Yes, I suppose she will be expected at Vacca tonight but you are not paying," Mr. East said, "This is my treat."

"We shall see," Alex said, with a wink."

Greta grabbed Miranda's hand excitedly and pulled her into Miranda's room.

She wanted to see Miranda's dress in real life.

"Oh, it is gorgeous," Greta said when Alpha had deposited it into her hands, "but way too fancy for the dinner tonight. Do you have something to wear? I think I have the perfect dress for you."

Miranda agreed to wear what Greta had and Greta asked Alpha to bring it. She held out the dress for Miranda to see. It was a short blue silky halter dress, the same colour as Miranda's eyes.

"Put it on!" Greta said, "It is too short for me so it might fit you perfect! You can have it if you like. I wore it years ago at the annual Utopia Ball."

Miranda grinned from ear to ear, "Thank you so much!" She had learned previously that Utopia had an annual ball to celebrate peace on January 1st. Everyone had the day off and a huge outdoor festival was put on in every city which concluded with an outdoor ball.

She put the dress on, realizing the back was completely open, showing off her slender lower back. She had never worn anything like that except maybe as a bathing suit at the beach. She bit her lip and sent Greta a nervous glance.

"Wow, that looks better on you than it did on me," Greta assured her.

Miranda turned her back to the mirror and glanced behind her shoulder, staring at her bare, unmarked back. Her spine was more pronounced now and she bit her lip again, wondering when she got so thin. She had never worn anything that showed off her back like this. This was sexier than Helen's short skirt, but more of a 'classy' sexy instead. Miranda looked back to Greta, "I don't know. This is a little much for me." She chuckled and peeked again at her exposed back, "Or I should say too little for me."

Greta shook her head, as she stepped into a simpler yellow dress that she had brought into Miranda's room for herself, "Do not be embarrassed, you look stunning." Greta's dress was short as well and gathered to one shoulder.

Miranda stopped to admire her soon to be sister-in-law. She looked beautiful as well and Miranda was happy to have her in her life. She could imagine how much more difficult her time adjusting to her new life would have been without Greta. She needed the woman's perspective. Miranda thought about telling her everything but was afraid to scare her or get Greta involved. Instead, she just gave her a hug. Greta squeezed back tightly.

They both had their makeup and hair done by Alpha and Miranda looked in the mirror again at the finished product. Her hair was swept up into a hairstyle that would have taken her forever to do on Earth.

"Alpha, can you add my jewel pins to Miranda's hair," Greta asked, and the dome encircled Miranda's head again.

Tiny jewels that looked like diamonds were tucked into perfect places in her hair. Her eyes filled with happy tears. She was so happy to have Greta and felt guilty for shutting her out of her life for the past two weeks.

"Can I tell you something before we go?" Greta stopped her before she could leave.

"Of course."

"You really look great together," Greta smiled, her eyebrows raised. She motioned to the picture of her and Alex that had made its way to a frame on Miranda's desk, "I saw the article today. It was really nice."

Miranda looked away. Yes, they did photograph well together but she didn't want to have feelings for him. She couldn't! Not after Jackson.

Greta heard her thoughts, "Jackson will understand that you have to move on."

"I can't like him," Miranda said, her happy tears fading to real ones.

"Do not cry," Greta said, giving her a quick hug, "You and Alex have cared about each other so much, from the very first time I saw you both together."

"Am I that obvious?"

"So is he. I was sitting beside him on the couch during the show. I could not hear all of his thought but I could sense his confusion and his guilt. I really think the two of you need to talk about it and…"

Miranda shook her head, "I just can't Greta. I know he doesn't feel the same. He is a great actor."

Greta sighed. "From what I gathered, Evan and Griffin told him just to be nicer, not to pretend he was interested in dating."

Miranda frowned. She wanted so much to believe that he felt the same way but didn't at the same time. She took some deep calming breaths trying hard to get rid of her tears before they fell and she would have to redo her makeup.

"Miranda, I know that the last few weeks have been very hard. I wanted so much to try and help you in any way. Griffin thought I should just leave you and let you come around but I want you to know that I am here for you when you need to talk about it."

"Thanks," Miranda said, blinking away her tears.

"I really believe you two should talk," Greta said, motioning to the picture again, "I am sure Alex also feels guilty about his cousin but..."

"Ladies!" Evan interrupted from down the hall, "We are hungry!"

Greta cast an annoyed look over her shoulder at the doorway, then took Miranda's hands in hers. "We can talk later," Greta said with a sigh, as she squeezed her hands, "You look beautiful."

Miranda smiled, "You do as well." She gave Greta another hug before following her out of the bedroom and down the hall. The men were all waiting at the door in their suit pants and shirts, with their shoes on, ready to go. Miranda's dad smiled at Greta as she walked down the hall and when Miranda stepped out from behind her, his mouth dropped. He was stunned, speechless.

"Seriously," Evan said, shaking his head at Greta, "I am having enough trouble keeping the men in line when it comes to her." He motioned with his head to Miranda.

Greta laughed and shrugged. She smiled innocently at Griffin who shook his head at her as well.

Miranda laughed and rolled her eyes.

Forget it Evan, she is mine, Miranda swore she heard Alex think, but no one else seemed to react to it so she dismissed it.

"Oh wait, Miranda. I have got shoes to go with that dress!" Greta said and then told Alpha to retrieve them. A pair of high-heeled silver shoes were deposited on the floor. They matched perfectly.

Alex was beside her when she stood up after putting them on and held his arm out to her which she took with a smile. Greta had her arm laced with Griffin's and they walked side by side out the door. Evan and their father were last out and shut the door behind them.

The group went up to the parking garage.

"Ev, come with us?" Alex asked, "I am going to take her to the valet and up the gauntlet of reporters."

Evan nodded, a little reluctantly, and followed them to Alex's car.

Miranda took the back seat and her stomach danced with butterflies. She hoped all of Utopia had liked her debut as much as her family had. Alex kept Mr. East's car in his rear view mirror as they made their way across the city.

When they got there, Miranda noticed a large amount of reporters, more than she had seen the last time.

"There are extra reporters because they are expecting us," Evan explained, "This is a popular place to be on a Friday night, especially after a debut episode."

"Oh crap," she said, her hands started to sweat, "I don't think I can do this."

"You will be just fine. We will be there right beside you and we have done this a million times," Alex said and he pulled up to the front of the red carpet. The windows in the back were tinted so no one could see her but they saw Alex and Evan. "Stay right there," Alex said, turning to look at her with a smile, "I will get your door." His eyes were lit up with excitement again.

Both Evan and Alex got out of the car and before Miranda knew what was going on, loud clicks started going off everywhere. Alex ignored the shouts from the reporters and came around to Miranda's side of the car, opening the back door. He took her hand and pulled her out. The cameras once again started clicking furiously as Miranda smiled nervously. Questions came at them from all around.

"You do not have to answer anything you do not want to. Just smile," Alex instructed quietly, linking arms with her, again. They joined Evan, who had moved ahead of them. He was smiling and talking to a man about his interview in *Daytime Drama*.

"*City 217* newspaper!" a woman called excitedly, looking at Miranda and Alex, "Are you two dating now? You looked very lovely together on the pages of *Daytime Drama*!"

A few offered their condolences to Miranda for the loss of her boyfriend and to Alex for his cousin. Miranda tried to smile appreciatively but her eyes welled with tears.

"Mr. East! What is going to happen in the show next?" a man shouted, noticing their discomfort and trying to change the subject.

"I will not be giving anymore hints apart from what I already gave to *Daytime Drama*," Evan winked.

"Miranda, lovely dress! Who are you wearing?" another woman called out.

Miranda smiled and told her what was on the tag, though she wasn't even sure who that was since it was Greta's dress. But the woman smiled excitedly and made a note of it. They all posed for the camera. Miranda even spun and gave them her best over the shoulder look so that everyone could see the back of her dress, which was non-existent. It was a pose she had seen some of her favourite actresses on Earth do.

"Come on then! We are getting hungry!" Griffin called out from the door. He, their dad and Greta were already standing there. Mr. East had parked his own car, so they had reached the doors sooner.

"Excuse us," Alex told the reporters with a smile, "Our family and friends are waiting."

Once they had taken a few steps away, Evan stepped beside his sister, "And where did you learn how to pose like that, my dear sister?"

Miranda smiled at him, innocently, "Hollywood, darling," Miranda drawled and then giggled.

Evan rolled his eyes, "You are going to make my 'big brother' job very difficult."

Miranda poked him in the ribs with her elbow, "Leave that to Griffin. You, my dear brother, are only minutes older."

Once inside, they were seated quickly at a private booth. This one was a round table that was surrounded by a three-quarter circle of dark blue wall to keep the other patrons from staring. There were long horizontal mirrors running the length of the wall. Beautiful drop lighting lit up the space, dazzling off the crystals that hung from the lighting and off the mirrors.

Miranda sighed happily as she caught her reflection. *This is definitely something I can handle*, she thought excitedly as she rounded towards the back of the table. She'd never gotten so much attention in her whole life. It was only something she had ever dreamed of.

"You look beautiful," Alex whispered in her ear as he took the seat beside her.

She shivered at the feel of his breath on her neck, *Oh no, it is too soon*. She couldn't do that to Jackson. She sent Alex a smile as he sat down beside her but frowned when she looked away from him. He looked great as well. She noticed that they matched. He was wearing a blue collared shirt and a blue and silver tie, almost like they had planned it. His blue made his eyes look an even deeper blue. She tried not to stare at him but couldn't help herself, and she clasped her hands together to stop the urge to run her hand across the smooth tan skin of his hand that he had rested on the table near her.

Two

★ ★ ★ ★

It was a cheerful and fun dinner. Everyone was so excited for Miranda. Even Miranda let herself be happy, truly happy for the first time in weeks. Alex surprised Miranda during dinner by telling her he had planned a small party to celebrate her, the new cast member. He had invited all their coworkers that day and had sent messages to their friends in the building to come to his apartment that night. It was then that Miranda's dad snuck away to pay before Alex did. He pre-emptively bought another two rounds of drinks for those who were drinking. They stayed at the restaurant for just over two hours laughing and talking. Mostly about events that happened before Miranda arrived on Utopia.

"Come on, we have to take to the gauntlet one more time," Alex said to her as they were finally preparing to leave. He clasped her hand as they all rose from the table.

Miranda looked to Evan, who shook his head. "Most probably went home by now. I am going to go with them," Evan said, motioning with his head to the others and then smiled, "It is the two of you they want anyways."

Miranda had hoped her brother would go with them. It was hard to be alone with Alex. She glanced at her twin brother one last time who gave her an encouraging smile as she followed Alex out the front door.

There were only two reporters left and the questions started again.

"How was your dinner Miss East?" the same man who had addressed her brother earlier called out.

"Excellent, of course," Miranda gushed and smiled.

The reporter looked down at their adjoined hands as they stopped in front of him. He asked about their relationship again and the woman beside him looked at Miranda and Alex, hopeful to get exclusive news.

Alex went quiet and started to fidget. He let go of her hand.

Miranda wanted to tell them. She wanted them to know she would never betray Jackson like that. "No, we are not together."

Alex looked at her, with surprise.

"Alex is my best friend," Miranda told them. She squeezed Alex's arm, "I love him like a friend and a brother. We grew up together, we played together, we fought and we made up. I admire him so much but we will only ever be friends."

She saw Alex nod in agreement out of the corner of her eye. The two reporters looked disappointed and made a note of it.

"We are having a party," Alex said, "You are both welcome. The entire cast will be there."

Both smiled and thanked Alex for the invitation.

"Why didn't you want to answer that question?" Miranda asked once they were in his car and in the air, "By not saying anything, it seems like we are hiding something."

"Not in Utopia. We do not misinterpret silence as we are hiding something here. Not like they do on Earth." He didn't look at her, his eyes on the road. After a moment, Alex shrugged, "You gave a good answer. Everyone will understand that we are just good friends. We grew up together which is why we work so well together."

Yes, they did look great together but not because they grew up together. *So why?* Miranda went quiet, wondering if they should talk about their feelings, like Greta had suggested.

"Perhaps we should" he mumbled, glancing her way.

Miranda chewed on her bottom lip. She knew she hadn't blocked her thoughts and was hoping Alex would say something but now that he did, her palms started to sweat. She wished she hadn't said anything. She took a deep breath. "I guess I just want to know what is going on with us and if I even want there to be an us. I'm confused about how I feel about you. You pretended to be nice to stop me from dating before, so I am not sure if that was real or just acting. You said..." Miranda stopped and took a breath, thinking of the conversation they had as he had held her close after one of her nightmares.

Alex's mouth snapped shut and he looked away. The words, *his* words, echoed in his head as well. His hands whitened as he gripped the steering handles. He cleared his mind. *No*, he muttered in his mind. He closed his mind from her.

"What? What's wrong?" Miranda asked. She scolded herself inwardly for letting that all out. Maybe Greta was wrong and she shouldn't have started this conversation or taken it to the next level.

"You really are a great person," he delivered in a monotonous tone, staring out at the window, "but I cannot be with you now." He didn't even look at her when he said it.

Miranda's heart almost stopped. She stopped breathing for a second as she felt her already broken heart rip again. It was fine, she tried to convince herself. She was fine. This was what she wanted anyways, right? She opened and closed her mouth, thinking of something to say. "So everything today, taking my arm, calling me beautiful. It was an act?"

Alex looked at her again then out the window, "No, Miranda, you are beautiful..." He paused. "I… you… you made your decision, Miranda. You wanted to stay with him."

Miranda was happy that they pulled into his parking spot just then. She wanted to get away from Alex. Of course she had chosen Jackson, she had to! They were meant to be together, the Legend had said so. Even though Alex didn't know any of this, she was furious that he put the blame on her. She had to stop all this with Alex. It wasn't fair to Jackson even now that he was gone. "Fine," she said, her tone steady, which even surprised herself. She stuck her hand out, "Friends?"

Alex looked at her hand, a mixture of emotions on his face. He hesitated before he took it. "Friends," he said flatly.

Miranda got out of the car and slammed his door shut. She walked briskly ahead but the wait for the elevator gave him a chance to catch up.

Miranda kept her thoughts in check. It *was* what she wanted.

"So?" Alex asked.

"So this is my fault?" Miranda snapped. Forget fairness, she was angry at him for blaming her. She had no choice in the matter!

"No," Alex replied, sadly, "I blame myself. We just should not be together."

Miranda sighed, frustrated, "Fine. I said just friends."

The elevator doors opened and they stepped inside. "Would you like to know my opinion on why?" Alex asked.

Miranda let out an angry breath. "Whatever the reason, Alex, if it is coming from you it is obviously twisted and screwed up and I do *not* care," she snapped, haughtily. The doors opened to their floor and loud music. People were spilling out of Alex's apartment already, and Miranda was all too happy to be separated from Alex by everyone.

"It is about time the guests of honour showed up!" Britany shouted. She seemed to stumble towards them in her short animal print skirt, apparently already feeling the effects of her drinking. She snagged Alex away and he readily followed.

Alicia ran up and pulled Miranda to the living room, excited to talk to her. They took a seat on Alex's couches. Alicia was Miranda's very first friend she made in Utopia and Miranda had not seen her since the funeral, even though Alicia lived in the same building. Her father was the building manager. Miranda noticed that Alicia had dressed up in a red strapless mini-dress. Her long blonde hair was swept up into a pile of curls and she wore red lipstick. She took a peek at everyone around the room. It was a pretty elite party, she supposed. Most of the cast were there, all dressed up. Alicia told her she watched the show and thought she did excellent.

"I cannot believe you get to be with Alex on the show! And you never told me!" Alicia laughed.

Miranda sent her an apologetic smile, "Sorry Alicia. I was not allowed to say anything."

"I understand," Alicia took her hand, "How are you? I have not seen you in weeks and I was afraid to call."

Miranda nodded, "I am OK." Miranda squeezed her hand, "And you? How are you holding up?" Miranda felt bad. Alicia had lost her best friend, Tina, in the attack on the school. Miranda was selfish to feel like the only one grieving. Miranda would be beyond devastated if Helen, her best friend on Earth, had been killed.

"My mother wants to move," Alicia frowned, her eyes swam with tears, "Dad is trying to talk her out of it."

"Oh no!"

Alicia held her tears back. She brushed her cheek with her hand checking to make sure none had fallen. "I am coping. It is hard to wake up every day and remember that Tina is not here anymore. But I do not think leaving will help. I cannot wait for the school to reopen and put this whole thing behind us. Get back to some normalcy. Are you seeing the grief counselors?"

Miranda shook her head. She had declined the invite when it came. She had too much in her mind that a therapist would be able to read. Her father had wanted her to, but Miranda adamantly declined until Mr. East finally gave up.

"They really help," Alicia said and frowned again, "I am not as sad as I was before."

"I am so sorry, Alicia," Miranda's eyes had filled with tears as well, "I have not been a good friend. I should have called you to ask how you were. I have just been so consumed in my own grief."

Alicia shook her head, "It is fine. I have also been keeping to myself. We will both be better friends now."

Miranda agreed.

"So what else can you tell me about the show?" Alicia asked, reaching for a new subject, "Anything exciting?"

Miranda thought about it. The sixth script was sure going to be interesting. The one she had practiced with Alex in his bed. They had gotten carried away and only stopped when Miranda's phone rang. They would be taping that episode on Monday, "Well, just wait five days. That should be an interesting episode." She looked for Alex in the crowd.

Alex was talking to one of the other cast members by the stereo and she caught his eye. They held each other's gaze a moment before she turned away first.

"Wow," Alicia exclaimed excitedly. She looked at Alex and back at Miranda, "You get to do that with Alex? Or should I say pretend to do that!"

Miranda went pink. She had given away the story line.

"I will not tell, I promise," Alicia said, seriously. "You looked upset when you got out of the elevator with Alex. Anything you want to talk about? I am here if you need it."

Miranda shook her head, "Thank you, but I really don't want to talk about him right now. Maybe we can talk another day."

Mr. East, Evan, Griffin and Greta joined the party, after going back to their own apartment to freshen up.

After spending some time with Alicia, Miranda tried to talk to everyone and get to know the cast members. She had never felt so popular. It seemed like everyone wanted to talk to her. She really got along with Britany, which was great, because Britany invited her to go out dancing sometime in the near future. Miranda excitedly agreed. She wanted to see some new places in the city.

When Miranda finally made it around the room to her group of friends she had made from the apartment, she was feeling pretty tipsy. She spent the first few minutes catching up with Rebecca, Jane, Greg and Nathan. These friends were all out of school and in the working world and reported nothing too exciting going on in their lives since they last spoke. Jane did get to see her favourite band, Illuminous, the previous night which she gushed about but Miranda had never heard of them. Jane pulled out her phone and pushed a few buttons.

"I have sent you their songs," Jane winked and slipped her phone back into her pocket.

Miranda heard a faint sound coming from her purse and thanked her. Aside from the one concert she had been to of Alex's favourite band, The Trees, Miranda had not been exposed to much Utopian music.

Nathan complimented her on her show.

"You watched it?" Miranda asked, excitedly.

"Of course I did," he laughed, "Everyone watches it." Rebecca and Jane nodded in agreement.

"Wow, I almost did not believe it when Greta told me how popular it was."

"It is a great show!" Rebecca smiled, "And you did so well!"

"Everyone loves the show," Greg added, "It is fun to see another culture alive on the screen since there are so few actual sentient beings in the universe. There is another show called Zeta One about the destruction of the planet Ingrid. The people there are very similar to us though. They all moved to another system when they realized their sun was about die out."

Miranda smiled though she had never seen or heard of the show. There was a lot of things she didn't know about Utopia. It had been just about two months since she had moved here and a lot had happened in those two months.

Nathan stepped in close, putting a hand on the exposed small of her back. "Can I interest you in a walk?" he asked.

Miranda knew Nathan liked her from the moment he had met her. His hand was warm, though it made her shiver slightly. She looked around and saw her brothers were each immersed in conversation. Greta was beside Griffin. Alex was across the room talking to a female cast member.

"Sure," she agreed and turned to the others, "We will be right back."

Luckily the elevator opened when she pushed the button. She knew Griffin had seen her walk out Alex's door with Nathan. He had made a motion towards her but she ignored him completely. He was probably telling Evan and Alex right now. Her brothers had warned her against Nathan that they saw him with plenty of girlfriends and they did not like that very much. She needed to get ahead before they came looking for her.

Miranda and Nathan took the elevator down to the bottom floor, walked through the swimming pool room and out into the warm night. It was dark and the sky was full of stars. Miranda drew in a deep breath of the warm night air and gazed longingly upwards. She wondered what her Earth family was doing right now. What was Helen doing?

"How have you been?" Nathan asked. He was quiet, shuffling his feet as Miranda led the way towards the treed path that led to the river.

"I've been OK," Miranda said. She felt guilty that she had never told Nathan about Jackson, but he must have known and seen their picture on the front page. Plus their relationship was all over the news when she lost him. Miranda fought back her tears and looked up at him, "How have you been?"

Nathan frowned, "It is hard, but I am coping."

Miranda did a double take. She had no idea Nathan had lost someone too. She stopped walking. That was why she had seen him at the funeral home. What a horrible friend she was! "Oh Nathan, I am so sorry. I am such a horrible friend. I had no idea." She reached a hand out and put it on his arm.

Nathan shrugged, "How would you? We don't know very much about each other."

"Who was it?"

Nathan fidgeted and frowned, "My mother was a teacher at the school."

Miranda put a hand to her mouth in shock and then she pulled Nathan into a hug. "I am so, so sorry!" She rubbed his back, "That is horrible. I feel terrible I did not know. I was just so upset at the funeral I had to leave. I didn't even stop by to pay my respects."

"It's OK, really," Nathan said, "I have been going to grief counseling and it helps a lot." He returned her hug, running his hands over her bare back.

"I hope you find comfort, Nathan," Miranda said, pulling away and looking him in the eye, "If you need anything, let me know."

"Thank you." He kissed her cheek. "And to you as well."

"I'm coping as well. Not very well, but I'm trying."

They walked a little further down the grass path. The grass in Utopia was genetically modified to only grow a couple inches so all the paths were well maintained. Nathan ran a nervous hand through his hair. "I was wondering if maybe you would like to try for a date again," he asked, hopeful.

She gave his hand a squeeze, "I would love to go out on a date with you. We never really did make it out to one did we?"

"Really?" Nathan was shocked she had agreed so easily. He almost smiled.

Miranda nodded, "Of course!" She didn't hesitate. Nathan was a nice guy to her and he was very cute. Although she had not seen him in a couple weeks, she had never seen him with another woman. Every time she met up with them in the game room, he had been alone and he never tried to pick up girls when they went out, only her.

They walked silently hand in hand for a bit. Miranda glanced down at his clothes. He had dressed nicely for the party as well. His striped button-down shirt clung to his biceps. He seemed much bigger than he was the last time she had seen him. "I know my brothers might not be happy with me going on a date. They did not like Jackson either, so please do not take it personally," Miranda said, finally breaking the silence.

Nathan frowned slightly, "And Alex?"

"Well, Alex is like a brother too, I guess," Miranda shrugged. "All of them."

Nathan rolled his eyes and took her hands, forcing her to face him. He looked down at her in earnest, "Please, don't believe him. It makes me so angry. I know he has spread lies about me to you. I do not have a lot of girlfriends. Sure, I have had sex before, but not like him. I thought I was in love, but I wasn't. Plus I was never going to save myself, just as he didn't."

Miranda looked away from his intense gaze. She couldn't believe her admitted that to her. She felt a little awkward.

Nathan continued despite her discomfort. "I know he told you I am with a lot of girls but that is Alex, not me," Nathan said, desperately, "I hope you will believe me."

"Alex told me he has never…" Miranda started to say and was interrupted.

Nathan snorted, "Oh please, my friend's sister is always gloating about being with him and so are a lot of girls. You haven't been around long enough to hear what they say."

Miranda frowned.

"I really do like you, Miranda," he said, "I am not going to allow Alex to poison your mind against me."

"I won't let that happen," Miranda said, trying to smile at him, "You have nothing to worry about."

Nathan finally dropped her hands, though he kept hold of one and started walking down the path again. Miranda was lost in her thoughts though she was careful to make sure Nathan couldn't hear them. She didn't know what to believe anymore.

Nathan's phone rang, interrupting the silence.

"Nathan, are you ready?" a voice said from the other end, when he had excused himself to take the call.

"Just a minute, dad," Nathan replied, annoyed. He sent an apologetic look to Miranda.

"OK, I need you home soon."

Nathan hung up and sighed, "Sorry to cut our walk short. My dad needs me. He's been a little lost since my mother died."

"You go ahead," Miranda said, encouragingly, giving him a squeeze on the arm. She had a lot on her mind and was feeling a little tipsy too. She wanted to stay outside and enjoy the fresh air. It felt good to be out in the fresh air, having spent the last few weeks in her room.

"Are you sure?" Nathan replied, running a hand down her back again.

Miranda nodded and sent him a small smile, "I know the way back."

"Can I call you tomorrow to talk about our date?"

"Sure." Miranda agreed and he kissed her cheek then left, oddly taking a different route then the one they had come from.

Miranda shrugged and continued on. She heard the sound of the river and followed the path to the bank of the crystal clear water. It wasn't a very large river. Only about 20 feet across and fairly shallow, though she had only ever waded out a couple feet and the water was to her knees. It was lined with rocks and there were a few larger boulders which she normally took a seat on. This time she sat down on the grass near the edge of the rocks and leaned back on her elbows, staring up at the sky. She wished she could talk to Helen again, who would know what to say to comfort her. She just wanted someone to talk to. Someone she could tell everything to, the whole truth and not just the made up version that everyone here but Jackson, his mother and a select group of people knew.

Miranda sat up on the grass, plucking a few pieces. They felt strange to her, more soft but tougher than Earth grass. She twirled the pieces in her fingers as she continued her internal struggles. She tried to count the amount of women Alex had been dating since she moved here and shook her head. It had to be about four or five by now. She had not seen Nathan with anyone else, though she had to admit, she didn't see him often. It didn't matter about Alex anyways. He made it clear he didn't want to be with her.

Her eyes welled with tears. It had been so easy with Jackson, why did she even bother with Alex? She felt so guilty and wondered if it was because of her that Jackson didn't have any powers. Was it because she had never truly been in love with him?

Feeling oddly like she was being watched, Miranda decided it was time to head in. She started to stand and stopped abruptly. A mysterious wind picked up and blew her hair wildly around her face. She was sure that the ground trembled slightly and looked around feeling eyes on her again, but there was no one. She put a hand on the ground but it wasn't moving. She must have imagined it.

"Miranda!" she heard Evan call. She looked back and saw him coming down the path. He was running.

Miranda rolled her eyes, even though she knew they were likely to be looking for her.

"Did you feel it?" he asked frantically, when he reached her, "The ground shook. Are you alright?" Evan's phone rang and he answered, "Yes we are all fine...Yes, Miranda is with me...We will be up soon."

Miranda's jaw dropped. The ground actually moved? It wasn't her imagination? That meant the evil ones weren't gone. Her phone rang as well, she sighed with relief when she saw Nathan, "Are you OK?" he asked before she could say anything.

"Yes, are you?"

"I'm fine, I was worried about you. I shouldn't have left you alone."

"I am OK. I'm so glad you called so I know you are safe as well."

Nathan gave her a half smile, "I will call you tomorrow."

She nodded and pushed the button to end the call.

"Who was that?" Evan asked.

"Nathan."

"Were you with him? Did he just leave you out there by yourself?"

"I am fine, just leave it alone," Miranda snapped and started up the path towards their building, and then she snapped back over her shoulder, "I know the way back."

Evan followed closely, looking over his shoulder every few seconds. He spotted Alex up the trail and flagged him down. Alex looked relieved to see them and waited for them to catch up.

Miranda eyed him warily as they approached and was shocked when he threw his arms around her and hugged her tight.

"Why did you come out here with him?" Alex asked, holding her at arms length, "Where is he now?" He looked over Miranda's shoulder, expecting to see him following.

Miranda shrugged, "I just wanted to walk and he went home. I was just out by the river." She motioned behind her.

"You should not go out by yourself, Miranda," Alex chastised, releasing his grasp of her shoulders, "What if something happened to you?"

Miranda narrowed her eyes at him, "I am perfectly capable of taking care of myself."

Alex made a face. He was about to say something else when his phone rang. He pulled it out of his pocket.

"Mom? What is wrong?" He could tell she was crying. "Where is Dad? Are you both OK?" Alex got more frantic with each question.

Mrs. West sniffled and let out a sob, "Your dad is fine," she managed to choke out, "But Alex, your grandmother. She was attacked." She broke down in tears again.

"No," Alex said, quietly. He swayed a little on his feet and Miranda took his arm to steady him. Her anger evaporated and was replaced with concern for him.

His mother sobbed and continued, "Come home tomorrow. We will need to make funeral arrangements. Your grandfather is beside himself with grief. Your father went to get him and bring him here with us."

Alex nodded, "I will see you tomorrow," he replied. His eyes were filled with tears and he hung up. Once he did, he threw his phone hard at the nearest tree and put his head in his hands. The phone hit the ground with a thud.

"Alex, I'm sorry," Miranda said, rubbing his back while he took deep, shaking breaths.

"The evil ones are not gone," Alex said, through his hands.

"I did not expect they were," Evan said, quietly, "There were so few in the last attack, I knew it could not be true."

Alex took his hands away. Evan and Alex stared at each other for some time but Miranda couldn't get a read on either of them.

"We should get upstairs," Evan said finally, looking to Miranda. He looked like he had won whatever internal conversation he had with Alex. Alex's frown deepened. Miranda nodded and took Alex's hand while Evan picked up his undamaged phone and handed it back to him.

"You will stay with us tonight?" Miranda asked Alex when they got in the elevator. She looked at Evan to see if it was alright with him. Evan nodded.

Alex agreed, numbly. They could still hear music coming from Alex's apartment as they exited the elevator.

Miranda knew Alex did not want to deal with anyone right now, "You two just go to that apartment." She said, motioning to her own. She paused and then answered their thoughts, "It is fine. I am just going to kick anyone else left out and then tidy up. I can do it alone."

Evan nodded and led Alex to the East apartment.

Miranda took a deep breath, hoping no one was left before she opened the door, but the only person remaining was the waitress Alex was, or had been, dating. Miranda hadn't even seen her all night and wondered when she arrived.

"Where is Alex?" she asked. She was sitting on the couch alone amidst the mess.

"I am not sure," Miranda lied, "I am sorry you waited for him. I just came by to help clean up."

"Oh?" she pouted, "You have not seen him?"

Miranda shook her head and started gathering empty bottles.

"Here, let me help," she said as she stood and started collecting the bottles from the floor.

"Thanks," Miranda sent her a smile, "I am sorry I do not remember your name."

"Kristen," she smiled at her, "I watched the show today. You were great!"

"Thanks," Miranda smiled in reply and they cleaned for a bit in silence. She went to get a cloth from the kitchen to wipe down the surfaces and Kristen found a kitchen gadget to do the floors.

"I like cleaning the floors myself sometimes," Kristen said aloud, "I know it can be done for you, but there is nothing more satisfying than doing it yourself." She smiled wistfully as she ran what appeared to be some kind of mop back and forth over the floor.

Miranda nodded, though she had no idea the floors cleaned themselves, but after she thought about it a minute, her apartment was always clean. Something must be cleaning it.

"Did everyone leave?" Miranda asked her.

"Yes," she answered, with a frown, "Right after the ground shook. I was worried about Alex so I waited for him to come back. He is not answering my messages."

"I am sure he is fine. He is probably with my brother. I talked to Evan after the ground shook and he would have said something if he had not heard from Alex. They are best friends."

"Um..." Kristen started and Miranda looked over at her. She was chewing on her lip and deep in thought, "Alex seems like he is avoiding me. Do you know what I did? You seem to be close friends as well."

Miranda made a face, not wanting to discuss his love life with her, "If you want the inside scoop on Alex, you have to ask him yourself."

"But you do not know at all?" Kristen looked at her, hopeful.

Miranda sighed, feeling bad for the girl. "I think Alex thinks you like him because he is famous. He gets that a lot. He does not want a girl who wants him for his fame. He needs someone who cares about him, the real him."

Kristen went quiet, thinking. She leaned on the floor cleaner, "OK," she said finally, "I will talk to him about it. Of course, the fame is always in the back of my mind, but Alex is really cute and is a great person. I do like the real him."

"Sometimes he doesn't realize that not everyone is after his fame." Miranda rolled her eyes.

"Yes," Kristen agreed, "Perhaps he does not realize what a great person he is."

Miranda nodded. "I think he also wants to take things slow," Miranda added with a shrug as she went back to wiping the table tops.

Kristen looked at her with a raised eyebrow, "Slow?" She snorted. "He did not seem to want to take it slow the other night." Kristen frowned and leaned the floor cleaner up against the wall. "I think I will just go." She picked up her purse and just before she left, she spun to face Miranda, an angry look on her face, "Tell Alex I do not want to be the next in line to be cast away. I am done with him."

Miranda watched her go, stunned. When the door closed, she sighed loudly. Alex was the least of her worries now. The evil ones were alive and she was on her own. She would have to start training again, alone.

Miranda took the floor cleaner to finish what Kristen had started. It kept her mind off of things for a bit. When it was done, she sat on the couch to think and ended up falling asleep.

"Miranda?" Alex called, coming in his front door. He wasn't able to sleep and was worried when she didn't come back.

Miranda turned over, away from the voice.

He sat down on the couch and shook her gently, "Maddie, do you want to go to bed?"

Miranda's eyes opened slowly. She reached up and put her arms around his neck, resting her head on his shoulder. She lifted her knees so he could put his arm under, expecting him to carry her, as her eyes drifted closed again.

He smiled a bit as he lifted her. "Thank you for cleaning," he said, quietly, as he headed towards the East's apartment and down the hall to her room.

"Uh huh," Miranda murmured sleepily. She yawned and came around a bit as he laid her down on her bed, "Kristen helped. And I am pretty sure she is mad at you now."

Alex shrugged, "Are you going to change?"

Miranda nodded and asked Alpha to bring out her sleepwear.

"You can't sleep?" Miranda asked when Alex passed her pajamas to her. She rubbed her eyes with her free hand.

Alex shook his head and turned to leave.

"Just stay in here," Miranda said, standing, "Get in bed. I'm going to change." She went to the bathroom, changed and brushed her teeth. She took her time and when she got back, Alex was already asleep. She crawled into her bed beside him and fell asleep as well.

Miranda woke up early after a nightmare. She sat up, taking some deep breaths and jumped a little when she heard moaning beside her. Alex looked to be having a bad dream as well. Miranda put a hand on his arm, hoping to calm him and he stilled. When she was sure Alex was sleeping peacefully, she got out of bed. Her dreams had returned so the evil must have too. Since it was so early, she went down to the gym to work out. It was time to stop feeling sorry for herself. She had a job to do, a destiny to fulfill and she had to get back to training.

When Miranda got back up to the apartment, Alex and Evan were in the living room on the couch. Alex looked anxious.

"How are you?" Evan asked, eyeing her curiously. She hadn't gone to work out since before the attack at the school.

"I couldn't sleep, I went to the gym," Miranda replied, motioning to her workout clothes, "I'm going to shower."

"Wait," Evan stopped her. "How well do you know the sixth script?"

Miranda thought about it for a minute. She had looked it over a few times and knew it fairly well. She looked to Alex, who wasn't looking at her. "I know it, why?"

Evan looked at Alex as well and back at Miranda, "It is just a good time to pause. I was hoping we would be able to film Alex's parts for the next two scripts before he leaves today. I have been up all night thinking about it and the scene in the sixth is a good time to stop and allow the audience to think about the plot. That way, I can edit him out for the next week."

Miranda paled, knowing exactly which scene he meant. She took a deep breath, "Of course. I know the sixth script well enough."

"OK. You will be able to have the next week off as well. Maybe I can even write in that you took a vacation together."

Miranda nodded. She paused, thinking for a minute before asking, "Are we going to the funeral too?"

"Yes, we will go once it gets settled," Evan said, sadly.

"Can I go with Alex?" Miranda wasn't sure why she asked but she wanted to be with him. He was going straight to the attack zone. What if the bad people were still there? She had no idea how or where they moved but they had been in his parents' city last.

Alex looked at her, a mixture of emotions.

"Uh?" Evan wasn't sure what to say as Mr. East entered the living room from the kitchen.

"Good morning everyone," he said, standing behind Alex on the couch. He gave his shoulder a comforting squeeze, "How are you today?"

Alex shrugged his shoulders a little and frowned.

"Dad?" Miranda asked, "Can I go with Alex today?"

Mr. East looked down at Alex and back at Miranda, "Is it OK with him and his family?"

"I can stay at a hotel. I will try not to be a bother," Miranda promised Alex.

"Have you ever even used your own money?" Alex asked, wearily.

"Well... no," Miranda said, looking at the floor. She didn't even know if she had money.

"You should," Evan said, "We *are* paying you. You can check by scanning your bank card with your phone."

She took out her phone and went to get her bank card out of her purse. In her bedroom, she scanned the card. Almost 175,000 flashed on her screen.

She swore aloud and went out to the living room, "Holy crap Evan! Have you been paying me for not working? What the hell is my salary?"

"Did you not read your contract?" Evan shrugged, "You make three million a year, whether you work or not."

Miranda looked down at her account and shook her head, "Well, I am pretty sure I can afford a hotel."

Alex looked deep in thought. He didn't want to admit out loud how happy he would be for the company. Sometimes he found it difficult to be with his parents since his sister died.

"Please Alex?" Miranda pleaded.

Alex bit his lip and took out his phone, "I will ask my mother." He went into the dining room for privacy.

"It is very nice of you to go with Alex," Mr. East smiled, "He will need a friend right now."

Evan smiled as well, hoping in his mind that it would lead to being more than friends.

Miranda rolled her eyes at him and looked pointedly at their father.

Mr. East looked from Evan to Miranda, "Are you more than friends?"

Miranda shook her head, "No dad. Alex is like my big brother. I just want to be there for him."

Mr. East scratched his chin in thought but no one could hear what he was thinking. He got up from the couch. "I just have to finish getting ready. Be safe today and Miranda, let me know if you are going with Alex."

"I will, dad," Miranda said. She gave him a quick hug, "You be safe too."

Alex came back into the living room, "My mother said it is fine with her. She will not have you stay in a hotel though. They have a room for you."

Miranda smiled, "Really? It is no trouble?"

Alex shook his head.

"OK. I will go pack."

"Just ask Alpha for a travel bag for five days. She will pack your necessities then you can tell her what clothes you want," Evan called after her.

"OK!" she yelled back from down the hall. She did just that and then made sure she packed her black dress and some black heels and other clothes she would need for a few days. She packed for an entire week or more because she couldn't decide what to wear or how long Alex intended to stay. She was determined to stay with him for as long as he needed. Then she went to shower and get ready for the day.

Three

★　★　★　★

Once she was ready, she went back out to the living room. Alex was still on the couch and looking stressed. He had his head bowed, his elbows rested on his knees and he was alone.

Miranda went to sit beside him. He didn't move from his position so she put a hand on his back.

"Are you going to be OK, Alex?" she whispered.

He nodded but didn't look up.

"Are you sure you are fine that I go with you?"

Alex reached over and put a hand on her knee, giving it a gentle squeeze, "Yes, I am glad you will be there."

"Did Evan leave?"

Alex nodded.

"Shall we go then?"

Alex started to bounce his knees nervously. "Are you ready for today?" He looked into her eyes and answered her question with one of his own, anxiety all over his face.

Miranda bit her lip and nodded.

"I do not know if I am," Alex said, looking down at his clenched fists.

Miranda put a hand on his knee to stop it. It was making her nervous. "We will be just fine," she tried to assure him.

Alex looked at her doubtfully, so Miranda leaned in and kissed him. When she felt the familiar pull and her body heat up, she pulled away. She thought maybe now it wouldn't happen, but the feeling had returned full force.

"Oh, this could be bad," she forced a giggle. Her cheeks went a bright pink.

Alex gave her a small smile. He stroked her cheek with his thumb, "I agree, but thanks for that."

Miranda stood and pulled Alex up with her, "Well, shall we go and get the scene over with?"

Alex nodded and together they put their shoes on and headed up to Alex's car.

Once they reached the studio, they were both ushered off to their dressing rooms right away. The stylist didn't do much with Miranda's hair that day. She thought it would be best to leave it down.

"I love your hair," she said as she spread some sort of lotion on it.

"Thanks," Miranda smiled. She was pretty fond of her hair now. It had softened a lot since she had been in Utopia. It looked a lot like her mother's hair from the pictures she had seen.

After she was done with her hair, she had Miranda dress in a strapless beige bra, which was the colour of her skin tone, so that it would look like she was wearing nothing. Over top, she put on a short jean skirt and a pale pink top for the first day of filming.

The scenes that had Miranda and Alex in them were filmed first so they could leave. The sex scene was last since the others were mostly outdoors. Once they reached the indoor set, Miranda changed into her next outfit, a simple pair of jeans and a white cardigan and waited off to the side with Alex, who was pacing nervously, while they fixed up the set.

Evan walked over to them, taking in their apprehensive faces.

"Are you both ready?" he asked.

Miranda nodded and Alex didn't answer.

Evan sighed, taking in their looks of nausea, "Do not worry about making any noises, if you know what I mean. There is going to be music playing."

Miranda paled, thinking about what happened last time she had to kiss Alex on set in front of her brother.

Evan put his hands on her shoulders, looking at her directly in the eye, "Miranda, you are a great actress. That is all this is, acting. You and Alex make a great couple... on screen," he added quickly when she gave him a sharp look, "To make it a little less awkward for you, I will step out for this scene."

Miranda eyed him, suspiciously, "You are not watching?"

"No, I already let Melissa know that she can handle this scene and she is thrilled to take over. I will watch the replay to make sure it looks good."

Evan left them. Alex came close to her and put his arms around her waist, "I am sorry."

"For?" Miranda asked warily, looking up into his eyes. What could he have possibly done this time?

"For what might happen. I cannot help it." He gave her an adorable half smile.

Miranda shrugged, relieved that it was nothing worse than a simple apology for something they had no control over. "It is OK to be reckless."

Alex chuckled and placed a kiss on her cheek, "Your brother is right. You are a great actress. We can do this together."

"Pick me up," Miranda commanded, "You have to carry me through the door."

Alex took her legs and heaved her into his arms, "You enjoy this a little too much."

Miranda giggled nervously, remembering that she had made him carry her to her bedroom last night. She shrugged, "It's a fireman thing, I guess."

"Fireman?"

Miranda didn't have time to explain since Melissa yelled, "Action!"

Alex carried her through the door and put her on her feet. Just as he leaned in to kiss her, a slow and sweet ballad started to play.

Miranda felt the familiar feeling rush through her. She pulled away for a second, long enough to bring his shirt up over his head, smiling shyly. Alex brought his arms slowly back down around her. From there, things were a blur. Miranda had no idea how long she had been kissing him but they had managed to make it to the bed.

"OK, stop for a minute," Melissa said. But the two didn't stop. "Um... Hello?" Melissa tried again as they moved further onto the bed. She paused the music and yelled, "Cut!"

Miranda and Alex sprang apart.

"Sorry Melissa," Alex said, his face red.

Melissa shrugged, "I need you to start again. You are moving too fast. It was good until you got his shirt off," she giggled before she continued, "then it got a little fast."

Alex groaned, a little frustrated, as he got off from on top of her. He put a hand out to help her up. Miranda smiled at him and saw a million feelings pass through his eyes including regret, guilt and a small amount of excitement but she couldn't read his thoughts. It was confusing. She stared at him.

"Hello? Miranda? Alex?" Melissa said, trying to get their attention. She had been speaking.

"Sorry Melissa," Miranda said, tearing her eyes away, "What did you say?"

Melissa laughed again, "You can start where you just got his shirt off so you need to put yours back on."

Miranda looked down and was shocked to see she was just in her bra. She located her shirt and threw it back on. Then they both took their places beside the bedroom door.

"OK, start up the camera and you both go ahead whenever you are ready," Melissa said.

Alex did not waste another minute and Melissa shrugged at the camerawoman as she focused on the couple.

Miranda kept her focus by trying to recite the alphabet backwards. Alex seemed to be listening to her thoughts so he filled in the missing letters whenever she drew a blank. She especially drew a blank when Alex had moved his lips to her neck. She gasped a little bit and hoped it wasn't too loud. Alex had heard it and he gave her a mysterious smile, then he told her in her mind that she had been on the letter 'J'. They successfully moved to the bed and finished the scene without being stopped again.

"OK, we are done filming," the camerawoman said as she backed away from the camera, talking into a headset, then she turned to the couple, "It looked very convincing from my view."

Miranda looked up at Alex, who smiled at her. She fought the urge to kiss him again, reluctantly getting up to put her shirt and pants back on.

Neither said a word to each other as they sat on the edge of the bed waiting for everyone to come back. Miranda chewed her thumb nail nervously, hoping they would not have to do it again. Evan came back after 15 minutes, after watching the replay.

"It looked great," Evan said, smiling, "Very convincing. You can both go."

Miranda smiled.

"Really?" Alex asked, smiling, as he stood.

"Yes, you both looked great together," Evan commented, his voice full of hope.

Miranda frowned and shook her head. Alex didn't want to be with her and she couldn't be with him. She wished Evan would just get over it. She sent Evan a warning look and then turned to Alex, "Are you ready to go?" His car was packed with their things. She had to forget about being with him, focus on saving the world and be friends just like they agreed last night.

Alex nodded.

"Take care of her," Evan said to Alex, then hugged Miranda, "We will see you soon."

Miranda had never left her family for the night since she moved to Utopia. It made her a little anxious to leave them behind, she thought as she worriedly glanced back at Evan as they walked away. Evan looked worried as well but he sent her an encouraging smile.

Since they were both already dressed in normal clothes, neither needed to change. Miranda followed Alex to the elevator and up to his car. It made Miranda more anxious to leave Alex. The attack had happened in his parents' city and he could be going right into the hands of someone evil. She wished his parents were coming here instead and that the funeral would happen here. She couldn't remember what happened to the ashes after the body was cremated. Did it really matter where it happened?

"They get put back into the earth," Alex answered her thought, quietly.

Miranda looked at him, she had forgotten to block her thoughts.

"We will be fine, Miranda," Alex added, "Try not to worry."

She gave him a weak smile over the roof of his car and got in.

"How long will it take to get there?" Miranda asked, once Alex had exited the parking garage.

"I have not decided if we should drive or get an express flight," he frowned, and turned to her, "If we drive, it will be four hours and if we fly, only 15 minutes. I want my car, which is why I would like to drive but it is very long. What do you think?"

"It really does not matter to me," Miranda said with a shrug, "I have been in a car longer than that and that was my parents' little Earth car." She stretched out and settled in for a long ride. "If you want your car when we get there, then we should take your car."

"OK," Alex smiled, "I will drive." He reset the destination and it planned out his route. He rose in the air another 60 metres and then settled in himself.

"So tell me about driving," Miranda requested, after about 20 minutes. She could see another little city coming up on the right. This one had a greyish mountain range along the edge and from far away it looked moss covered at the peaks. But the town looked the same. No buildings above the treeline, plenty of greenery, and a swarm of cars in the air as people moved about their business. It looked like a swarm of bees or birds from this far away, but then Miranda remembered that Utopia had neither of those. They had gone extinct. The car ride had been silent until then and she turned to him. "Do you think you can give me that lesson now?"

Alex nodded, happy for the 'safe' topic. "Well, just like an Earth car, there is a stop and a go pedal. We do not have gasoline. Like everything else, our vehicles run on solar energy," Alex explained. "Every time you drive, you set your destination first. The car will calculate your navigation and indicate which altitude you should remain at. Each vehicle is programmed to fly at different altitudes so that you will never hit another vehicle. Sometimes there might be someone else at the same height, but they are normally not within your trajectory. When I set the vehicle to race mode, it ignores all this so that I can fly at the same height as the others."

"That is very cool," Miranda smiled, "I can't wait to try it."

Alex chuckled and continued, "All vehicles are push button start." He pointed to the button. "It may look complicated, but all these other buttons just need to be pushed once the car is started. They start up the navigation, stabilization and everything else the car needs. I turn some off when I race."

Miranda smiled and lapsed into silence for a bit. It was slightly uncomfortable. She felt like they had so much left unsaid. She tried to think of something else. "Have you ever gone on vacation?" she asked after several minutes.

"Yes," Alex said with a smile. He reminisced about his camping trips with his family. Camping, to Utopians, involved going out into the forests surrounding the cities in small shelters. Miranda told him they called them tents on Earth. He smiled at her Earth word as he continued. Normally, people would set up near streams for swimming and there were designated hiking areas that were maintained by the nearby city it was associated with. He told her about his few vacations to the islands, where he windsurfed and went scuba diving.

"I know how to windsurf," Miranda smiled and then she remembered how she had learned and frowned. Jackson had taught her on their first date.

Alex went quiet, hearing her thoughts. It was several uncomfortable minutes before he asked her about her family trips.

"I went camping with my family as well," she said. She told him about Ontario's provincial parks and how they had probably visited every one of them. Then she told him about her first trip to the Caribbean, how she loved the blue green water and white sand and then about her trip to Alberta to see the mountains and lakes. She went on to describe Newfoundland, where her family went on a whale watching tour in the cold Atlantic Ocean.

Alex smiled at her when she finished, "Sounds like you got around."

Miranda shook her head and gave him a small chuckle, "Well, unlike here, there are continents and people on the other side of Earth. I never went overseas, though I might have liked to see a few places." She tried to describe Paris and Italy, and some of the other places on her bucket list. "I guess I will have to make a new list," she ended with a frown. She had learned a lot about geography from Jackson, but Utopia's culture was so integrated, that all the people were the same. Everyone had the same history and any significant old buildings were long demolished. It was sad that their history was gone, even though it had been over a billion years since Utopia had become one culture. There were very few historical records on what it had been like before. Most of the history she had learned from Jackson was about the evolution of technology and animals, never the people. It was like they intended it that way to forget.

"You can go visit other planets for vacation," Alex said, glancing her way, "My family just chose not to. And now that I am hearing about Earth, maybe someday we could go see more of it. It does sound interesting."

Miranda looked at Alex, confused. He wanted to go to Earth with her? She thought he hated Earth. Alex caught her eye and didn't turn away.

Yes, of course I would go with you, Alex said in his thoughts.

As friends, I guess, Miranda answered in her mind. *I suppose that would be fine*.

Alex gave her a quick look of longing before he echoed, *as friends*.

"Don't you have to watch where you are going?" Miranda asked, breaking the stare.

Alex shook his head and turned to stare out the other window, "It drives itself. I barely have to do anything unless I am in race mode."

Miranda bit her lip and turned her gaze out the window. She watched as they passed by another city to the right, it was further away this time but she could see the swarm above it. She sighed, quietly.

"Are you hungry?" Alex asked. It had been at least an hour since either of them had spoken, "We are almost there."

Miranda shrugged, "I could eat."

Alex gave her a half smile, "I am sure my parents will have something ready, but we could go out first."

"I am sure your parents are anxious to see you," Miranda said, putting a hand on his knee, "Let's go there first."

Alex wrinkled his nose, still worried about being with his parents for several days, but nodded. He had not spent more than two days with them in a long time, though he did visit for the day, at least once a month.

It was another five minutes before a Miranda could see a city straight ahead. There was no ring of mountains that surrounded the city like their own, only the snow-capped one she had seen from Alex's pictures in the distance. Miranda looked down as they flew over a big lake. She loved the colours of Utopia. They were so vivid. She could see people swimming and boating in the blue expanse below. Alex's parents lived near that lake and they arrived quickly after. The parking garage looked so similar to the one at her own apartment complex, they could be in City 217.

Alex's parents were both in the living room when they walked in. Miranda started to feel nervous that she invited herself along.

"Alex!" Mrs. West said with a small smile as she rose from the couch to hug her son tightly. Mr. West was right behind.

"Hello Miranda," Mr. West said. He pulled her into a hug, "Welcome to our apartment. I am so happy you accompanied our son."

Mrs. West hugged her next, "I am so glad you are here."

Miranda sent her a smile when she let her go, "Thank you so much for having me here, Mrs. West."

"Please call me Erica," Mrs. West said.

Mr. West took her hand and squeezed it, "And you can call me Ryan."

Miranda smiled at them both, but it faded when she remembered why they were here, "I am so sorry to hear about your mother."

They both nodded and Mrs. West sent her a smile, though her eyes glistened with tears. She turned to her son and hugged him again, "I hope you had a good drive but we were thinking of heading out again. We wanted to take you out to dinner, is that OK?"

Alex nodded, "Where is Grandpa?"

Erica made a face, "He insisted he go home. He said that is where he belongs. Your dad is going to stay with him tonight."

"But the attack?" Alex asked, "Where did it happen?"

Mr. West shook his head, "Not at the apartment. Your grandmother was out with a friend for a late night meal. They were walking to their vehicles when it happened. Her friend was only unconscious when they found them but she could not remember what happened. Only that your grandmother had told her to run and she did."

There was a moment of silence as Alex digested that information.

"Alex, you can take the first room on the right," Mr. West said, then paused for a second, "I do not know the situation between the two of you but Miranda you are welcome to stay with him or take the second bedroom on the right."

"The second bedroom is fine," Alex answered before Miranda could. She was going to say the same thing.

Mrs. West looked between the two of them before she led the way up the hallway and everyone followed her.

She stopped at the first door on the right and turned. "The washroom is the first door on the left." She motioned to it before continuing, "If you wanted to freshen up before we go."

"Thank you," Miranda smiled. She noticed the apartment setup was much like hers, minus one bedroom at the end of the hall.

Mrs. West showed her to her bedroom and Miranda went inside to change before dinner. The room was decorated in pinks and greys. It had pictures of the family, but most of them were of Alex's sister and what looked to be her friends. Even though she was gone, her parents had still made it her room.

Alex was sitting with his parents in the living room when Miranda returned. "Do you like seafood?" he asked her.

Miranda nodded.

"Excellent," Mr. West smiled, "We should go before it gets too crowded. You will love this place, Miranda."

They all went up the elevator and to Alex's car. Mr. West talked excitedly about Alex's racing as they made their way to the restaurant.

They arrived at the restaurant, which looked like a big fish tank. It was lit up with blue lighting and its walls actually *were* a big fish tank. Live fish swam around the glass. Miranda stared at it in awe. She could see the people dining inside the restaurant. A neon sign floating in the centre above the front doors read, *Urchins*.

"Oh wow," Miranda said, as they walked up the path to the front doors, "That is so neat!"

"Clean?" Alex asked, giving her a funny look.

"It means cool. It's just slang," Miranda shrugged.

Alex smirked, "And cool is not defined as something that is not quite cold?"

Miranda rolled her eyes and shoved him playfully.

Alex chuckled, "You say some funny things."

"I'm glad there are no cameras here. Do they see our show out this way?" Miranda asked, changing the subject.

Mr. West held the door open for them as Alex answered, "Of course they do. It is shown all over Utopia."

Miranda smiled, "I still can't believe I'm on a show like that."

Alex sent her a smile and a wink, "Watch this." He stepped up to the host stand where a woman about their age was fumbling with a stack of the electronic menus. "Hi," he said to her, "I was wondering if you had any private booths available."

The woman looked up and her mouth dropped. She managed to knock over the whole stack of digital menus she had been fixing. She looked horrified at what she had done and blushed deeply as she bent down to pick them up.

"Here let me help you," Alex said and bent to help her pick up the menus.

"Oh, no Jeff, uh, Alex, er... I mean Mr. West," she stumbled over her words as she gathered them together, "I am so clumsy." He helped her anyways, while Miranda looked on, a smile playing at her lips.

The hostess straightened up and placed the menus back beside her in a neat pile, "I am so sorry. Yes, we do have a private booth available," she said, flustered, "Please follow me."

Alex sent Miranda a smile and motioned for her to take the lead. Miranda followed the hostess through the restaurant and to the back. Alex's parents followed behind them with amused looks on their faces.

"Please sit here," she said, her face still pink, "I am sorry. I forgot menus. I will be right back." And she hurried away, her black hair swinging behind her.

Miranda shook her head at Alex, "You should not do that to people. That is mean!" But she burst out laughing.

"He does that all the time," Erica smiled as she took a seat on one side of the booth. Ryan sat beside her, leaving the other side for Alex and Miranda.

"I cannot help who I am," Alex chuckled, "It is different when we leave our City. They are all used to seeing us around. But here, they do not expect it."

The hostess came back around with the menus, "Please enjoy your meal. If you need anything, I will be up front."

Alex smiled at her and her eyes widened. She tripped a little as she sped away. He chuckled again and turned to Miranda, "I do have to warn you though. We may have some company when we leave."

Miranda looked up at him from the menu, "Oh?"

"Well, like I said, since we do not get out of our city often that when we do, word usually gets around. I bet she is on her phone now telling her friends."

"I suppose we should have driven separately," Mr. West groaned. "Last time we took Alex for dinner, we had to wait an hour for the crowd to leave."

"I better get used to it, I guess," Miranda bit her lip and looked down at her menu again. She hoped she wouldn't attract any evil towards them and regretted her decision to accompany Alex. What if she put him and his family in more danger? But the waitress really hadn't noticed her. She was still new to the show. Perhaps when she texted her friends, it would all be about Alex.

She snuck a peak at him out of the corner of her eye. He looked deep in thought, staring, but did not appear to be reading, the menu.

A few minutes later a waitress came around to their booth, "Oh, she was not lying!" Her face went as red as her hair. "Hello Mr. West. Oh! And you play that new girl!" She smiled at Miranda, "I was so sad to see Jeff and Janet break up but the two of you together have such chemistry! I am a huge fan of the show!" she went on, rambling a little. She looked at Alex's parents, "Oh you must be their family. You must be so proud of them."

Miranda bristled, *So much for not being noticed*. She managed a smile back at the waitress.

Mrs. West nodded, "Yes, Alex is our son and Miranda is the daughter of our good friend."

The waitress smiled and then remembered she was supposed to be serving them, "My name is Shelly and I will be your server this evening. May I bring you a drink?"

Miranda and Alex's parents ordered a drink with alcohol.

"Just plain water for me," Alex added.

The waitress nodded and left.

"Do you know what you want?" Alex asked Miranda.

"I think the shrimp pasta," Miranda said as she scrolled through the menu again. When he spoke to her, she could feel his breath on her neck and it made her shiver.

"Oh?" Alex said, "I was thinking the same."

Miranda smiled as she put the menu down, "Sounds good. What are you having?" she asked his parents.

"Lobster!" they both answered at the same time and then laughed. Mrs. West smiled at Miranda, "We get that every time we come here." Neither of them had even picked up a menu.

The waitress returned with their drinks and Alex told her what they all wanted.

"You may have a picture and our autograph," Miranda said before she left. She knew that was what the waitress wanted. She could hear it in her mind, "We will not get you in trouble."

The waitress looked around and then smiled at Miranda. She moved closer to the booth so no one around could see, "Thank you so much! I was afraid to ask!"

"Not to worry. Would you like to sit by Alex and I will take your picture with him?"

Shelly nodded enthusiastically, a wide smile on her face. Miranda stood and took her notebook that she held out to her. Shelly sat in the booth beside Alex. She looked nervous. Miranda took the picture and handed the notebook back to her.

"Will you sign it please, Mr. West?" Shelly asked him.

Alex nodded and took her notebook from her. He pulled out the stylus and signed the picture.

"Now will you take one of us?" Shelly stood beside Miranda. Miranda complied and put an arm around her. Shelly put her arm around Miranda, and Alex took the picture.

Shelly took her notebook back from Alex, "Will you sign as well?" she asked Miranda.

"Of course!" Miranda said and took the phone and stylus. She signed the picture that had just been taken with a flourish. "That is a good one," Miranda said, handing Shelly back her phone with a smile.

"Thank you both so much! No one will believe I met you!" Shelly exclaimed, "By the way, you were so great in your first episode and you both looked so cute together in the magazine."

Miranda smiled at her as she took her seat again. Shelly went to give the chef their order.

They all laughed quietly, as Mrs. West described the last adventure they had the last time Alex had visited, until another person, a man this time stopped by their booth.

"Hello, I am Jonas Graham, the owner of Urchins," he shook each of their hands, "I am sorry to disturb you. I just wanted to introduce myself and tell you I am a very big fan of the show."

"Nice to meet you," Alex replied.

"I hate to ask, but can I get a picture of the both of you to put up on our wall. It is very rare that we get famous people in our City," he asked. He sent an apologetic smile to each of them.

"Of course," Alex said.

"Shelly, come here please and take our picture?" Jonas asked Shelly, who was a few tables away.

Shelly returned and took her boss's notebook. Both Alex and Miranda stood on either side of Jonas, and Shelly took the picture.

They both signed the picture and then he beamed the picture to a nearby frame so it could be on display.

"Thank you both very much. Please enjoy all your meals on the house, and if you need anything. Just let me know."

Alex and Miranda took their seats again. "How am I supposed to spend this stupid amount of money if people give me free meals all the time?" Miranda grumbled.

Mr. West laughed, "Ah, famous people."

Miranda stuck out her lower lip, "And I was going to buy dinner."

Alex shrugged, "Next time."

The waitress brought Miranda another drink, "Your meal will be out any moment," she smiled.

Miranda had a great time talking with Alex's parents as they ate. They were also big into hockey so they had a lot to talk about, and they were also curious about Earth. It became apparent that Alex had talked to his parents a lot about her. The phrase 'Alex said that' or 'Alex told us' was used a lot.

Miranda could tell his parents cared about him deeply. She didn't understand why Alex would think otherwise.

Once they were done, Shelly asked if they needed anything more.

"I think we are great!" Mrs. West answered, "Unless you would like another drink?" She looked to her husband and Miranda. Alex wasn't drinking since he was the driver.

"I am fine," Miranda said, "Thank you." Mr. West agreed that he was finished.

"The owner has got the bill. Please take all the time you need," Shelly said and smiled again, "Thank you both again, and I hope you both enjoy our city."

"Thank you so much," Alex said and Miranda smiled. They stood and Alex led the way to the front of the restaurant. "Are you ready for this?" he chuckled, stopping just before the front door.

"Ready for what?" Miranda asked, a confused look on her face. Alex pointed outside and Miranda followed in the direction of where he was pointing.

A large crowd had gathered outside of the restaurant.

"What the hell?" Miranda swore. Mr. West groaned behind them.

Alex cast his parents an apologetic look and looked at his watch, "I will give them a half hour of our time."

His parents nodded. "We will wait in the car," Mr. West said and turned to his wife, "It's best we get out before them." They went ahead.

Alex turned to Miranda, "Just smile and sign their notebooks. It is simple. Do not give any of the show away and do not answer any questions if you do not feel comfortable."

Miranda's stomach dropped. The large crowd out there was for them. She tried to convince herself that they must all be fans of the show, but couldn't help think there may be someone evil out there.

"Deep breaths," Alex instructed with a smile. He opened the door and a buzz started throughout the crowd.

Miranda pasted a smile on her face as she followed. The crowd all moved in excitedly, blocking the path from the restaurant doors to the parking area.

Alex paused at the top of the stairs so that he was over the crowd, "Hello everyone!" he shouted through cupped hands, and the crowd calmed so they could hear him, "Hi," he said again and dropped his hands to his side. He took Miranda's hand in his. "Miranda and I are excited to see you all here. Thank you so much for supporting *Northern Shores*. It would be nothing without its fans. To ease the traffic in and out of the restaurant, Miranda and I will be over here," he pointed off to the side, "We will be able to sign autographs and take pictures, so if you would please form a line, it would be appreciated, especially by our friends here at Urchins."

Miranda spent the next hour in a high-alert daze. There were so many people, but she tried to keep her eyes sweeping the crowd. Most wanted pictures with the both of them so they posed and signed the notebooks of almost 50 people.

Miranda shook her wrist as they headed back to Alex's car, happy they hadn't been attacked. It was the most writing she had done since she left Earth. Alex laughed when he saw it, none the wiser that she had been looking around paranoid the whole time.

"Sorry it took so long. We could not leave anyone behind. I would not feel right," Alex said. He said the same to his parents, who were sitting on the hood of his car, relaxing when they reached them.

Miranda laughed, "I can't believe so many people were here."

"Well, between the waitress, the hostess and the owner passing messages to all their friends and so on, it adds up."

"Evan doesn't mind us getting pictures with everyone?" she asked Alex.

"Not at all! It helps with publicity," Alex told her as he started up the car with everyone inside.

"Does each city have a studio? Do they have their own celebrities?"

"Not every city. Well, each city has a news station for local news," Alex explained.

"That was kinda fun," Miranda lied easily. It would have been fun if she hadn't been so tense. "Do you get that every time?"

Alex sighed, "Every time I go somewhere outside of our city."

"Well, at least the show is popular!" Miranda smiled.

"It is very popular," Mrs. West said. She smiled proudly at her son.

"Oh Alex, you look exhausted," Mrs. West commented when they returned to the apartment.

As if on cue, Alex yawned, "It has been a long day."

Mrs. West looked sympathetic, "Go to bed. We do not mind." She turned to Miranda, "Well, Miranda. If you cannot sleep, please feel free to roam around as you wish. You are so welcome here. We have a pool and work out room downstairs but no game room or movie theatre. The nearest is in the building to the north."

Miranda thanked her, but she was also tired and went into her temporary room to lie down on the bed. It *had* felt like a long day. She wasn't laying for long when the door opened. Alex came in and shut the door. She sat up on the edge of the bed.

He stood at the door for a second before he took a seat beside her. "I know my mother said to roam around as you wish but I cannot sleep thinking you might be going anywhere by yourself."

Miranda shook her head, "Oh Alex. I am almost 19. I can..."

"Just please," Alex cut in, "Please do not go anywhere alone outside of the building." He looked anxious, almost as anxious as she had felt earlier. "The attack happened here in this city just last night. I was so worried the whole time you were standing out there exposed. I should have sent everyone away."

Miranda gave him a pitying look, not knowing that he had been just as anxious as she was. "I was worried too," she admitted.

"I know," Alex said, "I felt your tension."

Miranda pursed her lips. "Do you always feel what I feel?" she asked, "I find you are the best at reading my moods, even when I'm trying to block you out."

Alex chuckled a bit and shrugged, "I am pretty good at it, especially with you."

Miranda sighed. It was hard to keep him out. She wondered if it was because she liked him so much or if because he was a West. Jackson seemed pretty in tune with her as well, though she never tried to block him out. She didn't have to since he knew all about the Legend, of course.

Miranda looked at Alex. He looked tired and anxious so she crawled over to one side of the bed and opened up the blanket, inviting him in. He did and she lay down on his shoulder and cuddled close. He put his arm around and held her tightly. "I promise I will not go anywhere without you."

Alex sighed with relief, "Thank you."

"Can you stay with me for a bit?" she asked, resting her hand on his chest. Miranda couldn't help it. Every time she slept beside him, she always had a good sleep. It sometimes helped to keep her nightmares away.

"Yes, of course," Alex said, sleepily.

It didn't take long before the both of them fell asleep.

Miranda woke up early after a dreamless sleep. She was still engulfed in Alex's arms. It felt amazing and forbidden.

Miranda closed her eyes as she traced patterns on Alex's stomach. She shouldn't think that way. She couldn't focus on boy drama anymore. What she needed to think about was the evil that had returned. She needed to start training again. She sighed, sad that her moment with Alex was over so quickly. She wondered if her life would ever be normal.

While moving as little as possible so to not disturb him, she checked the time on her notebook which she had put on the bedside table. It was 5:49. She had slept nine hours which was pretty decent.

Miranda's intention was to go down to the gym, but Alex awoke while she was trying to extract herself.

"What time is it?" he asked, stretching a bit.

"It's only 6," she replied.

He sat up, "I slept really well."

"Me too," Miranda agreed, "I was going to go to the gym. Do you want to come with?"

Alex nodded and got up to get ready.

Miranda met him in the foyer. She knew she wouldn't be able to exercise her mind with Alex there, but at least she was doing something.

Alex's parents were in the dining room when they returned from their workout. Alex's dad had just returned from his father's apartment.

"I did not realize you were both awake," Mr. West smiled, "I guess fame is really exhausting."

Miranda smiled, "We had a long day yesterday. We had to be at the studio early before leaving."

"Would you like breakfast, or did you want to shower first?" Mrs. West asked.

"Go ahead and shower first, Miranda," Alex offered, "I will have breakfast."

"You are welcome to use Alpha to do your hair and makeup," Mrs. West offered, "I can program you in now." She got up from the table and followed Miranda down the hallway and to the bedroom she was staying in.

Miranda smiled at her appreciatively as Mrs. West called for Alpha and programmed her in.

Mrs. West was looking at the bed when Miranda stepped away from being scanned. She had a small smile playing at her lips. "It is nice to see Alex with a girlfriend. He has never brought one to meet us," Mrs. West sat on the bed, "I was worried after Andrea passed away that he shut down from loving completely." Her eyes glistened with tears, but she still smiled serenely. "We took her death very hard, but Alex was completely devastated and became so withdrawn."

Miranda frowned and she looked down at her clasped, sweaty hands, "I am sorry but Alex and I really are just friends."

"But you both have feelings for each other," she said, knowingly, "Every time I talk to Alex he has something to say about you. I can hear his affection for you in his voice. And you seem very fond of him."

"I am, Mrs. West," Miranda said.

"Please call me Erica," she cut in.

Miranda gave her a small smile, "I do have feelings for him and I love him like a brother, but..."

"But?" Erica asked, "That seems like a good start for a relationship."

"Well... I was dating Jackson when he died," Miranda said looking down at her hands, her eyes filled with tears.

"Ah, yes," Erica said, sadly, "Alex did tell us that. Jackson was a fair and kind-hearted man. He did not deserve to die so young."

Miranda nodded. There had been so much promise in her relationship with Jackson and it was all taken away.

"Come sit with me," Mrs. West said, comfortingly. She patted the spot beside her and Miranda sat. Mrs. West put a hand on her back, "You must have had a rough time since you came here, first your mother and then Jackson. But I know Jackson would want you to be happy."

Miranda nodded as a tear escaped down her cheek and landed on her lap.

Mrs. West leaned back a little, deep in thought, "I remember when you were just born. Alex loved you right away. He called you his baby."

Miranda gave a little gasp and turned to her quickly. She wasn't sure if she heard her correctly. "Excuse me?"

"Before you were brought to Earth, Alex spent the first and only day with you and he cried for days when you left. He was almost 2 years old but they forget easily so young," Mrs. West said.

Miranda's mouth dropped. Alex's mother had known about her!

"Your mother and I were the best of friends," Mrs. West sighed, sadly, "She told me she was worried about having three children and that she would be sending you away. I tried to get her to talk to someone, but she was adamant that you should go to Earth."

"So I *was* born here?"

Mrs. West nodded, "I felt awful for not telling your father but it was her choice and I would never give away her secret."

Miranda wiped her face hastily as the tears slipped down and waited for Mrs. West to continue.

"Miranda, you were so loved by your mother," Mrs. West said, stroking her hair, "It tore her up inside to let you go. I will never understand why she did not try to ask the council if she could keep you."

Miranda nodded her head a bit. She had hoped Mrs. West had known of the Legend. She just wanted someone to talk to and someone who understood all that she was going through.

The door opened and Miranda looked over to see Alex standing there.

"What is wrong?" he asked and he turned to his mother, accusation in his eyes, "What did you say to her?"

"She knew about me," Miranda whispered, "She knows I am Evan's twin. My mother told her everything."

"Her and Evan were both born here?" Alex asked his mother and she nodded. He put an arm around Miranda and she leaned into him, "Well, that explains that part. I do not understand why no one would tell Mr. East."

"It was not my secret to tell," his mother shrugged.

"Why? Why did she send her away?" Alex asked his mother, irritably.

Mrs. West frowned and shook her head. She didn't know but she had supported Miranda's mother and her decision.

Miranda stood abruptly and said she was going to shower. She left the room before her thoughts could give anything away. Miranda knew *exactly* why she was hidden and no one else did. She had no one to talk to except Jackson's mother and she felt too guilty to talk to her.

Alex put his head in his hands once she had gone. His mother scooted closer, pushed his hair back off his forehead and planted a quick kiss.

"You are deserving, Alex," Mrs. West said, "I love you very much and so does she."

Alex shook his head, not looking at her.

"You are not to blame for anything," she continued and hugged him tight, "You were always a wonderful person, Alex, and you still are. I am so proud of you."

"No, I am not," Alex said, pulling his hands away from his face, "I do not deserve anything." He stood and left the room.

His mother frowned, watching him go, wondering if subconsciously he remembered her. Did he ever stop loving that little baby?

Once Miranda was ready, she went out to the dining room where Mr. West fixed her breakfast. They chatted about the show and then about Alex's car racing.

"He always liked to drive fast," Mr. West smiled, when Miranda commented on his driving.

She nodded in agreement.

"There is a race here tonight," he said, "We should go see it."

"Oh, that would be great!" Miranda agreed, "We will have to ask him."

"Ask me what?" Alex asked, entering the dining room.

Miranda turned to him excited, "There is a race tonight. Maybe we could all go?"

Alex shrugged, "OK."

"We will go to the funeral parlour for the meeting," Mr. West said, "You can take Miranda to the lake if you like."

"You do not want me to help make the arrangements?" Alex asked his father, "Mom can take Miranda to the lake."

"We can take care of it. We just wanted to spend some family time with you, Alex," Mr. West smiled sadly, "We miss you and at times like this, it is important to have your family close. We can meet you both at the lake afterwards and maybe even rent a boat."

Miranda smiled at that while Alex nodded slowly.

Mrs. West entered the dining room and stood beside her son. She had gotten dressed and looked elegant in a long brown skirt and matching suit jacket. Miranda felt under-dressed. She had only put on her black shorts with a flowered tank top. Mrs. West gave Alex's shoulder a squeeze but he did not look at her. He stared stonily at the ground, his hands in the front pockets of his khaki shorts. His parents shared a concerned look.

"Well, we should get going," Mr. West said, checking his notebook for the time.

Alex did not say anything so Miranda jumped in, "Sounds great, Mr. West. We will let you know where we are."

Mr. West sent Miranda a smile, then he and Mrs. West went to put on their shoes and left.

"Are you OK?" Alex asked her when the door closed behind them.

Miranda nodded and her eyes softened, "I should ask you. Are you alright?"

Alex nodded.

"What's wrong?" Miranda asked, reaching out to touch his shoulder. She didn't believe him for a second. He seemed out of sorts, but she assumed it was because of his grandmother, or perhaps being near his family brought back the hurt from his sister. She didn't know.

Alex shrugged her hand off and changed the subject, "Would you like to go to the lake?"

Miranda nodded, "I'm glad at the last minute I decided to pack my bathing suit." She tried to smile though she was sad that he had shrugged her off. She wondered if he treated all his girlfriends like this. Did he never let anyone get close to him? Perhaps that was why he went through so many.

Four

★ ★ ★ ★

They drove in silence to the lake. As they flew, Miranda looked around curiously. The city and the buildings were the same. Everything was the same. She sighed.

"We used to have different cultures long ago, just like Earth," Alex said, hearing her thoughts, "But after billions of years, everything finally just became one. Everyone finally just agreed that peace was the most important of all. Peace, beauty, love..." Alex trailed off.

"I guess," Miranda said, staring out the window, her cheeks turning pink at the mention of love. She ignored her blush and continued, "I just can't picture Earth ever becoming like that."

"Maybe it will, over billions of years?"

Miranda frowned and looked out the window, "I missed a lot of learning."

Alex shifted, uncomfortably, "How far did you get?"

Miranda shrugged. They were too busy training mentally and physically to put a full effort into all her classes.

"Training mentally? What do you mean?"

Miranda's eyes widened in horror. She thought that out loud. Quickly she put up her mental block and tried to think up some lie.

"Well..." she started, "I had to learn how to read people's minds and move stuff. I thought it was more important, and it took me some time to do it."

Alex looked at her doubtfully, but Miranda had closed her mind to him. He waited for her to speak again, but she went quiet.

"It's a beautiful day," Miranda commented. She looked up at the cloudless sky. Alex nodded, disappointed she changed the subject.

"Oh, I left my phone in the car," Miranda said about halfway to the beach. They had parked with all the other vehicles in the large grassy area. It was a Sunday, so the beach was full of people. "I should get it just in case my family tries to call. I don't want them to worry."

"I will get us a spot," Alex said, and Miranda turned to head back to the car.

With her notebook in hand, Miranda didn't have a hard time finding Alex. He was surrounded by women. Miranda groaned, but knew she couldn't get irritated with fans. She put on a smile as she walked up.

Alex was posing for a picture when he spotted her, a girl on each arm and a wide smile on his face. It was the first one she had seen on him all day. Both girls were very pretty, and Miranda had to push away her jealousy. She had no claim on Alex and it shouldn't bother her. Before the next group of girls could grab Alex for a picture, he waved to Miranda. Miranda smiled again as the attention turned to her. Only one woman in the crowd recognized her. The others, it seemed, were not caught up with their episodes.

"I forgot my hat," Alex whispered to Miranda when she reached his side. He put his hand on her arm, just above the elbow and gave a small squeeze.

Miranda reached into her purse and pulled out his sunglasses that he had left in the car. She had assumed he would want them for the beach so she grabbed them.

"Nice!" Alex said, as he put them on. He gave her a kiss on the cheek and let his hand brush her upper arm, "Thank you."

It was a very affectionate touch and it made Miranda almost feel giddy, but she knew it was his way of getting rid of the crowd and she allowed him to use her for that purpose. She smiled up at him and rested her hand on his forearm. He reached over and tucked a wayward hair behind her ear.

There were still a few women who were trying to get a picture, but the others started to disperse, noticing Alex had a companion and they did not want to disturb him, just as he intended.

Miranda turned to the crowd, "OK, just a few more." She held out her hand for their notebooks, "I can take them."

The women smiled and Miranda was handed five notebooks. She took five pictures and handed them back.

"Can I get one of the two of you?" the woman who had recognized her asked.

Miranda nodded and stood next to Alex. He wrapped his arms around her so she rested her head against his shoulder.

Once they were gone, Alex sighed with relief and sat down on the blanket.

"Thank you for the rescue," Alex said. He was smiling and stopped abruptly, remembering that she had actually saved his life before. One of the evil people had attacked them and Miranda had narrowly saved Alex from a deadly flash.

"No sweat," Miranda said, with a smile taking a seat beside him. She gave him a playful nudge, trying to keep it light.

"I can guess what that expression means," Alex smiled again. He leaned back on his elbows taking in the sunshine, "What would you like to do?"

Miranda shrugged, "I'm going in the water. Are you going to be OK here by yourself?"

Alex nodded, "I suppose."

Miranda got up and took off her purple cover-up. She noticed Alex's eyes had wandered over her body, so she bunched up the dress and threw it at his face.

He chuckled as he pulled it off and put it on the blanket beside him.

Alex joined her in the water after about 15 minutes. He was tired of people coming up to him as he sat by himself watching Miranda in the water. The sunglasses weren't working since the fans knew he was there already and word seemed to be spreading.

Miranda had been watching him get harassed while she swam farther and farther out, but was enjoying the water too much to go sit with him. The water was warm and shimmery blue. She watched some bright green fish that were swimming lazily around and a few white fish which she could only see because of their red fins. When she saw Alex coming her way, she swam to meet him.

"I should have come out with you," he laughed as he met up with her. A light breeze rustled his hair. His laugh stopped abruptly as the wind picked up and the ground trembled. His eyes went wide and they automatically moved closer to each other, panicked. The wind was so ferocious that it picked up sand from the beach. Miranda felt the granules hit her face before she buried it in Alex's shoulder. The calm water became rippled with waves.

Miranda looked around him as a scream rang out from the beach and then the ground stopped. Just as the night of the party, it lasted only seconds but it had shook roughly. The attack was nearby.

"No," Miranda whispered and started to make her way towards the commotion. Alex followed right on her heels. Miranda struggled against the water which slowed her forward motion, but managed to finally reach the beach. She ran across the beach, away from their own belongings, with Alex right at her heels.

They reached the commotion. Several people were shaking and crying, gathered in a circle by the edge of the beach. Others were packing up their things hastily.

"What happened?" Miranda asked the first person she came across near the scene of the attack.

"A young girl was attacked," the man replied, his voice shaky, "Her brother was taken."

"Taken?" Alex repeated, aghast. He took Miranda's arm, instinctively.

The man nodded. "The poor girl was killed," he said, grimly. He frowned quickly towards the people gathered in a circle and went right back to packing his family's belongings.

Miranda paused. There was nothing she could do now. She turned to Alex and was engulfed in his arms. "That was so close," she said, shaking.

She felt Alex nod.

Miranda pulled away, "We should check our phones. My dad is probably calling."

Alex nodded again and his hand slid down her arm to take her hand as they headed quickly back across the beach. They had almost reached their blanket, when a reporter spotted them.

"Oh, Alex!" the man called out. He made his way over to them, his face lined with worry, "I am Gerald Kane. I write for *City 980*

News. It is nice to meet you both, but not under these circumstances. I heard you were both in town." He turned to Miranda, "I am so sorry, I forget your real name, Cara."

"Miranda," Alex answered for her, "I am sorry Gerald, but we must check in with our families. They must be worried."

Gerald nodded, "I understand. Do you mind if I follow?"

Alex shrugged.

"You make a lovely couple," Gerald commented, looking at their entwined hands.

"No, we… " Miranda started to say, but Alex said "Thank you." Miranda shot him a glance but Alex just looked determined to get to their phones.

Miranda could hear hers ringing as they walked up to the blanket so she let go of Alex and hurried to get it.

It was her father and brothers, all calling so she tapped them all. Alex's phone started ringing as well, and he bent to retrieve it.

"Oh Miranda, we were so worried," her father said. He looked frantic.

"Sorry, we were away from our phones. Alex and I are just fine. I got back to my phone as quickly as I could."

"I got word that the attack happened there," Evan said, anxiously. Of course he would, he worked at the television station. "What happened?"

"It did, but we are all fine," Miranda said, grim. "A young girl was attacked." She didn't tell them that it happened very close to where she was. She didn't want them to worry.

"I do not like you being there," Griffin said, worried, "It sounds like the evil ones are still there." Miranda could see Greta's face in the frame with him. She looked worried.

"We will go back to Alex's parents' place and stay there. I won't go anywhere," Miranda promised them.

"I love you, Miranda," Mr. East said, "Call me later, please?"

"Love you too, dad. I promise I will call and we will be safe."

Once they disconnected, Miranda looked at Alex. He was pale and talking with Gerald.

"Is your family OK?" Miranda asked him.

Alex nodded.

"So, you are here visiting family?" Gerald asked, and Alex nodded again. Gerald turned to Miranda, "Can I get your account of the incident?"

Miranda took a breath and looked quickly out at the water where they had been. It looked so serene like nothing dangerous had just occurred. "We were out in the water when the wind gusted and the ground started to shake. I heard a scream and that is all. It was over so quickly."

Gerald frowned, "Yes, just as the last one, very quick."

Miranda put up her mental block as she wondered if the evil ones were attacking quickly, so as not to give her enough time to react. How could she think of even stopping the attack when it was over so fast?

"We should go," Alex said with a frown as he bent down to pick up the blanket, "My parents are meeting us at home. I am sorry to cut our beach day short."

Miranda waved his apology away. There was no sense in him shouldering any blame. To her surprise, he put an arm around her waist. He was being very affectionate and she assumed it was because he was afraid with the attack happening so close.

"Well, thank you both for talking to me," Gerald said and headed to the scene of the attack. Most people had already left, though there were a few who seemed determined not to live in fear. They were sitting on their beach blankets, stiffly, looking around for anything strange. The lake was now devoid of people.

They didn't have many belongings to collect and were in Alex's car shortly afterwards, heading back to his parents' apartment.

Miranda took a deep breath and turned to Alex, "A lovely *couple* Alex? I was OK to pretend to get rid of the women who wanted pictures, but you can't tell that to people if it's not true."

Alex didn't look at her but he shrugged, "It is no point arguing it when we are so far away from home. Besides, everyone is concerned with the attack. He probably will not even remember."

Miranda paused for a second as she caught his passing thoughts. "Alex!" she swore at him, calling him a few funny names that he didn't know the meaning of. "You did that because Gerald thought I was pretty!"

"I was just trying to help you," Alex snapped, "Are you really going to go on a date with a reporter from another city?"

Miranda rolled her eyes. "Yes, right after they scraped the dead girl off the beach!" she snapped sarcastically, "You are crazy, Alex." Miranda turned her head to look out the window and crossed her arms, "I, unlike you, don't date everyone who talks to me."

"I do not date everyone who talks to me," Alex snapped.

"Oh sorry," Miranda said, "Only the women."

Alex sped up, his typical reaction when he was irritated.

Once they were back at his parents' apartment, Miranda went down to the pool by herself and stayed there for hours, away from Alex so she could clear her head. She went into the hot tub for a bit which had a view of the weights in the gym. She lifted them up and down with her mind. Luckily they were already set to a heavy weight so she got a good mind workout. How could she react faster next time? What if her powers had diminished since Jackson was gone?

When she grew tired of lifting the heavy weights, she jumped back into the pool and the coolness of it perked her back up. Her phone rang just as she was about to get out.

Miranda saw it was Nathan so she answered, "Hi Nathan!"

"Hi beautiful!" he replied.

She smiled, and a faint blush appeared on her face. She hardly thought she could look beautiful right now. Her hair was plastered to her face and dripping. But it was nice that he called her beautiful. It really made her feel special.

"I'm sorry I did not call you yesterday," Nathan said, "I forgot all about a meeting I had with work."

"Not to worry," Miranda said, "I am actually not in town."

"You're not?" he asked.

"I should probably be back by Friday. Would you like to go out then?" Miranda asked, hoping he wouldn't ask why she was away. She didn't want to tell him that she was with Alex. It would just potentially cause an unnecessary argument.

"Yes, that would be great!" Nathan agreed.

"Cool," Miranda smiled, "I cannot wait to see you."

Nathan smiled, "Me too. Have a great trip!"

"Thanks Nathan." They hung up. She went and stood under the dryer and then put her cover-up on before going back upstairs.

Alex's mother was reading while his father was watching television when Miranda walked in the front door.

"Did you have a good swim?" his mother asked, looking up from her notebook.

"Yes, I am just going to change," Miranda said from the foyer.

"OK," his mother replied, "We are still going to the races. Would you like to come?"

Miranda nodded and headed down the hall to change. She worried about another attack. The evil ones were so close by. She couldn't let anyone else get hurt, especially Alex's parents. She knew she needed to react faster this time and tried to think of ways she could practice. If only there was someone who could train her or at least train *with* her, like Jackson did. Miranda's only hope was to ask Jackson's mother to put her in contact with whatever group of people knew about the Legend, surely one of them might want to help her.

"Where is Alex?" Miranda asked his father when she returned to the living room. She hadn't seen him when she had walked in. Alex's mother was in the kitchen fixing something to eat for everyone.

Mr. West frowned, "He left right after you went downstairs and then he just messaged five minutes before you got back that he met up with a friend and would meet us at the race."

Miranda bit her lip. A friend? She had no idea he had any friends here.

Mrs. West called them both to dinner. Miranda felt a little awkward alone with Alex's family. She sighed, a little angry with Alex for leaving her and not even telling her that he was leaving.

At dinner, Erica told Miranda the funeral would be on Tuesday. Miranda's family would arrive that morning by express flight and their plan was to leave the next day, but Miranda was welcome to stay as long as she liked. Although it was terrible that they had the funeral to go to at all, Miranda was happy it was not going to be on her birthday, which was Wednesday. She wondered how she should celebrate her birthday, though right now she didn't feel much like celebrating.

"How is Alex?" his mother asked. She and Alex's father shared a look. Now that he wasn't there, they were free to ask.

Miranda looked between them, "He is fine." She looked down at her plate wondering where he was and who he was with. Why would he just leave her without saying anything?

"It is just that he does not talk about himself much when we call or visit," Mrs. West said, "I know he blames himself for his sister's death but surely he cannot believe that still?"

Miranda bit her lip, "Yes, I think he still does."

Mrs. West frowned and looked sadly at her husband, "He should have moved with us. I knew we should not have left him alone."

"He did not want to leave his friends or the show, Erica," Mr. West said, reaching out to take her hand, "You know that." He turned to Miranda, "We thought about staying in the city, but both our parents are here and we wanted to be close to them."

"We just could not stay in the same apartment," Mrs. West said with a sniff. Her eyes glistened with tears, "I miss him, though, and I try to call him at least once a day. He used to tell me everything, but now he will not open up to me anymore."

"I'm sorry," Miranda said. She put her fork down. She didn't know what else to say and she was very mad at Alex for leaving her to go out with some friend while she was here making up lies to his parents for him. He was probably with a girl. She wasn't going to tell Alex's parents that he dated a lot of girls and she took special care not to think it so they could hear. "Alex has never shared anything with me. He did not even tell me he had a friend to visit."

Mrs. West bit her lip, "We did not know he had a friend here either."

Silence ensued. Miranda barely touched her dinner and apologized when Mrs. West cleared her plate for her. Mr. West said they would leave shortly. He knew some of the drivers and was going to take them to the driver area prior to the race.

"I will message Alex to let him know where we will be," Mr. West said, taking out his phone.

The track was set up on the opposite side of the city. It had a lot of dips and curves that were displayed high up in the air. Since there were no mountains, like in Miranda's city, they would be able to see the whole race.

Mr. West led the way through the driver area where, to their surprise, they found Alex. He had removed the under-panels of his car and it was set to race. Miranda stopped in her tracks while Alex's parents moved ahead to check out his car detailing. He was given the number '82' for the race and it decorated his door.

Alex smiled when he saw them, "I am in the race tonight."

Mrs. West looked thrilled, "Oh that is wonderful, Alex! I have not seen you race in years!"

Mr. West happily ran a hand across the hood while Miranda stayed back, folding her arms across her chest. She glared at Alex, who completely ignored it.

"Yes, my friend races. She told the crew. I will be racing as myself and not under my alias," Alex smiled and he finally looked at Miranda, "There were reporters here earlier to do an interview." He turned his attention back to his parents when Miranda didn't say anything. "They wanted to encourage people to come out after the attack today. They do not want them to live in fear."

Miranda silently fumed. She couldn't believe he just went on television and announced to everyone to come out after that attack. What if the evil showed up again? What if they went after Alex? Miranda looked down as her eyes filled with tears. Didn't he know she couldn't do this without Jackson? Miranda wiped at her eyes, hastily, hoping no one would sense her panic.

Alex didn't seem to notice, or care, that she was upset. "I told them we would be available after the race to meet the fans," Alex said to her.

Miranda bit her lip and nodded, forcing her tears away. It didn't help that at that moment, a pretty blond-haired woman bounced over to stand beside Alex. She wore a bright green racing suit that hugged her curves. She took Alex's arm and smiled at him.

"This must be your family," she said brightly, her voice somewhat nasal.

Alex's mother smiled over at her.

"This is Kelsey," Alex said and introduced his parents, "She used to race in City 217 but she moved here six months ago. I thought I would surprise you all by entering the race tonight. Kelsey helped." He turned to Miranda, "And this is Miranda. She is on *Northern Shores* with me."

Miranda was able to force a smile out. This was Alex. What more could she expect?

Kelsey smiled at her, "Nice to meet you. You did really well. I watched your episodes today." She turned to Alex, "I normally catch up on Sundays." She turned to Alex, "Anyways, I have to go if I plan on winning the race."

"Maybe come in second," Alex challenged.

Kelsey gave him a playful nudge, "Yes, *you* can come in second." She gave him a quick kiss on the cheek and headed off, a little bounce in her step.

Once she was gone, Mrs. West looked uncomfortably between Alex and Miranda.

"I think we will go find a spot before it fills up," Mr. West said, obliviously, as he stepped back from Alex's car, "Have a great race!"

"Yes, have a great race," his mother agreed and kissed his other cheek.

Miranda just turned from him without a word and led the way back to the field. There were reporters near the entrance to the field who saw Miranda and motioned her over to them. She sent an apologetic look to Alex's parents and told them she would meet them on the grass.

"We will try to stay near the edge at the start/finish line so you can find us," Mr. West smiled.

Miranda went over to the reporters, unsure of what she would say. She hoped they wouldn't ask her too many probing questions.

"Hello, Miss East!" one woman called out.

"Please, call me Miranda," Miranda smiled.

"How are you enjoying our city?" she asked.

"We are here to visit Alex's family, but I am enjoying myself," Miranda explained. "It was a very unfortunate incident earlier today," she frowned. "I was at the beach with Alex when it happened."

"So, you really are a couple?" another asked. "My sister sent me a photo of the two of you at the beach. We are hoping to have your permission to print it."

"No, we are not," Miranda said to everyone, "Alex is my best friend and our families have always been close. Can I see the picture?"

The woman pressed a few buttons on her notebook and the picture of Alex and Miranda together at the beach showed up on the screen. She passed it to Miranda.

Miranda tried not to frown. It was the one the last girl had taken of the two of them in each other's arms. She shrugged as she gave the woman back her phone. "Perhaps not tomorrow, not with what happened there. Any time after tomorrow is fine."

The woman nodded in agreement, "I completely understand, we would definitely not put any spotlight on your presence here when such a devastating event occurred. I will file it for the news on the following day."

Miranda nodded and smiled in thanks.

"How do you feel about Alex racing?" a man with a video camera asked next.

Miranda turned to him, "Alex is great at everything he does and that includes racing. He is really dedicated and I admire him for it."

"Have you ever raced?"

"No, but I have been in the car with Alex," she made a face, "He likes to drive fast all the time."

There was a small chuckle around the group. "Can you tell us what is to come on the show? Is there to be an official breakup of Jeff and Janet?"

"Sorry everyone, but that is a secret," Miranda said, "My brother would be mad at me if I told!"

"Ah yes, Evan is your twin correct?"

Miranda nodded, "I am so proud of my brother and his show. He has an amazing imagination and our writing team is the best with him at the lead."

"This is your first job in acting?"

"Yes," Miranda said and explained, "I used to travel often with my mother but I prefer acting and I had a great teacher."

"Did you shadow Alex?"

"Yes," Miranda lied, closing her mind so no one would know, "He taught me everything I know which is probably why we make such a great couple on screen."

Everyone nodded in agreement.

"I was very lucky a position opened on my brother's show," Miranda continued. "He had no idea it was what I wanted most, and I begged him to let me try out. He had no idea how good I had become." She winked.

"Well, he made a great choice!"

"Thank you everyone," Miranda smiled, "I really should go before the race starts."

She said goodbye and headed towards the seating area. She pulled out her phone and sent Alex a message that if anyone asked, she was his shadow and that she learned everything from him. He messaged back that she would do well to keep listening to him. She ignored that comment and tucked her phone into her pocket.

While she walked, she had an idea. She went over to where they sold the race shirts and bought herself a hat which she pulled low over her face. Maybe that would buy her some time before she was recognized.

Miranda spotted Alex's parents and joined them.

"New hat?" Mr. West asked.

Miranda laughed. She had no idea whose number it was. She just picked the black one with the number '24' in blue on it which matched her blue shirt.

"I thought it would help me get through the race before fans recognize me," Miranda smiled.

"It would help a bit if it weren't for your long, beautiful brown hair," Mrs. West said, motioning with her hand.

Miranda pulled an elastic out of her purse, tied her hair back and returned the hat to her head, tucking her ponytail neatly through the opening in the back. "Better?" she asked Mrs. West, who nodded.

No one recognized Miranda. There were so many people at the races that they had to turn some away. Alex came in second place and his parents were ecstatic. They were so excited the whole time watching as their son zoomed around the track. Miranda could tell they absolutely adored and missed him terribly. Mrs. West gushed about his 2nd place finish as they made their way back to the driver's area.

"Oh there he is," Mrs. West pointed to him about 50 feet away. He had just walked into view with another pretty girl on his arm. Mrs. West frowned and looked at Miranda.

Miranda shook her head slowly and then a slow rage filled her. His words from earlier rang in her head. How can he say they were a couple just because some reporter thought she was pretty, but then flirt with all these other women? She took off her hat, pulled her hair out of the elastic and ran her hand through her hair a few times, hoping it looked OK. She turned to Mrs. West, "Can you hold this just a minute?" she asked sweetly.

Mrs. West nodded, curiously, and took her hat.

Miranda put a big smile on her face and started to run towards Alex. "Alex!" she called out happily. Alex spun to face her. She practically jumped into his arms, he had to catch her and spin her around which had forced him to let go of the woman. "Oh Alex, my sexy cuddle bear, I am so proud of you! That was a great race!" Miranda pretended to notice the women beside him and continued to talk baby talk, "Oh I am so sorry. I just could not help myself." She turned back to Alex and gave his cheek a pinch, perhaps a little too hard, "Who could leave this gorgeous face for more than five seconds, never mind a whole race!"

"Oh yes, Miranda!" the woman smiled, "It is great to meet you! Can I have your autograph as well?"

"Sure," Miranda smiled wider, reluctantly letting go of Alex. She took the woman's notebook and signed it.

"I did not realize you were a couple," the woman said when she had taken her notebook back. There was a little disappointment in her voice.

"Well, it is very new," Miranda smiled. She put her arms around Alex again and gave him a squeeze.

"Well, it was nice to meet you both," the woman said and turned to walk away. Alex's mother burst out laughing and his dad chuckled once she was out of earshot. Miranda let go of Alex and he gave her a disgusted look.

"Was that necessary?" Alex snapped.

"Listen here, jerkface," Miranda snapped, "If I cannot even have someone think I am pretty, you cannot throw yourself at the first woman who bats her eyelashes at you." She poked him hard in the shoulder.

"I was just being nice," Alex said, shaking his head at her.

Miranda snorted, "Sure."

Alex's parents shared a look of discomfort. There was a few seconds of silence before they both spoke at the same time in hopes of breaking the tension.

"Great race, Alex!" Mr. West had said, while Mrs. West had said, "Nice second place finish!"

Alex sent them a small smile, "Thanks."

"We should go celebrate," Mr. West said.

"We are going to have to say hello to the fans first," he told them, "Do you want to meet us there?"

"Yes, we will go and get a table," Mrs. West said, "The place is called *Checkered Flag*."

"We will try not to be long, but there are a lot of people here," Alex said.

"Not to worry," Mr. West said, "We can wait."

They both left arm in arm and Miranda watched them walk away. She almost wished she could go with them, knowing that Alex was now mad at her.

"Sexy cuddle bear?" Alex asked, angrily, fixing her with a glare.

Miranda snickered, "It was the first thing that came to mind."

"Could you at least pretend to sound like you are from this planet?" he snapped and started walking away.

Miranda bit her lip. Of course that wouldn't be a term of endearment here. She had no idea what they used as their pet names. She had never heard Greta and Griffin call each other anything but each other's names. Nathan called her beautiful and her dad had called her sweetheart before. Alex called her Maddie, but that was just after a tiny wild cat, and she knew he did it to mock her shortness. She sighed.

"Are you coming?" Alex snapped as he spun back around towards her.

Miranda frowned and caught up to him. She didn't understand why he was so mad, unless he had really wanted to hook up with that girl.

They walked in silence until they reached the edge of the driver's area. Even from far away, they could tell there must be a thousand people standing there.

"Well, I hope your hand is better. We have to get through this quickly. No personal pictures and no, we are not a couple," Alex snapped.

"Good!" Miranda said, matching his anger, "Why don't *you* remember that when it matters?"

"As long as you do," Alex crossed his arms, staring her down.

"I remember just fine, Alex," she glared back.

"Uh, Alex?" a nervous-looking race official cut in, "Sorry to bother you both but can I get you over here for a minute?"

They were forced to end their staring contest and Alex turned to go, "Just go over there and start with that crowd. I will be there in a minute." He didn't look back as he headed away with the race official.

Miranda headed towards the crowd, nervous. They had set up a makeshift stage with a table and two chairs on it for the two of them. Miranda slowed her pace. She had no idea how to address a large crowd like this. It was different when she was up on stage acting. She had lines to memorize. She took a look over her shoulder. Alex was posing for pictures with the winner of the race and his trophy.

Miranda reached the stage sooner than she wanted to. A few of the race officials were acting as ushers, forming a group of people, mostly women into a line.

"I am glad you are here," one of them said, "We were worried you both would leave and we would not know what to do with the crowd." He smiled.

Miranda sent him a nervous smile, "Alex will be here in just a minute."

"The stage is on so they will be able to hear you in the back," he explained, "We have only allowed the first 100 people to get to the race a chance for an autograph since there are so many. I am sure you would not have had enough time to get to them all. We have them lined up."

Miranda nodded, but had no idea what he meant until she stepped on the stage and could hear her footsteps echo. The backdrop projected the show's name on it and hers and Alex's name on either side with a large picture of the pier in behind. It looked so real, Miranda had to pause a second. Everyone burst into applause when they saw her and many pulled out their phones to take a picture.

"Hello everyone," she said when she reached front and centre. She smiled and the crowd hushed. "Alex will be here in just a minute, but I just wanted to thank you all for your continued support of the show." She copied Alex's lines from the restaurant last night, "We would be nothing without our fans and we thank you for watching. I am looking forward to being a part of this already amazing show."

The crowd roared again and Miranda smiled. She thought it was for her but she heard footsteps behind her. Alex had walked onto the stage. He put an arm around her and kissed the top of her head. It was a nice act, considering he was so mad at her. Miranda smiled brightly. She could act too.

"Yes, thank you very much everyone," Alex added, "I am happy to have such a wonderful co-star who is also one of my best friends. We have a lot of great story lines coming up and hope you will continue to watch."

They both smiled to let the crowd take some pictures then Alex nodded at the race crew who cut the stage microphone.

"That was good," he whispered to her.

"Thanks," she mumbled, "I stole it from you, of course."

Alex laughed under his breath. They both took a seat and the line started to move. Each person took a picture and had both of them sign it. They answered any question that they could.

By the time they were finished, Miranda could barely lift her arm and her face hurt from smiling. She rubbed her jaw with her left arm, "I think I need a drink after all that," she laughed.

Alex looked at his notebook and started typing, "Well, we should go. My parents have been waiting for two hours. I let them know we are on our way."

Miranda and Alex waved to the people who were left, they cheered for them as they made their way offstage.

The ride to the bar was quiet. It was pretty and looked a lot like Ernie's in their home town. It had a race car on display in green lights near the front doors and two large checkered flags announcing the name of the bar.

They found Alex's parents and each ordered a drink.

Miranda told Alex's parents all about the post-race crowd while Alex wandered around socializing with the other racers. Miranda preferred the company of his parents and they seemed to really like her.

Several drinks later, Alex's parents were ready to leave.

"I think Alex has been drinking too," Miranda said, "Shall I go get him so he can come with us?" She hadn't seen him at all in the last hour and wondered if he was even still there.

"Yes, thank you," Mr. West said, checking his watch. "I should go check on my father." He took one last long drink from his water glass and set it down empty.

Miranda wandered around the bar looking for Alex. He was talking to a woman at a far table. As she headed towards them, the woman leaned in and kissed him. Miranda stopped in her tracks, her stomach dropped to the floor. Would it ever stop bothering her that he made out with every woman he met and was a complete liar? She shook her head and frowned. She fought the urge to storm up to Alex and give him a piece of her mind. Instead, she turned on the spot and walked away quickly, meeting up with Alex's parents at the door.

"Alex is not coming," Miranda said. She closed her mind so they would not know she was upset or what she saw, "He is busy being Alex."

Mrs. West smiled, "Would you like to stay here with him?"

Miranda shook her head, "I hope you do not mind but I am really tired. I would prefer to go."

"Of course we do not mind," Mrs. West smiled and Mr. West led the way to the car.

When Miranda got back to the apartment, she excused herself, changed into her pajamas and hopped into bed. Once she was settled, she allowed the tears to come and she cried herself into her nightmares.

"Miranda, wake up! You are having a nightmare," Mrs. West shook her gently.

Miranda's eyes snapped open and she sat up quick, her eyes wild. She frantically looked around the room, still feeling like someone was after her. The lights were dim, casting shadows around the room and she shrank back in the unfamiliar bed.

"It is OK, sweetheart," Mrs. West put her arms around her to calm her, "You were having a bad dream."

"I am so sorry to wake you," Miranda whispered, taking deep breaths to calm herself.

"Not to worry," Mrs. West said, "I am a light sleeper."

"Is Alex home?" Miranda asked, without thinking, as she scanned the room again.

"Want me to check?" she asked.

Miranda shook her head. As much as she did want to know, she also didn't want to find out that he was not home. She glanced at her notebook. It was 4:15.

"I will get him," Mrs. West said, and left before Miranda could tell her not to.

Miranda's eyes filled with tears as the night's events came flooding back to her. She thought she was finally getting somewhere with Alex, at least as friends. They were having such a good time until that attack happened.

"No, mom," Miranda heard Alex whisper just outside the door, "Go back to bed. I can take care of her."

She didn't want to see him so she laid down and rolled away from the door. Alex closed the door behind him and went to stand over her.

"Are you OK?" he asked, sleepily.

"I'm fine," Miranda whispered in reply. She was worried if she spoke any louder, he would be able to tell she was crying.

She felt him sit down on the bed beside her.

"Don't touch me," Miranda snapped. Alex who had just been reaching out to rub her arm, pulled his hand back.

"Why did you ask for me then?" he snapped back.

"I didn't," Miranda whispered, "Your mom assumed I wanted you but I don't need you."

Alex sighed, "Fine. I have things I want to do tomorrow and will probably be gone for the day."

"Fine," Miranda snapped. He probably wanted to go out with some girl. He was such a jerk. Miranda heard him retreat and she rolled over and glared at the closed door. There was no way she was going to stay here. She was so mad at him for leaving her that day without an explanation and then hooking up with who knows how many women. And now he had made other plans that didn't include her. She should have never come with him. It had been a horrible idea. She needed time away from him to remind herself why they couldn't be together. There were several hotels in the city. She would find one, she thought, as she threw the covers off.

She packed her things and sent a message to Evan telling him that she was going to a hotel. City 980 was four hours ahead, so it was still very early for Evan. He wouldn't get the message till he awoke and by then, he wouldn't be able to tell her to stay. Once she had everything together, she waited another 20 minutes in hopes everyone would be sleeping again and then she crept quietly through the apartment.

On the rooftop, she pushed the bus call button so it would know to pick her up. It wasn't long after that it showed up. It was exactly like the buses at home, with a picture of some kind of wild cat as the City emblem. It read 'City 980 Bus Services'.

Miranda smiled to the driver as she climbed aboard.

"I am looking to get to the hotel," she told him.

"Certainly!" he smiled, "It is not very far and I have not had many people out tonight. I can take you straight there. Have a seat!"

"Thank you so much," Miranda said, swiping her identification card as she took a seat near the front.

The bus driver dropped her off on the rooftop of the hotel. She took her bag, thanked him again and headed down one floor to the hotel lobby.

An older woman was at the front desk. She looked sleepy but was playing on her notebook when Miranda approached the desk.

"Hello, I would like a room please," Miranda smiled at her.

"Welcome to the hotel, for how many nights?"

"I will be leaving Wednesday morning."

"Great!" the woman smiled. She took Miranda's identification card to type in her details, "Oh I barely recognized you but I heard you and Alex were in town. I watch your show!"

Miranda smiled, "Just here visiting family."

The woman typed in her information and deducted money from her account.

"Just a single bedroom? I will upgrade you to a suite, free of charge!"

Miranda thanked her with a smile.

"Perfect! We have one single bedroom suite left." She handed Miranda back her identification.

"If you will hold still a moment, I will program you into Alpha." Miranda stood still a moment while a dome came down from the ceiling and she was scanned. "Excellent, Alpha will know which room you are in and you will be allowed to access it." She explained to Miranda that they had all the amenities she would need. A pool and fitness room, a game room, a restaurant with an excellent menu and a movie theatre. There were also stores on site with personal stylists and a salon if she wanted to be pampered. "You are in room 206 which is down one floor. There are six rooms per floor. You will be at the end of the hallway."

Miranda smiled and thanked her. She could definitely use a massage later. She picked up her bag and headed back to the elevator.

Miranda had Alpha turn on the lights when she arrived in her room. It was really nicely furnished in bright colours and opened to a living area. There were two doors, one on each side of the large screen television mounted on the wall. She opened the first which was the bathroom. It had a large tub with jets and a stand up shower. The other door opened to the bedroom which had a king size bed. She smiled and jumped on the bed, happy that she was away from Alex now.

She jumped off the bed and headed back into the living room. There was a large corner bureau beside the sitting window which had an oven and a cupboard. There were small bottles labelled ice cream and cookies that she could use for snacks and a dozen bottles of alcohol in different flavours. She smiled. This was way better than staying with Alex. She felt bad for leaving his parents, they probably wouldn't understand why she needed to leave anyway. That would be up to Alex to explain. She didn't have either of his parent's contacts, so she could not leave them a message that she had left for the hotel.

She couldn't sleep anymore so she grabbed a blanket from the bed and brought it out to the couch, making herself comfortable. She used voice commands and decided to watch the episodes of *Northern Shores* that she missed. She had only watched her first day and had missed the last two days.

Her phone rang, which woke her up. It was Alex so she pushed ignore. Did he really think she was going to answer? It was 8:29 so he must have finally realized she was gone. *Good*, she thought. If he wanted to leave her with his parents and go out with a million different women, then fine. But she didn't have to put up with it.

Her phone rang three more times and each time she pushed ignore. She knew Alex would be so angry but she didn't care. He deserved it after ignoring her the previous day.

She restarted the episode that she had been watching.

Her phone rang again and she would have shut it off if she knew that eventually someone in her family would call. Sure enough, this time it was Evan.

She answered with a smile, "Hi Evan."

Evan rolled his eyes, "Hello, dear sister." He yawned. He had probably been sleeping.

"So, Alex called you?"

Evan nodded, "You want to tell me what happened? I really do not like you being there on your own, especially with the recent attacks there."

"I am fine. I checked into a hotel and there is a lot I can do here. I promise I will stay here and you will all be here tomorrow morning anyways."

"And Alex?"

"Please do not make me go back to him," Miranda pleaded, quietly. She squeezed her eyes shut in hopes he wouldn't make her. There wasn't much he could do though, except tell Alex where she was and then Alex would probably come get her.

Evan sighed, "Do you want to talk about it?"

Miranda shook her head, "I couldn't stay there anymore, but I would not have left if it wasn't for a good reason."

"What did he do?"

Miranda frowned. She didn't want to admit to Evan her confused feelings for him.

There was a pause as Evan carefully watched her face. She looked so unhappy. "I will tell him to leave you alone then," Evan frowned when she didn't answer. He sighed, "I will not tell him where you are either."

"Thanks Ev. I will see you tomorrow." She tried to smile.

"Be safe Miranda. Message me if you need anything."

"OK, love you!"

"I love you too."

Miranda hung up, happy he hadn't forced her to go back to Alex. Five minutes later she received a message from Alex. *I am sorry. Please come back.*

She messaged back that she just wanted to be left alone and that he could do *whoever* he wanted, she didn't care.

Her phone rang again and she ignored it again.

Please just tell me where you are, was the message she got back. She just typed back, *No*. She smiled a bit, knowing Evan had kept his promise. At least he was on her side.

After she finished catching up on *Northern Shores*, she went down to the salon and got a massage. The woman who was working there knew who she was so she also included a manicure and a pedicure, free of charge. While she was there, she got a call from Greta, who asked if she could join her that afternoon. Miranda knew it was her brother's doing, but thought it would be nice to have the company, so she agreed.

Miranda jumped back, frightened when she found Alex sitting on her couch. He looked miserable with his head down and he had her bag at his feet. *So much for the massage*, she thought as her stress returned in full. "What are you doing here? How did you get in?"

"We do not use locks, Maddie, you know that. See how easy it is for someone to go after you?" Alex looked up at her, a pained expression. He stood. "Come back with me, Miranda. I packed your stuff."

"No," Miranda said, stubbornly. She picked up her bag from his feet and put it back in her room. "Greta is coming later and I will spend the day with her. Just go away! I thought you had things to do?"

"Why?" he asked, following her.

"You are missing the point of this. You cannot tell me I am not allowed to date someone and then turn around and shove your tongue down the throat of every girl you meet!" she snapped, turning to him.

"So that is what this is about?" Alex asked, "You are just mad that I said we were a couple to Gerald? Do you want his number? If I get it will you come back with me?"

"No, Alex!" Miranda snapped, "I do NOT have any interest in Gerald! And I am NOT going back with you."

Alex took a deep breath and asked calmly, "Please?"

"Tell your parents I am sorry I had to leave," Miranda said and went around him back out to the living room. It was uncomfortable being in the bedroom with him.

"No." He followed.

"Fine, then I will tell them tomorrow," Miranda snapped, "Just go AWAY! Go do whatever you want with whoever you want!" She was trying so hard not to send him flying across the room. She stomped over to her cupboard where she knew there was some alcohol and pulled a bottle out.

"You know I am not like that," Alex insisted.

Miranda snorted, which made her choke a little on her drink.

"I was so worried when I woke up and you were gone. Do you have any idea how scared I was to find your bed empty? I searched everywhere," Alex sighed, sadly, "I thought something happened to you. You promised you would not leave."

Miranda shrugged, "I saw you last night, Alex."

Alex looked puzzled, "OK? We were at the bar last night. Of course you saw me."

"I saw you kissing that girl," Miranda snapped.

He let out a frustrated laugh, "Seriously? You saw one girl try to kiss me and you run away?"

"You left me with your parents too. You didn't even tell me you were leaving and look where you went, right to some girl."

Alex ran a hand over his face and sat down on the couch. It was a full minute before he spoke. "I needed to think. I was out driving around when Kelsey messaged me. She found out I was in town. I barely spent an hour with her and then I was at the track. I didn't mean to be gone for so long and I am sorry I did not message you or tell you."

Miranda took another drink, a little embarrassed for overreacting. "And what about today? You said you were going to leave me again."

"I was mad, Miranda," Alex said, "I was tired and my mother woke me up. You said you did not need me."

Miranda rolled her eyes, "So quick to blame me all the time."

Alex frowned, "No, I did not mean it that way. I was half asleep. I do not have any plans today. I just assumed we would spend the day with my parents."

Miranda shook her head and took another drink. "I really think you should just go," she said after a moment.

"I said I was sorry," Alex said, quietly, watching her.

"I need some time too."

Alex sighed and stood, "Greta will be here later?"

Miranda nodded.

"Fine," Alex said, "Just stay safe." He frowned at her and then left.

Five

★　★　★　★

Miranda was sad she had let him go. She felt silly for overreacting, or did she? From what she remembered of the girl kissing Alex last night, he hadn't tried to pull away. She wasn't sure how to feel anymore. It was all so confusing. She liked Alex, a lot, but she needed to focus and she was having a hard time doing that. She couldn't stop thinking about him. While she waited for Greta, she had a few drinks. At about 18 hour, there was a knock on the door and Miranda was so happy to see Greta. She hugged her tight and tears sprang to her eyes.

"Oh Miranda," Greta said, upon seeing the tears, "What happened?"

"I don't know," Miranda said, sullenly. She told Greta everything from when they left City 217 till now. "I don't think I overreacted. Alex didn't show any restraint," Miranda frowned, as she finished her tale, "He doesn't feel the same way."

"Of course he does," Greta tried to console her, "He just does not know how to express it."

Miranda snorted a laugh, "He goes out with other women all the time. How does that mean he feels the same?"

"I think he is afraid," Greta explained, "And I think it is because of his sister. I think that he thinks he could lose anyone he loves and it frightens him."

"I just have such a hard time believing it. Especially with all the other girls. And I can't love him anyways. I feel so guilty."

"You are both so in love," Greta said with a wistful smile, "You both have been through so much that you both deny it. You deny yourself the thing that will make you the most happy because you do not think you deserve it."

"No," Miranda disagreed, "Alex doesn't feel the same way."

"Yes he does," Greta insisted, giving her arm a comforting squeeze, "Alex feels the exact same way. I know it, your brothers know it and I even think your dad knows it. Everyone knows except you and him."

Miranda pressed her lips together in thought, "So what do I do?"

Greta's face lit up. She looked like an idea popped into her mind. "How important is it to you?" Greta asked.

"How important is he?" Miranda asked. She thought about it a minute before she answered. There was no point in denying herself anymore. She had so much affection for Alex that it would just eat away at her if she kept denying it. "I would give my life for him." Miranda closed her mind so Greta could not hear what she thought next. Although evil had returned, Miranda needed the little love she had left in her life to help get her through. She would protect Alex to her dying breath, even if it meant telling him about the Legend.

"And you almost did!" Greta said, reminding Miranda that she had saved his life before by putting herself in danger. "So just wait."

"Wait?"

"Yes, just wait. What are a few months when you will most likely spend the rest of your life with him?"

Miranda remembered saying almost the same thing to Helen on Earth. She had told Helen that it didn't matter if Helen and Bryan spent a few years apart going to different schools when they would likely spend the rest of their lives with each other after. This was different though, since she had to watch Alex date other women while she waited. And then of course, her guilt returned. "What am I waiting for? Waiting for him to realize that it is me he belongs with? What about Jack?" Miranda frowned, "I will always be tied to him."

"Yes, it would be dishonourable not to keep a close memory of Jackson. But you cannot live your life in the past. You have to move on," Greta smiled, and gave her an encouraging hug, "You just wait. Alex will realize what he needs."

"OK. I will try to be more patient," Miranda agreed, doubtful, "But I cannot help but get upset when he goes out with other women."

"Yes and I truly believe that he is dating other women as a means to deny his feelings."

"That is a horrible thing to do," Miranda said with a frown.

"Just you wait," Greta said, putting a reassuring arm around her, "He will realize his mistakes. Now, we should do something fun. I hear the lake is beautiful."

Miranda nodded and bit her lip, "That is where the attack happened yesterday. Alex and I were there."

Greta frowned, "You were right there? You should have said so!"

Miranda shook her head, "I didn't want to scare you all. It happened pretty far from where Alex and I were. A young girl was killed and her brother was taken."

Greta put the hand that had been resting on Miranda's arm to her mouth. She looked in thought for a minute and then put her hand down, "Well, I will not allow them to scare me. We cannot live in fear. This is our planet and our peace."

Miranda looked into Greta's eyes and knew she meant it. "OK, let's go to the beach."

They spent the rest of the afternoon on the lake. Greta suggested they rent a small speed boat. She told Miranda she grew up in a city that had a beautiful lake as well and had spent most of her life on the water. She was an expert sailor. Although Miranda worried the whole day that there would be another attack, there wasn't. It was a fun day and Miranda was happy.

That night, Miranda's dreams were jumbled images of the previous attacks. She had to re-live saving Alex, and Jackson's death. She saw the face of every evil person that had been in the school that day including the woman who looked so familiar. Greta had to wake her in the middle of the night. They both slept on the king size bed and Miranda had awoken her with her thrashing.

As Miranda lay awake in the early hours of the morning, she convinced herself that it was her feeling for Alex that was responsible for Jackson's death. She didn't live up to her end of the Legend. She was never in love with Jackson because her heart always belonged to someone else. She didn't understand her feelings for Alex, because she had never been in love before. Was this what it was like? *Love sucks*, Miranda thought glumly as she finally decided that more sleep was hopeless and hopped in the shower.

Greta was awake when she got out. She was looking at Miranda carefully as she left the washroom. "You still have bad dreams?" she asked.

Miranda nodded, "All the time."

Greta frowned, "I thought they were gone. We just didn't hear you screaming anymore."

Miranda shrugged.

"What happens?"

"Just the past events. I keep re-living them."

Great shivered visibly, "I wonder what we can do to help."

"I have tried everything," Miranda said, taking a seat on the couch beside her, "going to bed hungry, going to bed full, staying up till I'm absolutely exhausted, thinking happy thoughts. The only thing that works sometimes is sleeping beside Alex." Miranda frowned and then remembered, "Except for the one night his grandmother passed away. It seems we both had nightmares that night though."

"Hmm," Greta said, thoughtful, "it did not work to sleep beside me. It looks like even your subconscious is trying to tell you something."

Miranda gave her a weary look, "I get it. He doesn't."

After Greta was showered and ready, they went down to the restaurant for breakfast and then went shopping. Miranda bought a black skirt and a printed black and navy shirt. She was tired of wearing the same black dress to all the funerals she had to attend. Was this what her life was going to be here, funeral after funeral? She was going to have to do something, but she had no idea what.

Greta got a call from Griffin once they had arrived in the city and they all agreed to meet up at the funeral parlour. Griffin, Evan and her father were waiting for them right by the elevator on the roof as soon as the girls arrived.

Tears sprung into Miranda's eyes as she threw her arms around her dad first. She hadn't realized how much she missed them.

"Oh Miranda," he said, soothingly, "Are you OK?"

"I just missed you all so much," Miranda said, trying to stop the tears from falling, but she couldn't. She let go of her dad and hugged her brothers next.

"We missed you too, sweetheart," Mr. East said. "How was your trip aside from missing us?"

"It was good," she said, giving them a brief synopsis but leaving out the bad parts.

"Sounds like you both had fun," Griffin said, putting an arm around his fiancée. Greta smiled reassuringly at him.

"We were worried about you after the attack," Mr. East said with a frown as he turned finally to push the elevator button.

"We were fine," Greta said, giving them a small smile.

Miranda took a deep breath as the elevator doors opened. She knew she would be seeing Alex really soon and her palms started to sweat. The reception area looked a lot like the one in her own city. It had darker walls and a rustic feel. There were ivory couches and plants dispersed in a pattern around the large gathering room they entered. She followed behind her family and, of course, Alex and his parents were close by the elevator door greeting everyone. They turned to Miranda's family with hugs. Finally it was Miranda's turn. She waited until her father was out of earshot before she apologized to Alex's parents for leaving.

"Oh Miranda," Mrs. West said, "I wish I knew what had happened. We were so worried when Alex was not well. He spent the entire day in his room and would not come out for anything."

Miranda apologized again, "I should not have left. I really enjoyed meeting the both of you and I hope you will have me again."

"Yes, definitely," Mr. West said. Mrs. West nodded and added, "We would be happy if you would come again."

Miranda smiled in thanks and turned to Alex. Alex was trying not to look her way. He looked tired and miserable, unkempt. It was very un-Alex-like

"Can we talk later?" she asked and he nodded. He caught her hand as she was about to turn away.

"I really am sorry for the way I behaved," he said, quietly, "You deserve an explanation."

"I'm sorry too," Miranda replied, "I shouldn't have overreacted."

Alex gave her a curt nod, "We will talk later."

Miranda could see Jackson's family across the lobby. She was almost afraid to go over to them but that was the direction her family was headed next. Marcy, Jackson's mother, was the first they reached. Marcy was the only one who knew the whole truth. She was the only one Miranda could actually confide in but she felt she couldn't because it had gotten her son killed. She didn't want to bring it up to her over and over again.

"It is great to see you all," Marcy said, tearfully, "I am glad you could make it."

Everyone offered their condolences. Marcy caught Miranda's eye and motioned for her to follow.

They walked to a darker corner behind a large plant where Marcy threw her arms around Miranda, who let her cry for a few minutes.

"Oh, I am so sorry," Marcy said, finally pulling away and wiping her eyes, "I cannot believe I am acting like this. It is just my James, my only other child. What else can a mother do?"

Miranda was confused. What did she mean? What about James?

"The Legend," Marcy explained, "James holds the power of the West now. I want you to tell him with me. I want you to help him understand."

Miranda's mouth dropped open. "No!" she almost shouted and took a step back from her. The room was getting busier now and several people turned their way.

Marcy pulled her farther behind the plant, her eyes wide, "There is still evil out there, Miranda. You cannot defeat it alone."

Miranda's eyes filled with tears again and finally spilled over. She couldn't train someone else to take Jackson's place only to lead them to their death. "No," Miranda shook her head again, "I cannot. I will do it alone before I bring him into this."

Marcy touched her cheek, "You are so brave, Miranda, but this is how it has to be."

Miranda continued to shake her head. She would not let this happen again. Was she expected to love James now? She didn't even know him! A wave of nausea came over her and she clutched her sides trying to keep herself calm and not go to pieces in front of everyone.

Marcy could see her falling apart. "Miranda, OK," Marcy said, reluctantly, "We will wait."

"Wait?" Miranda repeated, numbly. It was a word she had already heard once too much recently. She wavered on her feet a little.

"We can wait and see if this escalates," Marcy explained. "If it continues with small attacks then I will not tell James. But as soon as the attacks get larger and we can see that evil has grown in numbers, we must tell him."

Miranda took a deep breath. "I cannot agree to that either. If we wait, James will not be ready. I have to do this alone," she insisted.

"I have already lost one boy," Marcy said, with accusation in her tone, "*I* will decide whether my other son will be brought into all this."

Miranda turned her back on Marcy's glare and walked away. She had to, before she threw up. She went to the elevator, feeling Marcy's eyes on her. When it opened she got in and took the elevator to the top of the building. She needed to be alone to think, and the confined roof would have to do. She needed fresh air.

Miranda hid herself between two cars and sat on the ground with her back against the roof ledge. Marcy had reminded her why she was here, her purpose on the planet. Her small drama with Alex was nothing. She could never be with him because now she was supposed to be with James? The thought made her sick again and she wished she had gone to the washroom instead. She took deep, heaving breaths, trying to hold back a complete breakdown. James was only 15, and he was so innocent.

Miranda had no idea how long she had been outside when she heard her phone beep and pulled it out of her purse. It was Evan who messaged to ask where she was. Miranda wiped her face as best she could before she went back down to the lounge. She couldn't miss the funeral. Her family was near the elevator. All of them were looking in different directions, trying to find her.

Mr. East saw her first, "There you are!" He looked anxious.

"Sorry dad, I was in the washroom."

"Oh, I thought Evan checked the washroom," he said with a quick look at his son.

Evan shook his head at her then turned to their father, "I guess I did not look hard enough." He pulled Miranda aside while the family went ahead. "Tell me what is wrong," Evan said, putting a hand on her shoulder.

Miranda stared at him, wanting someone to talk to.

Evan gave her a hug, "I can see you are upset. Please do not hide from me, talk to me. Tell me everything. Do you want to go?"

Miranda shook her head. It would be rude to leave now and she couldn't tell Evan. She couldn't tell anyone, she thought, as she pulled out of his embrace.

"You can tell me," Evan insisted. "You can tell me anything even if you think I will not like what you have to say. Even if you think it will scare me. You have to tell me."

Miranda looked up into his eyes. He was her twin brother. Maybe she could tell him. She would definitely have to think about it. "Maybe later," she said, hoping that would satisfy him.

Evan nodded and led the way to the cremation room, where Alex's grandmother lay on the table. Miranda went to stand by her father, who put his arm around her.

Alex's grandfather stood close to his wife with his sons on either side of him. He looked to be leaning on them heavily.

Once everyone was in the room, the director of the funeral parlour joined them and stood at a podium. Miranda looked around. She had never been to a full funeral. She always left before the body was put into the fire.

The director thanked everyone for coming. "Just as when you are born and married, you are reminded of the basics of life, earth, water, wind and fire. We are made from the earth and drink in the purifying waters, our lives are like the wind which helps to ignite the flame of death and we are left again as earth. It is a cycle. So as we remember Geneva West, we remember that though her body is gone, she remains alive in the earth. I hope you find comfort and will all keep your memories alive as we give Geneva to the flames and back to the earth." He stepped down from the stage and opened the door. A roaring fire was beyond the door. It made Miranda jump a little as she felt the heat and she gripped her father's arm tighter. The director pushed a button and the table supporting Alex's grandmother disappeared into the fire.

Miranda felt awful. She was at the funeral of the West's grandmother who had been attacked by the evil ones. She had to stop her hormones and stop chasing after Alex. It meant nothing. She was put on this planet to protect it from evil and she had failed. Two others were dead.

Fifteen minutes after the body had been engulfed in flames and after 15 minutes of silence, the fire receded and went out. There was nothing left but ashes.

Miranda turned to her father, "Dad?"

He hugged his daughter tight, knowing this had been her first full funeral, "I am sorry you had to see that."

"It was so fast," Miranda said, as her silent tears slid down her cheeks.

"We can make our fire burn a lot hotter than on Earth," he told her with a frown.

"I want to go" Miranda said and looked up at her father. "Can we go?"

He nodded.

"I am taking Miranda back to the hotel," he told his sons. "You can come with us or stay with Alex."

"Please, take my car Mr. East. My parents will drive everyone else," Alex, who had overheard, said as he joined them. "Miranda, you are still welcome to stay at the apartment."

"Evan can stay with you," Miranda said, not meeting his eyes. She spun and left the room. Her father thanked Alex for the use of his car, said a quick goodbye and followed.

Six

★ ★ ★ ★

On the way back to the hotel, Mr. East asked if she wanted to change her room so they could all stay together.

Miranda shook her head, "I think I will stay by myself. I have not tried the bathtub yet. Is that alright?"

He sent her a smile, "Of course. Are you sure you are OK? I get the feeling something is wrong."

"Alex and I had a fight," Miranda frowned, "That is why I would not stay with his family."

"Well, you will both work it out," Mr. East said, knowingly and patted her leg, "When you love someone, forgiveness comes easily."

Miranda nodded.

"I am very happy for you both," he continued, "Alex is a wonderful person and I am so glad you are together."

Miranda turned to him with a frown, "Why would you think that? Alex and I are not together."

He gave her a confused look, "No?"

Miranda shook her head.

"Well, you are still young," he said. "I guess I was just hoping."

Even her dad hoped that they would be together? She went quiet and quieted her mind. She didn't want to worry her dad at all, but now she couldn't even be with Alex. It had to be James. She gave her head a shake, not wanting to even start thinking about that in front of her father. She might lose it completely.

They drove in silence and Miranda told him she was going to lay down for a nap, since she had not slept well. They parted ways when Mr. East went to check into the hotel, but not before he told her they would be having dinner with Erica, Ryan and Alex at 24 hour.

Miranda sat on her couch. She thought about James. He was so young and skinny and he was the same height as Miranda. However, she was tough. She certainly had a power that no one else seemed to have. Perhaps James would have it, even though his brother didn't.

Could she really bring him into this? James was hardly an adult. He was just 15. If it came to it, she didn't think she could. Miranda debated this in her mind for at least an hour, weighing pros and cons. The only pro would be that she wouldn't be alone. Didn't she just wish the other day that she had someone to practice with? The cons list was so much longer, and the worst point was that James could die and it would be her fault again. She couldn't ever let Marcy allow her other son to be a part of this. She could never love Jackson's brother.

Miranda sighed and drew herself a bath. She slipped into the soothing warmth, wishing her problems would just go down the drain. When the water had gone cold, she got out and the dryers activated to dry her hair and body. She tried to take a nap, but sleep wouldn't come.

At 23:40, there was a knock on her door. Miranda had just finished getting dressed and went to answer it.

"Are you ready for dinner?" Alex asked when she had opened the door. He still looked tired.

Miranda nodded as her phone rang behind her. She went to check it as Alex let himself in and closed the door behind him. Miranda saw that it was Marcy West so she took a few steps away from Alex and answered.

"Hi Marcy, I..." she started to say but Marcy cut in.

"Oh Miranda, I am so sorry about earlier. I am just such a mess with my mother in law passing away. I do not blame you at all. I hope you know that, but we have to tell him. I am just so upset that James could be next."

Miranda had tried to interrupt her three times to tell her she wasn't alone.

"What about James?" Alex asked.

Marcy's eyes went wide and her mouth formed an 'o'. "You were trying to tell me you were not alone?"

"Alex is here," Miranda sighed, frustrated.

"What about James?" Alex repeated, taking a step closer to Miranda.

"He is fine, Alex," Marcy said quickly.

"What is going on?" Alex asked, irritably, looking at the phone and at Miranda.

Miranda ignored him, "Listen Marcy, do not do anything until we talk in person. Can we meet up next week?"

Marcy agreed and they disconnected.

"What is going on?" Alex repeated.

"Nothing," Miranda lied as she moved around him. "We should go."

"Wait, I thought we could talk," Alex said and Miranda stopped with her hand out about to reach for the door opener. She turned to him and waited for him to talk but he didn't. He looked so unsure of himself. Alex had always been confident.

Miranda jumped in, since he wasn't saying anything, "I am sorry Alex. I did overreact, I just…"

"I completely understand why you are angry and I do not blame you. I do not even understand myself these days," he sighed, frustrated with himself.

"You understand?" Miranda bit her lip. Of course he did. How many subtle and not so subtle ways did she show that she wanted to be with him? Miranda got a chill, unsure of herself.

"And I know you understand why we could not be together."

Miranda's stomach dropped again, hearing those words again. "Why?" she had to ask this time.

Alex frowned. He looked forlorn as he put his hand on her face and stroked her cheek, "You know why."

Jackson?

Alex nodded.

Miranda's eyes filled with tears and she turned her face so he let his hand fall. This was the way it had to be anyways. It felt like she was the one getting dumped though.

"I need you to ride home tomorrow with me," Alex said.

"Oh," Miranda looked away, "I thought I would just get the express with my dad. Evan will ride with you I am sure."

"I want to talk more," Alex urged, "There is so much more I need to say."

Miranda bit her lip, "I really don't think that's a good idea. Just tell me now."

Alex shook his head, "Please, just come with me. I just… I need some time to think first."

"Fine," Miranda sighed. She couldn't say no to him.

"You do forgive me?"

Miranda closed her eyes and sighed before looking up at Alex. "Yes. Do you forgive me?"

Alex nodded. He put a hand on each of her shoulders, "I need you to remember that."

"Why?" Miranda asked, apprehensive. What could he need to say that she would need to forgive him for? What more could he have done?

Alex closed the distance and hugged her. Miranda was stunned and nervous. Whatever it was, it was going to be bad. Then Alex did something that made all her thoughts disappear. He kissed her lightly. It was quick, but it made her forget what she had been thinking about. Alex was frowning when he pulled away, his face dark. He reached around Miranda and opened the door. "Everyone is probably waiting," he said. He moved around her and led the way without another word.

Their families were waiting at the hotel restaurant since it was the most convenient. Miranda hoped they wouldn't have to deal with any more fans. She had enough paparazzi the past few days, so she brought up the rear of the group with Alex in hopes of a normal dinner at a normal table. They were seated at a table in the open with the other diners, though it was not very busy.

Miranda thought Alex would have sat beside her, but instead he was as far away as possible. Greta took the seat beside Miranda and sent her a reassuring smile.

"Did you have a good nap?" Greta asked.

Miranda nodded, even though she hadn't slept at all.

It was a quiet dinner. Obviously the server didn't watch the show. Either that or she never really got a good look at Alex. Alex's parents chatted with Miranda's dad and Griffin the whole time while Greta and Evan commented once in awhile. It was only Miranda and Alex who were silent.

Miranda hugged Mr. and Mrs. West goodbye and thanked them. They wished her well and hoped to see her again soon.

Evan went with Alex and his parents and the rest of the East family went up to their rooms.

Miranda had her usual nightmares. It was the one she had most often where a very large male with the evil marking above his eyes was stalking her and trying to kill her. He caught her, but this time he didn't try to kill her. Instead he threw her to the ground and got on top of her. He threatened her, telling her to keep quiet in a deep, booming voice. She stopped struggling because she didn't want to die and he started touching her. She could feel his hot, sick breath near her face and tried not to cry for help but a scream accidentally escaped from her mouth. He hit her across the face and laughed, but was suddenly thrown off of her by a strange force like someone had used their mind to pick him up and toss him. No one could move something that size but her. Miranda looked around, hopeful. It had been so long since her saviour had been in her dreams.

"Miranda," a voice said.

She turned, hoping to finally see who it was but her dream was going blurry. Someone was waking her up. She became aware of a gentle shake on her shoulder and opened her eyes slowly. Alex was sitting on the bed beside her, looking down at her concerned.

"Did you have a bad dream?" he asked.

Miranda nodded, "What time is it?"

"It is almost 9. I thought we should go soon."

"Ok," Miranda nodded, "Just give me a minute to get ready."

Alex covered her hand with his, "Happy Birthday."

Miranda gave him a small smile, "Thanks."

He got up and left her to get ready. Miranda picked up her phone. She had four messages from her family all wishing her a happy birthday. Her dad went on to say that they had to leave to catch their flight but that they would see her at home. She messaged everyone back her thanks and also wished Evan a 'happy birthday' as well.

Alex watched her quietly as she moved from room to room, getting ready and packing her things. Once she was ready, he reached out to take her bag and carry it for her.

"Thanks Alex."

In reply, he held out a hand which she took and he led the way out, holding her hand all the way up to the parking garage. He was so confusing.

Miranda expected him to start talking as soon as they were in the air. She wondered what it could be. She was really nervous to find out because of the way he acted yesterday. It certainly didn't give her any reason to be hopeful and it didn't matter, she thought and bit her lip. She shut her mind down. It didn't matter anymore, even if he did want to be with her.

After the first hour of silence, she gave up waiting for him to start the conversation and turned her attention out the window.

"Did you have a good time despite the funeral?" Miranda asked him, breaking the silence.

Alex gave her a weary look so Miranda dropped the subject and it lapsed back into silence for most of the trip. With nothing to do but think, Miranda put up her mind block and thought about the evil ones. She worried about Marcy telling James. How could she possibly have romantic feelings for James now? Just turn off her feelings for his brother and Alex? Her guilt returned in full force and she shook her head to clear her thoughts again. She couldn't think of this now. Alex was so attuned to her thoughts that she might slip and she didn't want him involved. She tried to think of other things, like that fact that it was her birthday and it was supposed to be a happy day. She was far from happy. She was 19 on Utopia, when on Earth she would just be 17. She was a little sad she had missed her 18th birthday. It seemed like an important year on Earth. She would have been considered an adult.

"I can hardly believe it is my birthday," she commented, mostly to herself. "My birthday is usually later in November."

Alex glanced her way, "Oh? Which day?"

"November 25th," she said with a frown. "When is your birthday?"

"February 14th," Alex said, keeping his eyes on the road.

"Valentine's Day?" Miranda smiled.

"What day?" Alex finally looked at her.

"Oh, nevermind," Miranda sighed. "Earth thing I guess."

"A holiday?" Alex asked, with a smirk.

Miranda shook her head, "Not really. It is a day to celebrate love, but it is really commercial nowadays. I never had a valentine, so I never understood it, but when you are young, the teachers let you exchange cards and parents give you heart shaped chocolates and candies."

Alex laughed, "It does not sound so bad."

"When is Griffin's birthday?" Miranda asked, changing the subject. She didn't want to talk about Valentine's Day with Alex.

"April 18th," Alex said.

"My dad?"

"March 1st."

"Greta?"

"July 20th."

Miranda sighed again, "I am going to miss being 18 on Earth. It is a pretty special birthday. You are considered an adult."

"You are an adult at 15 here," Alex reminded her.

Miranda's frowned deepened, "Well, I missed that one too."

Alex glanced at her again, his expression unreadable, and he reached into his pocket and pulled out a small box, "I have something for you." He placed it in her hands.

"What is this?" Miranda asked, shocked that he had gotten her anything at all. She picked up the box gingerly and turned it around in her hands. She heard a small clink inside. It looked like a box that jewelry would come in and it sounded like it too. She slowly opened the lid, as her heart hammered in her chest. Inside on a small blue silk cushion was a necklace, a black pendant on a silver chain. She turned the box so the pendant flipped over. It was a tiny compass but it looked to be broken. The compass hand hung limply and did not point North.

She lifted it out of the box. It felt warm in her hand and all of the sudden the compass face emitted a faint glow. The black pendant turned to a dark green and the compass hand sprang to life, pointing directly at Alex. Miranda wasn't sure if that was North but it didn't seem to be the correct direction.

Alex spared a quick glance her way, seeing the glow out of the corner of his eye. He quickly looked away again. It was a few moments before Alex said, "My grandmother gave that to me when I was 15. It has been in our family for ages. She told me I would know who to give it to when the time was right."

Miranda stared at the pendant. It was part of her Legend, she knew it.

"I do not know how you found out or how Jackson was involved," Alex continued. He took a deep breath, "But I am the first child of the West." He didn't look at her when he said it, staring out the window ahead.

Miranda drew in a sharp breath, her head snapped towards him. She felt like she couldn't breathe. Had she just heard him correctly? "You knew this whole time?" she accused, narrowing her eyes at him.

"The question is, how do you know, Miranda?" Alex asked, turning to her. His voice was full of emotion. "What happened? What did I miss?"

Miranda's eyes narrowed, "No. I asked you first. You are telling me you knew this whole time?"

He nodded. "Your brothers know as well. Your mother had a book in which she placed her digital will. It marked a page which told of our Legend," he told her, his eyes on the road, "Evan was holding the book and read the passage. He showed it to Griffin and I and that was when I knew what that pendant meant."

"How could you not tell me?" she glared at him, "How could you let Jackson die thinking he was supposed to protect me!" She took a few deep breaths, feeling a little hysterical.

"Of course we had no idea, Miranda," he said, sadly. He looked down and out the window, anywhere but at her. "I had no idea you both knew and that he thought he was the first child, not until it was too late."

Miranda took a deep breath to try and calm herself. "But Marcy..." Miranda started to say.

"I have no idea where she found out about it or how."

"Her and my mother belonged to a group of individuals who traced their lineages before we were born. They knew they would birth the chosen children. It is not you, Alex," Miranda insisted, "It was Jackson and now that power has been passed to James." There was no way it could be Alex. They wouldn't have made that kind of mistake.

"No," Alex insisted, "I am the first child born in the generation. I am your protector. My grandmother told *me*. She was the first in her generation and that pendant was passed to her by her grandfather. He gave her the pendant and told her the Legend when she came of age. I went to see my grandmother once I found out and she told me the truth. She told me the story of how she insisted my grandfather take her last name like all the female Wests have to do. She never had the book, but she had the passage memorized. She said she had waited to tell me since there was a rumour that you existed. She heard a conversation between our mothers."

Miranda's eyes filled with tears. Alex was her protector? That meant Jackson died for nothing.

"It *is* my fault," Alex agreed as an escaped tear fell down his face, "Like I said, Miranda, I was a coward. I did not want to accept my fate right away and look what that cost." He brushed his face roughly.

"Don't lie to me, Alex," Miranda said, in denial. "You can't even look at me because it's all a lie."

Alex turned his face to her, frowning. "Of course I would not lie about this," he said quietly.

Her denial was replaced by anger again. "And my brothers? Jackson died because you were all liars!" Miranda asked. They had known the whole time. They had brought her here to protect their planet.

"Your brothers feel awful about it. We all had no idea you had found anything out. How could we? How could we expect that Marcy had been misinformed and that Jackson thought..."

"Well, he did!" Miranda yelled and turned away. She couldn't look at him anymore. She wanted to get out of the car. To run away from this new information. She couldn't handle it.

"Your father was the one who wanted to bring you home. After reading the passage, your brothers tried to convince him to leave you there, but he would not listen. You were brought here because you are wanted and not to save anyone."

"Oh, right. That's just an added bonus." What did they think was happening when someone had started fighting back?

"We did not know it was you. We thought you still did not know and that there was just some sort of resistance happening. You were nowhere near any of the fighting. How were we supposed to guess that you could throw your powers around like you can?"

Miranda shook her head. This couldn't be happening! How could they have all known and not told her. She put her arms across her waist and bent over feeling sick.

"Are you OK?"

"No!" Miranda shouted as she took deep breaths. Her world was falling apart. This changed everything completely. Everything she had been struggling with and all of her guilt and sadness.

"I will protect you, you know that right?"

Miranda stared through blurry eyes at the floor. She looked up and saw they were approaching their city. She could see the red mountains. "This is why you hurt me the way you do. You really don't have feelings for me," she whispered, "You just feel obligated."

Alex didn't answer, knowing she wouldn't accept anything he said to her right now.

Miranda sat back and took a deep breath. Her heart felt like it was going to pieces. If he knew he was supposed to be with her, why did he date so many women? It was obvious he did it because he did not want her. He probably felt forced. "How can I ever trust you?" she whispered, "How, after all that you have put me through?"

"Yes, you can trust me," he said as they reached the traffic of their city.

"Trust you?" Miranda asked, incredulously, "When all you and my brothers have ever done is lie to me?"

"We did not lie. We just kept it from you," Alex pointed out.

Miranda huffed angrily, "No, you had opportunities to tell me. You all tried to keep me from dating anyone when you knew all along that it was supposed to be you and me together. Do you really hate me that much?"

"I wanted to tell you. Your brothers told me to wait. When someone started fighting back, they thought you would never have to know. I could not go against their wishes and I just wanted you to have a normal life. I did not want to burden you with this if I did not have to."

Miranda sat back in her seat. Jackson wouldn't have listened to her brothers. Alex had his own mind. He didn't have to listen if he cared at all but he didn't care. He never did.

When they reached the top of their building and he had parked his car, Alex turned to her, "Your family has planned a party for you. It was supposed to be a surprise, but I had to tell you so you could fix yourself up."

Miranda frowned. How could he have let Jackson die? How could he not have told her the truth right away? A lie of omission was still a lie in her books. She broke his eye contact first and looked down at the pendant that was still warm in her hand. She felt compelled to put it on, despite it being from Alex. She opened the clasp and put it around her neck where it rested just below her shirt line. A steady warmth filled her from that spot, like the warmth from the pendant was seeping into her skin. Alex put a hand to his chest, the same spot where the pendant rested on hers, and a small gasp escaped his lips.

"What is it?" Miranda asked, angrily. She was curious but it still didn't stop her anger.

Alex took a deep breath and turned away, "Nothing." He opened the door and got out of his car.

She slipped the small wooden box into her purse and got out as well. Alex opened the trunk for her and she pulled out her makeup case. She did what she could to look presentable. She was not excited about any party, especially one where she had to pretend she wasn't angry at her brothers. Everything they did since she got here was a lie.

Alex waited patiently for her.

"Why don't you just go on ahead?" Miranda snapped, finally.

"No," Alex replied stubbornly, "I will be spending a lot of time with you so get used to it."

Miranda laughed, "You are joking, right?"

Alex shook his head.

Miranda sent him a glare, "That is ridiculous. You have no idea what I have done on my own so far." She snapped the case closed and put it back in her bag. Then she lifted her bag out of the trunk and headed to the elevator.

"No, I do not and I blame myself," Alex said after her.

Miranda ignored him. It finally dawned on Miranda why Alex had hated her in the beginning. Who wants to be forced to love someone? She was unsure at first when it came to Jackson, but he had been so easy to be with. On the other hand, she had a strange attraction to Alex from the moment she laid eyes on him. Now she knew it was all some stupid pull of destiny. She looked down at the pendant which still pointed at Alex and sighed, angrily.

Griffin and her father were already stringing up a big digital banner that read 'Happy 19th Birthday Miranda and Evan' in big blue lettering, when they walked into the apartment.

She forced a smile as they turned to see her walk in.

"Surprise!" Griffin said, excitedly. "Happy Birthday!"

"Happy Birthday, sweetheart," Mr. East said coming over to give her a hug.

Evan came out of his room with a smile, "Happy Birthday, little sister."

Miranda shot him a glare when her father's back was turned as he went back to decorating. Evan stopped in his tracks, his face fell. He looked at Alex who gave him a curt nod. Evan made a face and turned to Griffin. Griffin frowned. Miranda shot him a glare too before she pasted the fake smile on her face.

"Thanks big brother," she said, trying to sound happy. There was a little catch in her voice though and it sounded strained, "Happy Birthday to you as well."

Greta came in the door behind them all.

"You are home!" she said excitedly, waving a little bottle around with her hand, "I just picked up the cake for the both of you. Happy Birthday!" Greta hugged her tight.

"Thanks Greta," Miranda smiled and closed her mind. Greta must not have known. She would have been the first one to tell her. Miranda didn't understand why her brothers would do this to her.

They made so many poor judgement calls when it came to her. They kidnapped her from Earth when they could have just explained it to her and she might have come to Utopia on her own time. They had Alex be nice to her so she wouldn't date anyone when all they had to do was let her go and learn for herself. She might have come to the right decision anyways. Now these secrets were the worst of all. They may have been trying to protect her, but she had found out anyways, and Jackson had died fighting a fight that wasn't his.

Miranda turned away from Greta's embrace and went into the living room. She tried so hard to hide her tears.

Greta followed, knowingly. She put a hand on her shoulder, "What is wrong, Miranda?"

Mr. East heard the question and he turned to his daughter. He frowned when he saw her tears.

"N-nothing," Miranda stammered, her voice faltering. She tried to think of something quickly, "I just hope you did not go to too much trouble for me."

Mr. East went to her and hugged her again, "Of course not. Birthdays are a celebration on Utopia. It is expected."

"I just... I..." Miranda trailed off. She wanted to tell him that she didn't feel much like celebrating right now, but she couldn't. It wasn't his fault and he probably wouldn't understand. "I guess I am just missing a couple years of my life and it feels a little overwhelming," she said instead.

Mr. East frowned, "I am so sorry. I guess we never thought of it like that." He took her hand and gave it a squeeze. "I have so many years to make up for not being with you."

Miranda finally managed to control her tears and she looked up at her dad. He looked so genuine and Miranda knew she would be able to put on an act, for at least a few hours while the party was on, just for him. She smiled, "You don't have to make up for anything, dad. This party will be great. Thank you so much."

Two hours later, the party was in full swing. Her friends and family even brought her presents, though she hadn't expected anything. It was interesting to learn that there was no wrapping on Utopia. Presents were just given to the birthday girl or boy upon arrival. Miranda got some new clothes, a pair of sunglasses, a necklace and some new earrings. Nathan brought her a bouquet of flowers that smelled amazing.

Miranda spent a lot of time with Leah, her cousin, who was the closest to her own age. She told Miranda stories about her mother. Miranda also asked her cousin about herself, about growing up on Utopia and was jealous. Leah had everything Miranda would have wanted for herself. Both her parents were alive and she had grown up happily and normal on Utopia.

Despite the jealousy, Miranda instantly knew that Leah would be fun to hang around. When Miranda told her she met the band, Leah even invited Miranda to the Trees concert she was going to in a couple weeks.

Evan turned off the music and put on *Northern Shores* when it was time for the episode to air. Not a single person complained, except for Miranda. As soon as the episode started, she knew exactly which one it was! It was the bedroom scene episode. She stood up in front of the television.

"This is supposed to be a party! Do you all really want to watch television?" Miranda asked the room with a smile.

"Yes!" Almost everyone shouted back.

Miranda's face coloured slightly and she wrinkled her nose, "Fine, but no comments." Miranda tried to disappear into the floor.

Her dad was watching too! She wasn't planning on having a drink at all that night, but now she definitely needed one. So, she grabbed one from the table and sat on the floor beside Alicia.

The scene stunned so many, and everyone was buzzing once the episode had finished saying how real it had looked.

"Obviously not," Miranda said, laughing. "Evan doesn't make pornos!"

That sent a chuckle through the crowd.

"That is not a word here, Miranda," Evan laughed.

"Oh, um," Miranda's face coloured. Pornography probably didn't even exist on this planet. She shrugged it off and got another drink. Then she talked to everyone in the room except her brothers and Alex. She avoided them all night.

Mr. East found her daughter talking to Alicia, "Before I go to bed, Miranda," he interrupted, "I wanted to give you my gift." Then he turned to the room, "For everyone who wants to see, you can accompany us up to the parking garage. It is up in my car."

Miranda followed him, curiously, into the elevator up to the parking garage. The whole family went as well as Leah, Alex, Alicia, Nathan and Rebecca. Inside the parking garage, Mr. East led them towards his car. Miranda thought her present must be in his trunk, but once Mr. East got to his trunk, he turned and motioned to the dark purple car beside his own.

Miranda's mouth dropped, "A car?" She stopped walking. Was it really all hers?

Her dad smiled and nodded. Miranda practically jumped on him, giving him a hug. She was so excited. Now she wouldn't have to be chauffeured around anymore. It was perfect timing too, since she really wanted nothing to do with Alex and he was the only one besides her father who had a vehicle.

"Now, we will have to teach you to drive, but it is all yours," he said to her.

Miranda shyly went over to the car and ran her hand along it.

"Wow!" Alicia said, joining her beside it, "The colour is beautiful!"

"This *is* nice!" Rebecca said, and patted Miranda's father on the back. "Great choice, Mr. East!"

"Oh this is great!" Leah smiled. "Hope you learn to drive before the concert! We were going to take a bus since none of us have a vehicle. You can be the driver if you want!"

"This is from all of us," Mr. East said to her, a big smile lighting his whole face, "The whole family. Greta and Alex as well."

"Thank you so much!" Miranda said excitedly as she hugged her dad again and even gave her brothers a quick hug, so her father wouldn't get suspicious. Greta got a hug next, a good one, and then Alex, briefly.

"Promise me you will not drive until I teach you," her dad said.

"I won't. Will you teach me soon?"

"Yes," he smiled. "Go ahead and open it. Take a look inside."

"Shall we move this party to my apartment?" Alex suggested to everyone as they all headed back to the elevator after admiring Miranda's new car.

Miranda sighed and reluctantly agreed, knowing her father would want to go to bed. Once in Alex's apartment though, she was drawn toward Nathan. In the back of her mind she knew that this would make everyone angry, but she liked Nathan. After all, at least *he* didn't lie to her.

"Congratulations on the car," he smiled at her.

"Thanks!" Miranda smiled. "How have you been?"

"Great and you?" he asked. "How was your trip?"

"I had a really nice time," she smiled. "I had an autograph session and had some quality salon time." She laughed and showed him her nails.

He took her hand and studied her nails which had been painted a pale pink. Then he gave her hand a squeeze. "So how about that date?" Nathan asked.

Miranda smiled and nodded, "I will let you know. My schedule for work is busy right now but I will definitely have a free night next week." She lied because she had been stirring up a plan in her mind for what she would do the next few days. She was still off of work until Monday.

Miranda noticed her brothers were still hanging around as the night got later. Normally they would have gone to bed long ago, especially since it was a work night. Miranda had a suspicion they were waiting to talk to her. She was dreading talking to them as people started to head home.

Nathan was the last to leave. Alex was cleaning up but her brothers were on the couch talking quietly and shooting daggers in Nathan's direction.

"Well, I should be going," Nathan smiled at her, "I have to be at work tomorrow as well." If he saw the glares he was getting, he sure didn't react to them at all.

Miranda walked him to the elevator, promised she would let him know a good day for them to go on their date and then she kissed him goodbye.

"Can we talk?" Griffin asked from Alex's door.

"Talk about what exactly, Griffin?" Miranda snapped, and took a threatening step in his direction, "Talk about how you lied to me? How all you ever did was lie to me from the second I got here? How, because of you, Jackson is dead? Is that what you would like to talk about?"

Griffin hung his head, "Miranda..."

"Fine, let's talk!" she cut in and marched back into Alex's apartment.

Evan was on the couch looking miserable and Alex was pacing behind it.

"Miranda," Griffin said from behind her. She spun to look at him, "We want to take you back to Earth."

"What?" she screamed and looked at Evan on the couch, who didn't look at her and turned back to Griffin, "Are you joking?"

"We need to protect you and we think the only way to do this is to put you back into hiding again," he continued.

"Speak for yourself," Alex snapped. He had stopped pacing and looked directly at Miranda, "I do not agree with this." He looked at Griffin, "Miranda is here now and she knows everything."

"Well congrats," Miranda said to him sarcastically. "Finally got a mind of your own?"

Alex rolled his eyes at her so she turned back to Griffin.

"I am NOT just going to walk away," Miranda said. She stomped her foot, knowing it was a childish move, but she needed to get her point across. "Do you have any idea what I have already been through? I know exactly what I am doing."

"We never wanted you to be involved," Griffin pleaded with her, reaching out to her, but she sent him such a deadly glare that he backed away. "If you never found out about the Legend, we hoped we could just protect you from anything."

"And just let the evil ones keep attacking innocent people when I could put a stop to it?"

"No Miranda. You put yourself in danger too many times already and we cannot allow it. Evan and I want you back on Earth," Griffin said, though it did not sound convincing. "Anything is better than the danger you are in here. We would rather know that you are safe."

"Well I won't let you leave me on Earth again," she said, forcefully. She turned to Evan, who hadn't said a word yet. "Evan, you agree with this craziness?"

Evan, who had been quiet and anxious, looked up at her. He had tears in his eyes as he searched her face, "No."

Griffin made an exasperated noise behind her, "Evan, we discussed this. It is for the best."

"I know but I cannot do it," Evan said, rising to his feet. "This is my twin sister and I want her with me."

"I am not going anywhere anyways," Miranda said, "but now that I know this is how you feel, you *can* take me home. *After* I rid the planet of the evil."

"No, that is not *our* plan," Alex cut in.

Miranda turned on him, "Our plan?" she let out a sarcastic laugh, "*Our* plan? You must be kidding me. I am alone in this. I do NOT need you."

"Alex is your... your…" Evan didn't know how to say it.

"And that is why you have always pushed him and I together isn't it?" Miranda turned her glare on him. "Let's make this clear. Alex and I will *never* be together. And in fact, I do not want anything to do with any of you. I am done with all your lies."

"But…" Griffin started.

"We do not want to lose you," Evan said quietly. He reached out to his sister but she stepped away from him as well.

"But you will take me back to Earth?" Miranda asked, crossing her arms over her chest, "That doesn't make sense."

"Just to protect you," Griffin jumped in before Evan said anything.

"Well, you did fine without a little sister before right?" Miranda snapped, throwing her hands up, annoyed. "And I was doing a lot better without brothers like you both."

"But..." Evan started and Miranda cut him off.

"Now I am going to bed, if you will excuse me," Miranda said, angrily spinning towards the door.

She stormed out of Alex's apartment and went to her room. She knew exactly what she was going to do now and it wasn't going to be sleep. Miranda opened her suitcase and took out her dirty clothes, and then she had Alpha bring her some clean clothes. She had been formulating this in her head all night and after all Griffin had said, she was definitely going to do it.

Seven

★ ★ ★ ★

Miranda waited hours until she was sure everyone was asleep before she left her room. She left her bag in the hall and went into her dad's room.

"Dad?" she whispered, touching his arm lightly.

Mr. East groaned, his eyes opened slowly. "Are you OK, sweetheart?" he asked sleepily.

"Yes, Dad," Miranda whispered, "I have to go."

"Go?" Mr. East said aloud, concern immediately taking over his face. He sat up and took in her clothes. She was dressed. "Where are you going?"

"I have a trip to make, but I promise you that I will be back in a few days. I need you to know that and I couldn't leave without telling you," Miranda frowned. She knew he wouldn't understand the full situation and she didn't want him to think that she ran away.

"Where are you going?" he asked again.

"I need to go to Earth," Miranda said, her eyes filled with tears, "There is something I need to do."

Mr. East's expression softened. He threw the blankets off, "I am driving you to the space centre then."

"But..."

"Miranda, if you must go then I can at least take you there," he insisted, "I will meet you in the living room."

Miranda bit her lip, feeling badly that she woke him now, but she turned and left his bedroom so he could get dressed. She took her bag and carried it down the hall so it wouldn't make a sound. She waited in the dark without putting any lights on.

Mr. East was quiet as well. She barely heard him come down the hallway and jumped a little when he walked into the dark living room. He led the way up to the parking garage and looked sadly upon Miranda's new car before climbing into his own.

Miranda knew that he was worried she wasn't coming back, that the car, her room and a couple months of memories would be all he had of her. "I am coming back, Dad," Miranda insisted, "I promise. I will be back soon."

Mr. East nodded, reassured, "I believe you. I suppose I am just worried because it is obvious you did not want your brothers to know you were leaving." He set the destination and they started off.

Miranda pursed her lips, in thought. "Well, I didn't think they would be happy with me sneaking out to go."

Mr. East chuckled, "They have been more protective of you than I have ever seen before."

Miranda sent him a smile, but inside her stomach churned. Yes, a little overprotective and completely bone-headed.

"I was going to suggest this visit before and I probably should have. You have had a very rough time here and I was afraid you would visit Earth and not come back," he admitted, quietly.

Miranda gave him a pitying look, "I do miss them very much but my place is here."

Mr. East tried to smile. They drove in silence to the space centre. There were not many people there except for a few travel administrators. Miranda was happy to have her father's help. It would make it much quicker.

"Sit here and I will get everything arranged," Mr. East said, once they got inside the building and to the proper area.

"I want to pay for it," Miranda told him, reaching for her card.

He took her card, "OK, but let me get it all arranged for you."

Miranda sat on the chair and watched as her dad arranged the trip. He came back with a smile on his face.

"All done," he said. "The pilot is getting the transport ready. You can leave in about an hour and the pilot understands that you may stay a few days to a few weeks."

"Dad, really," Miranda frowned. "I promise it will be just a few days."

He gave her a half smile and a nod, "I know. I just do not want you to feel rushed. I am sure Evan can delay your return on the show if you needed to stay longer." He led the way out to the transport, talking as he went. "I know your driver very well. He knows your situation and knows where to go. There are a lot of confidentiality laws that you must understand though," Mr. East explained. "I know your Earth parents are aware of the existence of other planets, but I will leave it up to your judgment whether you feel any of your friends can keep one of the greatest secrets of their lives."

"Yes, I know," Miranda said. Jackson had grazed over some of the laws in her lessons. "Is it the same driver that brought me here?"

Mr. East nodded and handed her a stack of money, "Here is some Earth money."

Miranda looked at the stack with a surprised expression. There must have been over a thousand dollars in her hand, all in twenties.

"Is that enough? I assume you will be staying with your parents?"

Miranda nodded and let out a small laugh, "Yes, it is plenty."

"Our exchange rate is very good," Mr. East chuckled.

Miranda raised an eyebrow but he didn't elaborate. Instead he explained that all the food she would need would be provided. If she didn't want to eat Earth food, she wouldn't have to.

"The driver will bring you right to Woodstock and he will stay nearby," Mr. East continued. He looked around, saw the driver and waved to him.

Miranda nodded. She started to get nervous for her flight and even more nervous about leaving her family. What if she came back and they had all been attacked? Miranda would have changed her mind right there if she hadn't remembered that Alex would protect them. Surely, as the first child of the West family, he must have some powers. Plus, she knew he would never let any harm come to her family, even if he didn't have any powers.

"Have a great time," Mr. East said. "I would say to call me when you get there, but I guess you cannot." He hugged her tight.

"I will be safe, Dad," Miranda replied. "Be careful while I am away."

"Would you like me to tell your brothers anything?" he asked, almost hopeful.

Miranda sighed and shook her head.

"Excuse me, Miss East," came the driver's voice. It rang throughout the bedroom, so there must have been some kind of intercom.

Miranda had made her way to the bedroom of the motor-home spaceship and had fallen asleep as soon as they left Utopia. "Yes?" she answered sleepily.

"We have almost arrived on Earth. Could you please come to the front?"

"I will be right there," Miranda said, quickly waking up. She couldn't believe she slept the whole way. Miranda straightened her clothes and headed to the front. Tim, her driver, was seated in the driver's seat, his hands were on the wheel handles. The dashboard in front of him was lit up and he seemed to be communicating with someone on Earth, telling them of their imminent arrival. He provided some co-ordinates of where they would be landing.

Tim flashed her a smile, "Are you happy to be home?"

Miranda nodded, "Thank you for leaving so late at night."

"Not to worry, Miranda," he said, his eyes on the way ahead. "I just happened to be working. I do not mind going to Earth. It has some interesting cultures."

"Yes, it does," Miranda agreed. "Have you visited often?"

"Oh yes," Tim said, excitedly, "Normally I accompany anyone who takes a trip to Earth. We must always land in Canada, but from there I have been to Egypt, Italy, Germany and Japan. The airplanes are very slow. I wish we could drive ourselves, but it is still exciting to fly on the primitive vehicles."

Miranda giggled, "I'm sorry we aren't going anywhere too exciting."

Tim smiled and shrugged, "Woodstock is nice."

"Have you been to other planets?"

Tim nodded, "Yes, but there are only six habitable planets across the discovered universe. They are the ones we can go visit without an oxygen mask or temperature controlled suit."

"Cool," Miranda said.

"There are 47 others that I've taken day trips to. They have some pretty exciting landscapes but not a lot of life," he explained, "Only certain planets have the right mixture of oxygen, carbon, water and a good temperature to have life."

"I will have to read up on them," Miranda said with a sigh. She still felt pretty dumb compared to the other Utopians but she didn't even want to think about going back to the school. She couldn't handle it.

"Well, there it is," Tim said, motioning straight ahead with his chin.

Miranda felt a flood of emotions, excitement and longing. She missed them all so much. They slowed drastically but Miranda couldn't feel it. It was an amazing view. There were millions of stars strewn across the blackness and planet Earth got bigger and bigger as they got closer. She could see large glowing splotches on the land to the south, indicative of populous cities but to the north and straight ahead, there were clouds. It must not be a nice day.

"I was told it is only four in the morning where we are going on November 28th," Tim said, and he tested the word, "That is so different for me. The 28th of November." He looked at Miranda, "I guess you are used to that though."

Miranda nodded. She wasn't used to the 26 days a month that they had on Utopia. She had her eyes fixed straight forward as they headed into the clouds. She wondered how Tim could see through all this.

"It practically drives itself," Tim said, smiling at her again, "The clouds are thick, but we will be through them shortly and you will be surprised how close we are to the ground."

Just as he finished his sentence, the clouds dispersed and the ground appeared.

"How is it no one sees us?" Miranda asked, curiously. Surely someone would see them coming out of the clouds, especially so close to the ground.

"We have what we call 'invisibility' technology," Tim said. "It keeps us protected from their eyes. I am told it is also very cold on Earth. I hope you have dressed warmly."

Miranda frowned, "Honestly, I forgot, but I should be OK. My family on Earth still has some of my old clothes, I hope." It was always warm where her family lived on Utopia and she had completely forgotten it was almost winter on Earth. There was a lot on her mind that was more important than the weather.

They landed on the outskirts of town. It was a smooth landing, one second they were in the sky and the next, they were travelling along the road.

"Now, here is what I needed *you* for," Tim said, "I almost remember where I am going, but I just wanted you for confirmation."

Miranda smiled, excited, "That should be easy. I know exactly where we are." She had travelled this road many times on her way to Stratford.

Another 20 minutes later, and they arrived in front of her old house.

"Well, here you go," Tim said, stretching. "I have to put a call out to Utopia and do an inspection of the vehicle. I will stay mostly on your street for the duration. If you ever have an idea of when you would like to go back, just let me know and I can prepare."

Miranda smiled excitedly and sprung up from her seat, "Thank you!"

Tim stood to stretch as Miranda left the driver area. She went to the back of the transporter and opened the door with the intent to scope out her old house. She knew it was early, and that her parents may still be asleep.

The first thing that hit her was the smell. It smelled a bit like exhaust fumes mixed with something rotten. It felt heavy in her lungs, and Miranda started to cough right away. Tim appeared in the doorway with an anxious look.

"Oh I am so sorry, Miranda," he frowned. "I was just coming to warn you about the smell."

Miranda coughed a few more times and waved her hand. "It's OK," she said between coughs, "I forgot." She turned and closed the door again.

"You will get used to it," Tim said. "It takes some time. I would suggest leaving the door open to let the smell in so your nose can get used to it."

Miranda wrinkled her nose. She didn't want to, but she opened the door wide as Tim suggested. She didn't cough this time but she could feel the heaviness in her chest. She looked over at her old, familiar house with sorrow. She had missed this old house so much. A million memories from of growing up in it entered her mind and she had to take some deep breaths, to hold back her tears. She had cried too much the past several weeks. It was becoming exhausting. She came here hoping to talk to Helen and to see her Earth parents. She needed to talk to someone and she missed everyone so much. Miranda knew she could never tell her Earth parents what she was up against on Utopia. They, like her brothers, would insist she stay on Earth, but Helen she knew could keep any secret.

Miranda had to wait a few hours before she saw a light flicker on the main floor of her old house. Tim had gone out to do his inspection and Miranda grabbed her bag from where she left it and headed out.

She nervously climbed the steps to the front door. Normally she would have walked in, but she knocked instead. It wasn't her house anymore. She bit her lip as she heard footsteps approach the front door and she saw the blinds sway as someone peeked out. Seconds later, the door opened and Jim, her Earth father, was there with a wide smile.

"Hi Dad," Miranda smiled.

"Oh Miranda! Look at you," he exclaimed and threw his arms around her. "I am so happy to see you! You got taller!" He pulled back and held her at arm's length to study her.

"Did I?"

Jim nodded. His face said it all. He was happy to see her and it did not matter that she had left them. She was always welcome back.

"Sara!" Jim yelled into the house, "Miranda is here!" Jim pulled Miranda inside and shut the door.

Sara called down from the second floor, "What did you say, dear?" But he didn't need to answer. She saw Miranda standing at the door. "Oh!" she said, bounding down the stairs as quick as she could. She engulfed Miranda in a hug.

Miranda squeezed her back tightly, "Hi Mom. I missed you so much."

Sara pulled back, her eyes sparkling with happy tears, "I missed you too. She hugged her adopted daughter again. When she pulled back again, she bit her lip, "Are you... here to stay?"

Miranda frowned a little, "Umm... just for a visit."

"Well, I can accept that," Sara gave her a small smile. "I am so glad you can at least visit."

"I can," Miranda smiled. "I can visit whenever I want to. I am not sure how much it costs since my dad paid for me, but I know I can afford it. I will come back all the time."

Sara smiled widely.

"Listen to you. You sound like your brother now," Jim commented on her lack of slang.

Miranda blushed slightly. She didn't realize she sounded exactly like them now.

"Come," Sara said, pulling her into the kitchen. "We were about to have Sunday breakfast. You arrived on the perfect day!"

Miranda's stomach grumbled in response. Jim laughed, and asked if they were feeding her well in space.

Over breakfast in her mother's familiar kitchen, she told them about her planet, her school, her new job and her family. She left out the attacks, wanting to paint a good picture for them in their minds.

They talked for hours, throughout the morning and into the early afternoon.

"Wow, an actress," Sara repeated, star-struck. She squeezed Miranda's hand, "I am so proud of you."

"Funny thing is, it is a show about Earth," Miranda laughed.

"It sounds absolutely perfect," Sara commented.

"Well, almost," Miranda said with a shrug. She pulled out her notebook in hopes she would at least be able to show them her pictures. She wasn't sure if it would work here but it powered on without any problems.

"*That* is pretty cool," Jim smiled, taking it out of her hands. Like anything new, he wanted to play with it. He pushed all the buttons on the clear screen pulling up different options and menus, until he came across her pictures himself, "Oh!"

Sara leaned across to look as well.

"Hold on. Let me see that," Miranda said with a sly smile. She took her notebook back and pulled the frame. The notebook got bigger and she handed it back to Jim who looked down at it in awe. Sarah gushed over the first picture, which was of her photo shoot with Alex.

They poured over her pictures and asked her to point out her friends. They asked a lot about Alex and Jackson, who were in so many of her pictures. Miranda didn't tell them she had dated Jackson, or that he was even dead. She didn't want them to know what she had been through, but she did talk a lot about Alex, explaining that he played her love interest on the show.

"He is very cute," Sara winked, "I thought so the first time I met him."

"What are these?" Jim asked, as he fiddled with her phone, and Miranda looked over. Her face fell. She forgot she also had all the articles stored in a folder. She went to reach for her phone, but Jim pulled it out of her grasp.

Sara leaned over again and together they read about her relationship with Jackson, Alex's compliments, Evan's article and then they found the article on the attack at the school and Jackson's death.

Miranda held her breath as they read through.

"What is this?" Sara asked, with tears in her eyes, "I thought the planet had no crime?"

Jim sat in stunned silence.

Miranda looked away, refusing to cry.

Sara stood up and moved around the table. She threw her arms around Miranda, "I'm so sorry."

"I'm OK," Miranda said, determined to be exactly that. "There is one evil on our planet but most were killed in the attack on the school."

"But why?"

Miranda shrugged, "No one knows, but I was told it stems from some ancient legend of good and evil. It is the only thing wrong with the planet." Miranda's frown deepened, "I didn't say anything because I didn't want to give you a bad impression."

Jim put his hand on Miranda's arm, "You know you can tell us anything."

"I know," Miranda said, looking down at her hands. "I just had a rough time and I came home for some time away. I really needed to see you both but I also wanted to talk to Helen. How is she? What did you say to her?"

Sara and Jim shared a look. "She was pretty angry," Sara said, carefully. "We told her that your real family found you and that you left with them, but we didn't say where exactly you went. She called every day for weeks wondering why you hadn't called yet. We didn't know what to say and then she got angry and told us to tell you that if you called, she didn't want to speak to you anymore," Sara frowned.

"She still calls, though not as much," Jim added. He leaned forward towards Miranda, "I know she would forgive you if you wanted to call her."

Miranda frowned.

"Want me to call her for you and see if she will talk to you?" Sara suggested.

Miranda shook her head. If Helen was mad at her, she needed to explain it herself in person, though the last thing she needed to deal with was Helen mad at her. "I think I will go for a walk," Miranda said, looking at the time. The clock in the kitchen said that it was just after noon. "Wow, I didn't realize how late it was! I hope I didn't keep you both from anything."

Jim shook his head and Sara replied, "No. It was going to be a usual Sunday."

Miranda smiled wistfully. Their usual Sundays had consisted of housework and homework. If it had been summer, Sara would have been out in the garden. Miranda sighed and stood, "I will head over to see Helen."

"I'm sure she will talk to you," Jim said, reassuringly.

Miranda got to the front door and realized she didn't have a jacket. "Mom," she called out, "Do you still have my jackets? I forgot to bring one."

"They are up in your room," Sara answered from the kitchen.

Miranda took the steps two at a time and entered her old bedroom. It looked exactly the same as the day she had left it and even her cat Tinsel was asleep on her bed.

"Oh Tinny," Miranda said, scooping her off the bed. She hugged her to her chest and nuzzled her face. Tinsel started to purr. "I missed you," Miranda murmured, and held her up to get a better look at her, "You got fatter."

Tinsel meowed, indignantly, as if she knew what Miranda had said. Miranda laughed and instead of getting her jacket, she sat down on her bed to give some attention to Tinsel.

An hour later, covered in cat hair, she was finally ready for a walk. After Tinsel was done with her, Miranda opened her old laptop and went through her pictures, lost in her memories of a time that seemed so much simpler. No matter how perfect Utopia had seemed, her life was still difficult there. She made a mental note that she needed to get some of these pictures printed so that she could bring them back to Utopia. All her pictures had been destroyed.

With her black winter jacket on, Miranda told her parents she would likely be awhile. If Helen would even talk to her, she had a lot of explaining to do, so she headed out into the brisk afternoon. The spaceship wasn't there. Tim must have gotten bored already.

Miranda took the long way to get to Helen's to give herself a long time to think about what she was going to say. She hoped Helen would at least give her a chance and not slam the door in her face. Before Miranda knew it, she was standing in front of the familiar red door. She took a deep breath and knocked.

Miranda had not known what to expect, but she didn't expect the whirlwind that happened next. Helen's mom answered the door and gasped with surprise. She pulled Miranda in the house, asking hundreds of questions as she called for Helen. Helen's half-sister Gabriella ran down the stairs first and threw her arms around Miranda. She had always admired Miranda and had evidently missed her. Then, Helen herself appeared in the doorway. She couldn't even pretend to be angry she was so excited, and now her eyes glistened with tears. They were sat down on Helen's bed, and Miranda had told her the whole story. She told her everything, from the moment she left Earth until now.

"I hope you are going to tell me next that you are home to stay," Helen said and hesitated. She took some deep breaths and threw her arms around Miranda.

Miranda frowned, "I just can't... not yet. They aren't safe. I needed to see you. I need your advice."

"My advice would be to stay the hell away!" Helen said with an angry cry. She stood and started pacing. "What if you died? How would I ever even know?" Helen let out a sob. "You just left and I had no idea what happened. I thought you would call or come back eventually. I never understood why you didn't try to call me. Now that I do, you will be lucky if I even let you out of my room!" Helen stopped pacing and went to check and make sure her bedroom door was still locked.

Miranda frowned, "Helen, I wish you could be there, more than anything in the world, but I am glad you are not. It is dangerous for anyone to be close to me there."

"That's why you have to stay here," Helen said, firmly.

Miranda shook her head sadly, "You know I can't."

Helen turned her back on Miranda. Miranda knew she hated to cry. "Your brothers sound awful," Helen sniffed.

"They really aren't," Miranda insisted, surprised even at herself for defending them. "You would like Evan, since he is just like me. Griffin is just being overprotective, just as you are of your younger siblings. What would you do in their place? What would you do to protect Gabby from my fate?"

Helen let out a strangled sob. "I would probably do anything," she said, quietly, "And it would probably be something stupid with your help."

Miranda paused and drew in a sharp breath. Just like Alex had done. Alex and Evan were best friends and he had done whatever Evan and Griffin wanted, including lying to her and pretending to like her, because they had asked him to. Just like Miranda would have done for Helen and Gabriella. Did she have any right to be mad at him?

"It sounds like you know what you are going to do anyways," Helen said, sadly. "Why did you tell me anything?" Helen turned back to look at her. Her tears had stopped but their traces remained on her face.

"I missed you so much," Miranda replied, "I think I just wanted you to know what happened to me and why I would leave without a word and what could happen. I want you to know why I may never return again."

Helen choked back another sob.

"I can come back. We are allowed to travel and I will come back often. Alex said he wanted to come with me," Miranda continued.

Helen held her gaze for a moment. Then she sighed and sat on the bed beside her again. "He confuses me," Helen said, thoughtfully.

Miranda snorted, "Me too."

Helen started thinking and Miranda heard every thought. She was weighing the possibilities. It was possible he was in love with her and was scared, guilty about Jackson, but then again, he might not be. Just as Miranda thought, he might feel forced into this relationship and keep fighting against it every step.

"That's what I thought," Miranda frowned.

Helen scratched her head, confused for a second. "Stay out of my thoughts," and she sent her a small smile.

Miranda shrugged, "It is as easy as if you were speaking to me."

"You repressed it for years," Helen said, "I am sure you can do it again."

Miranda bit her lip and pretended to shut it off, but she could still hear Helen's thoughts. At first, Helen had tested it a bit, thinking silly thoughts and Miranda did her best to keep from laughing or even smiling. It wasn't until Helen started thinking about Bryan that Miranda reacted.

"Ew!" Miranda said, waving her hands in disgust, "Why would you think that?"

Helen laughed, "Stay out of my thoughts then!"

Miranda made a few gagging noises and shook her head with a sigh, "We know I'm going back, but please tell me what to do about Alex?" Miranda looked down at the pendant. The compass needle hung limp again but it warmed when she covered it with her hand.

She could feel his heartbeat. Miranda drew in a sharp breath, "I feel him, even now so far away. It is so weird."

"I really do think he loves you," Helen insisted, "He must if you both have that kind of connection."

Miranda bit her lip and her eyes filled with tears, "I think *that* is my real problem. It is not the lies, the Legend, or the pain in seeing him date other girls. I just don't want him to die like Jackson. I could not handle that."

Helen hugged her tight. "I wish I could assure you that won't happen but I know you will do everything in your power to stop it from happening."

Miranda nodded.

"So he does love you, but now what should you do," Helen said. She sat back and thought about it.

"I left them so angry," Miranda said, "I never expected to come here and understand why they did what they did."

"Sometimes you just have to take a step away to gain a little perspective," Helen said. "I seem to remember you were the one who always gave me great advice like that. I was the one who had boy or makeup or clothes advice. You always solved the life issues."

Miranda had never thought of it like that.

"I give terrible life advice," Helen said with a small laugh, "If it were me, I might yell and scream a lot. I probably wouldn't talk to them ever again."

"I have considered that," Miranda admitted looking down at her hands, "And maybe it is best if I do stay mad. If they weren't around me as much, they would be safer."

"That's true," Helen said. She waved a hand in the air, "I think I have had enough to take in for one day. How long are you staying?"

"Probably one or two days," Miranda said, "I have to get back to work."

"I want to see a movie and Bryan won't see it with me. I've been missing you so much, especially lately. You know your birthday just passed, right?"

Miranda nodded, "Actually yes, even on Utopia. My birthday is November 2nd."

"They have the same months as us?"

Miranda snorted, "Well, they did introduce their calendar to us." She let out a laugh, "They thought the way we kept track was too complicated and dropped some hints into Pope Gregory's mind. He is the guy who invented the modern calendar, supposedly."

Helen rolled her eyes. "Anyways... Let's have a normal night out and then I'm skipping school tomorrow."

Miranda nodded in agreement. A night out with her best friend sounded like the best thing to happen in a long time. She used Helen's cell phone to call her Earth parents to tell them where she would be. As if on cue, Helen's mom called them down for dinner and Helen told her their plan. She wasn't too keen on letting Helen take a day off school.

"Shouldn't you be in school too, Miranda?" she asked her.

Miranda bit her lip, "Yes, but it was my only chance to come back before Christmas."

Helen's mom asked her many questions. Miranda told her the story that she had made up in her mind as she walked to Helen's. That her real family was from the Bahamas and they were having phone trouble because of the hurricane. Somehow Helen's mother did seem to remember a hurricane reported and Miranda sent Helen a secretive smile.

"Oh, alright," Helen's mother said finally. "You can have tomorrow off."

Both girls cheered.

After dinner they headed out to the movie theatre and Helen told Miranda all about what was going on in her life. Helen whispered throughout the whole movie, earning them a few nasty looks from those around them. Luckily, since it was a Sunday night, the theatre was fairly empty and Helen completely ignored the glares. Apparently Bryan had decided to stay local with his university choice and Helen was ecstatic. It made Miranda a little jealous that Helen's life was so normal.

As if he knew he was being talked about, they ran into Bryan after the movie just outside of the theatre. He just happened to be with Scott. Miranda had gone out with him once, just before she went to Utopia. Scott had been her first and only crush on Earth. She stopped in her tracks, unsure of how many people she wanted to see while she was back on Earth. How many people did she want to lie to? But she was happy to see him. He still looked gorgeous.

Bryan hadn't noticed her yet, but Scott stopped, his mouth dropped open.

"Hey babe," Bryan said to Helen. "We decided to see a movie too." He motioned to Scott and saw that he had paused. Then Bryan finally noticed who Helen was with. "Miranda!"

Miranda tore her gaze from Scott and smiled at Bryan, "Hey Bry." She turned back to Scott, "Hi."

"Hi," Scott said, staring.

Miranda tried not to blush but now that she could hear Scott's thoughts, she couldn't help it. Scott was thinking about how hot she looked and a few naughty things too. It also passed through Bryan's mind that Miranda was looking pretty fine.

There was an awkward silence.

"I-uh," Miranda stopped and started, not sure what to say. "I guess you both heard that I went to live with my real family."

Both nodded.

"Sorry I could not say goodbye," Miranda continued.

"Are you back to stay?" Bryan asked.

Helen and Miranda shared a frown and Miranda turned back to the boys, "No. I am just here for a visit."

"Well you look great!" Bryan said, throwing his arm around Helen, "Helen's been missing you a lot. Everyone does."

Scott agreed with another up and down look at her. He started thinking dirty things again and Miranda wondered if he had always thought that way around her. It definitely made her feel uncomfortable. She tried not to be offended. He was an Earthling and had no idea she was listening.

"Shall we skip the movie?" Scott suggested to Bryan. "I would like to take these lovely ladies out somewhere we can catch up!"

Sure you do, Miranda thought sarcastically knowing he would like to do more than 'catch up'. They all agreed and headed next door to the bowling alley.

Aside from his first thoughts, Scott turned out to be just as she remembered. He was funny and attentive to her. The four of them had a great time bowling. Miranda couldn't remember the last time she felt so normal. This had been what she had hoped for, a boyfriend like Scott who treated her like she was the most important person, who didn't care that she was now taller than him and certainly didn't make fun of her height. She had also always dreamed that she would date someone to go on double dates with Helen. But, of course, this dream also couldn't last.

In the car back to Helen's, Miranda almost convinced herself she would just stay on Earth but knew she would feel guilty for the rest of her life if she did. She would also miss her real dad, and maybe her brothers too. It was such a hard choice but Miranda knew she had to go back to Utopia. She would just plan on coming to Earth more often once the evil were gone. If they were every truly gone. Miranda was in for more pain and heartache when she went back.

When Bryan parked in Helen's driveway, Miranda leaned over and kissed Scott goodbye.

Scott looked stunned and silence fell throughout the car.

Bryan motioned to Helen with his eyes and Helen nodded. "We'll, uh," Helen paused, "Give you both a minute." Bryan and Helen got out and headed around to Helen's backyard.

Once they were out of sight, Scott leaned in and kissed her again, emboldened by her forwardness.

It felt nice and made her tingle all over, but it was nothing like kissing Alex, it felt wrong. She pulled away and as she did, all thoughts of staying on Earth completely evaporated.

"Sorry Scott," Miranda said, a little breathless, "but I am not staying. I leave to go home in two days."

Scott looked downcast, "I'm sorry. I just really like you."

Miranda sighed sadly, "I like you too. I just... if things were different, I mean..." Miranda struggled, not sure how to let him down gently.

"What about university next year? Will you be coming back to Canada?" he asked, hopeful.

Miranda bit her lip and shook her head. "I have a job in the Bahamas. I am on a local soap opera," she lied, "I really like it and I was thinking of maybe just doing that for now. It will get me a lot of experience."

Scott gave her a half-smile, "Congrats. That is amazing."

"Thanks," Miranda tried to smile but it turned into a frown, "I really am sorry that I have to go back."

Scott brushed her cheek with his thumb, "So am I."

"What was that about?" Helen asked once they were back in her bedroom. Her eyes seemed to bulge out of her head.

Miranda looked confused, "What do you mean?"

"Scott!" Helen exclaimed. "You just kissed him!"

"Oh that?" Miranda snorted a laugh. "That was nothing."

Helen's mouth dropped, "Who are you?" She laughed as well. "I have never seen you so flirty."

Miranda shrugged, "Well, he *is* gorgeous. Plus, it was just a kiss."

"Again, who are you?"

Miranda smiled proudly, "I am a huge star on 'the most watched daytime drama series in Utopia'. Think about it. I have to kiss Alex almost every day, whether I want to or not. Plus, I have been dating. Plus, I sometimes give a kiss on the cheek to guys who want autographs. Really, it means nothing."

Helen sat on her bed, bewildered, "I saw the way Scott looked at you. I even caught Bryan looking at you. What were they thinking? If Bryan thought anything about you, I'm gonna kill him!"

Miranda laughed, "Aside from thinking that I look pretty good, Bryan is a perfect gentleman. It is Scott's thoughts, wow! He is not quite a gentleman in his mind!"

"Really?" Helen giggled as Miranda sat down beside her on the bed and told her some of his thoughts. Helen's giggling died away and a look of disappointment crossed her face, "I guess I missed a lot. I missed all your firsts, but you were there through all mine. All my heartaches and all my joys." Helen bit her lip, "You haven't done anything, uh, else?"

Miranda shook her head.

Helen unexpectedly threw her arms around her. "I'm so sorry that I couldn't be there when you needed me most, especially recently."

Miranda squeezed Helen back and tried not to cry. "It's not your fault," she muttered.

"This sucks," Helen said, leaning back, "I don't like this and I can't control it."

Miranda sent her a half smile, "How do you think I feel? Tonight was awesome and it almost made me want to stay here forever but I just can't."

Helen frowned, "I know. I have thought about it too, and I have an idea."

"Oh?"

"My mom started taking this self-defence class which is, conveniently, tomorrow night. Come with us. My mom has been begging me to go with her. She says she's learning a lot. It's taught by two ladies who are brown belts in jiu jitsu."

Miranda looked uncertain, "How will that help me? We're talking about people who throw boulders, plus this weird force they can wield like a laser beam. Hand to hand combat isn't really a Utopian thing."

"Well, make it one," Helen insisted, "If it comes to it, wouldn't you like to know a few moves?"

Miranda thought about it for a minute. It wouldn't hurt to learn, and it was just one night. It wasn't like she could keep taking classes. Finally she agreed. Helen really wanted her to and she couldn't say no.

Eight

★ ★ ★ ★

Miranda slept at Helen's that night and then spent all Monday with her, talking and laughing. They went to all their usual hangouts. Miranda had a lot of good stories about Utopia that she hadn't had time to tell Helen about. She told her about Utopian hockey, car racing and she told her more about the show she was on. Helen asked her a lot of silly questions about robots. Miranda had to tell her that robotics were a thing of the past. Utopia valued humanity more than robotics. It was part of their life balance. However, they didn't talk anymore about what Miranda should do with Alex and her brothers but Miranda gained a lot of perspective just by being away from them. She did miss them a lot, but it was hard when Helen talked about Bryan. They had a normal, healthy relationship, while Miranda was stuck with someone who didn't seem to be in love with her at all.

Miranda's Earth parents met them for dinner at Miranda's favourite restaurant, just outside the mall.

Over dinner, Miranda asked them what they had been up to the last few months.

Sara took Jim's hand and smiled, her eyes glistened with happiness, "We're expecting a baby soon."

Miranda's mouth dropped, "What? Why didn't you tell me yesterday?"

"We were just so interested in you, that it slipped our minds," Sara said with another smile at her husband. "The baby is due next week. A teen mother is putting her up for adoption. We have already spoken with her."

Miranda smiled, "Do you know what she is having? Where is the baby's room? Why didn't you use my old room?"

Sara bit her lip, "We couldn't remove your things. We are using my office. It's all painted and ready to go. It's a girl, and the mother is letting us name her."

"What name?"

Sara and Jim shared a look and Jim answered, "We have a few we like but haven't decided yet. We want it to start with an M."

Miranda bit her lip to keep the tears away. It was sweet that they wanted it to start with her initial.

"We were thinking Melanie or Melody. Maybe Mia, Megan..."

"Madeline," Jim chimed in.

Sara playfully punched him, "Oh no, you know I don't like that one."

"Well I like it," Jim said, "We could call her Maddie."

Miranda made a face, "That's what Alex calls me."

"What, Maddie?" Helen asked with a giggle.

Miranda rolled her eyes, "Yes. It's after a Utopian animal that looks like a tiny leopard cat with an angry growl and a big appetite."

Sara and Jim shared another look and laughed.

Helen laughed as well, "Seriously?"

"Well, it's called a Maddixon on our planet but he shortened it."

"Hmm," Helen sat in thought, "I like it better than Mandy. It's really cute, but you aren't exactly small!"

Miranda turned towards her as the waitress brought their food to the table. "Don't even think about it," she threatened with a smile. She waited till the waitress was gone, "I am actually short on Utopia."

"Really?" they all asked together.

Miranda nodded.

"I kind of like it now," Sara admitted.

"Oh no," Miranda shook her head, "Not you guys too! How about Marilyn? Famous actress!"

"Jim nixed that one," Sara said.

"Aw, Dad," Miranda laughed, "How come?" Miranda stopped laughing abruptly and bit her lip. Should she have called him Dad? She had called him dad the whole time she had been her, but what if they didn't want her to anymore. Jim beamed, happy that she still considered him her father.

"I like Mary-Lynn better," Jim shrugged.

After dinner, although Miranda really didn't think it was necessary, she joined Helen and her mother for self-defence. Helen's mother was excited for the company. She paid for everyone and introduced them to Anna and Jen, the two instructors, who were sisters. It was obvious, with their matching blue eyes and golden blond hair both tied back in high ponytails. They were even dressed similarly in black yoga pants and white t-shirts.

Once the warm-up was complete, Miranda learned how to throw a proper punch, as well as kicking and kneeing several sensitive points on a body and a few grappling moves. Somehow, Helen managed to get Anna, the younger sister, to stay an extra hour.

"I'm not exactly sure how you managed to get her to stay without paying her," Miranda said in the car.

Helen looked at her mother pointedly and then shot Miranda a smug smile, "I just asked her for some extra pointers. Not my fault she took an hour."

Miranda rolled her eyes. She heard clearly in Helen's mind that Helen had made up some huge lie about Miranda having a stalker and being frightened for her life. Anna was happy to help ease her mind and teach her a few extra things.

Once they turned on Miranda's street, Helen got quiet. "When are you leaving?" she said as they pulled into the driveway.

Miranda frowned, "Probably in the morning. I have to get back to work."

Helen's mother glanced back at Miranda, "Work?"

"School, I mean. Feels more like work," Miranda said, her face went a little pink at her slip up, "I am in some advanced classes at a private school. Pre-university study."

Helen's mom smiled, and then she looked sternly at her daughter, "See, now Miranda is studying hard. Why can't you put a little more effort in?"

Helen scowled at Miranda, then turned to her mother, "Miranda was top in our class before she even left. Give me a break."

Mrs. Beauchamps smiled at her daughter, "You are smart too, baby. If you tried more."

Helen rolled her eyes and changed the subject. "I'm going to come and see Miranda off tomorrow morning before school. I might be late so can you call it in, please?" Helen pleaded.

"Of course," her mother smiled indulgently at her daughter, and turned back to Miranda, "When will you be back next?"

"Hopefully in a couple months," Miranda shrugged, "Our phone should be fixed soon, so at least I will be able to call."

Helen gave her a half-hearted smile, knowing that a phone call was definitely not something she would expect though she wished with all her heart that she could speak to Miranda again on a regular basis. She was afraid for her friend. "I will see you in the morning."

Miranda waved as they drove away and then headed over to the motor home sitting across the street from her parent's house. She found Tim reading from his phone at the table and let him know she would be ready to leave in the morning. She would have loved to stay a week, but perhaps next time. She didn't want Evan to have to change any scripts.

The night felt it went by so fast. All of a sudden it was morning, and Miranda was ready to go. She hadn't slept well at all. She was worried about her family back on Utopia and also worried she may never see Earth again.

As promised, Helen showed up. She pulled Miranda aside and thrust a bag into her hands.

"What is this?" Miranda asked.

"My dad's hunting rifle," Helen replied. "I want you to take it with you."

"What?" Miranda practically shouted. She pulled Helen away from her parents' ears and set the bag down at Helen's feet. "I can't take this. There are no guns on Utopia. The self-defence was a great idea but this goes against everything we stand for."

"How do you defend yourselves then?" Helen snapped, frustrated. "What if you are attacked by people from another planet or aliens or… something!"

"Our space explorers travel everywhere. I am sure we would know and determine the best defence."

Helen looked scared, "I'm afraid for you." Her eyes welled with tears.

Miranda gave her a hug, "I'm scared too but I can't shoot a gun. It would feel so wrong. I just have my powers, whatever they are."

Helen hugged her tighter, "What if I never see you again?"

Miranda buried her face into Helen's shoulder, "Just know that you are the best friend I could ever ask for and I will do everything I can to see you again."

"You better," Helen said, finally letting go. "Take the gun though."

Miranda shook her head, "I'm sorry. I can't."

Helen rolled her eyes and bent down to open the bag. Miranda started to protest, but saw Helen was reaching for a book. "Well, if anyone can learn from this, it would be you."

Miranda took the book and laughed. It was a self-help book on martial arts.

"You do realize that without you, Garrett is going to be valedictorian. He wasted no time in making that known around the school."

Miranda let out a laugh, "Well, now that I know what I am and what my mind can do, it wouldn't have been fair to go up against you Earthlings." Miranda sobered quickly. "I will try to come back soon," she promised.

Miranda watched her parents and Helen all the way down the street, until the spaceship turned the corner and they were out of sight. Then she panicked, wondering if that was the last time she would ever see them. She had kept it together the whole time, trying to be strong, knowing if she let herself cry, she might even consider staying on Earth forever. She broke down now, deep wracking sobs and went to the back bedroom for some privacy, not wanting Tim to hear her breakdown. She cried herself to sleep.

She woke an hour before they would land back in Utopia, so she made herself something to eat, even though she wasn't very hungry, and sat at the table with her thoughts. She thought about everything that she had talked over with Helen and everything Helen had said. It was true, how could her brothers have thought that she found out about the Legend. She never told them and they didn't tell her that they knew. It wasn't all their fault that poor Jackson had died because Jackson was misinformed. However, they could have prevented it if they had said something. What they knew could have saved his life, they had to understand that. She went over the conversation with her brothers in her head and while they seemed repentant, they never once apologized and only defended what they did. Griffin was talking about sending her back to Earth. How could he even consider that option? It was ridiculous.

She sighed. Talking to Helen had only fuelled her fire. She had every right to be angry, and anyways, it was better that she stayed angry with them. She needed to keep them away from her, especially Alex. Anyone near her could be killed, just like Jackson. Miranda couldn't bear to even think of something happening to her family or Alex. It would crush her.

It was in the late morning hours when the spaceship touched back down in Utopia. Tim told her it was Sunday morning. Miranda thanked him and got up from her seat. She just happened to glance down at her pendant as she exited the spaceship. The needle had come to life and was pointing to her left. Miranda stopped short as she noticed Alex standing right there on her left.

"Where is my dad?" Miranda asked, worried.

"They do not know you are back," Alex replied, chewing on his lower lip. "I have been calling the space centre frequently and finally they told me your transport was returning. I was not exactly sure if you would be on it."

"Of course I am," Miranda snapped, as she started walking again. "I said I would come back, and I always do what I say I am going to do."

Alex frowned. Miranda walked past him, headed towards the buses to go home.

"Wait," Alex said, turning to catch up to her, "I came to pick you up. Just come with me."

"Why?" Miranda shot at him. "'Cause you are my protector and are here to make sure nothing attacks me?"

"No," Alex said and paused, "because I missed you."

Miranda spun on him, "What? You haven't had any dates? Are you going to play all happy to see me and then run off tomorrow with some other bimbo?"

Alex looked taken aback and he sighed heavily, "I had hoped you would not be so angry when you returned. I thought talking to Helen would make things better."

Miranda frowned, "Yes, right. Watching my parents in their normal, happy life and Helen in her perfect relationship with Bryan would make me *so* happy. I only feel worse now that they know. I lied to my parents and told them I was just a bystander when they found the articles on my phone, and Helen couldn't handle it. She threatened to lock me in her room and I'll have to admit, that it was tempting to let her do it." Miranda let her bag fall from her hands. She rubbed her face in frustration.

Alex had silently moved to her side, "I knew you would come back."

Miranda eyed him warily, "I didn't come back for you."

Alex nodded, "I know."

"In fact, I went out with Scott while I was home. We had such a great time." Miranda couldn't help it. She wanted to hurt him like he hurt her and to keep him away.

He picked up her bag, silently, ignoring what she had said completely, "We should go home."

Miranda sighed and followed him to his car.

"Were there any attacks while I was gone?" Miranda asked, breaking the silence of the car ride.

"Yes," Alex replied, "A quick one. Someone went missing again."

Miranda's stomach dropped. Why were they kidnapping people now? Were they recruiting or taking hostages? "Where was it?"

"Not nearby," Alex replied.

Miranda sat back to think. How could she react quicker? Sometimes it seemed to take her power awhile to build and the more she concentrated, the more she glowed and the more she could do, especially when it came to stopping the whole planet from shaking.

"The whole planet?" Alex asked, quickly glancing in her direction.

Miranda sighed. She hadn't blocked her thoughts.

"You do not have to block them anymore," Alex said. "I know everything."

Miranda sent him a glare. "No, you don't," she said angrily, "You have no idea how hard I've worked or about all the things going on in my head."

"So tell me," Alex said, softly. "I want you to be able to trust me."

Miranda's mouth opened and closed until finally she pressed her lips together firmly. This nice guy routine was not going to fool her and she couldn't let herself get close to him again. "No. I don't trust you at all. Not after how much you hurt me."

Alex went quiet. Miranda didn't know what he was thinking, though he looked deep in thought.

Mr. East was happy to see his daughter and so was Greta. Griffin had hoped she would have stayed on Earth, so Miranda didn't even acknowledge him. He hadn't moved from the couch. She was forced to hug Evan because he didn't care if she was mad at him, he was just glad she came back at all.

"Griffin," Greta chastised, turning to him confused. She had jumped off the couch at Miranda's arrival and now she turned, surprised that Griffin was not at her side. "Are you not happy to see your sister?"

Griffin sent Greta a reassuring smile, "Of course I am." He turned to Miranda, "Welcome back."

"Thanks Griffin," Miranda said icily.

Greta looked between the two of them with a frown.

"I sent you the new scripts," Evan said, breaking the silence. "You will need to be ready to film tomorrow."

Miranda nodded. She hadn't turned her phone on yet.

"If you want to practice together, I am not doing anything today," Alex said. He had followed her into the East apartment.

Miranda nodded and bit back a sarcastic thought that was about to cross her mind. She didn't want to start any fights in front of her father. He was already suspicious of the anger between her and Griffin, though he didn't say anything about it. "I should go unpack," Miranda said, feeling the tension. She took her bag down the hall and just as she got into her room, she heard Greta ask Griffin why he was acting the way he was. She didn't wait to hear the reply and shut the door.

She turned on her phone and started to unpack. She had several messages waiting for her. One from Nathan, two from Alicia and surprisingly, one from her neighbour, Rebecca, asking her if she wanted to go out that night. Miranda checked the time on the message and it was from today. Rebecca had sent it an hour ago.

Miranda messaged Rebecca back first, saying she would love to head out that night. She replied to Alicia, telling her she had been away for a week and was sorry she had missed her. She made plans to hang out with her on Monday night after work. Then she called Nathan and scheduled their date for Tuesday night. Finally she got around to looking through the scripts. Did Alex actually believe she wanted to practice with him?

Apparently he did because he knocked on her bedroom door an hour later. Alex slipped past her and into her room when she answered the door.

"What do you want?" Miranda snapped at him.

"To go over the scripts for tomorrow and maybe the next," Alex replied with a shrug. "You did not want my help?"

"You actually believed that?" Miranda asked, surprised, "I only agreed because my dad was standing right there."

Alex frowned, "You are going to have to get over this anger. Yes, we made a mistake and it cost a lot. But your brothers did it because they love you."

Miranda noted that he did not say because *he* loved her. "My brothers wanted to bring me back to Earth. They tried to run my life," Miranda explained, "When they learn that I can make my own decisions, then maybe I will speak to them again."

"Fine," Alex said, "be stubborn."

"And you as well, Alex," Miranda said. "Get out of my room and out of my life. I don't need you."

Alex stood his ground.

"And I meant what I said," Miranda continued. "Once we are done whatever we need to do, I am going back to Earth." She knew this would hurt him most. She thought of the time she spent with Helen, Bryan and Scott on Earth. She thought about how perfect it seemed and how she had kissed Scott. He even asked if she would come back to Canada to be with him. She fabricated a lie in her mind that she had said yes. She would try to come back so they could be together.

Alex looked hurt. He backed away from her slowly. "That is how you truly feel?"

Miranda nodded and turned her back on him. She took a steadying breath, trying not to start crying uncontrollably. She had to keep it together, so he would believe it. "Get out," she said, forcefully.

And he did. She heard the door close behind him and then she threw herself on the bed and cried.

Miranda stayed in her bedroom all day practicing her script. She skipped dinner, though her father had tried to coax her out. She told him she wasn't hungry and that she ate a lot on Earth. He spent some time with her in her bedroom, asking questions about her trip. He was so happy she had a good time and even happier that she had come home.

When Rebecca messaged to say she would be leaving in an hour. Miranda called for Alpha to get her black skirt and silver tube top. She accessorized with a red belt and some red heels. Then she had Alpha straighten her hair and do her makeup. She messaged Rebecca when she was ready and said she would meet her in the parking garage.

Evan and Alex were sitting in the living room. Miranda had wanted to sneak out, but they both turned to her when she opened the door.

"Where are you going?" Evan asked anxiously, rising from the chair.

"Out," was all Miranda replied without even turning around.

Evan pressed his lips together with displeasure, "With who?"

"None of your business!" Miranda snapped and faced them.

"We need you at the studio early tomorrow," Evan said with a sigh, "Have you practiced?"

Miranda nodded.

Evan bit his lip and looked at Alex, then back at Miranda, "Can we come with you?"

Alex looked at him like he was crazy and so did Miranda, "No Evan. I don't need you around," and she shut the front door.

Rebecca was waiting for her up in the parking garage and together they went to Club 217.

It was already crowded inside and Miranda started drinking immediately. She wanted to forget everything and have fun.

"I love this song!" Rebecca yelled and pulled her onto the dance floor once they each had a drink in hand.

Miranda smiled as she watched Rebecca do some fancy moves, "You have got to teach me to dance like you!"

Rebecca smiled, "It is easy, just watch and copy me."

Miranda did the best she could to copy her.

"You got it!" Rebecca shouted to Miranda. "You are a natural!"

"Thanks!" Miranda said and added in a little spin.

Rebecca copied her, "That was good!"

While they were dancing, a group of girls came up to them. "Are you Miranda?" one girl asked shyly.

"Yes?" Miranda replied, a little confused and a little frightened. Surely a group of girls weren't evil though.

The girls squealed.

"Oh it *is* you!" another exclaimed.

They all started talking at once.

"You are so amazing in the show!"

"I love *Northern Shores*!"

"What is Jeff, I mean Alex, like in person?"

"How do you become a star?"

"Woah," Miranda held up a finger, and smiled, "One at a time."

They all started talking again at the same time. Miranda giggled.

The first girl started waving her hands around to get everyone quiet, "OK, so can we get a picture with you?"

Miranda nodded and Rebecca took the picture for them. The girls hung around them all night and Miranda had a fun time. She had never gotten so much attention, but she ended up drinking a lot. Everyone kept buying her drinks whenever her glass was empty.

Later that night, Rebecca and Miranda headed out to the parking lot.

"Oh no, Rebecca," Miranda frowned. They were holding each other up, "How are we getting home? You can't drive like this."

"Oh, I forgot about that part," Rebecca giggled, "Do you know anybody awake that could pick us up?" She motioned with her head to the line-up at the bus stop. "I suppose we can wait but that is a long line."

Miranda only knew her brothers and Alex and she didn't want to call any of them.

"Oh, we should call Alex," Rebecca said, excitedly and pulled out her phone.

"You have his number?"

Rebecca nodded, "Yes, we date off and on." She waved her hand like it was no big deal as Alex answered.

"Hi Beck," Alex said, "What did you need?"

"A ride, handsome," Rebecca replied sweetly. "Where are you? You look like you are in a car."

"Is Miranda with you?" Alex asked, avoiding her question.

Rebecca nodded.

"I am not too far away. I will be there soon."

"So, you date Alex off and on?" Miranda asked once she had hung up. She tried to sound nonchalant but it didn't come out that way. Miranda started to feel sober and she frowned.

Rebecca shrugged, "Yes. He has always been a good friend but he is such a prude." Rebecca giggled, "Would I not love to get that boy in bed!"

Miranda tried to force out a laugh. That was the first time someone had outright admitted that they hadn't slept with Alex.

"It is great that he is saving himself and all," Rebecca slurred and put an arm around her, leaning against her heavily. "The poor boy! Everyone seems to stretch the truth about him. I have to say, I have lied about it too. No one wants anybody to think they were turned down. But facts are facts. We Utopians have a hard time pulling off a lie."

Miranda frowned. He *was* saving himself?

Rebecca started humming a song and dancing, forcing Miranda to dance too. "What an awesome time I had! You are so much fun. We should do this again very soon!"

Miranda nodded as Rebecca clutched at her arm. She was still dancing when Alex pulled up.

"Wow, that was fast," Rebecca said, as she let Miranda go and pulled open the door. "Were you stalking us?"

Miranda froze. Hadn't he been with her brother when she left? Why was he out?

"Why would I stalk you?" Alex laughed. "I was out on a date."

"Are you getting in?" Rebecca giggled, turning to Miranda. Rebecca had jumped in the front seat.

Miranda felt herself sobering up too quickly. She didn't like it, but she also couldn't start any arguments in front of Rebecca. Miranda got in the back quickly. She saw Alex's eyes on her in the rearview mirror.

Rebecca yammered on as they drove, completely oblivious to Miranda's silence. Alex answered her politely, but he kept looking back at Miranda.

"I thought you were on my level!" Rebecca laughed as she pulled Miranda out of the back seat.

"Oh I am," Miranda giggled, even though she didn't feel it anymore. To prove it, she leaned onto Rebecca, who seemed to be leaning back on her. They tried to take a few steps towards the elevator but Rebecca stumbled and almost took Miranda down with her.

Rebecca burst out laughing. "Oh, we should use him." Rebecca motioned with her head and turned to Alex, "A little help, please?"

Alex rolled his eyes dramatically and came around the car towards them, a sheepish smile on his face. Rebecca let go of Miranda, took Alex's arm and whispered something in his ear. Miranda only caught a few words but it sounded like she was asking Alex to come to bed with her.

Alex just laughed, "Thank you for the offer, but you know how it is."

Rebecca pouted, "OK, just take me home then," and she roared with laughter again.

Alex turned to Miranda and offered his other arm. Keeping up with her act, Miranda took it but she didn't lean into him.

The elevator door opened on Rebecca's fifth floor apartment. She kissed Alex's cheek, "Remember the offer still stands." She winked and laughed then she stumbled out of the elevator and towards the wrong apartment. She seemed to catch herself and laughed again before she turned to the correct door.

Alex stepped back and let the elevator door close. Miranda let go of his arm immediately.

"Did you have a good time?" Alex asked, making conversation.

"Up to a certain point," Miranda snapped as the elevator door opened again on their own floor. She sent him a glare, "Did you?"

"No," Alex sighed and stepped out into the hallway between the apartments.

Miranda followed, "Did you really have a date or were you following me?"

Alex frowned, "What do you think?"

"Seriously?" Miranda's eyes flashed.

"Do not get mad at me," Alex snapped back, "Evan asked me to."

She remembered her conversation with Helen about how she would do anything for her. "I'm already mad at you," she said, more to convince herself. She turned away and went into her apartment to go to bed.

Miranda wasn't sure what to expect when she left her room the next day. Evan already went to work, but Griffin was still there. He told her, icily, that she should go with Alex to the studio. Since Greta was beside him, Miranda did not contradict him, but when she was ready, she took the elevator up to the roof to get the bus. Griffin must have checked on her, because Alex was up there a minute later to get her.

"We are taking my car!" Alex snapped as he walked up to her and easily lifted her over his shoulder.

"Alex! Put me down!" Miranda screamed, "I have already called for a bus!"

"No, you are coming with me," Alex said calmly, and pressed the button again. The light went out and Miranda huffed angrily. Was it really that easy to cancel a bus?

She stopped struggling when they reached the elevator. "I can walk, you know," Miranda said, the blood rushing to her head.

"I will put you down in the car," Alex said as he reached over to push the button. The elevator opened right away. Miranda thought about grabbing the doorframe when they went in but did not want him to drop her and she knew he would.

Miranda sighed. At least there was no one to witness this indignity, or so she thought. Bill, Alicia's dad and the building inspector, was waiting to get onto the elevator from the parking garage. Miranda's face was already red from being upside down, so she couldn't flush anymore.

"Hello Alex," Bill said and chuckled. "Hi Miranda."

"Hello," Miranda managed to squeak out, embarrassed.

"We are just practicing for filming today," Alex said.

"You should probably just put me down *Jeff*," Miranda snapped.

"Not till we get to the car, Cara," Alex smiled and said goodbye to Bill.

When the elevator door closed again, Miranda let out a string of curses. "That was so embarrassing!"

"But you will never try to take the bus on your own again, will you?" Alex asked, amused.

Miranda snorted, "Yeah, we shall see about that." Miranda cheekily noticed that she had an awesome view of Alex's butt so she let herself hang down a little farther.

Alex set her down, "Miranda!"

"What?" Miranda laughed, feeling a little dizzy as the blood drained from her head. She had to put a hand on Alex's car to steady herself. "You are the one who wanted my face right there."

He turned away, opening the door to the passenger side. He turned back to her, "Get in," he snapped.

Miranda folded her arms across her chest, "No."

Alex took a threatening step towards her.

"Fine!" she said and climbed in the car.

They did not say a word to each other the whole way there,

Once they were at the studio they parted ways without another word spoken.

Miranda walked into her dressing room and Britany was there, "Hi," she smiled, excitedly.

"Hi," Miranda replied.

"How was your trip?" Britany asked, but then frowned, "Aside from the funeral. How is Alex anyways?"

"It was fine. He seems OK," Miranda said and she started to feel bad. He had just lost his grandmother and she wasn't being a very good friend. She shook her head, she had to keep him safe. She sent a smile at Britany, having blocked the last thoughts. "I had my first autograph session and a few run-ins with reporters. It is nice that there are so many fans of the show and that they recognize me so quickly." Miranda sat on her side of the room and spun in her chair to face Britany.

"Have you seen the pictures of you from Vacca?" Britany asked.

"I did not see any new photos after the last one up there." She motioned behind her.

"Check your notebook for the Saturday edition," Britany said.

Miranda opened it up and found it. There were several pictures. One of her in her dress in the behind-the-shoulder pose, one of the three of them, and one of her and Alex. They just happened to be looking at each other in admiration. She wasn't sure when that had been taken. It may have been on the way out.

"Are you and Alex together now?" Britany asked, curiously. "By the way you are looking at each other, it seems like it, but the article says you are just friends."

Miranda shook her head and bit her lip. She pointed her notebook at an empty frame and beamed the article over. Then she stared at the picture of her and Alex.

"Do you want to be?"

Miranda shrugged and closed her mind. Of course she still did.

"Well, come out with me sometime this week," Britany insisted. "We can find you someone else."

Miranda sent her a half smile and nodded, "How about Wednesday?" She was happily filling up her week, so that she didn't have to see her brothers too much.

The filming went by quickly. No matter how angry she was with Alex and her brother or how angry Alex was with her, their characters were still great together. Evan had no complaints.

"Are you doing anything tonight?" Evan asked curiously as they walked out of the studio together towards the elevator.

"Just out with Alicia," Miranda said.

"In the building?"

Miranda rolled her eyes, "Yes, probably."

"I have to stay late," Evan said. He shifted uncomfortably as he pushed the button to call the elevator, "Will you just go home with Alex?"

Miranda turned to her brother with a look of disdain. "Do I have to?" Miranda whined.

"I would really like it if you did," Evan said. He looked down at her, hopeful.

"There are a lot of things I would like," Miranda snapped, "but you and Griffin are too busy trying to run my life."

Evan's mouth clamped shut as they got in the elevator and he pushed the button for her floor and his own.

"You just don't get it," Miranda continued, "Neither you nor Griffin seem to think you did anything wrong! Jackson is dead! If you had just told me right away, none of this would have happened! He would be alive and maybe you would have your wish. Maybe Alex and I would have ended up together but now we never will!" The elevator door opened and Miranda left to go to her dressing room without a look back.

Alex walked into her dressing room without knocking. "Would you like an ungraceful exit or are you going to come willingly?" he threatened.

Miranda squealed with surprise. She was naked, aside from her undergarments and covered herself with her shirt.

Britany, who was already changed and fixing her hair in front of the mirror, laughed. "Have you not learned to knock Alex?"

Alex snorted, "Like I have not seen it before." He sent a cheeky grin over to Britany and added, "Both of you."

Britany sent him her most alluring smile and shrugged, knowing he was right. She went back to fluffing her hair.

Miranda hurried to put her clothes on. "See you tomorrow, Brit," Miranda said and grudgingly followed Alex out the door. Again, they didn't speak the whole way home. Once they were back at their apartment, Miranda went to her room to practice for the next day before she messaged Alicia. She met her downstairs at the pool.

Even after Alicia left, Miranda stayed downstairs as late as she dared. She didn't want to see her brothers or Alex and hoped they would be asleep. First she went to play games in the game room and then went back to the pool area to use the gym equipment. There was no one out this evening and Miranda had the whole floor to herself. She didn't mind, everyone was safer if they stayed away.

Evan checked his watch and glared at her when she walked into the apartment, "You have to be at the studio at 9 tomorrow," he snapped, "Do not be late."

Miranda smiled sarcastically, "Yes boss." She saluted him and went down the hallway to her bedroom. What was he still doing awake anyways? He looked exhausted.

"Get up!" Alex shouted and smacked her on the backside.

Miranda swore and rolled over, falling off the bed.

"We are going to be late," Alex snapped, as he left her room. "Get in the shower and fix yourself up."

Miranda groaned. She sent an angry glare at the empty door frame then stood. It was already 8:25 and she had forgotten to set her alarm. She assumed Alex woke her up late on purposed. He had probably been up for hours. She ran to the bathroom and was ready in ten minutes.

Alex was waiting for her in the living room. She was hungry but knew she had no time to eat. Instead she got her shoes, and led the way up to the parking garage. She knew Alex would never let her take the bus.

She started to walk towards Alex's car, but realized quickly he wasn't following. Instead, he was heading towards her car.

"Just what do you think you are doing?" Miranda yelled across the parking garage. She stopped walking and stared.

Alex didn't answer. He just got in her car and started it. Miranda crossed her arms and stood her ground. She stared stonily at him though she couldn't see him through the back windows. He drove it over to her and the door to the passenger side opened.

"Get in," he said.

"This is car-jacking!" Miranda yelled.

"I do not know what that means," Alex retorted.

"You are stealing my car!"

"No, your dad said it was fine that we use your car. I asked him this morning while you slept in."

"*We* are not using it. You are stealing it!"

Alex sighed angrily, "Just GET IN!"

Miranda huffed and looked at her clock. It was 8:40. Evan was going to be so mad. She got in the car.

Alex took off before she could get the door closed. She tsk-tsked loudly and clutched the sides of her seat.

Alex drove so fast, the world outside was a blur.

"Do all cars drive this fast?" Miranda asked, hanging on for dear life. She looked straight ahead so she wouldn't get nauseous, "Take it easy! She's brand new!"

"All cars are the same," Alex snapped, "Did you know that getting you a car was my idea but now I regret everything I have ever done for you."

"Does that include letting my boyfriend get killed?" Miranda snapped.

It stung. Alex cringed and it only made him drive faster.

He was out of the car before Miranda could even loosen her grip on the seat. The elevator arrived and he got in and closed the door behind him even though Miranda wasn't inside yet.

Her eyes filled with tears. She was so ungrateful, just like Alex had thought in his mind but she had to be. She needed to keep him away from her. She felt it was her only choice.

Evan was waiting for her outside her dressing room. He was looking at his notebook for the time.

"You are late," he snapped.

"I said something mean to Alex," Miranda said miserably. "Go check on him."

"You mean something more than you have already said?" Evan asked crossly.

Miranda nodded and a tear fell down her cheek.

Evan's face turned from anger to pity, and he brushed by her to go in search of Alex.

Miranda wiped away her tear and went into her dressing room. Her stylist was there waiting, since she needed to be ready quickly.

Miranda took a few deep breaths and started a bit of mental motivation. She needed to be happy. She didn't want to screw up today.

Before she knew it, it was time to go home. Again, she performed perfectly with Alex. Miranda was happy it wasn't in the scripts to kiss, but tomorrow was going to be different. They were expected to do another bedroom scene. Apparently, the last one was received very well by fans and the writers thought another one was warranted.

Miranda went to Evan after they were done filming before heading back to her dressing room to change. He had been talking to Melissa about the set up for tomorrow and making a change on his notebook, "Can I come home with you?"

"I have to stay late, Miranda," Evan said, bitterly. "Just go with Alex."

Miranda frowned. She felt horrible for what she said that morning.

"I hope you did not mean it. Of course we did not want Jackson to die," Evan snapped, looking up at her, "but you still have to go with him."

"No," Miranda said, stubbornly, "I am taking the bus."

Evan sighed angrily and walked away from her. He was so frustrated with the whole situation and it definitely was getting worse. He wished she would not put her life in danger. She was safer with Alex. He went to get Alex to make sure he took her home.

Miranda was waiting by her car when Alex found her. He looked irritable.

"Thank you for making me search all over the building for you." He was angry. "I thought you left."

"I forgot you stole my car," Miranda snapped. "There is no way you are driving this without me."

Alex rolled his eyes and he got in. He drove fast all the way home and didn't say another word.

Miranda did her best not to think anything. She didn't want Alex to know that she felt bad, that she didn't mean it, and that all she wanted was for him to hold her and promise that he would not die.

Miranda was working on her script when Nathan messaged asking when she wanted to have dinner. Miranda replied she was good to go any time.

He messaged back that he would get her at her door in half an hour.

Miranda changed into a knee-length ruffled black skirt. It billowed out when she spun and she did a few dance moves in front of her mirror. She would definitely have to wear it the next time she went to the club. She had her hair fixed and makeup redone and was ready the minute she heard a knock at the door. Both of her brothers were in the living room and they both looked over as she answered the door. Anger coloured Griffin's face and Evan frowned when they saw who it was.

Both of them looked like they were going to say something, but Miranda smiled, "Don't wait up," and closed the door on her brothers' flustered faces.

"So what do you feel like?" Nathan asked as they got to the parking garage and headed for his dark green car.

"How about pasta? Have you been to Joe's?"

Nathan nodded and he chuckled, "Of course. It is one of my favourites."

"Can we go there?"

"Yes, definitely.

Miranda and Nathan were seated at a private booth once they got to Joe's, since Miranda was recognized the minute she walked in the door.

Kristen was her waitress again, "Hello Miranda." She greeted her with a smile, then she turned to Nathan, "Hi Nathan, how are you?"

"Oh, you both know each other?" Miranda asked, an eyebrow raised.

"We went to school together," Nathan said.

We did more than that, Miranda heard Kristen say in her mind. Miranda tried not to react to that statement. Out loud Kristen said, "What can I get you to drink?"

They both ordered a drink with alcohol.

Miranda closed her mind. She wondered if Kristen was the girl Nathan had fallen in love with. She felt so inexperienced and now all of the sudden she was 19! Two years older than how she felt, mentally. Miranda sighed quietly.

When Kristen returned, she took their food order and soon after that, their meals were delivered to the table. Miranda talked about her two long days at the studio while they ate and Nathan complimented her on her acting. It was polite conversation with some awkward silences, at least they felt awkward to Miranda but maybe that was just because she felt badly for leading Nathan on.

As they were leaving after dinner, a woman approached, "Hi Miranda! I am from City 217 news. Can I have the exclusive?" she continued excitedly. "Who is this handsome man?"

Miranda tried to smile, "This is Nathan. He is uh..." She broke off, unsure of how to describe him. She still thought it was too soon to date after Jackson's death, and she didn't want to be judged.

"This is our first date," Nathan supplied an answer for her. "Though I would like it to be more." He smiled down at Miranda. Miranda finally realized how tall he actually was. He looked even bigger than the last time she had seen him.

Miranda smiled back at him, appreciatively.

"Can I get a better picture of you both?" she asked.

Nathan wrapped both his arms around her, and Miranda smiled.

"I am happy to see you are moving on after the tragedy," the reporter said sympathetically.

Miranda frowned, "Thank you."

"Thank you for the picture," the reporter said and she headed to her car.

"How about a movie?" Nathan suggested, "We can pick up some drinks from my apartment."

Miranda nodded. "Sounds great," she replied, half-heartedly.

It wasn't late enough when the movie ended. She knew her brothers might still be awake, so she invited Nathan out for a walk.

They headed down the path towards the river, walking hand in hand. Nathan carried a small bag that had more bottles of alcohol for them and they had a little picnic under the stars. When he started to kiss her, Miranda had to force herself to continue. It felt so wrong.

"That was nice," he said, huskily.

Miranda murmured an agreement even though she didn't think it was.

"Well, I should probably get you home," he said picking up the scattered empty bottles.

Miranda looked at her phone. It was past 1, her family should be in bed by now however Griffin and Greta were both on the couch when Miranda walked in the front door, though Greta had fallen asleep on Griffin's lap. She stirred and sat up when Miranda walked in. Miranda felt sorry for her. She must not have a clue about what was going on.

"Hey," Miranda whispered quietly.

"Hi," Greta replied, yawning. Griffin didn't look at her once, staring stonily ahead at the television.

"Well, goodnight," Miranda said, mostly just to Greta.

"Do you mind if we talk tomorrow?" Greta asked, sleepily, "I want to know what is going on."

Griffin finally turned away from the television, "I told you it is nothing, Greta. We all just had a misunderstanding and now we are all mad at each other. Do not worry about it."

Greta frowned and looked between the two of them, "Well, I think it is ridiculous that we have to stay up and wait for her. She is a big girl and can take care of herself," she said to Griffin.

"I am sorry Greta," Miranda said, apologetically, "but if Griffin hasn't told you, I can't be the one to tell you."

Greta frowned at Miranda and turned to Griffin expectantly. She sighed when Griffin ignored her stare.

"Goodnight," Miranda repeated and went to her room.

Miranda had a nightmare that night, but this time someone was going after Alex. Miranda tried to reach him in time, but the ground shook so hard she fell many times. By the time she reached him, he was already dead and she screamed in agony.

Miranda awoke with a start, tears sliding down her face. She got out of bed quickly, put on her bathrobe and crept quietly to the front door. A bad feeling washed over her as she listened through the metal panels. She felt like someone was standing outside, right there in the hallway between their doors. She drew in a breath, frightened. She was frozen solid, half torn between throwing the door open and attacking or running back to her room. In that brief pause she heard some motion, a rustle of clothing and the elevator door opened and then closed again. Miranda couldn't feel anything anymore and perhaps she had been wrong. She opened the door and stood there for a second, trying to think. Perhaps she had been just frightened of her dream. Maybe Alex had been out on one of his many dates? Still, she needed to check on him so she crossed the hallway and knocked.

He answered it after a stressful minute, while Miranda had anxiously knocked as quiet as she dared, still dressed in his clothes from yesterday.

Miranda didn't say anything for a second, thinking how stupid she was being. Her dream had scared her, and it was probably just another woman leaving Alex's apartment.

"What is wrong? Do you want to come in?" he asked and stepped aside.

She shook her head several times, feeling so silly for knocking on his door. "I just had a bad dream and I needed to see you." She felt terrible for treating him so badly and telling the lies to make him think she was going to run back to Scott after all this.

Alex shifted uncomfortably, "Is that all?"

Miranda spun away quickly and went to her apartment before he could hear what she was thinking. He was probably just out with another woman and that was making her furious.

She returned to her bed completely irritated at herself for going to check on Alex, but how could she be mad at him for it? She had just been out on a date as well.

Alex was asleep on their couch when Miranda left the bathroom that morning. He looked ready, so he must have dozed off waiting for her. She thought about leaving him there, but since she didn't plan on going home with him later, she figured she should wake him. Her plan for the night was to go clubbing with Britany and they had decided to make a whole evening of it by going to dinner and shopping before they went out.

"Time to get up, Alex," Miranda shouted, jumping on the couch. It was payback for how he woke her up yesterday.

He awoke with a start and had to draw in some deep calming breaths to still his fast beating heart.

"You look tired, didn't you sleep?" Miranda asked, jumping down off the couch.

"Not well after you left," he replied, tiredly.

"I'm not stupid. I heard someone leaving last night," Miranda told him.

"You are obviously hearing things," Alex rolled his eyes, adding in his mind, that yes, he did think she was stupid.

Miranda sighed, "I am ready to go."

Alex did a double take down at her clothes. "Thank you for waking me. Finally you realize..."

Miranda frowned and cut him off, "I would watch what you say next or next time I won't wake you."

Alex shut his mouth and rolled his eyes.

Miranda's phone rang as they made their way silently across the city. She looked down and saw it was Marcy. She forgot she was supposed to talk to her this week. Her stomach dropped. She would have to explain to Marcy that Jackson died for nothing. He had never been the chosen one.

"Hi Marcy," Miranda said. Her voice shook a little so she cleared her throat. She saw Alex glance at her out of the corner of his eye.

"Hi Miranda. I am sorry I have not called you yet this week. I have been so busy at work. I was wondering if we could meet up tomorrow evening?"

"Yes, that is fine," Miranda replied. This conversation was going to have to happen. "I will call you once I get out of work. Perhaps you can meet me at the studio?"

"Yes, that sounds great," Marcy said, forcing a smile.

They hung up and Miranda hung her head. How was she going to tell Marcy that her son died for nothing? Miranda's eyes filled with tears. It wasn't going to be an easy conversation.

"Do you want me to come with you?" Alex asked, sadly.

She thought about it for a minute before she shook her head, "I can tell her myself. I don't think it's a good idea for you to be there."

Once she reached her dressing room that day, Britany talked excitedly about what they would do that night.

She suggested they go to a place called Spicy Noodle for dinner.

"Thai?" Miranda asked.

Britany cocked her head, "Thai? I have never heard that word before."

Miranda tried to describe what Thai food was.

"Yes, spicy noodles," Britany nodded, "That is pretty much the idea of this place."

Miranda laughed.

"Do you like spicy sauce?"

"Yes, that should be fine."

"Thai food it is then!" Britany laughed, "Then we are going shopping. I have got to get you ready for this place we are going to tonight."

"What is it called?"

"*Black*," Britany replied, her eyes sparkled. "The dress code is black clothing. You should see the men that go there in tight black pants." She sighed dreamily. "They play classic music."

Miranda laughed nervously.

"It will be so fun. You will forget all about Alex!"

It was hard to forget Alex when she had to do scenes like this next one, Miranda thought to herself as she waited for them to set up the bedroom set. This time it was Jeff's bedroom. Miranda felt a lot calmer than the last time, but Alex still looked sick. He was across the room, pacing again.

Evan strode over to her. "So, just like last time, I will not be in here," he explained, all business-like, "and there will be music again so you do not need to make noise." He spun away without another word and went over to Alex. Evan looked like he was trying to console or reassure him. Miranda couldn't hear, but she saw Alex straighten and nod his head.

Miranda frowned as she watched. It wasn't fair that everyone was against her. She had every right to be upset. Why couldn't they just apologize for trying to run her life all the time? They lied to her in the worst way, and insisted she should go back into hiding. Evan and Alex had been against it, but still no one had offered an honest apology yet! Miranda's face grew red with anger as she watched Evan and Alex. At least they had each other. Miranda had no close friends or family at all.

Before Miranda could even stop herself, she marched straight up to them. "I don't want to do this scene," she said, angrily, "I want a re-write!"

Evan did a double take and frowned. He took a step back beside Alex. Alex's jaw dropped, "Why?"

"Re-write it," Miranda said, crossing her arms over her chest, "I am not doing it."

"Why?" Evan asked again.

Miranda pointed a finger up at him, "You can't push us together, no matter how hard you try. Just give it up already."

"Miranda, I did not even write this scene," Evan insisted, calmly "I do have other writers on my team."

"You approved it," Miranda snapped.

Evan looked at Alex, who shook his head in annoyance.

"I thought you were an actress," Alex said, forcefully. "You cannot allow your emotions to get involved. Yes, you are angry but you also have a job to do. You signed a contract and you knew that we would be doing this type of scene before you did."

"This character was not created for you," Evan added. "Cara was going to come into being whether you played her or not. She could have been any one of those girls that auditioned that day with you, and it could have been one of them doing this scene."

Miranda turned away. *Great*, she thought, *because I can't think before getting angry, I now know that I'm easily replaceable.*

Evan sighed, "Miranda, you are..."

Alex cut him off, "Are you doing the scene or not?"

Miranda didn't look back at them but she nodded.

"Good," Alex huffed, "Now stop being ridiculous, they are ready."

"I need a second," Miranda said, quietly and she left the studio to head up to the roof. She just needed five minutes to calm herself, embarrassed by her little tantrum. She almost blew her cover. She needed to stay angry at them and not act like she wanted them in her life. It was far too dangerous.

When she returned, only Alex, Melissa and a cameraman were there. Alex and Melissa were laughing.

"Sorry," Miranda said to Melissa.

Melissa smiled, "I can imagine a scene like this would make anyone nervous."

Miranda nodded.

"Ok, so today we would like to see more passion. The first time was slow and sweet," Melissa described. She looked like she was picturing it in her mind, "This time I need no hesitations, no shy smiles, just rip his clothes off."

Miranda's jaw dropped in horror before she reminded herself, again, that she was a professional. She took a deep breath and nodded.

Together they took their places just outside his bedroom door and Melissa told them to go when they were ready.

Alex led the way into the bedroom while holding Miranda's hand tightly. Miranda looked down at the bed and smiled wickedly at Alex, "I can see where this night is headed." And she launched herself at him.

Miranda didn't expect him to have any effect on her at all, not since the big fight, but the fire raged through her the moment their lips met, and she did exactly what Melissa had said. She tore at his clothes and he did the same.

"Ok, that was fiery!" Melissa said, once Miranda and Alex were through. The managed to get through the scene with only one take. Melissa strode over to the video booth, "Can you just play that back for me?"

"Do we have to start over?" Miranda asked, once she had gotten her clothes back on. She bit her lip. Her mind was reeling over that. It had been a hot blur. She couldn't even recall if she had done what she was supposed to.

Melissa shook her head and both Alex and Miranda breathed a sigh of relief. "It actually looks great. I sent it to be processed."

Alex stood up quickly, "I have to go."

Miranda turned to him, "Go?"

"Can we wait to see if Evan likes it?" Melissa asked, confused. Alex never left early.

"I am sure you made a good call," Alex said as he walked away and then added over his shoulder, "Tell him to call me."

Evan came back in a few minutes later, his expression unreadable. "Where is Alex?" he asked Melissa.

Melissa threw her arms up, confused, "He left once I said it looked good."

Evan turned on Miranda, "What did you say to him?"

Miranda looked taken aback, "Me? I didn't say anything!"

"I have to stay late," Evan sighed, "You are just going to have to wait for me then."

"Actually, I am going out with Britany," Miranda said. "She is probably waiting."

"Are you making plans every night now?" Evan asked, his temper rising.

"Yes," Miranda replied, sticking her chin out, daring him to stop her.

"So, that is it," Evan snapped. "You really do not want anything to do with us anymore."

"No, I don't!" Miranda yelled and spun on her heel. She heard Evan groan in frustration as the door to the studio closed behind her.

Britany had a bright cherry red car, which they took to dinner and then shopping. Britany showed her the outfit she had in her trunk that she would be changing into. It was a pair of tight pants that looked like they were made of some kind of shiny, black, synthetic leather and a matching tube top that would show her flat belly. And now they were headed towards a store in the shopping centre that Miranda had never been to.

"This is perfect for you!" Britany said pulling a tiny dress, made of the same material as her outfit, off the rack.

Miranda's eyes went wide and she shook her head, "There is nothing to that!"

Britany giggled, "Would you prefer this?" She pulled the same dress down but with geometric shapes cut out in the mid-riff region.

Miranda gave her a look of horror and took the other one from her, "I will try it on."

Britany laughed and watched her go to the change room.

It was the shortest dress Miranda had ever worn. It was so short that if Britany had not said it was a dress, Miranda would have thought it was just a long shirt. The material was stretchy so it hugged her every curve. She came out of the change room and Britany's eyes lit up.

"You look gorgeous!"

Miranda shifted uncomfortably and tried to pull the dress down.

Britany whacked her hands, "Stop it."

Miranda rolled her eyes and looked at herself in the mirror, "How am I supposed to dance with this tiny thing on? Do I get to wear shorts underneath?"

"No. You get some black underwear," Britany said. "And they will cover up the important part." She winked.

Miranda made a face and looked at herself in the mirror again but her mind drifted to the event at the studio. She was still reeling from it, even though she had tried to laugh it off when she told Britany over dinner.

"Alright, fine," she said, "I will get it." She did look good in black with her dark hair and light blue eyes.

"Good!" Britany cheered, "May as well leave it on. We can go to the bar early and get a good start on drinking before it picks up."

Britany went and got her a pair of black underwear from the store and Miranda went back into the change room to put them on.

"You really look great!" said the woman who owned the store when Miranda went up to pay. She was dressed in the similar shiny, black material, "And you will have a great time at *Black*. My family owns the club."

Next they headed to a shoe store and picked up a pair of black high-heeled boots for Miranda to wear. As they passed the sporting goods store, Miranda told Britany she was going in. She wanted a Knights jersey.

The cashier at the store knew exactly who she was and gushed about liking the same team as her.

As Miranda was leaving the store, she heard the woman on the phone, probably to one of her friends, saying that she had just had Miranda in her store and they liked the same team. Miranda smiled wistfully. It reminded her of her and Helen. They would always call each other first if something exciting happened in their lives.

Once they were parked on the roof of the club, Britany hopped in the backseat to change. She came out looking absolutely gorgeous. Miranda was jealous of her pants as she tried to pull her dress down again.

"You are just revealing more up top when you do that," Britany giggled.

Miranda looked down and her bra was showing. She had to pull the dress back up a little.

"Here, I have this," Britany said as she pulled out a silver metal chain and tied it around Miranda's waist like a belt. Britany adorned herself with large gold hoop earrings and a thick gold bracelet. She also put a tiny gold chain around her exposed waist.

They got their own private booth and talked and drank for the first couple hours till the place got busier. Miranda felt more comfortable the more she saw people wearing the same short skirts and tight clothes. It was either that or the alcohol that made her more confident.

Britany left a few times to go out on the dance floor. She would point out someone she thought was cute and then go dance against him. Miranda watched her in awe. She could never do that.

"That is it!" Britany said when she returned once again, "Get out here with me!" She smiled and pulled Miranda up. Miranda's head swam a little. She had drunk a lot in a short period of time.

On the dance floor, Britany pulled her onto one of the raised platforms so that everyone could see them. Miranda watched Britany dance a bit while she swayed to the music.

Britany looked at Miranda, "Come on!" she shouted over the music. "I know you can dance!"

Miranda gave her a small smile and then did the few moves Rebecca had taught her. Then she did a few she learned just from watching Britany.

Britany had stopped to watch her and smiled excited when she was done, "That was great!"

A group of girls joined them on the platform shrieking with delight when they recognized who they both were. Miranda laughed and joked with them while posing for pictures.

As the night neared its end, Miranda looked around for Britany. The last time she saw her, she was kissing some guy on the dance floor.

Miranda circled the club several times but couldn't find a trace of her. Not that it mattered, because Britany was too drunk to drive her home anyways. Who was she going to call? Or should she take the bus?

She thought of messaging Nathan, but she didn't want him to see her like this. She felt really drunk and she still didn't trust him completely. Miranda went up to the roof. The only time she ever took the bus by herself was when they had visited Alex's parents and she was the only one on the bus. Miranda looked at the lineup waiting. Was she putting herself in danger? If evil was coming for her, it was going to get her no matter where she was. Anyways, she didn't want Alex to be near her if it ever found her.

Miranda was fiddling with her contact list, trying to decide who to call when his blue car pulled up. Alex got out and came over to sit with her on the ledge of the building.

He took a deep breath, "I am sorry about earlier. I should have stayed. I just needed to think."

"It's fine." Miranda sighed, "You following me is another matter entirely. Perhaps you should apologize for that."

Alex shook his head, "No. I am doing it because Evan asked me to. I will not apologize for that."

"Do you always do what he asks?" She felt herself sobering up. He seemed to have that effect on her. It was annoying.

"Only if I want to," Alex admitted.

"So you want to follow me?"

Alex shrugged.

Miranda closed her mind. The only way to get him away from her so that he could be safe would be to hurt him so badly that he didn't want to follow her. She would have to think of something.

"Come on," Alex said, standing, "I will take you home. You were going to call me, right?"

"No," Miranda snapped, "I was going to call Nathan."

Alex narrowed his eyes, "Seriously?"

"Oh I am sorry," Miranda said, sarcastically, "I forgot only you are permitted to date."

"Yes, but I do not date just to make your brothers angry," Alex said and he opened her door for her.

Miranda got in and shut it. Once Alex had gotten in on the driver's side, she responded, "At least I don't date everything with a pulse."

Alex slammed his door, "Are you going to start that again?"

Miranda crossed her arms over her chest and stared out the window, "It is true."

"So, do you want me to stop? Stop dating everyone else?" He looked straight at her when he said it.

Miranda snorted a laugh and looked at him incredulously, "You would stop?"

Alex shrugged.

Miranda shook her head, "Don't bother."

Alex pressed his lips together, deep in thought but Miranda couldn't hear them.

Nine

★ ★ ★ ★

Britany was anxiously waiting for Miranda in their dressing room the next day. She had already called that morning to apologize for leaving her at the club. "Oh, I am so sorry," she said again when Miranda walked in.

"It's fine. Don't worry about it," Miranda said, waving her hand, "I made it home."

"Next time, I will not do that unless you have a hook up too," Britany said, with a secret smile.

Miranda wrinkled her nose, "No thanks."

"Really?" Britany asked, in shock.

Miranda had never thought about it really. She never even had the opportunity to ever say no to sex but she definitely wasn't going to hook up with some random guy at a bar.

After filming, Miranda took a deep breath and called Marcy. Marcy said she would pick her up shortly and they could go for dinner. It didn't take her long, she was anxious to talk. As soon as Miranda was in the car, Marcy suggested the nearest restaurant.

"Before we start, you have to let me talk first," Miranda said. She took a deep breath, "There is something you need to know that is going to change everything."

Marcy gave her a weary look, but was quiet.

"Maybe I should wait until we land," Miranda said, as she gazed out the window.

Five minutes later, they landed on the roof of a nearby restaurant. The sign read 'The Caffe'.

Miranda ordered a glass of water for each of them once they were seated.

Marcy took a deep breath, "I am afraid I am not going to like what you have to say."

"How did you guess?" Miranda tried to smile but her eyes filled with tears.

"Tell me please," Marcy said. Her eyes glistened at the sight of Miranda's. She picked up her napkin and started to fiddle with it.

"James is not the first child of the West and neither was Jackson," Miranda blurted out. Her voice faded away as she spoke.

"What?" Marcy said, shaking her head, "That is not true. The group told me that I would birth the first child of the west."

"They did not understand. You have to believe me. Your mother in law, Geneva, gave this to Alex before she died." Miranda pulled out her chain and started the lie she concocted so that Marcy had no reason to blame Alex for her son's death. She closed her mind and put her hand around the pendant which was pointed to the west. It warmed at her touch and she could feel Alex like he was standing right behind her. She let go of the pendant quickly. "When Geneva saw you give that book to me, she realized that we knew, but no one told us we had the wrong person. She gave this necklace to Alex to give to me." Miranda paused and then said, "We are the protectors."

Marcy was quiet as the waitress brought the water.

"We will need another minute with the menu," Miranda forced a smile at the waitress.

"Take all the time you need, Miss East," the waitress, an older woman, smiled knowingly.

Marcy looked ill, "My son died for nothing," she whispered, "because I was told that he was the first child."

"Please do not blame the group," Miranda said. "This is all because of the evil people. They kill everyone that is good, and Jackson was a very good person." Miranda repeated the words that her father had said to her before.

Marcy looked down at the menu, quiet, so Miranda did the same.

The waitress came back to check on them and Miranda ordered a chicken salad. Marcy decided on some chicken soup. She wasn't sure if she would be able to eat anyways. Not after this news.

"I had no idea Geneva knew anything," Marcy said at last. "It makes sense though, I suppose, that the story would be passed from first child to first child."

"It is passed to the first child born in the generation."

Marcy nodded slowly, "Are you sure? My husband was the first child so I assumed it would have passed through him to my first son."

Miranda nodded and then quietly confirmed, "But Alex was born first in that generation." She looked down at the chicken salad that the waitress placed in front of her. She was surprised at how well Marcy was taking this. She could read in her mind that she placed the blame on the evil ones and not the group who wanted to fight against them. Miranda watched as she picked up a spoonful of broth and took a sip until she decided to start eating herself.

"This news is shocking," Marcy said, once she had taken a few sips, "But I am happy that we found out before we told James. He will be safe from the worst part."

Miranda nodded slowly. Alex was the only one in danger now.

"I am sorry Miranda, I did not mean it like that," Marcy looked up, shocked by herself for saying that.

Miranda tried to give her a smile, "I understand."

"How is Alex taking the news?"

"He is having a hard time," Miranda said quietly, "and so am I. After Jackson, I just didn't want anyone else that I loved involved."

"Alex is very strong. He is the best person for you," Marcy said, putting a hand on Miranda's arm. "I love Alex and I will always be worried for his safety, but he is the kind of person meant for this role. He is strong and has always been a compassionate and caring person. He was an amazing brother to Andrea and also very protective of her. Plus, I can see how much you both love each other. It worried Jackson to see you together. He talked about it with me several times."

Miranda went pale.

"I know you loved my son too," Marcy said, putting a comforting hand on her arm.

Miranda nodded.

Once they were finished, Marcy brought her home. Before she left, she hugged her tight, "Keep in touch Miranda. And keep safe."

Miranda nodded and walked slowly towards the elevator. It would be the first time she was home in the evening all week. She didn't like it, and pulled out her phone. She messaged Rebecca to see what she was doing.

Rebecca got back to her right away. She was in the game room with everyone from the building, so Miranda went there instead.

Miranda went out every night that week, and even made plans for Sunday night with her cousin Leah, who had messaged her to ask if she still wanted to go to the concert on Tuesday.

When Miranda awoke on Sunday morning, she wondered how she was going to avoid her family that day. She started down at the gym, followed by a dip in the pool and that was where her dad found her.

"Hi Dad," Miranda said, pulling herself out of the water. She stood under the dryers and put her clothes on overtop.

Mr. East sat down on the lounge chairs and stretched out, so Miranda sat in the one beside him.

"I have not seen you all week," Mr. East said. "How are you?"

Miranda shrugged her shoulders slightly, "I'm good. How are you?"

"Busy at work," Mr. East said. He told her about his week and then he looked to her, expecting her to tell him about hers.

Miranda told him what she did every night, leaving out her date with Nathan. "I am going out with Leah tonight and then to the Trees concert with her on Tuesday. It is not far," Miranda concluded.

"It is nice for you to get to know your cousin," Mr. East said. "We are going hiking today. Would you like to come?"

"Is everyone going?"

Mr. East nodded and Miranda frowned, "No, thank you."

Mr. East sat up, "Why? What happened? I know something is going on."

Miranda shook her head, refusing to tell him.

Mr. East sighed heavily. He got the same response from Evan and Griffin. "How about I teach you how to drive instead? Everyone else can go for a hike."

"Really?" Miranda smiled. If she learned how to drive, she wouldn't have to be driven everywhere and she would be able to drive Leah and her friends to the concert.

Mr. East nodded.

"Let's go now!" Miranda said, excitedly, and stood.

Driving was so easy. Just as Alex told her, all she had to do was turn the car on, type in a destination, and the car pretty much drove itself. Mr. East had taken her outside of the city limits, so there were not many cars around, and she drove from there. What shocked her most, were the images that came up on the windshield in front of her. She had wondered why there were no side mirrors and this was why. There were images in front of her depicting every angle around the car, even one image of the passenger seat and the backseat.

"Wow!" Miranda asked, startled when the images appeared in front of her, "I didn't know you guys could see all this."

Mr. East chuckled, "Sorry. As a passenger, you cannot see them. I never thought to mention it."

Miranda drove for hours. Each time typing in a new destination and the car told her which altitude to maintain. If she wanted to go faster, she just stepped on the 'go' pedal.

Miranda drove her dad safely home.

"Thank you," Miranda hugged him, still in the driver seat.

"I wanted to take you to learn all week, but you never came home," he frowned.

Miranda frowned too, "I am sorry."

"I talked to the boys, but I am going to tell you as well. They know that this is not how it works in our home. We talk about things," Mr. East lectured. "I want this problem solved this week. I do not want my daughter out every night just to stay away from her brothers. You must be exhausted."

Miranda smiled, sheepishly, "I have to admit. It was a very busy week, but I did enjoy myself."

"I am glad," Mr. East said and kissed her forehead, "but I would still like this fixed."

Miranda sighed. She needed to say something to pacify her father, but had no intention of making up with her brothers while she was still a target. "I don't know what to do. They aren't even sorry for what they did. I cannot forgive them for what they aren't even sorry for."

"Well, what did they do?" Mr. East asked, inquisitively.

"They lied to me," Miranda said, "and they are a little too overprotective. They did something really dumb and it really hurt my feelings."

Mr. East sat back, thinking. He was quiet for several minutes but Miranda couldn't hear his thoughts.

"Well, hopefully they will realize how badly they have acted," Mr. East said finally. "I know I did some silly things to protect my sister when I was young, even though she was older than me."

"Did you?"

Mr. East chuckled, "I did. One time I even told her boyfriend that she was seeing someone else so that he would break it off with her."

Miranda shook her head, "And did he?"

Mr. East laughed, "No, he married her."

Miranda joined, laughing with her father. She didn't realize how much she had missed him that week. Avoiding her brothers had caused her to avoid her dad and Greta as well. Her heart ached.

"I do not even know why I did it. Ray is a great match for my sister," Mr. East said once the laughter died down, "Every sibling does silly things when it comes to their other siblings. No one is good enough for them. Evan also gave Greta a hard time for the longest time."

"Really?" Miranda asked, incredulously. "Greta is awesome!"

Mr. East nodded, "Come on now. Have dinner with the family tonight."

Miranda bit her lip and moved to follow her dad to the elevator, "Fine."

Dinner was a quiet affair. Greta and Mr. East did the best they could to engage everyone in conversation, but no one was talking. Miranda could tell her brothers were no closer to apologizing than they were last week, so that night she did her best to fill her schedule for the week.

On Monday, Miranda sent a message to Senika that she would be at the show the next day. Instead of writing back, Senika called her.

"Hi Miranda," Senika gushed, "I have been meaning to call you for some time, but things have been so busy with the Trees! I am the band promoter now!"

"That's wonderful," Miranda exclaimed, "I am so happy for you!"

"Oh I am so glad you will be at the concert tomorrow," Senika said, "I will put your name on the list to come backstage, and I have a favour to ask."

"Sure," Miranda smiled, "I will be with my cousin and her friends Breanne and Emma. Do you think they could come too?"

"Of course," Senika said. "You gave me an idea when you said you were coming. Do you think you could come earlier? Tomorrow is a big day for the boys. Their concert is going to be televised and they will be doing some interviews about their upcoming new release. Perhaps if you come and show your support, it will help."

"Yes, definitely" Miranda replied, "I can come out after work." It would be perfect. She wouldn't have to see her brothers at all.

"Great!" Senika said, "I am so excited to see you!"

"Me too. It will be great to see you again." They hung up and Miranda called Leah to tell her the good news, then she headed out with Nathan.

Tuesday morning, Miranda had to tell Alex that they would have to drive separately because she was taking her car to the concert that night.

He bit his lip in concern but didn't say anything, and followed behind her to the studio. Miranda wasn't nervous at all driving by herself for the first time. It was so simple.

After work, Miranda picked up Leah and her friends and they headed to City 219, which was only 25 minutes away. It was still fairly early and there were no crowds. They got into the auditorium, which looked much like the one from their own city, and found the aisle to head backstage. Miranda gazed up at the high glittering ceiling and smiled. Despite looking the same, it was still pretty and had a magical effect.

Senika was waiting just outside a set of double doors and she smiled wide and practically jumped on Miranda, hugging her tight. "Thank you so much for coming!" Her long blond hair was loose this time and she wore a bright pink shiny mini-dress. Her lips were pink to match.

"Thank you so much for inviting us back here," Miranda said. "It is so good to see you. You look amazing! I love your dress!" Miranda felt a little underdressed. She had just worn her band t-shirt and had on Helen's short black jeanskirt that matched the black band logo on her blue shirt.

"Thank you! You look great as well!" Senika said and turned to the other girls. Miranda introduced everyone.

Senika commented on how much Miranda and Leah looked alike. Leah did look somewhat like Miranda. They shared the same colour hair and face shape except Leah's eyes were hazel and she was taller.

"Follow me!" Senika said and she led the way, chatting excitedly, "The concert is going to be shown on television across the planet! The band is so excited! The reporters have already started the interview, but they know you are coming, Miranda."

The band members were lounging on two luxurious brown couches in the centre of the overcrowded room. There were so many reporters standing or seated around them. It was all very casual. There were food and drinks set aside for everyone.

Miranda's entrance caught everyone's attention. Aaron, the singer, jumped off the couch to greet her. "Thank you for coming!"

Miranda gave him a hug and kissed his cheek. She heard the telltale sound of the camera click.

Aaron turned to address the reporters, "You all know our guest, Miranda East, from *Northern Shores*. She is a good friend of the band and is going to help us continue to promote our music."

He smiled at Miranda and Miranda introduced her cousin and friends.

Aaron politely said hello to the others with hugs. Leah looked starstruck and her mouth dropped open in shock and delight when Aaron hugged her. She squealed to her friends as Aaron moved back towards Miranda. "I just have to borrow Miranda for an interview," Aaron smiled and took Miranda's hand and led her towards the couches. "I am so glad you are here. I hope you are well. I see you and Alex finally got together," Aaron whispered, "Who would have thought that you would get together after the last time we saw you."

"I thought you hated him," Senika added quietly with a little chuckle.

Miranda's smile faded and she bit her lip to keep from getting upset. She just couldn't let herself react in front of everyone. "We are not together," Miranda said and tried to force another smile, "Alex and I are just good friends."

Senika shared a look with the singer, confused.

"But we saw you in one of the papers together," Senika started to say, "And on television, you both have such great chemistry!"

Miranda shook her head, "That is all acting."

"Oh," Senika said, sharing another look with the singer, "I am so sorry. I guess we are not up to date on our news. Well, you look great together on television. We try to keep up when we can."

"We really like to watch, but have had such a busy schedule recently with the new release coming up," Aaron added.

"Do not worry about it," Miranda forced a wider smile, "Let's do this!"

The reporters took pictures of them all. Even the band photographer captured some shots for the band to use if anyone was to look it up on their phone.

"Can we get a statement from you, Miranda?" one man asked once they were all out of questions for the band.

"The Trees were the first concert I ever went to and I have been a big fan for a long time," Miranda smiled and sent Aaron a wink. She pulled the guitar pick out of her skirt pocket, "Aaron gave me his guitar pick and I got to go backstage. He was just so great. I just fell in love with their music!"

Aaron winked at her, "I cannot help but notice a pretty girl."

Miranda blushed and smiled. When the questions started coming about *Northern Shores*, Miranda put a stop to it, saying it that tonight was all about the Trees and she would not be taking any questions about the show.

Instead of going out into the crowd, Aaron asked Miranda and her friends if they wanted to watch the show from side-stage. Leah and her friends readily agreed, with more squeals of joy. Senika offered them all a drink but Miranda only had one, knowing she had to drive back later that night.

After a few songs, Miranda thought she heard her name echo throughout the auditorium.

"Miranda, come on out. You are going to join me for this one," the singer said.

Miranda's eyes went wide and she started shaking her head at the singer from the wings.

"You have all seen her, the newest addition to *Northern Shores*. She is part of my favourite television couple!" the singer continued and the crowd went wild.

Senika gave Miranda a little nudge, "Go on."

"No way!" Miranda laughed. "There are thousands of people out there and you said this is being televised!"

"You are on television every day!" Senika laughed.

"Yes but I cannot see them!" Miranda laughed nervously, motioning to the crowd. They couldn't see her, she was blocked by a privacy wall.

"Come on out, Miranda," the singer said while Miranda shook her head fervently. "Oh, I think she is a little shy everyone."

The crowd started chanting her name. Senika had pulled her towards the edge of the privacy wall and gave her a nudge so

Miranda was onstage. She looked around at the crowd nervously, and waved. The large crowd roared and Miranda was frozen to the spot. Aaron came over to her, grabbed her hand and pulled her to centre stage. Miranda sighed, all she had wanted to do was enjoy the show. She didn't want to take any attention off the band.

Aaron smiled at her and whispered, "We wanted to bring you out." He winked at her then turned to address the crowd. "Now, I met this girl while back even before she started on *Northern Shores*. I love the show so I had to get her back here because she said she loved my music."

Miranda smiled out at the crowd as she settled down a bit. This wasn't so bad.

"So, we are going to make sure she has been listening," the bass player added, pointing to his head, "because she is going to join us in this next song."

The singer turned to her, "You remember 'I Fall Apart'?" He winked at Miranda.

Miranda looked at him in horror. He wanted her to sing? Her heart rate spiked again and her palms started to sweat. Could she even sing? She had done a musical number at her high school on Earth but she didn't think she was that good. But she would have to try. She smiled and nodded, and then turned to the crowd, "I can NOT sing." Miranda laughed and turned back to Aaron, "Are you sure you want me ruining your song, Aaron?" Miranda was surprised at her voice as it sounded throughout the auditorium without a microphone. It seemed to ring confidently and sweetly.

Aaron smiled, "I sure do," he said as the first few chords began.

The singer took the first verse and Miranda joined in at the chorus. He looked to her for the second verse and she nodded knowingly before it started and he let her sing it. Miranda closed her eyes and let the words come out.

As they reached the chorus for the last time, Miranda caught Aaron looking at her.

"In the end, I hope you will see," they sang to each other, "That the reason I fall apart is you are not with me." The song ended and they kissed. It only seemed appropriate. The crowd roared.

"I would just like to apologize to Alex, who is hopefully watching at home," Aaron smiled, and winked towards a camera. "You have one beautiful girl here."

Miranda shook her head and bit her lip as Aaron gave her hand a squeeze.

"Well, I love that song as a duet!" the guitarist said, and turned to the crowd, "What do you think?" And the crowd went wild again.

Miranda laughed. Miranda could feel her face burning red as she waved one last time and returned backstage.

"I can't believe I just did that," Miranda said, waving her hand like a fan in front of her face.

"I did not know you could sing like that," Leah shrieked excitedly. "You just stood out there like it was nothing and you sounded so amazing!"

"You absolutely did," Breanne added, "Such a great voice! Have you sung before?"

Miranda shrugged a bit. She didn't know if they had musicals on Utopia and didn't want to tell Leah's friends that she was from Earth. "I have a few times, but it was never really a dream of mine and I have never performed in front of such a large crowd.

Senika headed over to the group that had surrounded Miranda. "That was so great! You can really sing!"

"Oh, that was amazing," Miranda smiled. "Maybe I will leave the acting behind and start a new career as a singer!" She laughed.

"I knew you would be good," Senika agreed, "All you actors have great voices."

Miranda smiled and shook her head at Senika, "Did you know he was going to do that?"

Senika put her hands up in surrender. "No, but I was telling him yesterday that I thought you would have a great voice for singing. He must have agreed!"

After the concert was over they all headed back to the backstage room with the comfy couches. Now that it was empty, Miranda could see the walls decorated with posters of musicians and their instruments. Some looked exactly like Earth instruments or variations of them with more strings or a different variety of keys or buttons.

"That really was great singing!" Aaron smiled at Miranda when entered the room and his eyes had found hers, "I am seriously considering turning that song into a duet and I might have you sing it with me Miranda."

Miranda laughed, thinking he was joking.

"No, I am serious," he continued and took a seat on the couch. "If I get you into the studio sometime soon, we can keep a recording of your voice to play at concerts and when you have time or are nearby, you can make a live appearance!"

Miranda shook her head in disbelief. "Really?"

"If that is something you might be interested in," the drummer added. "I agree with you Aaron. That song was great as a duet!" Senika, who was sitting across his lap nodded enthusiastically. "You were right, Sen, you have a great ear." He brushed a kiss on her forehead.

"Wow," Miranda said as they all waited for her answer. "Yes, I will."

"Great!" the singer said, "I have the next few days off and can make a trip out to City 217 while the others go off and do their own thing. I will book a session at the studio and we can start recording. Then I will let you know our concert dates and you can let us know which ones you can attend. That way we can promote it with your guest appearance."

Miranda was still in shock as she nodded along. She exchanged numbers with the singer so that he could contact her.

"I have to admit, this is going to help our band out as well," Aaron smiled to her. "Can we talk payment? We can offer you a percentage of ticket sales."

Miranda shook her head, "It is fine. I make enough as it is with the show. I would like to do this for you all and since I have no experience singing, you can show me the ropes."

Aaron shook his head, "We would not feel right if we did not pay you."

"I will tell you what," Miranda said, "Just pay my way to the concerts and we can call it even."

He shook his head again but Miranda insisted that she would not do it otherwise.

The singer looked to the others in the band who shrugged. So, he agreed.

Senika jumped up excitedly and pulled Miranda off to another couch. They talked and laughed all night. Senika was so excited that she would be joining them when she could. Leah and her friends mingled with the band and the other guests.

At 2 in the morning, Miranda gathered them up and said they should head home. She had to work in about eight hours. Evan knew she was going to the concert at told her she could be at work for 10 that morning. They said goodbye and the singer told her he would be in contact within a couple days.

Miranda was glad they stayed late. She was absolutely exhausted and would hopefully sleep dreamlessly.

Alex was asleep sitting on the couch when she got home. He looked so uncomfortable with his head back the way it was that Miranda had to wake him.

"Oh Alex," Miranda whispered, touching him gently. He jerked awake and looked around like he didn't know where he was. "Why didn't you just go to bed? I am perfectly fine."

Alex frowned and patted the spot beside him. Miranda sat. "I watched the concert," he said, putting a hand on hers, "You sang beautifully."

"Thank you," Miranda replied, moving her hand out from under his. He must have also seen her kiss Aaron then. She wondered how he felt about it. She looked into his eyes and saw into his mind clearly, the whole family sitting and watching the concert. Evan had called their father in when Miranda was called onstage. Greta commented how well Miranda sang and she felt Alex's heart sink a little when he saw them kiss, though his face remained blank. Everyone had looked at him to see if he would react but he was emotionless as he agreed that she had sung really well.

"I guess you did not feel the attack?" Alex asked, ignoring the scene he had just allowed Miranda to see in his mind.

Miranda's face fell, "There was an attack?"

"It was far away, so it was barely noticeable here. It happened during the concert."

"Did someone go missing?"

Alex nodded and Miranda sighed. She stood, "I am going to bed."

"Wait," Alex said quietly, but Miranda pretended she didn't hear him.

Miranda kept up her busy schedule for the rest of the week and there were no other attacks. On Friday, Aaron called her and she arranged to meet him in the recording studio after she was done filming. It was in the same building anyways, she didn't have far to go.

Miranda looked a little green as she followed him into the soundproof room. It had a large window which looked out into the other room until Aaron pushed a button and it turned into a one way mirror.

"So, you have never sung before?" Aaron asked.

Miranda shook her head. She was afraid if she opened her mouth to explain that she had been in a musical once, she might throw up.

Aaron chuckled, "How do you manage to film every day?"

Miranda shrugged.

"Well, we will have to get you to open your mouth at some point," he laughed and then spread his arms wide, "So this is where we record. The whole room is a microphone and will pick up anything we say."

Miranda smiled.

"I usually start by warming up my voice and singing a few notes," he said, "Can you repeat after me?" He sang some musical notes.

She repeated them and he smiled and sang more. She repeated him again. He tried some more complicated, going through his normal warm up routine.

"Not bad for a beginner," he said with a wink when they were done.

Miranda smiled in return, clamping her mouth shut again.

He pulled out his notebook and brought up the lyrics, "OK, so the band and I have discussed it. We like it exactly as we did it on Tuesday night, so I am going to take the first verse, we will sing the chorus together. You take the second verse, we sing the chorus together again, but then for the last two verses, I will take the first two lines and you take the last two. And then the final chorus together."

"Got it," she managed to squeak out.

"OK," Aaron said, addressing the mirror, "Start it up."

Miranda took a deep breath as the music started to play.

It took only four tries. Miranda was sure she sounded the same every time, but Aaron told her a different hint each time, to make it better.

"That was perfect!" Aaron said, after the fourth time. Aaron looked at the mirror and asked for a full playback.

Miranda's face flushed as they listened and she beamed widely at Aaron as the song finished, "That was cool!"

He chuckled, "You have a beautiful smile."

It made Miranda blush even more.

"I was wondering if you wanted to celebrate with dinner?" he asked, "We could go as friends or maybe… a date?"

Miranda bit her lip.

"That is unless you and Alex are...?" Aaron said, quickly.

Miranda shook her head with a frown, "No, we are not. I would love to go to dinner. I can take you somewhere the reporters will be hanging out tonight."

Aaron smiled, "Great! That way I can announce to the world that we recorded a new version of the song! Can we go now? I am starved!"

Miranda looked down at her outfit. She wasn't really dressed for Vacca and that's where she wanted to take him. "Sure, but first I am going to get changed up in my dressing room. Come with me. I will give you a little tour of the studio and you can see where we record the indoor scenes."

"Sounds great," Aaron smiled.

Miranda showed him the studio and introduced him to Melissa, who was still there completing some changes for the next day. Melissa was ecstatic to meet him. She was a fan of the Trees as well. Then Miranda brought him up to her dressing room.

"You can come in or wait around outside," Miranda said, "But I do have to get changed."

Aaron gave her a wide smile, "I will come in."

Miranda coloured slightly, and teased him, "Just so you know, you will not be watching me change."

"Too bad," Aaron said as he followed her in.

Once inside, he went over to her wall of photos while she tried to select an outfit she liked. Miranda's phone rang while she was looking. It was Evan.

"Miranda, where did you go after work?" he asked anxiously.

"Out," Miranda snapped.

Evan sighed, "Alex looked everywhere for you."

Miranda shrugged.

Evan seemed to squint into the phone, "Are you still at work? Stay in your dressing room. I am coming up." And he disconnected.

"Nice pictures," Aaron said, pointing at the wall, "I think you need one of me up there." He smiled.

"Maybe we will get one tonight," Miranda said, "My brother is on his way up."

"Older brother?"

"Just by a few minutes. If he does try and give you a hard time, just ignore it," Miranda sighed, "He sometimes does that."

"Older brothers frighten me," Aaron chuckled. "They have to be my worst fear, ever!"

Miranda laughed, "Well my oldest brother is worse, so you are getting off easy."

"Maybe someday I will meet him though," Aaron sent her a smile, "if I am lucky."

Miranda blushed as Evan walked in the door. He stopped short when he saw who was with her.

Miranda introduced them, "Aaron, this is my twin brother Evan. Evan, this is Aaron. You might recognize him as the lead singer of the Trees."

Evan smiled and shook Aaron's hand, "Wow, what brings you here?"

Aaron looked at Miranda, confused, "You did not tell your family about the recording?"

Miranda bit her lip and thought of something fast, "It was going to be a surprise." She turned to Evan with false enthusiasm, "Surprise?"

"Recording?" Evan asked, looking between the two of them.

"You saw the concert, right?" Miranda asked, and when Evan nodded, she continued. "Well Aaron asked me to make that song a duet, officially. I went to the recording studio after work."

"Oh wow, Miranda," Evan said, smiling. "That is really exciting!"

"And she is also welcome to any concert she wants to sing at," Aaron added. "In fact," he turned to Miranda, "bring anyone you would like to. They will also get in free."

Miranda nodded and turned to Evan, "Is there something you wanted because we are starving. Singing makes me hungry."

Aaron laughed.

"Oh, uh," Evan started, "I guess not. You are both headed out on a date?"

Miranda crossed her arms over her chest, "Yes."

Evan frowned and turned all business, "Try not to stay out too late. I was going to tell you that we are trying to get ahead, so I would like you here early tomorrow."

Miranda nodded, "How early?"

"Eight," Evan said, then turned to Aaron, "It was nice meeting you. Your band is great." He didn't sound so enthused anymore though.

"Thank you," Aaron replied, "I will have Miranda home early."

Evan gave him a half smile and left.

"OK, you have to get out too," Miranda said, "I have to change."

"And maybe I will also get to see that someday," Aaron joked on his way out. He chuckled as he shut the door behind him.

Miranda decided on a lacy black mini-dress. She found a small pink belt and some pink heels. Then she darkened her eyelids and put on some pink lip gloss to finish up. Luckily she had been watching her stylist carefully since they did makeup and hair manually here at her work.

Once she stepped out, Aaron did a double take and she smiled shyly.

"You look beautiful," he said and held an arm out to her.

"Thank you," Miranda smiled.

"I feel like I should go change into a tuxedo."

Miranda gave him a playful nudge, "You look great. Far from what the rock stars look like on Earth." She giggled. He had on black cargo pants and a dark green polo shirt.

He chuckled, "I would love to hear all about them."

Miranda didn't even know where to begin. She told Aaron about long hair and long beards, ripped jeans, black makeup, black nail polish and chains. She described some of the great icons of rock on Earth as they made their way up to the parking lot, into Aaron's sleek black car and headed to the restaurant. He laughed a lot.

"Oh, I am guessing that is the valet spot," Aaron said as the restaurant came into sight. There was already a crowd outside of the restaurant.

"Yes," Miranda took a deep breath. It was always nerve-wrecking to face the crowd of reporters and fans.

Aaron pulled up and Miranda could hear people talking excitedly.

"Stay there," Aaron smiled, "I will get your door."

Miranda smiled to herself, he was such a gentleman. She could hear shouts from the reporters as he made his way around the car. He helped her out, and Miranda flashed a smile at everyone.

"I have an announcement everyone," Aaron said, turning to the crowd. "Miranda has recorded a new version of the Trees song 'I Fall Apart' with me and it will be available on our next release out next month.

"I will also, when I have time, be travelling with the Trees to perform live at select concerts," Miranda added.

Everyone started talking excitedly at once and shouted to be heard. "I heard you perform it at the concert Tuesday and it was very well done, is that why you chose her?"

"Miranda, have you ever thought about a career in music?"

"Will there be any other new recordings?"

"Are you both dating?"

Miranda shared a look with Alex and they both laughed.

"Oh where do I begin?" Miranda laughed, "No, I have not thought about pursuing music. I love my role on Northern Shores and that will be my first priority."

"Yes, Miranda was amazing at our concert and because of her performance, we did select her," Aaron answered next. "We have a total of eight new songs plus the re-release of 'I Fall Apart' on the new album that the band and I have been working on for the past nine months. I started singing when I was very young, mostly at school where I met my band mates. And I would like to date Miss East but I worry her heart belongs to someone else."

Miranda looked at him and frowned. She bit her lip. *Oh no, why did he have to say that in front of everyone?*

"Who is that Miss East?" a woman shouted out.

Miranda sent her a small smile, "I think Aaron is misinformed."

They posed for a few pictures, and then made their way inside and up to the hostess stand where they were given a private booth.

"Sorry," Aaron said when they were seated, "I did not know it would hurt you at all to say your heart belongs to Alex. I saw your pictures and I see it in your face."

"Don't worry about it," Miranda smiled, "Alex and I are just friends though. Well not even that right now. We had sort of a falling out and now are not speaking to each other."

"You know the song we sang today?"

Miranda nodded. Of course she did.

"Well the reason I think you sing it so well was because it was about wanting and heartbreak. I wrote it about a girl that broke up with me years ago. I am over her now, but for a long time I fell apart not being with her," Aaron explained.

"I am not falling apart though," Miranda argued, "I am on a date with you." She sent him a smile.

"True," he said and chuckled, "I suppose I should not give up so easily."

The waitress came by to give them menus and take their drink order. Both ordered the purple one.

Miranda asked him about the attire of the rock bands on Utopia, anything to get away from the subject of Alex.

"Well black seems to come with the music, though the craziest I have seen is probably the Red Bones. They like to wear skeleton suits. But what you see me in now is what you get."

Miranda smiled at him. He looked pretty good. If he were on Earth, he would probably be the bad boy of the school.

"Should I take that as a compliment?" he laughed.

Miranda giggled and nodded. They both looked up as someone crossed by their booth. The hostess was leading Alex and a really tall, skinny red head to a table. She had a very loud voice to match her very loud dress. It was pink, with blue and yellow splashes of colour. She had a gaudy pink necklace and large pink earrings to match.

Miranda looked away, annoyed, but Aaron called out a greeting. Alex did a double take and stopped. The girl looked over and seeing who was there, started to shriek excitedly.

"Oh wow!" she said and stepped right up to their table. She held out her hand to Miranda who took it, suspiciously, "It is so nice to meet you Miranda. Oh, I know we will be such good friends if you hang out with Alex as much as I see in the news." She looked over to Aaron and let out another squeal, "You are the lead singer of the Trees! Wow!" She pointed between the two of them, "Are you both dating?"

Aaron and Miranda shared a look and both laughed. The girl still smiled and gazed between the two of them.

Aaron shook his head. "Would you both like to join us?" he offered.

The girl turned to Alex, "Oh Alex you have such great friends! Can we?"

"I think we should leave them to their date Jessica," Alex suggested, "And we can continue ours."

Jessica pouted, "OK, maybe next time."

Miranda smiled at waved at Alex, "Have fun!"

Once they were gone, Miranda and Aaron laughed.

"I have no idea why he dates girls like that," Miranda giggled.

"I have to admit, I have done it as well," Aaron chuckled, "Sometimes a girl will not take no for an answer. It is hard to find someone who will look behind the person you are onstage."

Miranda shook her head, "I don't understand it. I have no trouble finding decent men."

Aaron gave her a wink, "Maybe because you are so beautiful."

Miranda blushed into her menu, "What are you thinking of ordering?"

"I think the pepper steak and potatoes," Aaron said, looking down at the menu.

"Mm," Miranda said, "That sounds great! I am going to get the steak salad."

Miranda talked a lot about music on Earth. She had not had a lot of time for music on Utopia, so Aaron filled her in on some of his most influential bands and also sent her copies of their albums to her phone.

When they had finished eating and were just enjoying a couple drinks, the girl Alex was with came bouncing around and sat down beside Miranda.

"Oh I hope you do not mind if we join you now," she said, excitedly to Miranda, squeezing her arm with both hands, "Alex went to the washroom but he will pass right by."

"That is great!" Miranda said, in mock enthusiasm.

"Oh, I am having such a great night!" Jessica gushed, "Alex finally agreed to a date with me and we are such a good match. And now I also get to meet the both of you!"

"It is nice to meet you as well," Aaron said, indulgently.

Alex was passing by and saw Jessica sitting at the table. He paused and sent an apologetic look to Aaron as he took a seat beside him.

"Oh, Miranda, tell me about yourself?" Jessica asked, and without waiting for an answer continued, "You must love fashion, just like me! That Tessa Morgan dress you wore, wow! I bought one for myself the next day. I do have some advice to give though and I say this because I am studying to be a fashion designer. You really need some accessories, say, right here." She pointed to her neck region, "And maybe a bracelet." She pulled back Miranda's hair to peak at her ears, "And some earrings. You are too simple."

Miranda silently fumed, she shot daggers at Alex to shut her up. She hated being criticized by one of Alex's girls. Luckily, Jessica had kept talking so she didn't hear Miranda's thoughts. Miranda took a few deep, calming breaths. It wouldn't do her well to tell this girl where to go in her normal Earthly manner. Though her father did say her mother had a temper as well. The girl kept talking and Miranda could just hear blah, blah, blah. *Jeez, she talks a lot*, Miranda thought to herself. She sighed, the girl had done nothing wrong. Miranda was just jealous and she shouldn't be. She was out with Aaron. She couldn't be mad because Alex was with *another* woman. However, she looked over at the girl again and her mouth was still moving. She hadn't heard a single word. She looked at the two men. Aaron was nodding his head along with whatever Jessica was saying. Alex looked spaced out.

"Are you listening?" Jessica snapped her fingers in front of Miranda.

Miranda gave her a glare. "Of course I am," Miranda seethed, "Do not snap your fingers at me."

Calm down Maddie, she heard Alex say.

Maddie? Aaron asked.

Miranda rolled her eyes, *Don't ask.*

Jessica sat back a little, pouting.

"Perhaps we should go?" Alex asked, hopefully.

"I am not done my drink," Jessica whined, taking a sip. She took a breath, then shook her head and smiled again, "So I was thinking if Alex and I are going to be together, that he should get an acting twin for the kissing scenes."

"I am sorry, a what?" Miranda asked.

"Someone to kiss you so that he does not have to," Jessica explained like it was obvious.

Miranda's rage escalated again, *a stunt double? Is she friggin kidding me?* She sent Alex another glare.

Earth word Maddie, Alex said, *Relax.*

"Your brother is the creator and director of the show?" Jessica repeated, annoyed that Miranda had not been listening again.

"Yes," Miranda said, sulkily. Why wasn't Alex disagreeing with this?

"Well, you should ask him to get Alex an acting twin because no boyfriend of mine will be kissing someone else," Jessica said.

Miranda was about to blow a gasket but Aaron beat her to it.

"Do you really think after one date you can make silly requests like that?" Aaron asked, "You have absolutely no clue about the entertainment business. It is their job."

"But he is my boyfriend and I have seen the way she uses him," Jessica snapped.

Miranda opened her mouth to retort but again, Aaron took the words from her, "And you do not think he has feelings for her as well? Any fool can see that."

"You are so mean!" Jessica said to Miranda.

Miranda looked at her incredulously. She had barely said a single word. She was dumbfounded.

Aaron stepped in again, "Actually, Miranda is an amazing girl. She is kind and talented and extremely modest. Too modest actually. And just look at her. She is gorgeous. If I were Alex, I would not wait much longer because I am willing to challenge those feelings." Aaron sent Alex a glare. He could not believe Alex had not stood up for her. It was ludicrous that Jessica even thought to call Alex her boyfriend after one date. He wondered why Alex would not correct her.

Alex, who had been sitting quietly, looked up at Miranda and mouthed the words, *I am sorry*. He looked at Aaron, "You are right." And then he turned to Jessica. "It is my job, Jessica, and Miranda has done nothing wrong. If I were not such a coward, I would be with her."

"What?" Jessica almost shouted. Her mouth dropped open and she stared at Alex with tears in her eyes.

Miranda sent Alex a look full of doubt. Did he really think admitting that was a good way to get rid of Jessica? Did he actually want to hurt her that badly?

"I want to go home, NOW!" Jessica stood and stomped a foot.

"Someday I will erase that look of doubt from your eyes," Alex said before he stood and they were gone.

Miranda let out the breath she was holding. *What just happened?*

Aaron smiled at her, "So, when you both get married someday, I would like some credit with making that happen."

Miranda shook her head and her eyes filled with tears. How could he pretend just to break up with that girl?

Aaron moved to her side of the booth and passed her a cloth napkin, "Dry your eyes. He meant it." He put an arm around her.

Miranda shook her head.

"Come on. I will get you home," Aaron said, rubbing her back.

She dabbed at her eyes, knowing there would be reporters out there still and she did not need to explain why she was upset.

"I do not know what happened between the two of you but I would not wait any longer, Miranda. Be happy now. You never know what tomorrow may bring."

Miranda sucked in a breath. Should she really risk everything? Should she enjoy any time she may have with Alex even if something could happen to either one of them? Could she ever recover if she lost him? She closed her eyes and blanked her mind before she thought of too much around Aaron.

Instead she turned and snagged the bill, "I am paying." And she quickly got up to settle it. She heard Aaron protest.

He shook his head when she returned, "Well, thank you for dinner." He gave her a kiss on the cheek and they headed out the doors. The excited crowd started yelling in their direction, which stopped Miranda in her tracks. Obviously Jessica's exit had been an interesting one.

"Miranda, what happened in there?"

"Jessica explained that you ruined their date, can you tell us what happened?"

"Miranda, are you in love with Alex?"

"Aaron, can we get your opinion?"

"Jessica had some strong words about Miranda, can you enlighten us?"

Aaron put his hands up to silence everyone, "What happened in there is that Alex finally realized what is right in front of him. Miranda did not do anything at all. She is a very sweet woman and I am completely jealous of what she shares with Alex."

Miranda's eyes glistened with tears. He really needed to stop saying that, it made her feel awful. Aaron took her hand and gave it a squeeze.

"So there will be no relationship in the future between the two of you?" a reporter asked as it looked like she was removing something from her notebook.

"No," Aaron said, "Miranda and I are good friends. I like to tease her with my affections but even I can see that she belongs with Alex. I am sure you can all agree."

Everyone nodded and one man shouted out, "Yes, did you see them together in the last article?"

"And do not forget the magazine!" another person added.

Miranda's stomach dropped even further, but she tried her best to be happy. So it was true. Everyone *could* see it. She sighed and pulled Aaron through the gauntlet, waving goodbye to the reporters.

"I am sorry if your feelings are hurt in any way, Aaron," Miranda said, genuinely, once they were seated in his car.

"Not at all Miranda," Aaron said, "I liked you the first time we met but after that, I realized your true feelings when I saw you and him together. I just like to tease you."

"So you will not be writing a song about me?"

Aaron laughed and shook his head. Miranda giggled and went silent.

"Seriously though," Aaron said, after a minute, "talk to Alex. Do not waste any time being without him."

"I just don't know," Miranda frowned, "You don't understand the mess we have made. We have said some awful things to each other and have not spoken in weeks." Miranda's head was buzzing. What could she do now? Alex had all but admitted his feelings for her. Could she still keep up her act to keep him away? Should she?

"Really?" he asked, in shock. "You cannot tell at all from the way you both act on screen."

Miranda snorted, "You should hear some of the awful things we have said to each other. Or that I have said to him, I mean. He lied to me and I have been so angry." Miranda's eyes filled with tears again, which threatened to spill over. She waved her hand, "Can we just talk about something else?"

Aaron sent her a pitying smile, "Of course. So I will send you a list of our concert dates and locations. Let me know which you can make it to and we will put out a press release."

Miranda was happy for a change of subject. She shook her head a little hoping to clear the buzzing away. "I am really excited about this. I am so glad you picked me."

Aaron laughed, "How could I not after you sang that way at the concert?"

They had reached her apartment building. Miranda leaned over and kissed his cheek.

"I will talk to you soon," Aaron said.

Miranda nodded and got out of his car. She turned and watched him drive away. If it hadn't been for Alex, she would have definitely considered dating him. Miranda frowned, still uncertain about Alex's intentions. Instead of going downstairs to her apartment, she took a seat on the ledge of the building to think. She looked up at the sky, wondering which way Earth was. She had never asked.

Miranda wasn't sure how long she was up there, but the second sun's rays glistened off her pendant just as it set completely. She picked it up. The needle was pointed directly behind her and she looked over her shoulder. Alex was headed her way.

"I saw you," Alex explained as he approached, "up here all alone. What are you doing?"

"Thinking," Miranda frowned. She looked up at the sky again, "Which one is Earth?"

Alex put a hand out to her, "Come here."

Miranda hesitantly took it and he pulled her up and spun her around. Gripping her by the shoulders, he positioned her properly, stepping in close behind her. Miranda could feel him behind her although they were barely touching and she closed her eyes for a second, relishing in the closeness. She opened them again as he spoke.

"You see that one straight out. It is bright," he pointed up at the sky and moved in closer. Miranda looked. "That is the sun in your solar system. Like I said before, we are relatively close to it so it shines brighter than others."

Miranda sighed and turned back to face Alex, "No, the suns of my solar system just set. That," she motioned behind her, "is for Earth. I don't belong there."

Alex gazed down at her longingly. If he had kissed her, Miranda would have let him. Instead he stepped away, "I am sorry about the things Jessica said to you. *I* should have defended you, not Aaron."

Miranda frowned, "It is fine. Just pick a better date next time." Miranda walked briskly past him towards the elevator.

"What are you doing tomorrow night?" Alex called after her.

"Going out with Britany," Miranda said without turning back. Seriously? Was he about to ask her out for a date?

"Wait," Alex said.

Miranda stopped and took a deep breath before turning back to him.

"You have to talk to me," Alex pleaded, "It has been two weeks. You have had months to practice. I need you to help me."

Miranda's mouth dropped and she felt like her heart stopped, "Help you?"

"I do not even know what you can do," he explained, "Or what I am capable of."

The colour drained from her face. "No Alex! I will not train you to die!" Miranda spun again and ran to the elevator. The elevator opened as soon as she pushed the button and she didn't look back.

Ten

★ ★ ★ ★

Miranda was exhausted when she got out of bed Saturday morning. She hadn't slept at all. Alex wanted to train with her, but she couldn't lose him like she lost Jackson. It made her sick to think about it and all day she felt awful. She couldn't face Alex today. It wasn't until she had already left that she sent him a message saying that she drove herself. They didn't look at each other until they had to film.

She almost wanted to cancel her night out with Britany, but then figured a few drinks would take her mind of things and maybe she might get some sleep. She put her little black dress on, straightened her hair, and left without a word to her family.

One drink led to another and as it got later, Miranda's vision started to blur and she knew she had too much. She thought about sitting down, but she was having so much fun on the dance floor with Britany. They giggled as they held each other up.

A couple men came to dance with them. Miranda danced with them like she would any of her friends, unlike Britany who loved to be a tease until she finally chose one of them.

"Mandy!" Britany slurred, taking both of her hands. "This one is coming home with me. He is sober to drive my car. His friend likes you but you do not have to. We can bring you home."

"OK," Miranda replied with a giggle, she took a quick peek and saw the guy was staring at her. She looked back at Britany, "But I do not want his friend."

Britany laughed and shrugged. She nodded to the guy behind Miranda but Miranda missed it. She only felt his arms slip around her and she stiffened.

"You will forget about Alex," Britany said to her before she turned back to her guy.

That name reverberated in her mind for a second. Alex. She drank so much she couldn't remember what she had been worried about. Miranda let the guy put his hands on her hips and draw her close to him. She wasn't sure how much she liked dancing with him. He didn't have the same rhythm as her. She stepped away and turned around to face him. The guy took that as an invitation to pull her close to him again and he started kissing her neck. Miranda wished she could remember what his face looked like, but she was too drunk. When he moved to kiss her mouth, she turned her head so he ended up slobbering on her cheek. She stepped away from him and into the arms of someone else. That person spun her away from the guy who had tried to kiss her.

Miranda looked back, but Britany had disappeared. So she turned to face the new person and moved in close, feeling every muscle in him tense. She ran her hands across his chest, exploring. He wore a tight black shirt, which left nothing to the imagination. She liked him. He swayed in perfect time with her and she liked the feel of his hands as they ran down her spine. She kissed him deeply and pulled away quick, feeling her hormones ignite. Should she do what Britany does and take him home?

Miranda pressed her lips to his again, hardly noticing that her hair started to blow wildly around them and the ground started to shake, except the strong arms gripped her tighter. He stopped kissing her and she gazed deeply into the concerned eyes above her, which were a brilliant blue-green in the darkness that surrounded them.

The music went off as people around them started to panic and pull out their phones to call their loved ones.

Miranda's reverie was broken when she felt her notebook vibrate in her purse. She pulled it out and answered. It was her father.

"I'm alright Dad," Miranda said, trying hard not to sound drunk, "I'll be home soon." But the images blurred as soon as Miranda hung up again and she knew she went overboard on the alcohol that night.

Miranda looked around again to see if she could see Britany, but she was nowhere in sight. She started to panic, wondering how she would get home. She couldn't even think straight.

The man that she had kissed hung up his phone and turned to her, "I will take you home." He slipped an arm around her waist and helped her walk. She stumbled several times, but he held her straight.

Miranda told him where she lived and he drove in silence. Miranda put her head in her hands and tried to clear her eyes and the buzzing in her head, but all she could think about was how much she wanted this person beside her. When they reached her apartment complex, he turned to her to say something but she silenced him with a kiss, pulling herself onto his lap. He responded to her, making no move to push her away. She opened the driver side door and pulled him to the elevator. She tried to push six on the elevator buttons, but kept missing. He took her hand and helped her push it. She turned to him and pulled his face to hers again. They stumbled out of the elevator together and Miranda led him into her room, whispering for him to be quiet as they moved through the apartment. She was surprised but glad, that no one was waiting up for her.

Miranda was too warm when she woke up, and as sleep finally released its grasp on her mind, she realized it was because she had an arm around her. A flutter of panic gripped her chest as she tried to remember what happened that night. Flashes of images from the night before came back and Miranda sat up with a gasp. The arm that was around her fell away as the man groaned in his sleep and started to stir.

Miranda was almost afraid to look, feeling stupid for what she had done. How could she have let herself do that?

She heard the man gasp as well. At least she wasn't the only one in shock. "Miranda," he whispered.

Miranda knew that voice. She snapped her head around to meet his eyes, Alex's brilliant blue-green eyes. Miranda put a hand to her mouth in shock as a million emotions went through her mind. Relief and happiness that it was Alex, then sadness that it was him and finally anger, mostly at herself. She was supposed to stay angry with him to keep him safe.

Alex looked like he remembered something and sat up as well. He was just in his underwear and Miranda looked down at herself. It looked like she was wearing his black t-shirt. He looked around for his phone and not seeing it, he snatched up Miranda's from her side of the table to look at the time.

"Oh no," he said, dropping the phone on the bed beside her. He got up and started to hastily throw his clothes on, which were scattered all over her bedroom floor, "I am late."

"Late?" Miranda asked incredulously, "For what?" Was he really going to leave after that? She called for Alpha to bring her a tank top and shorts. She pulled her shorts on first since she had nothing underneath, and then turned her back to Alex to change shirts. She handed his back to him.

He paused with his shirt in his hands. "I am sorry," he said with a frown. He slipped his shirt on.

Sorry? Miranda asked in her mind. She felt nauseous. He was sorry for what happened? Why did he let it happen then? Miranda looked away, her eyes filled with tears and she sank to her bed.

Alex came around the bed and stood in front of her. "I am not sorry for what happened," he said, quietly and cupped her face with his hand, his thumb stroking her cheek.

Miranda looked up at him, a mixture of emotions.

Alex frowned again, "I did not expect this. Just know that I lost myself, just as you did," Alex released her face and bent to kiss her cheek, "I am sorry that I have to go." He turned and went to the door, hesitating.

Miranda could hear in his thoughts that he was worried about her brothers. That they might be right in the living room and he did not want them to know.

Miranda rose from the bed, resigned, "Just wait here, I will check." She opened her door and crept down the hallway. There was no one in the living room but she heard some movement in the kitchen, so she looked back at her bedroom door, where Alex waited, looking anxious, and held a finger up in the air.

Miranda went to the kitchen and sighed when she saw it was Evan. She would have to distract him and the only way to do that was to actually talk to him.

"Morning Evan," she said, a little too loud.

Evan started. He hadn't heard her come up behind him. "Are you talking to me now?" Evan asked, spinning to face her.

Miranda pursed her lips, trying to think of something. She saw his egg sandwich on the counter. "Not really but I was wondering if you could make me a sandwich like that." She pointed at it. "I don't know how to do that."

Evan sighed and turned back to the cupboard with the bottles.

Miranda looked back and watched as Alex crept to the front door, opened it silently and was gone. She spared one final sad look at the door before she turned back to Evan.

Evan, none the wiser, put the bottles on the counter with a thump.

"You know, just forget it," Miranda snapped, "If you don't want to it's fine."

Evan rolled his eyes, "This is the first time you speak to me in two weeks and you ask me to make you a sandwich?"

Miranda frowned, "You are not even sorry! Why should I talk to you?"

"Well of course I am sorry, Miranda!" Evan said, exasperated, "But you made it quite clear you were done with us."

Miranda bit her lip and gave him a doubtful look, "Then why didn't you just apologize? All I needed was an apology and a promise not to meddle in my life anymore."

Evan sighed and blurted out everything, "I am so sorry. I am sorry we kept everything from you and you have no idea how sorry I am that it got Jackson killed. I am sorry for pushing Alex on you. I am sorry for driving you away," he pulled her into one of his hugs, "I *am* sorry, Miranda. You have no idea how sorry I am to have hurt you so badly that you could not stand to be near us."

Miranda was quiet as she hugged her twin back tightly, confused. They'd all be safer if she didn't forgive him.

"Safer?" Evan asked as he pulled back and held her at arm's length.

"Safer, Evan," Miranda frowned, she tried to push him away but he wouldn't let go of her arms. "Safer because anyone close to me could die at any minute. Any time I get attacked, one of you could be caught in the middle."

Evan gripped her arm tighter. "You are trying to keep us safe by staying away? How could you, Miranda?" He looked angry.

Miranda gave him a questioning look. She had never thought Evan could be threatening.

"We are safer together," he insisted.

"You still lied," Miranda replied, gazing back at him intensely.

"We were about to tell you," Evan sighed and leaned back on the counter, "Do you remember when we said we had to talk that day of the attack at the mountain path? Alex was furious at us. He had a feeling you knew something and when he saw you glowing that day, he was sure of it. He demanded that we tell you that second."

Miranda remembered. Jackson had come over and she had shut the door on them. Then the next day, her brother had said they wanted to talk to her that night. That was the day Jackson had died. This changed everything, now it was her fault again. If she had just talked to her brothers that day, then Jackson might still be alive.

Evan watched as her face fell and heard the guilt return in her mind. "Wait," he interrupted her thoughts. He took both of her hands in his, looking down at her intensely. "This is not your fault. Jackson may have died that day anyways. You would have still gone to school. You still would have been there with him, and I know that he would have protected you whether he was supposed to or not."

Miranda took a few quick, calming breaths as her tears fell. Maybe that is true and maybe not. They would never know.

"Talk to me, Miranda," Evan insisted, "I want you to tell me everything and leave nothing out. We can spend the day together, just you and I."

"Let me go shower," Miranda said with a sigh. It was about time she let it all out, especially after what happened with Alex. Though that would be the last thing she would ever tell Evan.

"What about your sandwich?" Evan asked. He quickly put it together and put it in their oven. He pulled it out and handed it to her within a few seconds.

"Oh, sure," Miranda said and took the plate from him. She didn't feel hungry but ate it anyways as she went back into her room. She stared down at her empty bed and frowned. How could Alex have just left like that after what they did?

Once Miranda was ready, she headed out with Evan in her car towards a trail she had never been to before outside of the city, through the forest. The hike started out quiet. It took some time for Evan to decide on the right words to say. Miranda decided to let him talk first. She admired the scenery and took in the smells of the forest. It was fresh and flowery, and she loved it. There were very little flowers on the ground, but they decorated the tree canopy. Brilliant reds and pinks dotted the deep green of the leaves.

"So," he finally said, "does this mean you will stop going out every night? Once you, Griffin and Alex all start talking again."

Miranda sighed, "I don't know."

"Please Miranda. I am so worried about you," he pleaded, taking her hand.

Miranda stopped walking and turned to her brother, "I know Ev but I need to live a normal life. If not, then what is the point of it all? What am I fighting for?"

"I do not want you to fight," Evan said, pulling her along again. "We all want you as far away from it as you can be."

Miranda sighed, "Sorry Evan. But it is my job. My destiny."

"And Alex too," Evan commented, "but you seem to have forgotten that part."

Miranda went quiet, chewing on her lip as she walked. Of course she hadn't forgotten that part. After a moment, she asked, "How much do you know about Alex's love life?"

Evan made a face, "Alex and I are best friends and we do talk. He told me he is waiting. I know it is hard to believe with the rumours and all the women he dates. I know it bothers you, but he is telling the truth."

"But even after he found out about the Legend, he still went out with many different women," Miranda said, crossing her arms in front of her.

Evan nodded and shrugged a little. He did not want to brush it off, it angered him to see Alex date so much as well. Evan had many discussions with Alex about it. "It is a huge responsibility to take on. Yes, Alex has dated a lot but I always saw it as a search. Like his soul knew it was missing someone that it could not find. After we all found out about the Legend, it seemed as though he was trying to deny it. After," Evan paused, "that incident at the school. Alex felt he was undeserving. He is punishing himself."

"Why would he do that?" Miranda frowned, "Why can't he talk to me?"

Evan shrugged, "Do not think I condone what he is doing. I tell him all the time and do you know what he says?" he paused and looked at her. Miranda looked up at him, curious for him to continue. "He says he knows what he has to do, he just needs time."

She rolled her eyes. If he knew, then why date other people?

"He is a difficult person to understand," Evan continued, "After his sister was killed, he was never the same."

"What was he like before?"

Evan chuckled, "He was still arrogant but he laughed a lot more." His smile faded, "After it happened, we did not see him for a long time. He spent so long looking for her killers. He caught a glimpse of them running away. He thinks he could identify them if he ever saw them again."

Miranda nodded, her face paled. He had told her he was watching over his sister when it happened.

"I am surprised he even told you that," Evan continued. "He does not talk about it, ever. He closed himself to a lot of people and he never opened up to anyone new, until you came along."

Miranda snorted, "Me? He hardly tells me anything."

"I do not believe that," Evan said, glancing down at her, "I see you both. You talk a lot."

"Surely he talks to the women he dates," Miranda replied.

"Yes, about the show, about clothes, about them. He does not share a thing about himself, he told me."

"Why does he date them then?"

Evan shrugged, "He is scared. He does not want to lose anyone again like he lost his sister. If he never gets close to anyone, he could never fear to lose them. Now he is in love with you and you are in danger."

Miranda stopped walking and stared at her brother, tears in her eyes. "Evan," she said, and bit her lip, "I am afraid too."

Evan put an arm around his sister. "I know and I am too, but we will do this together," he said, trying to be brave. "So tell me everything from the beginning. How did you find out?"

Miranda launched into her story, leaving nothing out. She told him how she found out through a book that Jackson had given her, training with Jackson and what she could do which Evan asked if she could demonstrate. She located the biggest boulder she could see and lifted it into the air with her mind like it was as light as a feather.

Evan shook his head in awe as he watched. "No one could ever lift that much in history," he commented when she set it down again.

"It doesn't seem like much," Miranda frowned and lifted it again, up and down a few times.

Evan watched it with his head, nodding as it went up and down, "The way you control it too. Can you lift me up and down?"

Miranda put the boulder down and looked at him, her head cocked to the side, "I don't want to hurt you."

Evan squeezed his eyes shut, "Go ahead and try."

Miranda concentrated on keeping control. She took a deep breath and lifted him into the air.

"Oh!" Evan gasped as his eyes flew open. He froze, in case it broke her concentration.

Miranda smiled a little, he looked so funny up in the air, arms and legs spread out like a star. She raised him higher till he was about twenty feet in the air.

"OK," Evan said, a little panicky, "You can put me down."

Miranda moved him about five feet horizontally, testing out her ability before she tried to set him down gently. It wasn't such a gentle landing though, and she dropped him when he was still about a foot off the ground. Evan lost his balance and fell backwards.

"Oh Evan," Miranda gasped, kneeling down beside him, "I'm so sorry. Are you OK?"

"I guess you should work on the landing," Evan smiled and waved her away. He stood and brushed his shorts off. "I wonder if Alex can do that too."

"I really don't want to talk about Alex anymore," Miranda frowned.

Evan sighed heavily and put an arm around her as they continued on. He changed the subject to the past couple weeks, going into detail about what he had been writing for the show with the team. Cara was going to be pregnant with Jeff's baby.

After the hike, Evan took Miranda out to play croquet, which was invented by Utopians. Miranda compared it to mini-putt. There were fifteen different play areas, and the first person to hit their ball through the wicket, won that round and got a point. At the end, the winner was the one who collected the most points. Though Miranda did manage to get her ball through the first hoop on the first shot, which she whooped about for a while, it only got more complicated with more obstacles. She got more and more frustrated and cracked more jokes as they went on. Evan beat her 11 to 4.

"I like hockey better anyways," Miranda pouted when they went to give their mallets back to the rental store.

Evan chuckled.

Mr. East was in the living room when Miranda and Evan walked in the door, and he smiled seeing them together.

"I still say you shouldn't have gotten that last point," Miranda laughed and gave Evan a little shove as he was bent over taking off his shoes.

Evan chuckled and maintained his balance, "You hit the wicket! It did not go through!"

"Whatever," Miranda smiled.

"Did you learn croquet?" her dad asked, rising from the couch.

Miranda nodded, "We have it on Earth but it is just a little different."

"Ah yes. We taught them long ago," Mr. East nodded and came over to hug his daughter, "I was so happy when Evan told me you were spending the day together."

Miranda looked to Evan, "I suppose I can't stay mad forever."

"And I should have apologized sooner," Evan added.

"Good," Mr. East smiled between them and returned back to the couch, "Griffin is out with Greta but I hope you will work it out with him tonight."

Miranda looked up at Evan and back at her father, "Well, if he apologizes then I will." Evan fidgeted beside her and Miranda peered up at him, curiously. "He's not sorry?"

"Well, he is," Evan paused and looked at the ground, "But he still thinks he did the right thing."

Miranda huffed, her anger returning slightly, "Well, if he wants to speak to me again, he better change his attitude." Miranda spun and stalked down the hallway to her room.

A flashback from the night before entered her mind as she stared at the bed. It only fuelled her anger. She stripped the sheets off the bed with the intention of bringing them up to the laundry, when Alex's phone fell out.

Miranda picked it up and sighed. The screen showed seven missed calls and twenty messages. *Boy is he every popular,* Miranda thought, sourly. She figured she might as well bring it back to him. She would have to see him again at some point and she was sure he would need it back.

Curious, though she did feel sneaky, Miranda checked the callers list as she walked down the hall and out her front door. He had four calls from a girl named Lydia and two from a girl name Reena. The other was from his mother. Miranda sighed. She didn't even bother with the messages, sure that all twenty must be from twenty different girls. She felt her stomach turn as she stood in front of his door and took a deep breath before she knocked. She was sure he was home, since she had seen his car in the parking garage when she returned with Evan.

"Miranda," Alex said, surprised. He looked behind him into his apartment and back at her.

Miranda felt her face go pink, "I, uh, found your phone." She held it out to him with a shaky hand. She didn't think she would be so nervous to see him again.

He took it from her and slipped it into his back pocket without looking at the list of messages, "Thank you."

Miranda fidgeted, not sure what to say next.

Alex's ears seemed to redden as well, "Your father said you were out with Evan?"

Miranda nodded.

Alex bit his lip and looked inside his apartment again and back at her, "I want to talk as well but now is not a good time."

Miranda finally caught on. He had someone over. This time it was anger that flushed her face. Another girl over after what they did last night? Is that why he left so quickly that morning?

"It is not what you think," Alex started to explain when he was interrupted by a honey blond girl in a light pink sundress who came to the door.

"Hi!" she exclaimed, recognizing Miranda at once.

"Sorry, I didn't know Alex had company," Miranda frowned.

"Oh that is fine since it is you," she said, excited. "I watch the show all the time! You are doing so great!"

Miranda tried to smile, "Thank you."

"My name is Lydia. Did you want to come in?" Lydia paused and motioned to the apartment with her hand, "We just watched a few episodes, and here you are!"

"Oh no, that is OK." Miranda took a few steps back, trying to keep her composure. Lydia was the girl who had called him several times.

"Really? I wish you would! It would be so great! I just love Cara and Jeff as a couple." She looked between the two of them smiling.

"I wish I could, but I am just leaving," Miranda said, as she turned and pushed the elevator call button, "I am sorry. Maybe next time?" She knew there would never be a next time. She was done with Alex. It made her sick to know he left her that morning for another date.

"OK, definitely next time!" she replied, excited.

"It was nice to meet you." Miranda turned quickly, hoping the woman wouldn't see her tears.

"And you as well!" Lydia said and turned to go back inside.

"Wait," Alex said as the elevator door opened, taking a step towards her, "Let me explain."

Miranda ignored him and pushed the ground floor in the elevator. The door slid closed and Miranda looked down at her bare feet. How could he hurt her like that again? That was it! This was her fault for trusting him and for trusting Evan today. Evan was wrong. She managed to hold in her sobs until she got to the riverside where she crumpled down on the water's edge and let it go.

Miranda wasn't sure how long she had been there when she felt a presence behind her.

"I saw you at Black last night," he whispered in her ear.

Miranda turned her head, startled that someone had gotten that close to her without her realizing it. Her breath hitched when she saw it was Nathan. He stood up to his full height and glared down at her, hatred written all over his face. He raised an arm like he intended to hit her, so she scrambled away from him but he reached down and grabbed her foot, pulling her back towards him. She kicked at his arm with her other foot and he was forced to let go. Thinking of the only self-defense class she had taken on Earth, she kicked him again in the back of the thigh and he dropped down on one knee. Miranda stumbled as she tried to stand, giving Nathan a chance to recover. He jumped on her back and she fell forward onto the grass. She felt a tiny prick as Nathan's hand moved to her neck, and she felt the heaviness settle into her legs. Nathan stood and pulled her up with him.

"No," she gasped. She tried to run but her legs wouldn't co-operate as the drug he injected her with took effect.

"All this time," he said, as he brushed a stray hair off her face with one hand while the other held her up, "all I had to do was keep you from him and I failed."

Miranda's eyes filled with tears. There was nothing she could do. What was he going to do to her? She couldn't speak or scream for help.

"But at least now I can join them," Nathan added, waiting for her unconsciousness. He was enjoying the fear in her eyes. "Yes, I am one of them," he confirmed. His eyes darkened. "Or, I should say I will be soon. And you will regret what you have done."

Miranda should have known it all along. Nathan was one of the evil ones. He knew she was a third child. He knew the councilman had allowed her to stay. And then she remembered the woman's face that attacked at the school, the one that had looked so familiar. She had the same features as Nathan. *His mother!* Miranda's last wish, before the blackness overtook her, was for Alex. She needed him. Could he feel her and would he come?

Alex was pacing behind the couch, trying to decide if he should leave Lydia for just a few minutes to explain to Miranda. Lydia was so fragile though, especially today. He stopped pacing and looked down at her. She was watching the next episode of the show and for the moment, she had stopped crying.

Lydia was his sister's best friend and today marked the anniversary of Andrea's death. It had been three years since that awful day. Lydia had spent every year with Alex, every anniversary and every birthday since. It was a sad day for the both of them, and Alex couldn't cancel.

A pain shot through Alex's chest and he clutched at it. Something was wrong, he knew it. His vision went black and he could see the river. Something bad was happening. "Lydia," he breathed.

She turned to him in alarm and sprung off the couch, "What is it Alex? Are you OK?"

"I am so sorry," Alex said, standing straight, "I have to find Miranda. I just need to talk to her." He tried not to sound worried so she would not be concerned.

The door opened to the apartment, and Evan walked in. He stopped short, "Hi Lydia."

Lydia flushed slightly, despite her anxiety. She had always liked Evan. "Hi Evan," she squeaked out.

Alex looked over at Lydia, "Would you mind going over to the East apartment?"

"Uh, OK," Lydia said. She looked between the two men and left. They heard her exchange greetings with Mr. East before Evan reached over to shut the door.

"Something bad has happened," Alex blurted out, "I can feel it. I have to find Miranda."

"What?" Evan asked urgently, sensing the danger. "What happened?"

"Go back to your apartment," Alex said moving towards Evan at the door. He called for his shoes, "Just let me go."

Evan, who had his shoes on already, shook his head. He was already looking for Miranda and his first stop had been Alex's apartment. She wasn't in her room. "I am looking for her too. She is not in her room."

Alex didn't argue as Evan followed. He knew exactly where to look and he pushed the button to call the elevator. "Miranda saw Lydia. She got upset before I could explain. Then this pain, just now." Alex put a hand to his chest again. The pain was gone but he still felt an empty blackness. Briefly, he thought of last night.

Evan looked at him, his face flushed with anger and he clenched his fists, "Alex," he threatened.

Alex visibly paled. He hadn't meant to let that thought out, but he had been thinking about Miranda all day. He was surprised Lydia had not caught his passing thoughts. "Evan, I love her," he admitted.

The elevator door opened but Evan blocked his way. "And did you ever tell her that?" he demanded and then answered his own question, "No! You hurt her again and again. You do not deserve her."

Alex froze, a look of torture crossed his face. "I know all that but we can argue later. I can beg her to forgive me later. I think I know where she is and something is wrong."

Evan got in the elevator. He thought of just demanding to know where so that he could go himself, but Alex seemed so upset, he let him into the elevator as well. Alex pushed the button for the bottom floor.

Once the elevator door opened, Alex was running and Evan had to sprint to keep up with him. They headed down the path towards the river but when they got there, no one was there.

"She was here," Alex insisted, searching the ground, "I know she was."

Evan searched too, not sure what they were looking for when he spotted something small and silver on the ground, a phone. He ran over to it. Miranda's necklace was draped over it and he picked them both up.

Alex, right behind him, snatched the phone out of Evan's hands. There was one message on the screen and it was for them. It was from Nathan.

'You will never see her again. I would suggest you go back to your normal lives and she will be fine. Try to find us and we kill her. Do not even think of telling law enforcement or she will die.'

Alex clutched his chest again. He felt sick. Evan took the phone from him and read the message. His face went white. "From Nathan," he murmured. Evan looked up at Alex's face. Alex was flushed red in anger.

"I knew he was evil," Alex said, running an angry hand through his hair, "I always knew I just had no proof."

"What do we do?" Evan asked. When Alex did not answer and started pacing, muttering to himself, Evan pulled out his phone to call Griffin.

Griffin answered after a moment.

"Can you come home now," Evan said, sounding strangled, "Miranda has been taken."

"What?" Griffin asked, dazed.

"What is it?" Evan heard Greta ask.

"I cannot repeat it," Evan whispered, "Just come home now." He hung up before Griffin could say anything.

Alex had stopped pacing and was already moving back towards the apartment. He looked determined. Evan followed.

In the elevator, Alex pushed the button for the parking garage, and Evan pushed the button for their floor.

"Alex, you saw what it said," he mumbled, numbly, "We have to tell everyone and then decide what to do. We need a plan. We cannot just go run off."

"I just have to try," Alex said, ignoring his request, "I will be back soon."

Evan didn't want to argue and let him go. He kept Miranda's phone and held the necklace out to Alex. "Take this. I will explain to everyone."

Alex took it and stared down at the pendant. The compass needle was lifeless. He clutched it tight and the face glowed. The needle sprung to life pointing east. Alex took it as a sign that he needed to find Miranda. He put the pendant in his pocket, his face set. He nodded to Evan as the elevator door opened.

"Good luck," Evan said without another look back. He needed to explain everything to their father and it was a daunting task. Mr. East would be so upset with them, Evan knew, and now he regretted keeping him in the dark this whole time.

Alex took a long look at Miranda's purple car as he crossed the garage to his own. He had no idea what else to do but look for her. He hoped to get some sort of vision again so he put his hand around the necklace in his pocket but no visions came. He took a peek at it and the needle still pointed eastward. He thought that was strange since he knew it wasn't pointing correctly, but since it was pointing to the east, he assumed it was because he wanted Miranda. He slipped it back into his pocket.

Alex couldn't decide which way he should go as he left the parking garage but he could not stay home. This was all his fault, just like everything else, and he needed to find her.

After an hour of circling the city aimlessly hoping for a vision or a sign, Alex's phone rang. He answered quickly in case they had heard something. It was Mr. East.

"Any luck?" Mr. East asked, hopefully.

Alex frowned and shook his head.

Mr. East's face fell, though he had not expected Alex to have found her so quickly. "Come home Alex," he pleaded, "We need to all discuss our next steps together."

Alex's stomach plummeted. He didn't want to go home without her.

"Please Alex," Mr. East continued, seeing his face, "Come home."

Alex nodded reluctantly.

"Lydia was picked up by her mother. She is fine. She does not know what was going on."

Alex rubbed his face, feeling completely awful for leaving Lydia. He had completely forgotten about her. He nodded again and hung up, then headed back towards the apartment.

The family was gathered around the dining room table. Greta had made dinner, but no one had touched it. No one said a word as Alex took a seat. Miranda's phone was in the centre of the table.

"Was there another message?" Alex asked.

Evan shook his head.

"We thought maybe we should send Nathan a message, but we wanted to know what you thought," Mr. East said. He picked up the phone and read what they had so far, "Please give Miranda back and we will give you anything you want."

Alex shrugged. He knew that they did not want anything except maybe the two of them dead. He cringed, thinking maybe they had killed her already but they could not have. He would have known if they did, he was sure of that.

Mr. East pushed 'send' and they all sat in silence until the phone beeped again.

Alex grabbed it before anyone even moved, and read aloud, "Go on with your lives, make your shows, go to work. Forget her. This is the last message you will get from me." Alex, frustrated, pushed the 'call' button.

"I told you all I needed to say Alex. You will never win," Nathan said, answering the phone. Alex could see nothing in the background. Nathan could be anywhere.

"Give her back," Alex demanded, "Take me instead. Kill me even. Just let her go."

"No," Nathan replied, rolling his eyes. Then he sneered, "I can have much more fun with Miranda."

"You lay a hand on her and I will kill you Nathan!" Alex threatened, his face flushed in anger.

"We will come for you next Alex," Nathan smiled an evil smile, "Do not worry."

"I will be waiting," Alex assured him.

"I will be destroying this phone so you will not be able to trace it. I would not bother to tell any law enforcement. Go on with your lives. Replace Miranda on the show. We will be watching to make sure of this and once we are bored with her, you will be next." Nathan hung up.

Alex squeezed Miranda's phone in frustration and threw it hard into the wall. Everyone flinched. The room was dead silent and Greta's tears spilled down her face.

"I have something to show you. Come with me," Mr. East whispered after a few moments. He let out a deep breath, got up and went into the living room. Everyone followed silently.

Mr. East went to the picture he had taken of Miranda on her first day of school and pulled the frame easily down off the wall. Behind it, there was a small hole and he pulled out a small chip. He turned and plugged the chip into the television and turned it on. He looked at his family who were all frozen behind the couch. "You should sit," he said and waited till they all chose a seat before he told Alpha to 'play'.

The screen lit up and there was Mr. East and his wife, looking years younger. They were sitting in this very room on the exact same couch and each held a baby in their arms.

"Hi Miranda," Mrs. East said, smiling, but with tears glistening in her eyes, "Today I am bringing you to Earth so you will be safe, but your father and I wanted to leave this message for you in case something should happen to us." Her voice faded and she hugged the pink bundle in her arms.

Mr. East held up a book in his free hand, the other cradled a blue blanket. "As you probably have been told by now, you are something more than special but I am going to read this in case you do not know." He read through the passage, the *Legend of East*, from the book. The one they all knew, including Miranda. Mrs. East started to cry silently as he read.

"Your mother and I love you so much," Mr. East said after he finished, and Mrs. East nodded in agreement, "and this was the hardest decision we have ever made, but we want you to be safe until you are old enough to handle this. I know that you will make the right decisions and be the brave and beautiful girl that I know you will become."

"Marcy West, a friend of mine, is going to give birth to the first child of the West who will stay on Utopia. Her plan is to tell him when he is 16, and once he understands, we will bring you home as well," Mrs. East explained. "We had no idea, until a year ago, that this would come to be. We were found by a councilman, Mr. Hope, who asked both Marcy and I to meet with him. I was told to keep everything from your father, but I could not. He is your father and he had the right to know, especially when I found I was having twins." Mr. East put his arm around her just as two little boys ran into the camera view. A 2 year old Griffin jumped onto the couch beside his dad.

"Dad!" Griffin whined, "Alex is chasing me!"

Alex, who was nearing 2 years old, giggled and climbed onto the couch beside Mrs. East. He peered down at the tiny baby in her arms and smiled.

"My baby!" he laughed happily and put his tiny hand on Miranda's face.

"No these are my babies!" Griffin told him.

Alex shook his head at Griffin, "Share!" He turned his attention back to Miranda with a smile.

"Mommy, why are you crying?" Griffin asked, and climbed down from the couch to put a hand on his mother's leg.

"Oh honey, we are going to say goodbye to Miranda today," Mrs. East said.

"Why?" Griffin asked.

"She is going to live somewhere else till she is bigger," Mrs. East replied.

Alex leaned down and kissed Miranda. "My baby," he repeated. Only Mrs. East could see, but Miranda's eyes opened and she smiled.

"Oh look," Mrs. East said happily, "She is smiling!"

Mr. East looked between Miranda and Alex, "Sweetheart, are you sure that Alex is not this first child?"

Mrs. East looked between Alex and her daughter with a confused expression. Then she nodded, "Yes I am sure. Marcy is married to the first child of West, so he will carry the lineage."

Mr. East looked deep in thought.

"OK, everyone look at the notebook and say goodbye to Miranda," Mrs. East said to the boys.

They both turned and everyone chorused a farewell but loudest of everyone, little Alex shouted, "Bye Maddie!"

The screen went blank. Everyone was silent.

"You knew?" Griffin asked his father after a minute.

Mr. East nodded, "I knew it was her this whole time. Your mother and I agreed that as long as I lived, I should pretend not to know but I just could not pretend anymore. This is the lie? The one you all kept from each other? But how did you boys find out?"

"Mom left her will in that book," Evan said, "We saw the passage but thought you did not know."

The silence that ensued was broken, when Mr. East spoke. "I had a suspicion it was Alex right from the beginning," he turned to the boys, "I was right?"

Alex looked at him and nodded, "I do not know where Councilman Hope got his information from, but my grandmother gave me a necklace when I was 15 and said I should take special care of it. It would be for someone special and I would know who to give it to when the time came. She had the same book, which she did not give to me until after Miranda was here. I did not know Miranda knew until it was too late."

Mr. East nodded slowly.

"But who is this group?" Alex asked, "Who are they and how did they not know the truth? Their mistake cost so much."

Mr. East shook his head slowly, "I do not know. I have no clue how they got their information. Your mother went to meet with them and I was not supposed to know. They agreed the less people that knew, the better, just in case it ever got into the wrong hands."

"What do we do?" Evan asked quietly.

"You heard Nathan," Griffin said, urgently, "They will kill her unless we go back to normal."

Evan stood up, anger flushing his face. "Do you think I am going to replace Miranda on the show?" he asked, incredulously, "I cannot do that! I cannot just go back to normal life! Not while my twin sister is missing!"

Alex agreed, "I will not rest until I find her." Alex stood and was going toward the door when Griffin blocked his path.

"If they see you looking, she will die," Griffin said and planted his feet, fear all over his face, "Are you willing to risk that?"

"Now wait," Mr. East said, also standing, holding his hands up, "before anybody makes any rash decisions, we should make a plan."

Eleven

★ ★ ★ ★

Miranda awoke with a headache and tried to move a hand to her head, but she couldn't move her arm. She opened her eyes in a panic and had to blink a few times in the dim light. She looked up above her head. Both her hands were tied to stone pillars. She looked down and her legs were tied together at the ankles. Frightened, she looked around the room, her breathing quickened. The walls looked like they were made of red rock. There was nothing else in the room except for the stone table she was laying on and a few floating lights. She heard voices heading her way and she closed her eyes again.

"She should be awake by now," a male voice said.

"Yes," Nathan replied, "she should be." She felt rough hands on her face that forced her eyes open. Miranda couldn't fake unconsciousness anymore, so she turned her face out of his hands. "Good morning Miranda," Nathan smiled wickedly and forced her to look at them again.

"What do you want with me?" Miranda asked, terrified. She pulled against her restraints, willing them to break.

"We just want to have a little fun before we kill you," Nathan explained with a smile, "I am looking forward to torturing Alex."

"You won't get away with this," Miranda snapped. "I will get out and when I do, you will be the first to die."

Nathan laughed, "Our new chief, my *father*, brought Alex in just an hour ago. He is in the room beside you and anything you do to us will be brought down tenfold upon him."

Miranda's eyes widened in fright and disbelief, "I don't believe you."

Nathan shrugged, "I am going to untie you, but you will be locked in this room alone. If you do anything to us, we *will* kill Alex."

He undid Miranda's bonds, and then he kissed her. She struggled to push him away, but he held her tightly. She wound up and punched him in the side of the head. He backed away and she quickly got up. Though her head spun, she tried to keep her balance and she kicked him in the groin. Nathan went down on one knee, giving Miranda the opportunity to knee him like she had learned in self-defence. She grabbed his head, like she had been taught, and brought her knee up but he blocked it with his hands and her knee didn't have its full effect.

One of the other men in the room grabbed Miranda by the back of her shirt and pulled her away, throwing her against the wall. Miranda's body hit the wall and she fell forward. Nathan stood, his face red with anger. He nodded to the other man by the door, who nodded in return and left the room. Seconds later, Miranda heard someone, a man's voice, screaming in pain.

Nathan looked down at her, "Do you hear that, Miranda? That is Alex. I warned you and now he will die!"

"No!" Miranda shouted, but the screaming continued. She stood quickly and went for the door but one of Nathan's cronies blocked her way. "Alex!" Miranda cried, fearfully. She struggle with the man and when she couldn't get past him she went to Nathan, dropped to her knees in front of him and begged him to make it stop. "Please stop hurting him."

The screaming stopped and Miranda started to sob. She put her face in her hands and rocked back and forth. She couldn't handle this.

Nathan moved away from her with a look of disgust. He put a hand to his head to make sure he wasn't bleeding from where she hit him. When he was satisfied that he wasn't hurt, he turned and left the room. The door slid shut behind him.

Miranda cried for a long time, ignoring the throbbing pain in her hand. She had never hit anyone before and it hurt. Would she ever see Alex again? What would they do to her? She was terrified at what they had planned for them.

She put her good hand to her chest and panicked when she didn't feel her necklace. She looked down and it was gone. How would she know if they had him if it didn't point to him?

Miranda sat on the ground for a long time, her heart racing, fear gripped her. When she had finally calmed enough, she decided the most important thing to do would to stop panicking and think. She needed to get out. She got up from the ground and went to the door and felt around the door for a spot to open it but couldn't find anything. She moved around the room, feeling the walls, trying to find any exit. When that failed, she sat down on the table she awoke on, frustrated, cradling her hand and wondering if it was broken. She tried to move all her fingers and was able to without much pain. She flexed her wrist and sighed with relief. She hoped that without any shooting pains, it was likely not broken, just sore.

Turning her attention back to the door, she thought about using her powers to open it but realized she might be able to trick them if she didn't use her powers. Nathan wasn't at the school. He suspected she was the third child, but could she actually make them believe she wasn't? She had to be patient.

Alex lay in Miranda's bed that night. He wanted to feel as close to her as possible, though he was sure he would not sleep. He would not rest until she was found.

They had all decided to pretend to live their life normally, but he would continue to search for her after work. They put all their faith in him. If they were being watched, they had to do what they could to keep Miranda alive.

Alex knew she was alive and was terrified for her. He could only think of a few reasons why they would keep her alive. The Legend said they had to kill them both. Why would they risk anything by keeping her alive, unless they wanted to torture her, or worse. He felt sick at what Nathan could do to her.

He got out of bed when he knew he wouldn't be able to sleep and moved about her room. She didn't have many personal items, he realized. One picture of the two of them sat on her bedside table. That was all.

He looked through her desk drawers and found nothing but a book. He laughed at the title, a self-help book on martial arts, and took it back to the bed with him.

Alex read all night. He fell into a restless sleep in the early hours of the morning with the book still in his hands. He dreamt of Miranda. He was trying to reach her, but couldn't find her and when he awoke, he felt like he had slept on a rock. He put his hand down on the soft mattress, confused. He shouldn't feel uncomfortable.

Alex decided to head down to the gym to keep himself occupied. He was going to have to keep it together for filming today, though he was not sure if he could. He could not believe that Evan had found a temporary replacement for Miranda so quickly. Evan had spent the night calling around and had hired one of the girls who had tried out for the part. She was the only other tryout that had brown hair and blue eyes.

The girl, Valerie, was sent the scripts for the week last night and would be coming into the studio that morning to sign a temporary contract. She had been told that Miranda had to go on a week-long trip but that they needed to keep filming.

Alex still felt sick to his stomach, so he jumped in the pool instead of working out. He swam some laps. All he had to do was get through today and he could search for her again after work.

When he was done in the pool he dried himself and went back up to the East apartment. They were all in the dining room sitting in silence. Evan looked as bad as Alex felt. There were dark circles under his eyes as if he hadn't slept either.

"I cannot believe I have to replace her," Evan said, shaking his head sadly. He stared down into his plate. No one had taken a bite.

"It is only temporary," Alex assured him. Alex had spent a lot of time in the pool convincing himself that he had to be positive. Miranda was alive and he was going to find her.

They sat in silence for several minutes, until Evan decided that was enough and he picked up all their food and reversed it back to liquid form. No one could eat, no one spoke. They were all lost in their own thoughts.

Alex drove Evan to the studio and Mr. East took Griffin and Greta to the space centre where they would all try to have a normal day. Alex watched behind him but no one was following them.

Alex went down to Evan's office where Patricia was waiting anxiously for them.

"What is going on?" she demanded when Evan walked in.

Evan ignored the question and made his way around his desk and took a seat. Alex stood there uncomfortably.

Patricia looked between the two of them waiting. "This is not how things work around here," she continued, when no one spoke, "If Miranda needed a week off we could have wrote her out of the scripts or went into reruns. We have never replaced someone before. Is it this music thing she got into? Is she going on tour?"

"Sit down," Evan said, miserably. He turned to Alex, "Shut the door."

Patricia took a seat in front of Evan and looked at him expectantly. Once the door was closed, Evan told her, "Miranda has been taken."

She laughed but when she realized Evan wasn't joking, she stopped abruptly, "You are serious?"

Evan nodded.

"But that is impossible! Who would do such a thing?"

"The evil people," Evan said, miserably. "They took her yesterday and told us if we do not continue to live our lives normally, they would kill her."

Patricia gasped and her eyes swam with tears, "But why?"

Evan shrugged.

"She went on a date with someone evil," Alex cut in and Patricia looked to him, "He did not take her rejection well."

Evan nodded.

Patricia shivered visibly, her face paled.

"He came back for her," Alex said.

Evan's phone beeped and the voice of the secretary came through, "Valerie is here to see you Mr. East."

"Send her in," Evan said and disconnected. He turned to Patricia, "We were told we have to replace her and that is what I will do. Alex is going to try to find her but we cannot tell anyone about it if we want Miranda back safe."

Patricia nodded again as Valerie walked in.

Evan pasted a fake smile to his face as Valerie introduced herself and shook their hands.

Alex couldn't fake nice. He was miserable as he looked this replacement up and down. Valerie was too tall and aside from the brown hair and blue eyes, she didn't look like Miranda at all. He took a seat in the corner.

"I practised all night," Valerie smiled, "I am ready for today."

Evan nodded, "Thank you very much for doing this. It will be a good experience for you."

"Definitely," Valerie agreed, "Thank *you* very much for the opportunity."

"Patricia will show you to the dressing room," Evan said.

Patricia left with Valerie, and Evan sunk back down to his chair, putting his face in his hands, "I will meet you upstairs," he muttered in dismissal.

Alex nodded and left.

"I heard Miranda is off for the week and they are replacing her?" Wayne asked as Alex entered his dressing room. "I have never seen them do that before." Wayne had been on the show from the very beginning, just as Alex had. Wayne's stylist, Jennifer, was fixing his eyebrows and she looked over and smiled at Alex.

Alex shrugged.

"Where did she go?" Jennifer asked.

Alex didn't know how to answer. He hadn't discussed it with everyone last night. "I cannot say," Alex said finally, "You will have to ask Evan, but I do not think he wants to talk about it."

Wayne shrugged, "I just hope everything is OK."

"Everyone is fine," Alex assured him, but didn't sound very convincing.

Once Alex was ready, he went up to the set and watched miserably as they went through a few of the scenes. Evan wasn't himself. Usually he was calm and collected. He rarely ever yelled and was encouraging to staff, but today he yelled at everyone, which made them suspicious of what was going on.

Alex pulled his best friend aside after he had yelled at the makeup artist who did Britany's hair.

"Ev, you are not yourself," Alex said, "Everyone can tell."

Evan ran his hands through his hair, "I know!" he snapped, frustrated, "I just cannot do this."

Alex put a comforting hand on his shoulder, "Listen. I will find Miranda, but for now, you all decided we needed to go on like normal so she does not get hurt."

"I had nothing to do with that decision," Evan said, miserably, "I was on your side. We should be out there looking for her. All of us! There was no one following us this morning. How are they supposed to keep track?"

Alex shrugged, "Will you take that chance? I do agree with Griffin on that point. I will not risk her life."

Evan grimaced.

"Look," Alex said, "You cannot go off the way you are. Get in there and apologize and then leave it up to Melissa. Go take a nap in your office or something. You look terrible."

Evan snorted, "So do you."

Alex frowned but looked determined, "I am going to find Miranda."

Evan nodded and rubbed his face with his hands, "I have to tell them something. I just do not know what."

Alex shrugged, "I do not want Miranda to look bad and I also do not want to raise any suspicions."

"What you said this morning about the dating someone evil, that was good. We could stick with that," Evan said, "But for now, I do not want too many people to know she is taken." He turned to head back and Alex followed.

Evan marched up to the middle of the set and called for everyone's attention. Everyone went quiet.

"I want to apologize for yelling this morning. We have some personal issues going on in my family right now which is why Miranda is not here today. I cannot tell you about them, and I am sorry for that as well," Evan said, his eyes glistened. "I hope I will be able to explain everything soon. We hope this will be a temporary situation, but I do not know." He looked down in defeat.

"Evan," Melissa said and he looked at her, "I think I speak for everyone when I say that we will support you and Alex in any way we can. If you need to replace Miranda for a week, that is fine. We hope that you can come to us with anything." Everyone nodded in agreement.

A tear slipped down Evan's cheek and he wiped it away, hastily. He looked at everyone scattered across the room. "Thank you. I just need a few minutes. I am going up to my office."

Melissa nodded and turned to the crew, "OK. We can move on to the next scene.

Evan left to go upstairs. He would try to take a nap on the couch in his office, though he didn't know if he could.

Alex was in the next scene with Valerie. Luckily he didn't have to be happy. Jeff was going to find out Cara was pregnant and they were going to argue. Valerie changed the dialogue twice because she had forgotten her line and she was acting too happy. Melissa had to stop the scene.

"Valerie, I know you are excited," Melissa said, "but take some deep breaths."

Valerie laughed nervously and apologized.

"Alex, I also need you to put a little more energy into it," Melissa said, though she made a face, "I am sorry but you look too miserable. I know Jeff would have preferred the baby come after marriage but he is still going to be excited."

Alex made a face and rose from the table they were at, "I need a minute." And he left the studio. He sat on a bench by the wall, put his head down and gave himself a pep talk. It was the same one he given himself in the pool that morning. He needed to stay positive. He was going to find Miranda no matter what it took. She was still alive, he knew it, and because of that, he would never give up.

Alex went back out and they would have gotten through the scene fine if Valerie hadn't messed up again.

"Sorry," Valerie apologized.

They had to redo the scene five times and Valerie was getting upset with herself. Alex had to talk to her to calm her down and assure her it was OK to make mistakes.

"Thanks Alex," Valerie smiled. "They all said you were really nice."

Alex sent her a half smile.

They managed to get through that scene but Alex wasn't looking forward to the next scene. He had to kiss Valerie, and not just any quick kiss either.

When he went to kiss her, as soon as his lips touched hers, he pulled away. "I need a minute," Alex said and sat down on the couch in the scene. He put his face in his hands as tears came. He couldn't do it. He wanted them to rewrite the scene, rewrite the whole episode and the rest of the season, he wanted the writers to make them break up or something.

Valerie looked to Melissa, biting her lip.

Melissa went up onto the set, "Excuse us for a minute Valerie." Valerie moved off to the side and Melissa took a seat beside Alex, "Alex, I do not know what is going on, but you told me before that it means nothing. It is just a kiss. You know that we can rewrite this scene, but what about the next? Miranda understands that you have to do your job."

Alex sniffed and wiped his eyes, "Sorry Melissa. You are right." He looked up at her.

Melissa gave him a pitying look, "We should just cancel today, and maybe the whole week. Obviously there is something big happening."

Alex shook his head, "No, I will be right back."

Alex went to Jennifer, who fixed his face. Jennifer gave him a pitying look as she covered the dark circles under his eyes again. The look in his eyes kept her from asking questions and he went right back onto the set. He got through that scene without a rewrite.

* * *

Miranda pulled herself up to a sitting position. She slept on and off but she wasn't sure how much time had passed. It felt like days and she was so uncomfortable. She was also really starting to have to go to the washroom. Surely they didn't expect her to go on the floor. She looked down at her wrinkled pink and grey striped t-shirt and black shorts. She wondered if they would let her change or shower. She doubted it.

278

Her door opened and Nathan came in.

"I have to use the washroom," Miranda told him as she stood. She refused to show any weakness.

He lifted an eyebrow, "And what do you want? For me to bring you to one?"

Miranda nodded.

"Beg for it," Nathan replied, anger colouring his voice at her impertinence.

Miranda gave him a look of complete disgust so he turned his back on her.

"Wait, please?" Miranda begged. She wasn't going to be able to hold it much longer. "Please take me to the washroom."

Nathan looked back at her, he folded his arms across his chest.

Miranda forced herself not to roll her eyes and kneeled on the hard ground. "Please Nathan." She hung her head, pretending to be submissive.

Nathan smiled, "That is better. You need to learn to respect me." He grabbed her arm and pulled her ungracefully to her feet.

Miranda stumbled a bit as Nathan led her to the bathroom. It was directly across the hall.

Nathan grabbed her arm before she could go in. "Do not do anything stupid and be quick about it," Nathan snapped. "I will give you two minutes."

Miranda went into the bathroom. There was no way to lock the door, but she tried not to dwell on that too long. The bathroom only had a toilet and sink. Luckily there was plumbing. After she used the toilet she splashed water on her face and then cupped her hands to drink from the tap. She tried to make a plan that wouldn't get Alex killed. Could she just allow herself to be thrown back into that room and sit there obediently?

The door opened beside her.

"Your two minutes are up," Nathan snapped. "Go back into your room." He pointed as he said this.

Miranda went, a million scenarios played in her head.

"Do not try anything," Nathan said as he pushed her back into her room, "I will have you begging me for everything once we are through with you." He shut the door.

Miranda drew in a sharp breath. She was not sure what he meant by that and she didn't want to know. She sat on the floor and tried to think of a plan to get out.

Evan rubbed his face with his hands. He hadn't taken that nap, and now he was exhausted, upset and hungry. He hadn't eaten since yesterday morning, though he didn't know if he even could.

"We should get you home," Alex suggested. "Maybe you should eat."

Evan nodded and they climbed into Alex's car, "At least let me go with you so you will not be alone."

Alex shook his head slowly, "If anyone attacks you, I do not know if I can protect you or if my powers work like hers."

"I do not care," Evan replied, "I want to find her too."

Alex got out of the car and followed Evan down to his apartment. Evan made them dinner, but they just picked at it, and then he sent a message to his father to let him know that they were going out to look. His father messaged them back telling them to let him know the moment they found anything.

'Start with the mountain path,' Mr. East messaged next. 'Maybe that is why they attacked us there.'

Evan turned to Alex, "My dad suggested we try the area around the mountain path. Since we were attacked there before, maybe their hideout is close by."

Alex agreed and they left in Miranda's car, hoping they weren't being watched.

Miranda was starving but she was afraid to eat the food they had brought for her. She wondered if they had poisoned it. She had been staring at it for an hour as it sat beside her on the floor and her stomach growled. It wasn't much, but she was afraid to try it.

Someone had come whenever she knocked on the door to take her to the washroom, and this was the first time they had offered her food. She still had no idea of the passing time, if it was day or night and she didn't want to ask.

Nathan opened the door. She hadn't seen him in some time, but she had no idea how long it had been. He marched right up to her and smacked her hard. Miranda let out a yelp of pain and put a hand to her face and felt something wet. He had split her lip open. She wanted to attack him back but she was afraid they would hurt Alex.

"My father will be back tomorrow night and you better be on your best behaviour," Nathan said as he kicked her hard in the side. Miranda cried out again. "We will also be attacking tomorrow and you will not stop it."

Miranda clutched her side, "I don't know what you mean. Stop it, how?" she panted.

"Do not think I am some stupid Earthling, I know who you are," Nathan said as he grabbed a handful of her hair and pulled her head back.

Miranda grimaced as she felt some hairs pull away from her head. "I don't know, I swear."

A flicker of doubt passed over Nathan's face as he let go of her hair, but it went away. He hit her across the face again, which brought more tears to Miranda's eyes. "You killed my mother and you will pay."

"I didn't," Miranda cried, "I didn't do anything. I was just there."

"My father is planning an attack outside of the city," Nathan said, ignoring her pleas, "You try to stop it, and we will kill Alex."

Miranda shook her head, "I won't stop anything. I don't even know how."

Nathan hesitated again and left the room, flustered.

Alex hiked north from the parking lot and Evan went south. Alex kept to the mountain side and avoided the treed side. If they were in the mountains, then it must be some sort of cave.

"Oh Miranda," he whispered to himself aloud, "Where are you?"

After two and a half hours of searching, he and Evan met up in the middle.

"Nothing?" Alex asked.

Evan shook his head and they started their walk back to Alex's car. They went the way Evan had walked, just in case Alex could get some kind of feeling that Evan might have missed.

Nothing came, and both of them were tired and frustrated as they headed home.

The rest of the East family were sitting in the living room quietly when they returned. They stayed there long enough for Alex and Evan to explain they had found nothing, and then they all went to their own rooms. Alex headed for Miranda's room and sat on the edge of the bed with the picture of the two of them. He ran a hand over Miranda's face.

"Alpha."

"Yes Alex?"

"Can you bring me Miranda's Knights jersey?"

He took the jersey from the clamp and hugged it. It smelled just like her and his eyes filled with tears. As the closet door closed, he noticed her suitcases. He got up and opened the closet door again and pulled them out.

Twelve

★ ★ ★ ★

Miranda was shaken forcefully awake from her broken sleep.

"Stand up," a man said, nudging her roughly with his foot.

Miranda, who barely slept, came to her senses quickly. She glared at the man.

Nathan walked in, with a smile, but it disappeared when he spotted her untouched food, "Death by starvation? We have bigger plans for you. Eat next time or you will wish you had never been born."

Miranda looked down. She was worried they were trying to poison her. She was starving but didn't want to eat anything they gave her. She had been living on water from the tap that she drank when they brought her to the washroom.

"We are not poisoning you," Nathan grabbed her by her hair again and pulled her head back so she had to look at him, "When we kill you it will be painful and quick."

Miranda could feel hairs being pulled out of her scalp again. She affixed him with a glare, "What do you want?"

Nathan smiled, a mysterious and evil smile, and looked at his notebook, "My father is attacking in about two minutes. We are here to make sure you do not interfere."

Miranda remembered what he said last night. They would kill Alex if she interfered. What should she do? How much was Alex's life worth? It may be worth everything to her but to allow other people to die was wrong.

Nathan let go of her head and knelt down beside her. He put a hand on her face, "I also have some interesting plans for you, should you try to stop this attack."

Miranda's eyes widened with fear when she read his thoughts. Nathan was disgusting and perverse and she had to think of some way to get out of here before he decided to just go ahead with his plans.

Miranda's hair started to move, as if in a gentle breeze and she gazed, wide eyed, at those around her. They were all staring at her, waiting for her to make a move. Just then, the ground started to tremble. Miranda had to decide what she would do immediately. It wasn't shaking as bad as if it were a nearby attack, so it must have been in another city, but what if it was an attack on Alex's family? Or Greta's? It was someone's family and she couldn't let it happen.

The man nearest to her grabbed her, just as he heard her thoughts. They both struggled with each other as Miranda gathered all her strength and she started to glow. Another man and Nathan jumped in as well, but they both received a shock when they touched her. Miranda willed her power into the ground and it stopped shaking. Just before she lost consciousness, she was also punched in the face.

Alex had just gotten to the studio when the ground started to shake. At first he worried for Miranda's safety, but the shaking was not very strong, it was not an attack nearby but what if they had taken her far away? What could he do? Did he have the same power Miranda had to stop it?

Alex moved away from his dressing room where people would be able to see him. He concentrated hard but just as he thought he had seen his skin glow, the shaking stopped. Did Miranda just stop it? He panicked, afraid for her. He felt drained and all of the sudden he felt a jolt of pain in his eye. He rubbed it and then hastily made his way to Evan's office.

Evan was seated at his desk chair, his face devoid of colour. He nodded to Alex when he walked in and Alex took a seat on the couch in his office.

They both didn't speak for some time, sharing each other's thoughts.

"I am not going down to film today," Evan said, finally.

"And I am supposed to just keep going while you sit up here?" Alex snapped, angry.

"I left yesterday," Evan admitted, quietly.

Alex turned to look at him, "You did what?"

"I left to look for her," he said, looking down at his hands, "I figured they expect me to be at work, so I left."

Alex balled his hands into fists, "Evan, what if something happened to you?"

Evan shrugged and sat quietly. "You know, I just keep playing everything back in my head. All the things we did to try and protect her, which all failed miserably. I cannot believe she forgave me."

Alex looked at him with pity, "You had good intentions Evan. I know you were all afraid for her when you found out about the Legend. You and Griffin were trying to get her to be with me and I was not helping at all."

Evan ran his hands through his hair in frustration, "We should have just left her on Earth."

Alex gave him a doubtful look and sat on the couch. They sat in silence for several minutes.

"I have an idea," Evan said finally, "We will film for today and tomorrow. With the four day lapse until the episode is released, it will bring us to one week. I am sure we will find her by then."

Alex looked doubtful, "I am thinking that I might be siding with Griffin. I am afraid for her. We need to keep filming."

Evan sat back at his desk and crossed his arms over his chest, "You do not want the extra time to look for her? Do you really not care about her at all?"

"I did not say that," Alex retorted, "I will never give up on her. I will spend every night for the rest of my life looking for her if I have to. I am just afraid they will hurt her if they see that we have stopped. What if we cut her life short, when all we had to do was make an effort to film every day? Do not get me wrong. I hate working with Valerie. I hate kissing her when it should be Miranda." Alex stood. "But I am doing it for Miranda," he insisted.

Evan frowned, "She does not know this. I am afraid they will torture her with the show by forcing her to watch it when she is replaced."

Alex paled. If Miranda watched it, who knows what she would think. The last time she saw him, he had hurt her so much, again, and he had not meant to. She did not know it was the anniversary of his sister's death. If only he told her that. All he had to do was open up to her but he had been a coward.

"If only," Evan repeated Alex's thoughts, "if only you had told her everything and had not been afraid of your own destiny."

"I know I have done wrong," Alex admitted, quietly, "I will never take her for granted again. Please believe me."

Evan was quiet, thoughtful. He wanted to be mad at Alex, but there was no point. Not when his days could be numbered. Anything could happen to anyone at any time.

Alex took a deep breath, "Do you think that you can title Valerie in the opening credits as 'temporarily playing the role of Cara'? Maybe Miranda will see that and know she's not being replaced."

Evan's eyes lit a little, "Yes, we can do that. That is a great idea."

Alex nodded and stood, "Are you coming?"

Evan sighed, reluctantly, "Yes, I will be there shortly."

Alex went to get ready.

Miranda regained consciousness slowly. She felt drained. Her hands were bound above her head again, and her ankles were tied together. She tried to open her eyes but one of them wouldn't open all the way. Her entire body hurt.

"About time," Nathan snapped.

Miranda turned her face to him slowly.

He reached over and stroked her face gently, "I really need you awake for this next part."

Miranda heard his thoughts and her eye widened fearfully. "No!" she screamed and tried to struggle, but she was bound so tightly that it made no difference.

Nathan just smiled wickedly. He ran a hand down her face and down her side. She hated the feeling of his hands on her skin.

"Please, no," Miranda said as the tears spilled down her cheeks and into her hair.

He ignored her pleas and lifted her shirt. Where his hand touched her skin, it crawled.

"Stop! I will do anything but that," Miranda cried, nausea building.

"You do not have a choice," Nathan said and climbed on top of her.

Miranda tried to struggle more as he kept running his hands over her. She pulled tightly at the bonds, but they wouldn't give. She tried to think of anything but what was happening as he kissed her neck.

"Nathan!" someone yelled from the door.

Nathan sighed and rolled off of her.

"What did your father say?" he continued, looking sharply at Nathan.

"You saw what she did," Nathan retorted, "She is being punished. Though I must say, it will be more of a punishment for me."

"I have a better idea," the man said, ignoring Nathan's comment. "One she will not like at all."

Nathan smiled down at Miranda, though there was nothing pleasant behind the look.

Miranda's stomach rolled. As soon as they left again, she cried. It was hard to breathe with the deep sobs and she also couldn't wipe her face since her arms were tied, which only made her cry harder. She pulled at her restraints in earnest but they wouldn't give. She began to despair.

"I can't believe you, Jeff," Valerie cried. "You did this to me and it is a part of both of us."

"I know!" Alex replied, pacing on the set, "I am just frightened. I did not expect this to happen so quickly."

"Come sit with me," Valerie patted a spot on the sofa beside her. Once Alex sat down, she rested her head on his shoulder. "I am scared too. But I love you, Jeff. We will be fine as long as we are together."

"I love you too, Miranda," Alex said, without thinking. He barely noticed his mistake.

Valerie bit her lip and looked out at Evan who cut the scene. He sighed, "Alex?"

Alex looked deep in thought. The words came out so easily. Why was it so hard for him before? Why did he punish himself or deny her? So a stupid book told him he was supposed to be with her, he *wanted* to be with her. He had never wanted anything more in his life. Alex rose from the couch and excused himself. Evan watched him leave the studio with a pitying look. He called out that they should move to the next scene and followed Alex out to check on him.

Alex pressed his forehead to the wall outside the studio which felt cool on his cheek. It helped keep the nausea at bay. What if he never had the chance to tell her? All of this was his fault. If he had stopped her from leaving when she saw Lydia, she never would have been kidnapped.

Evan put a hand on his shoulder. "You will get a chance," he assured him, "It is not your fault. I am sure they would have found a different way to take her. You cannot blame yourself."

Alex turned and put his back against the wall. He let himself slide to the floor.

"You are supposed to be the strong one," Evan said with a sigh, "You need to keep us all positive."

Melissa came out into the hallway and took in the scene. Alex had his head in his hands and Evan looked like he had not slept in days.

"Uh..." she started to say, "I just had a question about the next scene but ..."

Evan sighed, turning to her, "I have to leave the show. I cannot do this anymore. Not without Miranda."

Melissa looked wide-eyed at Evan and then at Alex.

"I have to leave too," Alex mumbled into his hands.

"That is *it*!" Melissa snapped, "We are going to reruns! And I am not accepting either of your resignations without an explanation! Where is Miranda? What happened to her?"

Evan rubbed his face, "She has been taken."

"WHAT?" Melissa practically screamed.

"You cannot tell anyone, not even the law enforcement," Evan said, "They left us threatening messages to continue with our lives or they will kill her. We are afraid she might even be gone already. We have no idea."

Alex whimpered a little. Although his heart said she was still alive, there was a sliver of chance that it was wrong.

Melissa turned back to Evan and threw her arms around him, hugging him tightly. "Evan, do not give up hope yet. I guess I am right when I say the evil people took her? They are the only ones I can think of that would do something like that."

Evan nodded.

Melissa didn't let go for several minutes. He buried his face in her neck and took several deep breaths. Her warmth was calming.

"OK, at least now I understand the whole Valerie thing," Melissa said, still holding him. She pulled back so she could see his face, "You will find her Evan. Just keep hoping."

A tear managed to fall from his eyes and Melissa wiped it away. Then she kissed his damp cheek.

"Thank you," Evan whispered.

Melissa gave him a small smile and nodded. They both looked at Alex, still sitting on the floor with his face in his hands.

"We have enough Cara and Jeff," Melissa said to Evan. "I will make some changes and move some scenes from tomorrow into today to have a full episode. Go home, both of you, or go look for her. I will go finish up for the day." She went back into the studio.

"Come on Alex," Evan said, standing over his friend, "we will go look."

They decided to start by driving just above the mountains surrounding the city. Alex turned off the auto-pilot and navigated through the peaks to see if they could spot anything.

"Anything?" Alex asked frustrated as they neared their starting point. The ride had been a quiet one.

Evan shook his head. He decided to send a message to the rest of the family to tell them where they were looking. Griffin messaged back that they were walking through the forest around their house.

Alex frowned. "I do not like them looking," he said as he descended to land on the outer side of the mountain range.

"She is our family," Evan replied, "We would all give our lives for her just as you would."

Alex grimaced. He was worried for everyone's safety. He could not lose anyone else, it was getting to be too much. He refused to let Evan go off alone. Quietly, they hiked together for hours until the first sun started to set. They knew the second sun would set shortly after, so they headed back.

No one was home when they got there. Evan made something to eat for the both of them. They were famished even though it tasted dry in their mouths.

Griffin, Greta and their dad returned while they were just finishing dinner. No one had seen anything.

Alex went to bed. Miranda's jersey was still under the blanket and he tried to fall asleep with it draped over him. He couldn't sleep, so he thought a lot about her. He thought about how he felt when he had first seen her on Earth. She was beautiful and interesting, so different from anyone he had known. After only a week of watching her, he knew he could love her. It would be so easy to love her, and right now she could be hurt and there was nothing he could do. He fell into a tortured sleep.

When they returned, they untied her and an hour later when they brought her food, Miranda ate. Her stomach hurt and it was one less pain she needed right now. If it was poisoned, so be it. She was probably going to die anyways.

After eating, she stood and felt around the walls again, looking for any secret passage that she could escape from. There was nothing. She was tired of sitting around. She wanted to attack every single one of them and then find Alex and go. She began to doubt they even had him. Should she even care if they did? She was tired of being hurt by him. If she got out of this mess, maybe she *would* return to Earth.

When she was bored of looking for a way out, she sat and tried to sleep. It was hard to get comfortable when her body was covered in aches and bruises.

Nathan woke her with a rough shake. Miranda looked at him with fear and confusion. He looked angry.

"My father was taken into the law enforcement building after that attack, and now he has to be freed," Nathan snapped. He kicked her several times in the side and she cried out in pain, "We will be attacking again this afternoon to set him free. This time, we will make sure you do not interfere. I have big plans to carry out but you will have to wait. Don't do anything while I'm gone."

Miranda could hardly think as she clutched her burning ribs and through blurry eyes she watched Nathan leave. She collapsed onto the floor and cried, scared for whatever it was he had planned next. She had no idea what day it was, how many hours had passed. She fell into despair.

Griffin, Greta and Mr. East went to work the next day, and Evan and Alex headed to the studio. It all seemed to Alex like they were on auto-pilot, going through the motions because they had to. They all barely spoke. Their lives felt empty and meaningless without Miranda.

Melissa met them up in Evan's office with a plan. They would film all of Alex's scenes in the morning, no matter how inconvenient it was, and then they would have more time in the afternoon to look. Alex was excited that finally something was going his way.

After the morning scenes, both Evan and Alex headed towards the mountains to continue their search, even though Alex had hoped Evan would stay at the studio. Since he refused, Alex would not let Evan out of his sight, even if it meant they could cover more ground. Miranda would never forgive him if he did not protect Evan.

Later that day, Miranda's door opened again and she turned towards it. Someone entered that she did not know.

"Come with me," he said roughly and Miranda hastened to stand.

She limped a little as she followed him down the hallway and into a large open room. It had high ceilings and on the far side, there looked to be an altar that was surrounded by four pillars. Two of the pillars were broken, their crumbled pieces lay in piles on the floor where the pillar stood. Like all the other rooms, it was dimly lit with floating lights. There was a small gathering of people on the far side of the room beside the altar. They were encircling a person, but Miranda could not see who it was. She worried that it was Alex. Would they kill him right in front of her as punishment?

But when the people stepped aside, she saw it was her dad. His face lightened a little when he saw her alive. He looked unhurt. "Miranda," he whispered and his voice carried to her. He reached out and went to move towards her but those that surrounded him, grabbed him and held him back.

"Dad!" she shouted and would have ran to him, if she was not held back as well. She struggled in the hands that held her, "Why is he here? Leave him alone!"

"You got my father imprisoned and now I have repaid the favour," Nathan said, as he entered the big room.

"They came to get me at work," Mr. East said. "I needed to see you. Are you alright? What have they done to you?" He took in her ragged appearance, her swollen eye, her split lip and her dishevelled and ripped clothing.

Miranda's eyes filled with tears and a rage built inside her. She started to glow.

"Now Miranda," Nathan said, facing off, "Calm yourself. You would not want your father to die." A red aura formed around the others that surrounded him. The symbol appeared on their foreheads, staring at her like second sets of eyes.

Miranda took a step back frightened and the glow on her skin subsided, "No, do not hurt him!" she cried.

"My father will be rescued and if you try to stop this attack, your father will die!" Nathan shouted, "Right in front of you Miranda! Would you let your father die?"

Miranda looked at her dad, wide eyed with fright. Her fists clenched and unclenched. No, she would never allow her father to die.

Mr. East looked fearful as well, but he shook his head, "You have to stop them."

A man beside him, elbowed him hard in the stomach to keep him quiet. Mr. East doubled over.

"No!" Miranda shouted and took a step forward. "Don't hurt him!"

Everyone, seeing her advance, formed a tighter circle around her father.

"No, you have to kill me instead," Miranda cried. "Don't hurt my family! It is in the Legend! Why haven't you just killed me?"

"I will kill every member of your family," Nathan seethed "unless you do everything we say."

Miranda stopped resisting, "I will do whatever you want, anything you want, just let him go."

"No!" her father shouted from the middle of the circle, but he was silenced again with a blow.

"Stop!" Miranda shouted, "I will do whatever you want!" Just as she said this, her hair started to float around her and the ground trembled slightly.

"Interfere, and he will die," Nathan said to her.

Miranda stood still. She would never allow her father to die. Not for anyone. Besides, Nathan told her they were merely rescuing Nathan's father. Perhaps it was just a rescue mission.

"Miranda," her father said, "you really think they will not kill anyone? Do it! Stop it! I am not worth it."

"No Dad," Miranda shook her head, vehemently, "I cannot let you die." He was right though, they were probably killing as they went. She looked torn between her father and the evil surrounding him. Would she have time to stop the attack and rescue him? Could she take them all on? Just as she started to gather her power, the ground stopped moving abruptly.

"She did it!" someone yelled, "She stopped it, kill him!"

"No!" Miranda cried, "I didn't do anything, I swear." She didn't let her glow subside, gathering her strength in case they did attack him.

And they did. The circle moved in towards him. With their glowing red aura, it formed a dome around them. Miranda heard her father scream and she sent a blinding stream of white light towards it. They were all thrown about 20 feet backwards away from him. Two were thrown into the wall and slumped to the ground. Miranda attacked the man beside her, sending him flying into the far wall as well. She left Nathan alone. He had no power so was not a threat. She turned and ran towards her father. He was cut badly on his right arm and had pressed the other hand on top, trying to staunch the flow of blood.

"Dad, leave now," Miranda said, stepping in front of him. The evil ones were getting to their feet.

"I will not leave without you Miranda!" her dad shouted, it sounded strained.

"Dad GO!" Miranda shouted as a beam of red shot out towards them. Miranda deflected it by thrusting her hand out towards it. The ground started to shake hard and the wind blew wildly around her. A large gust raised all the dust in the room which blew towards her and she was momentarily blinded. She put her hands up in front of her and a glimmering shield formed. It stopped the dust from reaching her. She looked back quickly but could not see her father. She hoped he had finally decided to leave as she turned back towards the attack.

Her shield was holding strong. None of the attacks on her were getting through, but she couldn't just stand there. When she attacked, her shield would lessen as her powers would dissipate. She hoped she could hold off all five of the remaining evil ones, at least long enough so her father could escape.

Miranda threw her powers at each of them, while keeping behind her shield. All missed them in some way. Two evil ones deflected them, and the last three dodged them at the last second.

"Wait!" someone yelled, "We all should attack at the same time. It will be stronger."

They all got down on one knee and the red aura around them grew. Miranda took the opportunity to attack them with her powers but her white beams just ricocheted off of them. Then they all rose at the same time.

"No!" Mr. East shouted as he stepped out from behind a pillar, "Take me instead."

Without missing a beat, they all turned towards him and set their powers at him. Miranda screamed and tried to send her powers to protect him. It only deflected the red slightly. It still grazed her father's side, opening up a large gash. He fell to the ground and Miranda ran over to him, stumbling slightly as she went.

"Dad, no!" she cried as she dropped down beside him.

"I am sorry my beautiful girl," he said weakly, reaching for her with a shaky hand, "but I could not let you die. I am older and you have so much more left to live for."

Miranda clutched his hand and sobbed. The wound was enormous. There was nothing she could do. She gave no thought to the evil men surrounding them. She would lose nothing if they killed her now anyways.

"Alex needs you," Mr. East whispered.

Miranda looked at his face, "Alex?"

Mr. East nodded slowly, "He is looking for you. He will find you."

So they truly did not have Alex. That sparked some hope in her.

Mr. East's breathing grew shallow and Miranda held his hand tightly.

"Be brave, my darling," he said, as he took his last breaths, "I love you."

"I love you too Dad," Miranda whispered into his hand just as he stopped breathing. Miranda squeezed her eyes shut and large tears streamed down her face.

When her arms were bound behind her, she didn't struggle. She was expecting to be beaten, but instead they drugged her. She welcomed the heavy feeling and the blackness.

Thirteen

★ ★ ★ ★

Alex used his powers and sent them into the ground. The trembling stopped. He saw Evan running towards him as his vision faded, and he felt himself slip into unconsciousness.

"Alex!" Evan shouted as he dropped down beside him. He had been searching the mountain just ahead of Alex as the ground started to shake slightly.

Evan tried to wake Alex, but he was still unconscious as the ground started to shake violently. Evan looked around in fright, knowing someone was attacking nearby. He was frightened that they were going to attack them for searching, but no one came. He glanced back and forth. His eyes swept the trees. There was no one attacking them, but then he worried they were attacking Miranda. What if she was killed? They would have no way to know. What would they do with her?

The shaking lasted a few minutes and finally subsided.

Evan turned back to Alex and shook him again.

"Alex, quick!" Evan said, panicked, "Wake up!"

Alex started to stir. He groaned sleepily.

"Alex! Wake up!" Evan was frightened, "There was another attack close by!"

Alex's eyes snapped open and he sat up quickly. His head spun and he almost fell into unconsciousness again as his vision went black, but Evan held him up. Alex took a few deep breaths as he felt his energy returning.

"What happened?" Alex asked weakly.

"After you stopped the first attack, you fainted," Evan explained, "and then the ground started to shake even harder."

Alex rose shakily to his feet. Evan stood beside him to catch him if he fell.

"I am fine," Alex said stubbornly. What if they had attacked Miranda? Did she fight them? Was she hurt?

Evan's phone started to ring and he pulled it out. It was Griffin.

"Are you alright?" Griffin asked. Evan could see Greta beside him. She had tears streaming down her face.

"Yes, Alex and I are fine," Evan said, "Where is Dad?"

"I do not know," Griffin shook his head and looked at Greta, "We checked his desk as soon as the ground stopped but he was not there. We are just looking around the space centre now."

"His phone is here on his desk," Greta added.

Evan nodded. "Call me when you find him." And they disconnected. Evan looked at Alex, who looked to have gained his strength back.

"I have an idea," Alex said. "You know how the medical services and law enforcement track the attacks?"

Evan nodded and knew what Alex was getting at and handed Alex his phone. Alex called the emergency line to see if they would tell him where the epicentre of the attack occurred. After Alex turned on his charm, the lady on the phone gave him the location. He thanked her, quickly, and hung up.

"Yes, we should go and see," Alex nodded. "It may lead us to her."

Before they could go, Alex got a call from his parents checking on him and they both had to answer a few messages from family and friends. They started their walk back to Alex's car.

Evan's phone rang again a half hour later. They had been aimlessly walking near the epicentre of the attack. It was Griffin and he was hysterical.

"T-they found D-Dad," Griffin choked out, "He is dead!"

Evan's eyes closed slowly as his hand started to shake. "No," he whispered. Alex stepped in and took the phone from him.

"Where, Griffin?" Alex said, tears in his eyes.

Griffin shook his head, he couldn't speak for several minutes, "I do not know. I just got a call from the hospital."

"We are headed that way now," Alex said, trying to be strong, though he felt the world slip away, "I am so sorry Griffin."

Griffin nodded, "Greta and I will meet you there." He disconnected.

Alex let out a frustrated wail and put his face in his hands. If only he hadn't stopped that first attack, he would have been conscious to save Mr. East. He needed Miranda now more than anything. They were probably torturing her with the death of her father.

"Come Alex," Evan said, barely audible. "We have to go to the hospital." He felt numb by the news. Surely it was not true.

They continued back to Alex's car and headed to the hospital.

Evan and Alex reached the hospital before Griffin and Greta. They were taken in to identify Mr. East.

Evan nodded when the sheet was pulled back, he couldn't tear his eyes away from the blood.

"Where was he found?" Alex asked, with tears in his eyes. They had cried too much this week and now this.

The doctor held out a digital clipboard and brought up a map. "The epicentre was around here. That was the second one this week from the same location, but we did not find anything the first time," he pointed to the base of a mountain on the east portion of the city. "However, we found his body here about 250 metres away. I am so sorry for your loss and I hope you find comfort."

Alex led Evan away and into the waiting area to wait for Griffin. When Griffin arrived the brothers embraced. After a moment, Greta joined in sobbing. Alex stared at the orphaned brothers, feeling empty.

When Miranda awoke, she remembered everything, and her eyes filled with tears. She moved her hands to her face, which were free, and sobbed. Her father was dead and it was her fault. He was trying to protect her and she couldn't protect him.

The door to her prison cell opened and closed.

Miranda didn't look to see who it was. She rolled away and into a ball in the corner.

"This is no way for you to live," a man said, his voice full of pity.

Miranda did not recognize the voice and when she felt a comforting hand placed on her shoulder she pulled away, pressing herself into the wall. "Go away," she sobbed.

"I am sorry for what happened and I want to help you," he continued, ignoring her plea.

Miranda cried harder but he wouldn't leave. Finally when she calmed herself, she looked at him. He was tall, really tall, and dark. He was probably middle-aged, and he gasped when he saw her.

"Oh, what have they done to you!" he cried as he knelt beside her and reached out a comforting hand again.

Miranda squirmed away. She did not want any comfort from someone evil.

"Nathan!" he shouted out, which made Miranda jump with fright.

Nathan came in.

The man got up and went towards him threateningly. He smacked him hard in his face, "How dare you treat her this way! I told you to bring her in and take care of her, not beat her!"

Nathan put a hand to his face, "But father! She tried to attack us and she stopped your attack. We had to do something."

His dad pushed him hard into the wall, "Go get a medical kit." Nathan left.

His dad turned back to Miranda, who gazed at him warily with one good eye. He moved back towards her. "My name is Seth, Miranda, please let me help you. I am so sorry my son treated you this way. Can I get you anything? Perhaps an actual bedroom? A bathroom? Are you hungry?"

Miranda looked at him, torn. What did he want? She was afraid to find out and didn't trust his kindness at all.

Nathan returned with a medical bag, which Seth snatched from him with an angry glare. Nathan backed away and left the room.

He got out several creams and bandages. He started to apply them to Miranda's face and she would have turned her face away, if it had not felt so soothing. She felt the swelling in her eye recede immediately.

Seth smiled slightly as he saw the relief cross her face. "Are you hurt anywhere else?"

"I have bruises on my side," Miranda said, barely above a whisper.

Seth turned and pulled out another tube of medicine. He handed it to her. "I will let you take care of that yourself. I am sure you would like a shower and a change of clothes. You can apply that cream to the bruises once you have showered."

Miranda looked at him with a flash of hope crossing her face. She nodded slowly, still wary of his intentions.

"I only wish for you to understand," Seth explained, "I will bring you to the bathroom and get you a change of clothes. Then later, we can talk."

Miranda nodded and stood. She followed Seth out of the room and to the bathroom. He left her in there to use the washroom.

There was a knock on the door and she opened it. Seth handed her a towel and a change of clothes.

"These are my daughter's," Seth explained. "They might be slightly big. She is much taller than you, but they are clean."

"Thank you," Miranda whispered.

"I am sorry about your father," Seth said, "It was not my intention for them to do that and I know that it might not mean much coming from me, but I am sorry."

Miranda's eyes filled with tears and nodded. She closed the door and got into the shower. It was not like the one in her apartment. It stayed on, while at home hers would shut off automatically. She washed herself three times and then just stood under the hot stream of water until she was wrinkled. The water may have felt hot, but she was cold inside. Her parents were both dead. What would her brothers think? Would they know she tried to save him?

After, she had to dry herself, since there were no dryers, and she applied the cream to her bruises. She saw them fade slowly as soon as the cream was rubbed in. They were still tender, but the pain dissipated. She sighed with some relief and she got dressed. Seth had brought her another pair of black shorts, which were a little big, and a black tank top.

There was another knock on the door and Nathan was standing there, frowning.

"Come with me," he said with his head down.

Miranda shrank back into the bathroom but he grabbed her wrist and pulled her out. He pulled her right against him.

"My father can say what he wants, but you will still respect me," Nathan whispered, harshly. "Now come with me."

Miranda was forced to follow him. They went past her cell and into a room three doors down. It was fully furnished with a bed and a large comfortable looking chair. There was a throw rug in the centre of the room, though the floors and walls were chiseled out of the bare rock. All of the sudden she realized where they were. The bare red rock. Of course, how silly she had been. They were in the mountains surrounding her city.

A full meal was on the desk on the far wall. "This will be your new room," he snapped and then left.

Miranda went to the desk. She ate quickly and hungrily. It was delicious and they had given her so much. A lot more than she had been offered before. She felt full for the first time in days.

After she was finished, she went to the bed and laid down. It was soft and comfortable, and she curled up with the pillow, crying herself to sleep.

Griffin, Greta, Evan and Alex got back to the East apartment that night. They had accompanied Mr. East's body to the funeral parlour and arranged for the funeral in three days, in hopes they would find Miranda before then so they could all mourn together.

They spent the next several hours in a daze, contacting family and friends to tell them the terrible news. Reporters also began calling.

All of them were numb with grief and worry.

"I am going to bed," Alex announced after an hour.

No one looked at him as he got up and went down the hall to Miranda's room. He cuddled with her jersey and tried to sleep.

"Wake up Miranda," someone said with a gentle shake.

Miranda groaned and rolled over in bed. It was so comfortable that she didn't want to wake up.

The man chuckled.

Miranda's eyes slowly opened and she saw Seth sitting on the bed beside her. She sat up, quickly, and backed into the corner. Both her eyes were open. All her pains were gone.

"Do not be afraid of me," Seth said, gently, "I will not hurt you."

"Then let me go," Miranda pleaded. "You win. You hurt my family. I just want to go home and grieve with them."

"They do not want you back," Seth said, "They were trying to get on with their lives without you, and now they have to arrange a funeral."

Miranda's face scrunched as she fought back tears. Getting on with their lives? Were they even looking for her or did they assume she was dead? She tried to remember what her father had said to her last. It couldn't be true. He said Alex was looking for her. A tear slipped down her face.

"You slept a very long time," Seth said. He made no motion to soothe her. "I assume you needed it, but I would like to have a discussion now. Are you hungry?" He motioned to a bowl on the desk.

"May I go to the washroom first?"

"Of course, I will be right here."

Miranda left by herself. No one accompanied her. Should she run for it? There was no one in the hallway as she looked both ways.

First she went to the bathroom and cried, wondering if what Seth said was true. Did they already forget about her? If she did try to escape, would she go back to them or should she go back to Earth? Maybe if she promised Seth she would leave and never come back, they would let her go.

But deep down, Miranda knew she couldn't leave. What if they killed her brothers or Greta next? She wouldn't be here to save them and if she left for Earth and never looked back, she would never know what became of them. It would be a nightmare that would plague her on Earth.

She looked in the mirror. The bruises had faded, leaving her skin yellow, and the cut on her lip had scabbed over. Miranda washed her face and then headed back to her room. She had to make a deal with Seth, somehow. Maybe he would let her go if she just heard what he had to say.

Seth smiled at her when she entered, "I knew you were reasonable."

Miranda picked up the bowl of oatmeal and started to eat. She was hungry again and it was warm and soothing.

She sat in the chair and turned to Seth.

"Now Miranda, I just wanted to explain to you what we are and what we stand for," Seth started to say. He leaned back on the bed and made himself comfortable, "Now I know you think we are evil, but I hope to make you realize that evil is present in all things. You cannot have good without evil. That is the reason for the symbol that appears above our eyes. It is what you on Earth know as a ying yang. In all good, there is evil and in all evil, there is good. Natural dualities, you know, like light and dark, low and high, near and far. Our basics of life, earth and wind, fire and water."

"Yes, I know what it means but you kill people. It is wrong."

"Right and wrong. Miranda, you have to understand that one side needs the other. That is why you are still alive. I understand this balance. Utopia would spiral out of control without the other."

"How do you know?" Miranda urged.

Seth shrugged, "I did not ask to be evil. It came to me. You know that stone altar in the other room?"

Miranda swallowed hard as she recalled that awful room. Tears sprung to her eyes as she nodded slowly.

"Once, I was laid on that altar," Seth continued. "The pillars glowed and transferred their powers into me. It happened to all of us, as you say, 'evil people'. We did not ask. It just happened. It is an ancient, but not a lost culture. It is a part of the people of Utopia and still lives within them."

"How? Why would you stand in it?" Miranda asked.

"We were sought out. During every attack, what you do not know, is that we find someone whose spirit is calling for us and we bring them to the altar. Sometimes it requires a fight, but it is necessary."

"What about my mother?" Miranda interrupted, "You just killed her. Alex's grandmother? His sister? Those were single attacks."

"Sometimes the evil inside is so overwhelming and we are compelled into the single attacks. It helps to right the balance. It is necessary."

"But they are all relatives of the Easts and Wests. Surely, you cannot just kill off all of my family and expect me to stand by quietly."

"No, I do not expect you to stand by quietly. You must right the balance and perform an evil act yourself by killing."

Miranda shook her head in disbelief, "No, I am not like you. I just want you to stop. It is simple self-defence."

"But do you not see that you are killing as well?"

Miranda's mouth opened and closed. She did not know what to say. She recalled the first time she had killed someone. She had watched the paramedics as they brought him back from the woods on a stretcher. He had been running away and she had attacked him in her rage. Miranda started to shake her head and whispered, "No it is not evil. I do not mean to hurt anyone, but I have to stop the attack."

Seth's eyes flashed in anger but it subsided before he continued, "And we feel our attacks are necessary too. You do not understand that it is the evil inside and it is our culture."

Miranda stared at him, opening and closing her mouth like a fish. She didn't know what to say. It made no sense. What was she supposed to do, just accept it? "So, what do you want with me? What are your plans?"

Seth barked out a laugh, "I would never tell you."

Miranda's mouth set, "So, are you going to let me go? Let me keep stopping your attacks? You make no sense."

"Miranda, you are too funny," Seth laughed again, "No, we will not let you go now. But I do want to know what you think would happen to you if you stood in those pillars?"

Miranda was afraid to find out. She shook her head in fear. Was that the plan? To make her evil?

"If you believe yourself to be a completely good person, then stand in them. You will not be hurt."

Miranda stood. She needed to prove to Seth and herself that she was a good person.

Miranda's eyes went to the spot where her father had died when they entered the big room. It had been cleaned. It was as if there had never been a violent fight in this room just a day or two before? Or had it been mere hours? She had no idea.

Seth stopped just before the altar and turned to her. "Today Nathan will stand on this altar and become evil."

Miranda could feel other people entering the room behind her and she spun to watch. She took a step backwards in fear, but no one even looked at her.

Nathan was dressed all in black. He carried a short dagger in his hands which was laid on top of a book, the book that held her Legend.

Seth stepped up to his son when he had reached him and took the dagger.

"Are you ready, son?" he asked, looking down upon him fondly.

Nathan nodded.

Seth took the dagger and made two small cuts above Nathan's eyes, right where the symbol would be. Then he motioned for Nathan to step inside the pillars.

Once he did and laid himself down on the altar, the pillars started to glow red.

"For the water, the earth, the wind and the fire, I bring Nathan before you," Seth said, raising his arms in the air. The pillars flashed and streams of red light went from them and towards Nathan. They encircled him in a red glistening mist that reminded her of her own white shield.

Nathan, in the middle, put his hands out, palms up, as if he was accepting and welcoming the evil inside. It moved into his skin, making him glow red. The blood that had run down his face from the cuts over his eyes seemed to be drawn back into the cut. From there it turned black and formed the symbol above his eyes.

Miranda wanted to run. She was frightened, but stayed glued to her spot. She had backed right up against the wall. Now would be the time to run, with everyone's eyes on Nathan, but Nathan had turned his head towards her, his eyes fixed on her. Surely, he meant to scare her and it worked.

Nathan moved so fast, only his father had time to react. Nathan threw his power towards Miranda. Seth deflected it, but it still hit Miranda's arm, leaving a deep gash. Miranda howled in pain. Instinctively, she picked Nathan up and threw him against the wall.

"STOP" Seth bellowed. Those around, who were gathering their strength to attack, stopped glowing and turned to their chief. "Nathan, you fool. Get up and come here! And you," he turned to Miranda with a look of rage, "get in there." He pointed to the pillars, which were dormant again.

Nathan struggled to his feet. He sent her a look of pure loathing and went to stand by his father. As he walked, the symbol started to fade from his forehead and by the time he reached his father, they were gone.

Miranda took a hesitant step towards the pillars, visibly shaking. She was afraid of what would happen. Would she die in there? Would her powers of good protect her or was she evil?

Seth nodded his head to the woman closest to Miranda, who took her arm and pulled her.

"No!" Miranda screamed and pulled back. She tried to dig in with her heels but she was still barefoot.

Another man took her other arm and they dragged her between them. Together they threw her up on the altar and pinned her down. Seth stepped inside with them. He took the dagger and wiped it on his sleeve. The man beside Miranda pulled her head back by her hair, so she was forced to look up at Seth, who made the tiny cuts on her forehead above her eyes.

Miranda could feel her warm blood trickling out of the cuts and down her face. Then Seth did something she didn't expect. He backhanded her and it split her lip open again.

"That is for attacking my son," he said and grabbed her arm where she had been cut. He dug in and she winced, "This is what I want, Miranda. You seemed confused earlier. I will show you that you are not good. You are just as evil as any of us. I will take you for our side."

Miranda didn't care enough to move as the two that pinned her down stepped outside the ring of evil. She had hoped Seth would be her only means of escape, but now even that seemed hopeless.

Seth took his place outside the pillars, put his arms up and recited the same words. "For the water, the earth, the wind and the fire, I bring Miranda before you, the third child and the one who possesses the power of good. Take it for your own," he commanded

The pillars glowed red and went towards her. Miranda cried out but a mist of white erupted around her, absorbing the red. It turned pink as it did and swirled around her body like tiny fireworks. She felt warmed, renewed by the sense that evil was not taking her. She only had milliseconds to think and react. She was filled with a confidence she didn't know she could have at the moment. This could be it, a plan came to her. If she could pretend to be evil, she might fool them into escaping or killing them all. She rose to her full height and put her hands above her eyes, willing a symbol to show up there. When she removed them, she heard a collective gasp around the room and knew that something was on her forehead. The powers around her, a swirling of pink exploded outwards and everyone ducked as it passed over their heads.

Seth rose and looked at the unmarked wall and back at her, "How do you feel?" he asked curiously.

Miranda forced a smile at him, hoping it was an alluring smile, "Very well, Seth. I think I understand."

"What just happened?" someone asked.

"You saw," Seth snapped, "She has been taken by evil. She is one of us now."

The man looked uncertain, "But that has never happened before. The evil should have moved into her skin. The symbol is wrong."

Miranda's smile faltered only a millisecond, but she shook her head, "You know what I am. Evil had to battle for its position inside of me and it won! Surely that was just some kind of reaction." To prove herself, though it disgusted her to do it, she went to Nathan and took his hand. "Oh Nathan," she purred, "This is all thanks to you. I know I disgust you and I have disobeyed but please forgive me. I only want to please you." She managed a seductive smile, or what she hoped was one.

Nathan's jaw dropped in surprise and he hesitated only a second before a smile flashed on his face, "Of course, Miranda."

Seth frowned. He shot a furious glare at his son, who backed away. "We have to leave here. There has been too much activity and there are many people searching the area. We have to clear out for several days."

Miranda nodded.

"Go back to your room and we will get you later."

Miranda obeyed, quickly. By the time she reached her room and looked in the mirror, the symbol had faded. She was not sure what had been there but it had worked. She had fooled them. Now to keep up with the charade as best as she could, to keep herself alive until she thought of something better.

Alex was startled awake when the ground started to shake. The wind outside the window blew wildly against the pane. He didn't even have the time to think about stopping the attack that was happening before the wind died off and the trembling stopped. Evan, Griffin and Greta ran to Miranda's room. They sighed with relief to see that Alex was there.

Evan sat on the bed and pulled Miranda's hockey jersey out which had become tangled in the blankets. He hugged it to his chest, "Do you think she is OK?" he whispered.

Alex closed his eyes, hoping for a vision, a sign or anything. Instead, something else happened. His skin had started to glow around him, circling him like a shroud. He felt all his strength fade from his hands and feet and ball up inside his chest. He gasped for breath as he felt it escape him and move into the glistening aura that surrounded him.

Evan saw his friend start to glow and stood up, hastily. He backed away beside Griffin, who was staring down at Alex, concern all over his face. Greta took a step forward, but Griffin pulled her back just as a burst of energy, seemed to explode around them. Alex fell back onto the pillows, unconscious and the three closed in around him.

Greta felt for a pulse and sighed with relief when she found it. "He is alive," she said to the boys. Evan rubbed his face with a stressed hand and Griffin bent down to take Greta's hand. She gave it a comforting squeeze.

They had to wait an anxiously for Alex to come around. Greta had gotten a cold cloth for his head. Griffin was sitting on his other side and Evan was pacing as his eyes slowly opened.

"Alex," Greta said, relieved, "how do you feel?"

Alex blinked slowly. "Fine," he said flatly.

"Do you know what happened?" Griffin asked. Evan had stopped pacing and stared down at Alex.

"I think Miranda needed me. I think she is still alive," Alex said, thoughtfully. He tried to clear his throat, which felt so dry.

Greta rose from the bed, "I will get you some water," and she left.

"Do you think they hurt her?" Evan asked. He was still clutching her jersey in his hands.

Alex put his head down and shrugged. He hoped that he had at least done his job protecting her.

"I am sure you did," Evan said, trying to sound encouraging. He held Miranda's jersey out to him. Alex took it and brought it to his face.

"It does not smell like her anymore," he commented, mostly to himself. He felt as if she was slipping away and he wasn't about to let that happen. He looked up at Evan, "The new episode airs today?"

Evan bit his lip and nodded.

"I hope she does not see it," Alex whispered, sadly.

Miranda was left alone for a few hours and had lots of time to think. She had to mentally prepare herself to pretend to be evil. She couldn't slip once, she needed to infiltrate them and maybe it will help bring them down. If Nathan wanted to kiss her, she would let him and pretend to like it. Could she do more? If it came to it, she wasn't sure.

Seth came into her room, smiling "Come with me."

Miranda was on her feet in an instant. She had nothing to take with her so she just followed him. He led her down the hallway where Nathan and another man were waiting and together they went through the large cave room and a short tunnel, and suddenly they were outside. Miranda hurried to take Nathan's hand as they walked. She smiled a dazzling smile at him.

They hiked for a bit, until they came to a clearing where four cars were parked. Miranda recognized one as Nathan's car. Seth opened the back door for her and motioned for Miranda to get in, then climbed in beside her. Nathan hopped in the driver's seat and the other man took the front. Miranda looked at them all. Now that she had been with the evil ones for several days, she could link some characteristics together. Each had a faint scar above both of their eyes. They all tended to dress in dark clothes and the skin around their eyes looked darker, like they hadn't slept.

Miranda kept quiet, watching the world outside. She hadn't been outside in days, or weeks, still unsure of the passage of time. She was careful that they didn't hear her thoughts. She felt like she didn't belong to this planet anymore. What was everyone doing? Was Alex looking for her? Were Griffin and Evan planning their father's funeral? Would she even be able to attend? Miranda's eyes filled with tears. It was something she needed to do. She leaned over slightly. "Seth?" she asked, sweetly.

He looked at her, waiting for her to go on.

"Do you know when my father's funeral is?"

Seth looked at his son and back at Miranda, "Two days."

"I know it does not matter, but he is my father and I must go.

"If you prove yourself, then you can go," Seth said, "We are attacking tomorrow and you will join us. I believe you, but we must prove to everyone else that you are on our side."

"Of course Seth," Miranda smiled, "I would be happy to join in the attack." Inside, Miranda's heart beat wildly. She was going to have to attack people. How could she fake that?

"You must change your hair," Seth said, "and your identification. We will have someone come to the house this evening. But for now we will let you get settled. I have arranged for your clothes to be brought here." He pointed towards their destination and Miranda saw they were coming up on an apartment building.

Miranda nodded, "Good. These innocent curls have to go." She thought maybe that was a little overboard, but Seth nodded in agreement. "My own clothes?"

Seth nodded, "Derek was at your house earlier to collect your wardrobe."

Miranda nodded. Surely, everyone was fine or else she would have felt an attack.

Nathan parked the car and then Miranda was told to wait while the three men made sure the coast was clear. When it was, Miranda followed them down to her new prison, taking in all the surroundings. She tried to formulate a backup plan, not sure how long she would be able to pretend to be evil, especially since she knew she would never be able to attack anyone. She felt stupid for even thinking this would work.

Seth showed her to her new room and she gushed at how nice it was. This seemed to please Seth and he left her to unpack her things. Miranda opened her suitcase once she was alone. She shed a few tears and took a few deep breaths. She could do this. She was a great actress.

Nathan was sprawled out on the couch, making himself comfortable when Miranda joined them in the living room. Seth was perched on the arm of the chair.

"It is 23 hour," Nathan said, as if it should mean something. He sat up and patted the spot beside him.

Miranda sat beside him. She sent him a confused smile, not sure why the time would matter.

"Alpha, can you tune into today's episode of Northern Shores?" Nathan asked.

The television turned on and the show started. Miranda's mouth dropped open when another woman was in her spot in the opening credits. The name 'Valerie Bridges – temporarily replacing Miranda East' flashed on the screen. Alex showed up right afterwards, in his normal sequence.

Miranda sat back slowly, her mouth agape. Quickly, she straightened back up. She was evil. This shouldn't bother her, but what was going on? The first scene cut to one of Jeff and Cara. The new woman was in her spot, saying her lines. What was her family doing? Did they really continue on with their lives without her? Did Alex and Evan just replace her and continue the show? Were they even looking for her? Her father said Alex was looking, but then what were they doing with the show? Why didn't they just go to reruns or cut their scenes out?

In the next Jeff and Cara scene, Miranda already knew what was coming. Alex was going to kiss this other woman. "Alpha, stop," Miranda said, angry. The scene froze, of course, at the perfect moment, but she took a deep breath. She needed to keep up her act. "I am far better looking than that woman," Miranda said haughtily but inside she was screaming. How could they do this to her? "Change the channel. I don't want to watch this crappy show by my stupid brother."

Alex, Evan, Griffin and Greta decided after work to search the mountains near the epicentre of the earthquake. Late that night, they finally returned home empty handed. There was nothing out of place. Alex felt nothing, no presence of evil at all. Not a single sign of Miranda and it made him so frustrated. He should have told her right away, despite her brothers' wishes. They could have had months to plan and practice. Instead he listened to Griffin, who hadn't wanted his sister involved. He had wanted to protect her. But that was the wrong choice. Her destiny had found her anyways. Alex went to sulk in her bedroom but when he pulled back the sheets, he saw her jersey was missing. Confused, he went to her closet and saw on the screen that it was empty.

"Evan!" he shouted.

Evan ran down the hall and into his sister's bedroom. Griffin and Greta were close behind.

"Alpha," Alex repeated for all to hear, "Show me Miranda's wardrobe."

"Miranda's wardrobe is empty," Alpha answered brightly.

Evan sat in stunned silence on her bed. "She was here?"

Alex shrugged, "Or someone was."

Griffin almost smiled though, "But do you not see, this means she is alive!"

"Yes," Greta's eyes widened, as she nodded at Griffin, "She is alive. I hope they have not hurt her."

Griffin frowned at this and he gave her a hug. "I am sure she is fine," he said, trying to sound convincing but he was not sure if he believed it himself.

"They had to have moved her," Alex said, taking a seat beside Evan, "She would be too noticeable if they stayed."

Evan gasped, "No! You think they left the city?"

Alex stood and slammed a fist down on her desk, "How can we search all of Utopia? It would take forever!"

"What if she thinks we abandoned her?" Evan said, "You do not think they would let her watch the show today?"

Alex shook his head, doubtfully, but he tried to sound confident, "She knows we love her more than anything."

Evan looked at him warily, "No, she does not, Alex! And now she may be gone forever."

Alex turned away from his intense gaze. The guilt weighed on him. He was afraid and that was why he had never told her. He had already lost so many people he loved.

Evan looked down into his hands. Miranda probably felt so abandoned.

"No," Alex said, quietly, "She has to realize how I feel. If she believes at all in her feelings for me, she must know that I feel the same pull to her."

Miranda was in the room they gave her, worrying over her current predicament. Was she alone? Were they looking for her? She didn't think they would abandon her, they just couldn't. If anything, Miranda didn't doubt for a second that Evan would leave her on her own. Alex and Griffin, she wasn't sure about, but Evan was her twin and would never abandon her. Miranda's thoughts were interrupted by a knock on the door.

"Hello Miranda," she said, "I am Stacie. I am so glad you have joined us." She was very tall and really skinny. She had on tight black leggings and a red shirt with a black belt. Her red hair was spiky and short. Miranda noticed the thin scars above her eyes first. She was evil.

"Hi Stacie," Miranda smiled, "What's up?"

"I am here to do your hair."

Miranda sat up, "Why do I have to change my hair anyways?" She ran a hand through her soft curls. She loved the way her once frizzy hair had been replaced with luscious curls and didn't want to change it.

"So no one will recognize you. We all do it once we change," Stacie explained.

"Oh," Miranda frowned.

"I have a few ideas, but I would like for you to tell me which colour you would like your hair to be."

Miranda thought about it for a minute, "Blond, I guess."

"Perfect!" Stacie smiled, "You will look amazing as a blond. I have some pretty strong hair relaxers which will make your hair a lot straighter. It will take months for your hair to be curly again. But that should be OK because we will have to re-dye your hair by then anyways."

Miranda nodded but wanted to scream. *There goes my signature hair*, she thought, as she followed Stacie into the bathroom.

Stacie went to retrieve a chair for Miranda and set to work. First she applied the hair relaxer and the dye and let it work its magic for ten minutes. After that was rinsed out, she dried it and then gave her a quick haircut and added some layers. Miranda refused to look into a mirror until it was done. All she wanted to do was lie in her bed and cry but she had to shield her thoughts from Stacie, so she thought nothing.

"I just need to lighten your eyebrows a little and then we will be all finished," Stacie smiled at her work as she ran a mascara-like brush over Miranda's eyebrows.

Miranda nodded and once she was done, Stacie told her to have a look in the mirror.

Miranda got up and took a deep breath. She turned to face the mirror. She didn't look like herself anymore. The honey blond hair fell in waves around her face, stretching down to the middle of her back. She had no idea how long her hair had been. She ran a hand through it and brought a few strands up to her face. It was really blond. She couldn't believe how different she looked.

"You look great as a blond," Stacie smiled, "It is perfect, because I made you this and it looks just like you now."

Miranda took the card Stacie held out to her. It was new Utopian identification and it had a woman with Miranda's face and long blond hair.

"I know someone who works at a city hall in another city. He made that for me."

"How did you know I would choose blond?"

Stacie shrugged. "Just a hunch," she smiled.

Miranda turned back to the mirror. She would have to get used to the blond, at least for a few days. As for her curls, they would come back eventually. She looked down at the identification again. Her new name was Stephanie Night.

Stacie followed Miranda out of the bathroom and into the living room. Seth was there watching television and he did a double take when Miranda walked out. He smiled wide, "I hardly recognized you."

"My latest creation," Stacie said, and smiled proudly.

"She looks wonderful, Stacie," Seth said and thanked her. Stacie left, and Miranda was alone with Seth until Nathan walked into the living room from the kitchen. He stopped and stared at Miranda when he saw her. "Come here," he commanded.

Miranda obeyed. Nathan looked different as well. His hair had been buzzed off completely.

Nathan took her face, stroking her cheek gently. "You look beautiful."

Miranda smiled up at him, "Thank you. You look good too."

Nathan was leaning down to kiss her, Miranda knew, when Seth cleared his throat. Nathan backed away sending a curious look at his father.

Miranda looked at Seth, wondering why he just didn't let Nathan do what he wanted with her. Then she caught his passing thought and her stomach dropped in horror. Seth wanted her for himself. She tried hard not to look disgusted. He was twice her age! Immediately she put up a mental wall. She looked up at Nathan, who must not be aware of his father's intentions. His eyes still swept her up and down in admiration.

She sent one more flirtatious smile up at Nathan and went to sit by his father on the couch. "So Seth, about this attack tomorrow. What will I be doing?"

Seth smiled and took her hand. He was filled with smugness. "There is a man, and his spirit is calling. He is a strong presence, and will be an asset to us," Seth said.

Miranda nodded, "How do you feel his spirit?"

Seth shrugged and explained, "We feel pulled towards an individual's evil core and I felt a very strong presence in this next person. I have always been an excellent tracker, even before I became chief. The chief you killed was weak and lacked vision and now that I am chief, I am strongest of all. I make all the decisions for our group." His chest seemed to puff out as he called himself the chief.

Miranda could tell he was extremely vain. He thought he was invincible. "What are our numbers?" she pressed on.

"About three hundred," Seth said with a shrug as he started to play with her hair.

Nathan sent his father an odd look, wondering why he was playing with her hair. He had seen his father sit beside his mother like that. He sent his father a glare.

"We are located all over Utopia and always looking for people to recruit," Seth continued, "When they find someone, they meet with me and we talk about the next steps, including how and when to attack."

"Yes, I can see you are very powerful," Miranda said, pretending to be in awe of him.

Seth smiled, dazzled by her.

"So what are your big plans?" Miranda inquired, still smiling. She wanted to get as much information as possible.

Seth chuckled a little and rested his hand on her leg, "I will tell you soon."

Miranda tried not to look disappointed. She would have to prove herself first before he would tell her any of the evil secrets. She continued with different questions. "How many of us will be attacking?" Miranda asked. She hung onto Seth's every word, hoping he believed her actions.

"There will be just three of us. Nathan will be staying here. We are attacking at his home, so the only witnesses will be his family."

Miranda felt sick, but forced herself not to show it, "So he has children?"

"He is the child," Seth explained. "He is 19."

Miranda's hands shook a bit, so she pulled it away from Seth and clasped her hands together before he noticed. What if she had to kill someone? "So what will I be doing?"

Seth tucked a hair behind her ear, "You will be the one to convince him that he must come with us while we restrain the rest of his family."

Miranda forced down the nausea. Restrain? What did that mean? Could she allow them to kill and not do anything? Miranda took a few deep breaths. She needed to be careful about what she said, to protect everyone she loved. She had to pretend to be on their side.

Fourteen

★ ★ ★ ★ ★

Miranda was asleep but she awoke the minute her door was opened. She had all her senses on high alert since she had been kidnapped. This was the moment she worried about. She knew it was Nathan by his thoughts.

Nathan crept quietly to her bedside and looked down at her. Miranda pretended to sleep, taking long and slow breaths, hoping Nathan would be discouraged, but he wasn't. He pulled back Miranda's blanket and climbed in, wearing just his shorts. He put an arm around her and started to caress her shoulder and kiss the back of her neck.

Miranda had an idea. "Seth?" she asked, sleepily. "Back again so soon?"

"What!" Nathan whispered in shock. He sat up quickly.

Miranda's eyes widened, "Oh Nathan!"

Nathan got up in a hurry, looking disgusted. His disgust turned to anger and he left her room without another word.

Miranda smirked to herself. Hopefully Seth would fall for the same thing if he tried anything. This could be her plan. She could pit father against son in a fight over her. She wondered if it would work. She had a hard time falling asleep as she wondered how far she could take it. Could she shut off her emotions and be able to kiss Seth? Her stomach rolled just thinking about it. She could flirt, but anything more she didn't even want to think about. It made her sick.

Miranda's eyes snapped open. Someone was touching her face. She scolded herself for not being on alert.

"We really must do something about that face," Seth said, gently caressing it with his thumb. "Surely you cannot go to the funeral like that. People will wonder who the abused woman in the back is."

"I can go?" Miranda asked.

Seth smiled "Of course you can. You will need to be disguised."

Miranda nodded in agreement, "Naturally, no one can know I am there."

Seth got up from the bed and handed her a tube of medication, "You will not be going alone either. There will be a number of us there mixed in with the crowd."

"No!" Miranda said, without thinking. She stopped and had to think of something fast. "They are his killers. It does not feel right."

Seth look thoughtful for a minute and finally nodded, "You are right. I will make sure none that are responsible are there."

Miranda nodded, "Seth, not only are you so powerful, you are wise. That makes a great leader."

Seth beamed at her compliments. "Get dressed and come," he said as he turned to leave, "We will be attacking in one hour."

Miranda got out of bed and went to shut the door. She was worried about the deal she had made. She was supposed to protect all of Utopia and now she was going to join an attack. She sighed heavily and got dressed making a promise to whatever Legend or power was out there that she was only infiltrating the evil side to destroy it.

Once she was ready, they all went up to Nathan's car and this time Seth drove. Nathan was already gone, she hadn't seen him.

"Now, Miranda," Seth said into the rearview mirror, "I trust you and I believe you are on our side, but there are others who do not. They are all watching Evan right now, and should something go wrong today are only a phone call away."

Miranda held her breath. She tried not to show her fear and instead a spark of anger. "I will show everyone the side I am on," Miranda snapped. "What is Evan to me when I have all of you for my family?"

They were not far from their destination. Seth parked the car in a small clearing, close to a building, but far enough away that no one could see it. She followed Seth and Derek into the building quietly. Her palms were sweating and she wiped them on her black pants.

They got into the elevator and Derek pushed the button for the second floor. They knew exactly where they were going.

"We have been scoping him out for weeks," Seth explained. "We always do before we recruit."

Outside the door to the apartment, Seth stopped. It looked like he was meditating. Derek did the same and then both their skin started to glow red. Miranda backed away to the wall as the wind started to blow and the ground shook. Seth put his hands out, and the door burst open and people started to scream.

What happened next was a blur. Seth and Derek both attacked and the wall to the outside of the apartment crumbled, sending the screaming woman flying out the window. Miranda felt sick as she watched her disappear. Then Seth grabbed her by the front of her shirt and pushed her down the hallway.

"Go do what you are supposed to," Seth yelled.

Derek was attacking the man who had been with the woman, but Miranda couldn't watch. She turned away just as a brilliant white light illuminated the apartment. Seth was thrown into the wall with a force that knocked him out. Derek wasn't so lucky. He was tossed out the hole in the wall and Miranda could hear his screams as he disappeared. She froze.

She could hear the man whimpering and went to him. He screamed when she came close.

"I will not hurt you," Miranda said soothing, "but please, run."

The man looked at her, full of fright.

"Now!" Miranda yelled and he rose from his spot behind the couch that had been knocked over and left the apartment. He pushed the button to the elevator and was gone.

Miranda didn't know what to do as another man, a younger one, entered the living room. He was the one they were after.

"You are coming with us," Miranda demanded of him.

The man put his hands up in surrender, "It is about time," he snapped. "I have been waiting for years to be found."

"Wonderful," Miranda rolled her eyes. "So you would allow you parents to die for this. It is our blood that runs in their veins too. You have a lot to learn. He will teach you." She motioned to Seth, who seemed to be gaining consciousness. The markings on his forehead were fading and Miranda bent down to Seth's level. "Seth, we have to go. The law enforcement will be coming."

Seth's eyes snapped open, "Help me." He put a hand out, and Miranda pulled him to his feet. He leaned on her. The other man took his other side and together they went out into the hallway. They just barely managed to get under the cover of trees before people began arriving. There were bystanders coming to check what happened and help, law enforcement and reporters. So many cars had landed around the building and people on foot came from the paths. Seth was able to walk and the three of them ran for it. No one suspected them. Seth's markings were gone.

Alex was at the studio when the ground started to shake. As everyone moved together into the centre of the room, he slipped outside the studio doors. When he was sure he was alone, he put his hands on the ground, as he had seen Miranda do before, and he willed his power into the ground. He closed his eyes as a white light sprang from his palms and that was the last he remembered until he heard voices around him.

"I thought he was in the studio with us," Wayne said to the group. There were a few sniffles.

Alex felt a cool hand touch his face and he flinched.

"Alex?" came Britany's familiar voice.

Alex groaned and forced his eyes open. Britany was the closest to him. All his co-workers were gathered around, all staring, with concern, at him.

Melissa knelt down beside him, "What happened?"

Alex shook his head, "I must have hit my head."

Wayne chuckled, "Well, how can you miss it. It is so inflated."

"Ha... ha..." Alex muttered and tried to smile. He sat up and felt dizzy.

Sandy returned with a glass of water, "Oh good, he is awake." She held the glass to Alex's lips as he took a drink. Once he felt steady enough, he took the glass from her and thanked her.

"Here," Britany said, holding out his phone to him. "We talked to Evan and your parents and told them you were unconscious, but you will probably want to phone them back to let them know you are fine."

"Thanks," Alex said taking his phone. Everyone was hovering. "I am fine everyone, really. Thank you for your concern. I will be back in just a minute, you can all get back to filming." Alex got to his feet to prove it. That seemed to satisfy most as they made their way back into the studio. Britany and Melissa hung around.

"Where is Miranda?" Britany asked curiously, "I have tried to call her and left messages. I just tried to call her from your phone but she did not pick up. I thought she would want to know that you were unconscious."

Melissa and Alex shared a look.

"I am not stupid," Britany said, "I thought for sure she would be one of the first to call to make sure you were fine. Where is she?"

"She just needed some time away," Alex said.

"But she is coming for the funeral tomorrow, right?" Britany asked.

Alex shrugged.

"It is her father, why would she not be there unless she could not," Britany surmised.

Alex frowned. Britany had guessed correctly. "I cannot say, Brit. I am sorry."

"Why?" Britany demanded, "Does Miranda know she has been replaced on the show? I would not want someone in my place even if it was for a week. I..."

"Stop asking questions," Alex interrupted, "I will tell you when I can, but for now just trust me."

Britany sighed, "Fine but it better be a good reason." Britany turned on her heel and went back into the studio.

"No sign of her yet?" Melissa asked.

Alex shook her head.

"How is Evan?" Melissa frowned, missing him. She wanted to help, but was not sure how.

"Luckier than I am," Alex whispered, closing his eyes. Evan decided he did not want to be at the studio that day, but he wanted Alex to continue on with filming. Evan said he was just making funeral arrangements, but Alex knew he was looking for his sister. How long did he try to search out evil when his sister had been killed? Of course Evan would do the same and Alex worried for him.

"Do not tell Evan, but the team has written both you and Miranda out of the scripts starting tomorrow," Melissa said. When Alex looked at her, afraid, she continued, "That gives you a week to find her. We have already filmed a week of episodes. I know you can find her by then."

Alex was stunned by her faith in them. He nodded. "Thank you Mel." He hugged her.

"Tell Evan I miss him," she said before turning back to the studio.

Alex always knew how Melissa felt about her boss. She was afraid because she did not want to ruin their good working relationship. Alex vowed that if they survived the next few weeks, he would talk to Evan about it.

Miranda hated the new recruit. He had been filled in on everything as they sat at the kitchen table and had lunch, but he did not trust or believe her at all. He gave her a hard time and kept quizzing her.

"If your friend saw you attack someone, would you kill her?" he asked.

"Yes," Miranda said and rolled her eyes, "Stop asking me questions, Rob! I am on your side."

He gave her a look of complete distrust and turned to Seth, "You believe her?"

Seth shrugged, "It was her first attack. Everyone freezes."

Rob's lips formed a thin line of mistrust and he sat back at his seat with his arms crossed and glared at her. "I will never freeze."

Miranda tried to ignore it but couldn't, "I saved you all today!"

"That is true," Seth agreed. Miranda could have run once Seth had been knocked out, but she didn't. She did her job. She got Rob and then got Seth out of there when he could not do it himself. Seth looked at her fondly and reached over to play with her hair.

Miranda had to suppress her shudder at Seth's touch. Seth could have called Nathan when he awoke and had her brother killed. It was not for him she had stayed, but it was good he would think that. She flashed him a smile.

Rob glowered as he looked between the two of them. "When can I take on this power?"

"We had to vacate the sanctuary," Seth said, "There were too many people snooping around with all the attacks that happened there recently. We should be able to return in a few days and then you may take in the evil. You will be a great asset."

Rob huffed impatiently, "Fine."

"But you do not think she was attacked?" Griffin asked for the hundredth time.

"I told you Griffin, I do not know," Alex said, frustrated. Once he had gotten home, they had grilled him about the attack, but Alex had no idea where his powers went or who they helped.

Greta put a hand on Griffin's arm.

Griffin looked at her sadly and took the hand she had placed on his arm, "I miss her so much." He turned back to Alex, "I am sorry for asking so many times. I just cannot help it." Griffin sighed. "I should have apologized. I have acted horribly to her, and now I may never get a chance to make it right."

Greta patted his back.

Griffin hung his head, "I was just so scared for her. She must have thought I did not care at all." He looked at Greta beside him, "I told her I wanted to send her back to Earth. How stupid was that?"

"Do not dwell on that now," Greta said. She frowned, a little mad that she had not been included. They had kept all the secrets, even from her. She could have told them this whole time how silly they were being. Maybe none of this mess would have even happened. But it did and now she had to stay positive and hope that everything would turn out fine. She was afraid. Mr. East had been taken right from work, right under their noses. What if the same happened to any of them?

Griffin turned to her, took her face in his hands, "I am sorry, darling. I am sorry that I kept so much from you and now we have put you in danger. Just knowing my family is a danger. I am so sorry."

"It is my family too," Greta said stubbornly.

Evan walked in the door, his face white.

Alex stood, "Where have you been? I thought you would be here hours ago."

"I was being followed," Evan said, shaking. He went to the kitchen and brought back a drink. He sat on the couch and downed it.

"Followed?" Alex repeated, dumbstruck. He shook his head "You should have said something when I talked to you!" he said, in accusation.

"I was worried he would hear," Evan whispered as he put the bottle down empty and put his head in his hands.

"He?" Greta asked.

"Nathan," Evan said, through his hands, "He was following me all day. I could not even look for Miranda."

"But where did you go?" Alex asked, sharply.

"I went to the funeral home and then I went to the ocean and back. I thought of going to stay with family, but I saw Nathan following me as soon as I left this morning and I did not want to lead him anywhere. I just sat on the sand all day."

Alex stood up, anger radiated from him. Mostly because he had not been there, what if something had happened to him? "Do not ever do that again!" he yelled, "You tell me! You tell me next time!"

"If he wanted to kill me, he would have," Evan said. "I was prepared for him to do it all day, but he never did. He just watched me."

Alex felt sick as he sunk back down into his chair. Miranda would have been furious with him if he had let her twin die. He rubbed his face in frustration and stood again. "I am going to bed."

Miranda was happy she was able to avoid Seth all night by going to the gym with Rob. She was working hard to try to make him trust her and had pretty much told him her whole life story laced with lies about how much of a badass she had been on Earth, but he was still doubtful.

Rob was going to be one of the crew accompanying her to the funeral. Others would be there, but Rob had given himself the task of watching her carefully.

"Why don't you trust me?" Miranda snapped as they returned to the apartment. Dinner was ready for them.

"Just a feeling," Rob said, crossing his arms. He eyed her up and down.

Miranda made a face at him. She grabbed dinner and then stomped down the hallway to her bedroom.

No one tried to enter her room that night, but Miranda could not sleep, worrying that Seth would. Finally she got some sleep in the early morning hours and awoke with just an hour till the funeral.

She dressed slowly, hoping no one would recognize her. She was afraid of what would happen if someone did. Luckily she had an outfit she was sure she had never worn before. She was going to wear her hair down and some dark glasses, which wouldn't be out of the ordinary. She had seen others wear them, probably to hide their tears.

Stacie knocked on her door and Miranda let her in. She was there to do Miranda's makeup. She put on several layers to hide the bruises. There was not much she could do about Miranda's lip, except cover it with lipstick. It was still a little noticeable.

Once she was finished, she went to the dining room for breakfast. Nathan was there with a plate of bacon and eggs in front of him. He eyed her when she entered, looking her up and down.

"Good morning Nathan," Miranda said and took a seat beside him.

He turned away and returned her greeting. He was still angry about his father.

Miranda did not know what to say, so she sat quietly.

Near the end of breakfast, Rob entered wearing a black suit. He looked very dark, and Miranda frowned. She got a bad feeling off of him. She couldn't believe he was going with her, but it was a much better exchange than if one of her father's murderers were there, if only slightly.

Seth was right behind him, and he smiled down at Miranda.

"Good morning beautiful," Seth said and placed a kiss on her head.

Rob and Nathan both looked disgusted.

"We are going to the cave soon," Rob snapped at Seth.

Seth waved a hand in dismissal, "Yes, two more days."

Miranda stood and faced Rob, "We should go now." The last thing she wanted was for Rob to become evil.

"You can take my car," Seth said as they walked out.

Miranda flashed him a smile and Rob followed her out.

"Hold on tight," Miranda smiled as she set the destination.

Rob gave her a look, "Why?"

"I am still new at driving," Miranda smiled wider as the car started to reverse on auto-pilot.

Rob gripped the door handle, "I could have driven!"

Miranda shrugged with a laugh, "I like to drive." She stepped on the gas and the car punched forward. It told her to rise to an elevation of 1000 metres so she shot up into the sky.

"Slow down," Rob complained.

Miranda laughed, "Do not be such a baby. Driving is easy."

Rob looked a little green as he looked out the window, and Miranda smiled in satisfaction. It must have been how Alex felt watching her grip the seat.

They reached the funeral home in minutes and joined the throng of cars that were parking.

Miranda took a deep breath and climbed out. This was it. Hopefully no one would recognize her. She put everyone in danger coming here and she might have turned around now, if it wasn't for proving to Rob that she was one of them. He would be even more suspicious if she left.

There were plenty of people in the reception room that Miranda was easily able to hide. She went to stand by one of the tall potted plants for extra coverage. It was a perfect spot and she had a good view of her family.

Rob followed and stood beside her. Miranda took his arm to make it look like they were a couple. He gave her a funny look and shrugged it off.

"We are going to have to talk," Miranda said, "so we are not just staring. It will look suspicious."

Rob made a face and started making small talk. Miranda turned to him to converse but her eyes roamed over to her family every few minutes. They looked awful. Their eyes looked tired and red like they hadn't slept all week and their clothes were completely ragged. Alex was standing with them and he looked just as bad. Miranda was staring at him when he looked up and locked eyes with her. She immediately turned back to Rob. *Shit, shit, shit,* she thought, and did not look back.

Alex grabbed Griffin's arm, since he was standing closest to him. Griffin looked at him, curiously.

"I think Miranda is here," Alex whispered.

Evan heard what Alex had whispered and he and Griffin looked around. "Where?" he whispered.

Alex peered at the blond woman by the plant but she did not look back at him. She had Miranda's build. He moved to get a closer look but Griffin held him back.

"Wait, if she is here and she has not made herself known, it means she is hiding. We cannot know it is her."

Alex frowned, "I am not even sure it is."

"Who?" Evan asked impatiently, "Which do you think she is?"

"There is a blond woman with dark glasses across the room. She is talking to some man in an all black suit. I have never seen either of them before."

Evan took a quick peek, trying to make it look like he was scanning the room. He turned back to the group, excited, "I think it is!"

"We cannot do anything about it," Griffin said, sadly. "If she came here in disguise, we cannot draw attention to it. It could be dangerous. I have an idea though."

Miranda continued her conversation with Rob, telling him more about growing up on Earth when there was a bit of a commotion. Miranda paused and looked over to her family. Evan, Griffin and Alex were being confronted by Alicia, who had just arrived. Greta had disappeared.

Alicia was talking in a raised voice, "I have not seen her in so long. Where is she? She is not answering my messages!"

Evan tried to calm her, "She is just away right now, Alicia."

"It is her father's funeral! Surely, she would be here," Alicia said, just as loud. She was a bit hysterical as tears poured down her face, "Unless something happened to her. Why will you not tell us? What happened?"

"Nothing has happened," Griffin added, "She is away."

"When will she be back?" Britany asked, joining the conversation from across the room.

"Next week, we hope," Griffin said with a shrug, hoping that would end the conversation.

Alicia pursed her lips, not sure whether to believe them. Her parents were with her and they were trying to calm her as well. They led her away from the family.

Griffin just happened to look over at that time, and Miranda had to quickly turn away. Her pulse quickened. Could they know it was her?

Miranda glanced at Rob, who was looking at her darkly. Miranda bit her lip and shrugged, "I have to use the washroom."

Rob followed her. Miranda made a wide berth around her family and went into the washroom. She almost let out a squeal of fright when she went into a stall. Greta was standing there. She put a finger to her lips and then reached behind Miranda and shut the stall door behind her. "Go away," Miranda snapped through the door at Rob, "We earthlings are a little more self-conscious about our bathroom habits."

"Fine, but do not be long," Rob said and left.

"Greta," Miranda breathed and threw her arms around her soon-to-be sister-in-law. Greta sobbed. It took her several seconds before she could speak.

"They told me to wait in here for you. Alex and your brothers thought it might be less suspicious if I was missing for a while," Greta managed to whisper.

"Oh Greta," Miranda said. She couldn't let Greta go, hugging her tightly, "You all should not know I am here."

"Alex knew right away, Miranda, he could pick you out anywhere," Greta said, pulling away and wiping her eyes, "I do not have much time and I have so much to say. One, Alex wants you to know that Lydia is his sister's best friend and that day you were taken was the anniversary of her death. Miranda, he wants to be with you and he is doing everything he can to find you," Greta spoke quickly and continued, "Two, quickly tell me what you are up to. Three, Alex says whatever you are up to, stop. You cannot do it without him. Lastly, we miss and love you so much. Have they hurt you?" Greta reached out and touched her face lightly with her empty hand. She saw the fading cut on Miranda's lip but Miranda had hidden all the faded bruises with makeup. "They did not want to replace you on the show. They were told if they did not, then you would die. Now, quickly, tell me everything."

"They did some ceremony and now they think I am on their side, but I am not. They killed..." Miranda paused, and choked back a sob. "They killed Dad right in front of me." She took a deep breath, trying to get it all out before she had to go. Her mind was racing. "If I pretend I am on their side, they will not hurt any of you and I am waiting for the perfect moment to attack them. I can win. If they think I am on their side and they trust me, I just have to be patient. You all have to trust me. It is just acting and I can do that."

"You cannot do this alone," Greta insisted, "Alex needs to help you. The Legend says so."

"Tell Alex to keep looking for me and use the necklace. If the necklace works for him, like it works for me, it will point right to me," Miranda said, "That place that was the epicentre on the mountain *is* where they are hiding. There is a large boulder in front of the entrance to a cave, but we won't be back there for at least a day or two." Miranda paused and took Greta's arms, "The last thing I want is for Alex to be hurt though, Greta. Or worse, what if he dies like Jackson? I could not bear it."

"I have to tell him," Greta said, shaking her head slowly, "He will find you."

"And to answer everything, yes I am fine and I love you and them more than anything," Miranda said and hugged her again. "I have to go. He will suspect something."

Miranda left the stall quickly without a look back. She washed her hands and went back out to the main room, which was filling to capacity.

Rob was waiting for her right outside the bathroom. He didn't suspect a thing. At that moment, the funeral director said it was time for the funeral. She was glad for that, since she worried about someone else recognizing her.

Miranda stood beside Rob at the back of the group of people. She focused on making sure Rob couldn't hear her thoughts as her eyes filled with tears.

Mr. East looked so peaceful. The blood was gone from his clothes. Miranda let out a small cough to cover up the sob that escaped her throat.

The funeral director finished his speech and Mr. East's body was put into the fire. Miranda couldn't see it through her tears.

When the fire was doused by water, she turned to Rob, "We should go."

"What are you going to do now?" Rob smirked, "The proper procedure is to say goodbye and send condolences to the family before you go."

Miranda narrowed her eyes at him, "I have never done that before."

"It is customary. Come," Rob said and grabbed her arm to get in the lineup.

"What are you doing?" Miranda whispered, harshly.

"This will be the ultimate test," Rob replied, "We shall see."

"We didn't greet the family at the beginning, why now?"

Rob shrugged as the lineup got closer to the family.

Miranda's palms started to sweat. Rob expected her to talk to her family? Did he want her to slip up? Of course he did. He was probably prepared to tell Seth what happened and then everyone she loved would be killed.

"Seth is going to be so angry with you for doubting me," Miranda hissed.

"We shall see," Rob replied, calmly.

They had reached the family.

Miranda took a deep breath as she stepped up to Greta first, "I am very sorry for your loss, I hope you find comfort."

"Thank you," Greta replied, acting her part perfectly. Miranda moved down the line. It was the same with Griffin and Evan. Both thanked her like they didn't know her.

Alex was last.

She looked away as she took his hand, "I am very sorry for your loss…"

Alex gripped her hand tight, "I will not let you go. I…"

"Don't," Miranda cut him off. She looked up into his eyes. He looked ready to pour out his heart. "I have to go. Don't make a fuss, don't try to stop me. You will put everyone in danger." She gave his hand a gentle squeeze and pulled her hand away. "Just forget about me, Alex," she added, for Rob's sake.

Rob glared her down as they took the elevator to the roof.

"Are you happy? One person recognized me," Miranda snapped as they walked away, "You are a fool for putting me at risk, and Seth will be so angry."

Alex stared at the door Miranda just went through, wishing he had time to say everything in his heart. How could he have just let her go? What was wrong with him?

"You did the right thing," Greta said, putting a hand on Alex's arm, "Miranda knows what she is doing." Greta was sure now, that Miranda had charmed her way into their group. They must really believe that she was one of them. How else would they even let her attend the funeral?

"What do you mean?" Evan asked her.

"Miranda said to trust her," Greta said and explained everything Miranda had told her in the washroom.

"Well," Rob said, "Except for that one little snag, you pulled it off."

Miranda sent him a glare, "You should not doubt me."

Rob sighed. He gripped the seat tightly as Miranda drove them back to their hideout. "I still do. Do not think for a second I buy your affection for Seth. I will still be watching you."

Miranda allowed herself to go dreamy eyed at the mention of his name. It helped that her mind was on Alex. She had been given a renewed sense of hope that her plan would work now that she knew the truth. Her family didn't replace her and Alex was looking for her. Miranda sighed, "Seth is an amazing man. He is strong and courageous, and a true leader, but you are right. I do not love him. I love his son."

Rob snorted a laugh, "I do not believe that either."

Miranda rolled her eyes, "Whatever. I will be telling Seth what you did."

Rob rounded on her, his eyes narrowed, "I am not afraid of him."

Miranda stared back at him. She saw a blackness in him. Of everyone Miranda had ever met in her life, both on Utopia and on Earth, he seemed pure evil. She saw a lot of bitterness and hate in his mind, and wondered where he came from. She looked away and took a deep breath. Now was not the time to wonder. She couldn't slip up and give her thoughts away.

Miranda and Rob returned to the hideout apartment to find Nathan and his father both in the living room.

Miranda did just as she had said, and told Seth what Rob had done. "He was a fool," Miranda concluded, "He could have put this whole thing in jeopardy."

Rob scoffed, "What whole thing? What have we been doing? Sitting here hiding, that is all. I did not wait my life pretending to be a good citizen to do nothing."

Seth went red with anger, "What do you expect? We cannot just go out and attack all the time! This is not some little game. We bide our time. We collect people and grow our numbers and when the time is right, we change Utopia forever. We need to regain our strength again. We were so close to everything we wanted."

"A strength that *she* weakened," Rob snapped and pointed at Miranda.

"That is ENOUGH!" Seth shouted, "You are not to pester Miranda anymore. She is with us!"

"I will not wait here any longer," Rob said, shaking his head. He turned and opened the front door again. "I am leaving."

"Good riddance," Miranda said when the door closed behind him.

Seth, who had stood up during the argument, came over to Miranda. He put a hand on her face in a loving gesture, "You will have to get used to him, my dear. He has great evil inside him. I have to follow him and try to get him to stay."

Miranda was left with Nathan and an awkward silence fell, only interrupted by the television, which had been left on. He was purposefully ignoring her and staring out the window. Miranda took the opportunity to carry on with her plan.

"Nathan, can we please talk?"

"Why?" Nathan asked, glumly, looking back at her. He made a face, disgusted by the fact that Miranda had been with his father.

Miranda went to take a seat beside him, "Please?" She waited a few seconds but Nathan refused to look at her so Miranda threw herself at him. She even dredged up a few tears. "Oh Nathan,"

Miranda cried, "I don't know what to do. I want to be with you, but your dad doesn't want me to. He forced himself on me and I could hardly stand it, but I pretended it was you and that's the only way I got through. You didn't give me a chance when you came to my bedroom the other night. I wanted to explain to you. I'm in agony right now." She clung to him desperately, "Please say you love me and that we can be together no matter what your father wants. You are the only one who completely understands me, the only person on Utopia who has ever listened to me."

Nathan was in stunned silence. It took a minute from him to process that she was throwing herself at him, but when he finally worked it out in his head, he held her tight, "I will not let him keep us apart anymore." And he kissed her.

Miranda knew her routine. She had acted it out with Alex so many times. She coached herself along, knowing what came next. That's all it was, an act, she kept telling herself as he put his grimy, disgusting hands on her.

Seth's return interrupted them. "He got away so…" he started to say as he entered and stopped suddenly seeing what was going on. Miranda hastily broke the kiss. "Nathan, what did I tell you?" he fumed as he moved quickly into the living room. He pulled Miranda off the couch and away from his son. Miranda didn't fight him, she stood and backed away.

"No father," Nathan retorted, standing up to face his father. Nathan was taller but Seth did not back down. "I will not give her up. She loves me."

Seth snorted a laugh, "You fool. Miranda is powerful and she belongs with someone who matches her power. How dare you disobey me!"

"She does not want you, Dad," Nathan said, jabbing a finger into his father's chest, "Leave her be."

"Stop fighting," Miranda said, from behind Seth. She stood between them. "I cannot stand it. Just stop. We are on the same side. You must get along."

"Fine, Miranda," Nathan said, and held a hand out to her, "Tell him yourself. Tell him you love me."

Miranda smiled at Nathan and turned to Seth, who she smiled at as well, "I…"

"No, you tell Nathan that you want me, Miranda," Seth interrupted.

Miranda broke down in tears, "I cannot handle the fighting," and she ran from the room and into her room. As soon as she closed her door, she curtsied to no one. "And that, my friends, is a daytime drama." She laughed to herself, and then she shivered slightly and tried to brush off the feeling of Nathan's hands on her skin.

Fifteen

★ ★ ★ ★

Alex tried to recall where he had put the necklace. He remembered finding it by the water and had put it in his pocket. It dawned on him that it may have slipped from his pocket when he went out looking for Miranda the night she was taken.

"Where are you going?" Evan asked, as Alex hastened to the elevator. Evan followed quickly. They had just gotten back from the funeral home.

"The necklace. Miranda told Greta that I should use it to find her," Alex explained as the elevator arrived. He got in and pushed the button for the parking garage. "I think it may be in my car. I have not seen it since that night she was…" Alex broke off. He hated himself for letting her get taken. He should have been with her that day, not Lydia.

"Stop torturing yourself, Alex," Evan urged, "You really need to stop blaming yourself for everything. It is not your fault"

Alex was silent and remained that way until he had the necklace in his hand. He found it under the driver seat in his car. He held it tight in his hand, but the needle didn't move. It hung limply.

Evan had been searching the passenger side and he met Alex's unhappy stare.

"It is not working," Alex said, disheartened. He took a few deep breaths and sat down in the driver's seat. Evan sat down too, his hope deflating. It was a few minutes before Alex spoke again, "Do you know that I have always felt wrong?"

"What do you mean?" Evan asked.

"I never felt like I belonged here, in Utopia," Alex replied. He closed his eyes and took a deep breath. He was ready to tell Evan everything. All the questions of his existence that he kept locked away in his mind. "It is hard to explain I guess but everyone is always happy, always friendly, always loving and I am not. I have hatred in me. One that I cannot describe. When I found out I was supposed to be this protector, look what I did? I refused it. I sought out other women. I was jealous. I hurt Miranda physically and emotionally. Do you know that I grabbed her arm when I saw her with Nathan a long time ago? I was enraged. No one gets like that in Utopia. How am I supposed to be some protector of all that is good, when I am not good?" Alex's eyes filled with tears.

Evan did a double take. Alex was serious? Evan shook his head. "No Alex. No one is perfect. No one is completely good. I have anger, jealousy, and sadness as well. Everyone feels those things. We are human, Alex, not robots."

Alex sighed and rubbed his eyes, "No, you do not understand. I just do not feel right. I feel more emotions than I should. I feel like I could hurt someone and that is not a virtue of a Utopian."

Evan shook his head again. "Alex, you are one of the best people I know. Yes, you are emotional, then," he said, when Alex went to interrupt him, "But being a good person, like everyone else, you know how to calm your anger and douse your jealousy. That is what makes us good. We have control over our emotions. We stop ourselves from overreacting. Sure, some people slip up, but do you truly believe you are not a good person because of that?" Evan could tell he did not believe it and it shocked him. "Alex, I hate the bad people. I hate that they took my sister and I am so afraid of what they could do to her."

"But would you kill them?" Alex asked.

"I-" he paused.

"See, you would not. Well, I would. I want them to die for what they did to my sister and your parents, and taking Miranda. I miss her so much."

"But you are capable of fighting them and I am not."

Alex scoffed, "So? I *want* them dead."

"And they deserve to die," Evan agreed, "But that does not mean you are not good. Think of the thousands of people you would save by eliminating the evil people."

"It just does not sound like I am a good person," Alex explained, sadly.

"Alex," Evan said. He paused until Alex looked at him, "You have this remorse and *that* is what makes you a good person."

Alex looked thoughtful. Maybe Evan was right.

"I know this has been tough," Evan continued, he looked down at the necklace in Alex's hand and noticed the needle had shifted. "But maybe we should talk about Miranda some more." The needle jumped again.

Alex wasn't looking at the necklace, he rubbed his face with his free hand, "I still cannot believe I let her just walk away."

The needle of the compass jumped again and spun around, just once. "We had to," Evan said, "We would have put everyone in danger."

"I know. Did you see her though? They completely changed her appearance. I loved her dark hair."

The needle spun again.

"She still looked good though," Evan encouraged.

Alex agreed, "But they hurt her. They did a good job of covering it up, but you could still see it up close. I cannot believe they let her just walk right up to us."

"It was probably some kind of test," Evan shrugged, his eyes on the jumping needle. It was quiet for a moment and the needle stopped jumping. Evan's eyes lit up, he had an idea. "So, do you still love her?"

"Of course I do," Alex said, looking at Evan curiously. Evan's eyes were on the compass. Alex looked down at the spinning needle and gasped. "It is working!" All of the sudden, the needle stopped, pointing northwest. Excited, Alex got out of the car. He spun in a slow circle and the needle followed him around. It really was working.

"We should wait a couple days," Evan said as he came around the car, "We should wait until she is back in the cave. It is too much of a risk to seek her out now."

Alex nodded in agreement, "I think I have a plan."

The next day, Alex drove to where the epicentre of the last earthquake occurred. There was a small clearing for parking nearby. Miranda had told Greta that there was a large boulder in front of the cave, so that was what they were looking for.

"How are we going to be able to get in?" Evan asked, as they headed out from the car.

"I should be able to move it," Alex pointed out, "I have the same strength as Miranda."

"Are you sure?" Evan asked, "Have you tried?"

Alex nodded, "I have been working on it at the gym this past week. Miranda let it slip that she could stop the whole planet from shaking, so I thought about it and I realized why she had been going to the gym so often. She was lifting weights with her mind."

"Yes, she can lift incredible weights," Evan said, and told Alex about the day he spent with his sister as they headed down the trail to the epicentre that had been marked.

They reached the point and looked around.

"So, maybe just start tossing boulders," Evan said with a shrug.

Alex forced a smile at him and looked around. He started small, ones that would basically just hide a crawlspace.

After a few, Evan sighed, "You really think they would crawl?"

Alex rolled his eyes, "I am working up to the bigger ones. This takes a lot of concentration."

Evan sat down on one of the small boulders and sighed. He had nothing to do but watch, as Alex worked his way to bigger and bigger boulders. Evan could see by the sweat that poured from his face, that it did take a lot of strength and concentration to move such big objects. He thought about his sister. She had become so natural at it that it barely fazed her anymore. He wondered if he could lift anything heavy. He was her twin, surely something passed to him in the womb.

So, he busied himself with trying to lift one of the smaller boulders, concentrating hard on it, the way he would for any small object. Evan had just managed to lift it a centimetre off the ground when a rumbling started.

"Evan, it is a trap!" Alex yelled, "Run!"

Evan hadn't seen that a boulder Alex had moved was in fact rigged to start a landslide. He stood frozen, watching as various sized red rocks started to tumble down the mountain side.

Alex noticed Evan's hesitation and he ran to his friend.

"Evan, move!" he yelled.

Evan seemed to snap to his senses, "Where?" he panicked. There was nowhere to go but downhill, and the rocks were headed straight towards them.

"Just go, fast!" Alex yelled. All he could think of was that if he got Evan killed, Miranda would never forgive him. He should have never brought him out to look with him.

They ran as fast as they could down the mountain but could hear the rocks gaining on them, tumbling faster than any human speed.

When Alex could hear the landslide at his heels, he yelled out to Evan one last time, "Get down!"

Miranda hadn't seen Nathan or Seth since their argument. Even Rob was off doing something. The only company she had been left with was another man named Felix who had replaced Derek. She was angry when Felix had stopped her from leaving. She had insisted she was only going to do some shopping, but he had been given orders not to let her leave the building.

"That is ridiculous," Miranda had complained. "Everyone else gets to leave. Have I not proven myself that I am on your side?"

Felix had shrugged.

This morning, Miranda found Nathan sitting at the dining room table, and Seth was nowhere to be seen. She took a seat beside him.

"Hi," she said putting her arms around his neck, hoping that whatever had happened yesterday had caused a rift between father and son.

Sure enough, Nathan turned to her with a smile. "Hello, Miranda."

Miranda gave him a quick kiss and saw his eyes burn with desire. "I hope you and your father have worked it out. I would hate it if I caused any animosity between the two of you."

Nathan gave her a hard look, "Well, my father has not realized that you have made your choice. He wants me to stay away from you, but I cannot. We will have to keep what we do a secret for now, until he realizes."

Miranda pouted, "OK." She took her arms back.

Nathan reached out and touched her arm, "We will be together soon."

Miranda sent him a smile, "I hope so."

After breakfast, Nathan said he was going to visit a friend and left. Miranda was left with Felix again. She sighed and went to her room, knowing he wouldn't let her leave. At least she had the time to think and plan. What would her next move be?

Evan dropped to the ground as Alex said. Alex crouched over him just as the boulders were about to rain down on them, but that never happened. A white mist appeared around the two of them and the boulders were forced either over or around their bodies.

After several tense seconds, Evan could tell Alex was struggling to keep up the shield. His face was red and sweaty as if he had just run a marathon.

"I cannot hold it much longer," Alex gasped out.

Evan chanced a peek over Alex's shoulder, "It is almost over, Alex, just a few more seconds."

Alex closed his eyes, feeling lightheaded. He was losing consciousness. He tried to grasp at his senses to keep himself awake. He pulled every bit of strength left inside to keep the glow around them. Miranda could do this. She would do anything to protect her brother.

As a darkness settled upon him, he heard Evan tell him it was OK to let go as he fell into blackness.

Seth came home an hour after Nathan had left. He entered Miranda's room without knocking, and Miranda sat up, surprised.

"I have to know if it is true," Seth asked, his voice thunderous. "When were you going to tell me you love Nathan?"

"No, I don't" Miranda admitted, quickly, "Nathan came to my room the other night and… well, I had to say something. He frightened me. I am so scared to be around him."

Seth's face softened and he took a seat beside Miranda, placing an arm around her. Miranda leaned into him.

"I am afraid of what Nathan will do to me if I say no," she continued and let her eyes fill with tears. "Look what he already did." She motioned to the already faded bruises and the cut that had nearly healed.

"He is my son, but I will not let him hurt you anymore," Seth said and touched her cheek lightly.

Miranda smiled at him, "Can I just keep pretending so that he will not hurt me anymore? We can keep what we have a secret."

Seth nodded and brought his other hand up to her other cheek. The moment Miranda dreaded was finally here, she realized, as Seth moved in closer to kiss her. Miranda tried not to show any hesitation and hoped her quick intake of breath was mistaken for happy surprise.

Seth's kiss was disgusting. He slobbered all over her and when he was gone, Miranda went to the washroom. She was only going to wash her face, but she felt so disgusted that she decided to shower. Seth promised her they would be together soon and she hoped she would find her way home before either Nathan or Seth kept their promises.

Evan was relieved when Alex awoke. He was out for a long time and Evan had worn a path pacing nearby. He kneeled beside his head and gave him water.

Alex took the bottle from him, "Thanks."

"You feel OK?"

Alex nodded as he finished the bottle. "How long was I unconscious?"

Evan looked at the time on his notebook. "About 25 minutes," he answered, concerned.

Alex sat up but still felt lightheaded. He took several deep breaths.

"We should go," Evan suggested.

"I just want to see what the avalanche unveiled," Alex said as he shook his head.

Evan frowned, "I do not think that is a good idea. What if there is another trap, or if the avalanche alerted them."

Alex took his time as he stood, feeling his strength return. He looked ahead of them towards the car. The rocks that had chased them weren't blocking the path. They had all went straight as the path bent and ended up in the woods. They had done damage to the trees in their way. He took a look back towards the hillside, then turned back to Evan. "I have to see. Stay here and out of sight. I will be quick."

Evan protested, but Alex was determined to check and see if the cave opening had been revealed. When he returned, his look of disappointment was enough. Evan knew he didn't find anything.

"OK, we should go," Alex said, leading the way. He made sure to keep looking around for any sign of evil, but it appeared the trap wasn't being monitored. Alex worried that they might suspect someone was there and hurt Miranda, but there was nothing he could do. He couldn't put every rock back, especially now that he was so exhausted.

To pass the time, Miranda watched reruns of *Northern Shores*. She couldn't bear to watch the new episodes, even though she now knew that they had not replaced her permanently.

When she heard voices in the hall outside the apartment, she turned down the volume to listen. They sounded like they were just outside the door. She thought it could be Nathan and Seth, and she smirked, proud of her recent accomplishments.

"Yes, I know you said a few days," one voice snapped, "But we are wasting time here."

Miranda assumed that was Rob. He was still bugging Seth to go to the cave so that he could be changed into an evil person. Out of everyone Miranda had met, he was the worst, and he wasn't even one of them yet. What would happen if he were to become one? Miranda bit her lip and kept listening. Perhaps her next goal would be to keep Rob away from that cave but the longer they stayed here, the greater the chance Nathan or Seth could make their next move on her.

"You listen to me," Seth demanded.

Miranda heard a small thump and wondered if Seth had pushed him against the wall.

"I am in charge here, and you will obey me."

"Yes, chief," Rob countered, "I understand that and I do. I have respect for you but I know that I will be great. I feel it."

"I have no doubt about that, but you have to be patient," Seth snapped. "I will not hear this again. We will go when I say we will."

Miranda turned the television off as the door opened. Seth looked thunderous, but his eyes softened when he saw her.

"Hi boys," Miranda smiled as she rose from the couch. She went to kiss Seth's cheek, "Did you have a good day?"

Seth smiled at her.

"Are we going to be attacking soon?" Miranda asked. "I still feel embarrassed about the last attack. I completely froze and I want to make sure that I am worthy."

"You did wonderfully, sweetheart," Seth assured, squeezing her hand. "You got both Rob and I out."

Rob rolled his eyes as Nathan walked in the door. He saw their adjoined hands and scowled. Seth's eyes darkened and out of spite, he put his arm around Miranda's waist and pulled her close to him.

"Hello, Nathan," he said pleasantly. He turned and kissed the top of Miranda's head.

"Dad," Nathan returned coldly and then sighed. "We have an issue."

Seth was immediately alert, "What is it?"

Miranda's eyes darted between the two of them as she heard the exchange in their mind. Apparently the trap they set near the cave was triggered, but there were no bodies found. They suspected Alex, but there was no proof. The cave was still covered and they did a thorough search but found nothing.

"We should send him a warning," Rob suggested and turned to Miranda. "Kill her and send them her body."

"No!" both Nathan and Seth said in unison. Miranda didn't even need to protest. She eyed both of them adoringly.

Rob's face flushed in anger, "I see what you are doing!" He took a threatening step towards Miranda, "You are playing them both as fools!" He turned to Nathan and Seth, "Do you not see? Has she told both of you that she loves you?"

Miranda's face dropped in horror but she quickly disguised it as anger, "That is IT! I am sick and tired of you doubting me!" She turned to Seth. "You know what? Kill him! That would make me very happy. You and I are enough power for the evil. He does not belong."

"Oh, you are wrong, Miranda," Rob said, darkly. Instead of arguing anymore, Rob turned to leave, but before he did he turned back to Seth. "I expect to be taken to the cave in the next two days."

Seth's mouth tightened in displeasure. He was supposed to be the chief. No one ever questioned the chief in his long service with evil.

"I do not trust him," Miranda said, reaching out to Seth once the door had closed behind Rob. She touched his arm lightly.

Seth turned to her with a burning look.

"He has no right to speak to you like that. You are a wise and powerful chief," she purred at him.

"Yes, it is unfortunate that he must join our ranks," Seth sighed, his anger melted away.

"You cannot just cut him loose? Maybe kill him?" Miranda asked, hopeful, "You know he exposed me at my father's funeral. It was all his fault. He did it on purpose."

Seth shook his head, "He is one of us. You are still new, but one day you will feel the evil inside others. Evil would not be happy if we killed him."

Miranda pursed her lips in thought, "I have a lot to learn."

"What are we going to do about Alex?" Nathan, who had been observing them quietly, finally asked.

Seth rubbed his face and turned to Miranda, "What do you think?"

"I-uh," Miranda stuttered. What could she say? If she told Seth to kill him, he just might do it, but if she didn't think of something right away, they would suspect her. "If we were on Earth, I would say kill his dog to send a message," Miranda joked instead.

Nathan smiled at his father, "That is actually a good idea. Kill someone he loves."

Miranda tried hard not to cry or shout. She wasn't sure which she wanted to do more. As if they hadn't hurt Alex enough! They had killed his sister, his cousin, and his grandmother.

Seth agreed, "But who this time? He just keeps coming after us and now it is him stopping our attacks. Who do we kill this time to keep him away?"

They both looked to Miranda. Who could she say? Who could she sentence to death? She hoped she didn't look as green as she felt. Her stomach twisted. "Kill...," she took a moment to think, her mind reeling, "Kill me."

Nathan's eyes widened but Seth whooped, "That is a great idea!" He picked her up and spun her around, "This will be perfect. We can fake your death and have him watch it and everyone will just think you have died. It is better this way."

Miranda smiled and nodded enthusiastically, "Yes. I never understood why we couldn't have just said I died anyways."

Nathan shrugged, and asked with a smirk, "Well, how would you like to die?"

"Well, I *am* a great actress," Miranda smiled, "We could do an epic fight scene. With a little camera creativity and some fake blood, I think we can pull it off."

Seth put his arms around her, "You are brilliant," and he kissed her.

Miranda let herself go limp and as soon as reasonable she slipped away from him, "I am going to go write our script." She kissed his cheek and then went to her room thinking no amount of chewing gum or disinfectant would ever take away the disgusting feel of Seth touching her.

Sixteen

★ ★ ★ ★

"You ready for this?" Nathan asked, releasing Miranda's hand. They had almost reached the clearing where they would film Miranda's death. They had chosen a spot away from the city where no one would be expected to interrupt.

Felix and Seth had their heads together, going over the script Miranda had written the day before on a notebook. There were two other people that Miranda didn't know, but each had a professional looking video camera.

"Did you memorize your lines?" Miranda teased, elbowing Nathan playfully in the ribs.

He smiled down at her, "Of course."

"Good 'cause we will only be able to do this once," Miranda said, and turned to everyone. "Once the ground shakes we cannot start over and when we get this blood on my clothes, I cannot clean it off." She picked up the bottle of fake blood that they had stolen from the studio the night before. Miranda was in luck that it was a Sunday night so no one would have been there, especially Alex and Evan.

"Well," Nathan teased, "we will not be as good as you, but I think we can handle it."

"Now, everyone understands that no harm must come to Miranda," Seth ordered. He took in everyone's face and fixed his most stern stare on them.

Nathan, Felix and the two men nodded in understanding.

"Time for makeup," Miranda chuckled and opened the bottle of fake blood. "You can all do a quick run-through while I get ready."

Everyone else spread out in the clearing while Miranda, using her phone as a mirror, pulled out her makeup case. She used a special powder she had from Earth to redden her nose and dribbled some of the fake blood on her upper lip to make it look like she had been struck. Then, she bent down to pick up some soil and spread it on her left cheek and forehead. She had worn the clothes she was first wearing when she had been kidnapped, and although someone had cleaned them, they had several tears. She used some soil to 'dirty' them up again.

Once she was finished, she turned to her cast, "Well, how do I look?"

"Perfect," Seth smiled and kissed her forehead. "Even like that you are still beautiful."

Miranda returned his smile, "Thanks."

"It looks very real," Felix commented.

Miranda shrugged, "My friend was a makeup artist. She taught me some tricks."

"We should get started," Nathan suggested, "I think we have got it."

Miranda nodded as everyone turned to take their positions. She had carefully scripted it so that although it looked like she died, Alex would know otherwise. He would certainly know it was a fake. She had worried that Nathan would catch it, but he hadn't.

Miranda took a few deep breaths and allowed her eyes to fill with tears. It was simple now. All she had to do was feel sorry for herself in her current situation. She thought about the things she was being forced to do to save her family and her father. She crossed her arms around herself, trying to hold it together. She didn't want to go so overboard that she couldn't perform this scene. She needed to stay strong. She hoped to be home in a few days.

The camera was pointed at Nathan, since Miranda's family knew he was the prime suspect in her kidnapping. The man behind the camera made a motion to him to let him know that it was rolling.

"Alex, we told you," Nathan said, angrily. "You would not listen and now you have forced us to do this."

Nathan turned and threw a punch at Miranda. She had taught him how to do it that morning without actually hurting her, but the makeup would make it look like he had.

Miranda cried out and fell to the ground. "No stop, please!" she cried out but Nathan got on top of her and hit her again. This time, he got too close and actually grazed her cheek.

Nathan looked stunned for a second, but Miranda kept going so he got back into it. Miranda tried to hit him back but he forced her down again.

"Alex, why?" Miranda sobbed. She looked at the camera. "I told you to leave me alone and they told you not to look for me." She purposely wiped at her face with her left hand where she held some of the blood in a little pack. It was sticking visibly out of her hand and she hoped Evan might notice it.

"Quiet!" Nathan yelled at her and then looked back at the camera. "I warned you, and now she will die!"

"No, please," Miranda cried desperately, her tears falling in streams down her dirty face. She threw him off of her and tried to get up. When he climbed back on top, she used her powers to throw him off, but she made sure to catch him in his landing so that he didn't hurt himself. That was when the rumbling started. Felix and Seth came onto the scene and attacked her.

"How dare you!" Seth called out and sent a beam of red towards her.

Miranda dodged it, allowing her protective mist to form around herself. She took deep breaths, trying to make herself look exerted, as they threw more attacks her way. Then Nathan, who had recovered, snuck up behind Miranda and attacked her from behind. Her mist erupted as if it had been shattered like a mirror and Nathan was forcing her to the ground again this time on her stomach. He pulled her head back so the camera had a view of her face, which was etched with fear.

"Any last words?" Nathan shouted down at her.

"Go to Earth," Miranda managed to get out, breathing heavily. "Tell my best friend Sara that I'm sorry I won't be coming back." Nathan got up off her and back away towards the others. Together they all used their powers. Miranda closed her eyes and the three of them attacked her at once. She let out a loud, bloodcurdling scream, and released the blood pack, which spurted out at her side and the camera cut out.

They had practiced and had aimed their attacks to strike mere centimetres from her. It would appear to be an extremely realistic attack but Miranda hoped with Evan's editing programs, he would know it was a fake.

"We have to go, now," Seth said. "We can look at the finished product back at the apartment." Seth looked around, worried. Their act hadn't taken long, but who knows how long until emergency vehicles arrived. He held a hand out which Miranda took and he helped her up. Nathan stepped up with a smile and took her arm.

"She was coming with me, dad," Nathan glowered.

Seth sighed, "We will see you back at the apartment."

As planned, they all scattered, going different directions back to their vehicles. Excitement permeated out of Nathan as they made their way back to his car. "You did great," he said, smiling down at her. His smile hitched a little when he remembered he had hit her, "I am so sorry I accidentally hit you." Nathan squeezed her hand and looked down at her shirt. It had a huge blood stain.

Miranda smiled up at him to let him know she was fine. She chuckled, "It does look real."

Nathan nodded. "Alex is going to just die inside," he commented, excited again. "I cannot wait to deliver this video and we can be free."

Miranda took his hand, "I know. I cannot wait."

* * *

A knock on the door startled them all.

Alex was the first to rise and feeling the evil presence behind it, he first turned to the rest of the family. "Hide, please. It is only one person, but I would feel better if you were all out of sight."

Evan was about to protest, but Griffin took his arm and dragged him to the kitchen. Greta was close behind.

Alex waited until he couldn't see them anymore, before he opened the door.

"Alex," Nathan nodded his head in greeting.

Alex gave him a hard look.

"Stay calm, I am merely a messenger," he continued and held out his hand with a small microchip in it.

Alex took it wearily and without another word, Nathan turned and pushed the elevator button. It opened right away, and he was gone.

Alex stared down at the chip in his hand. A million horrible scenarios raced through his mind. The ground had shook that morning, but it was so brief and he had been so tired, he could barely muster up the strength to stop it. Before he had, it was over.

Evan had quietly approached behind him. He took the chip out of Alex's hand and went over to the television.

They all gathered in the living room, but no one sat down as they watched the scene.

"No!" Greta cried in horror as they watched Nathan deal the final blow and the screen went dark.

Evan and Griffin looked sick. Evan clutched his shirt, like a pain had shot through his heart.

"No, something was not right," Alex said, shaking his head, though tears filled his eyes, "Alpha, replay that."

Evan looked at Alex, stricken, as Alpha restarted the video.

"Pause," Alex said, when he saw Miranda wipe her face. He went over to the television and touched the screen. It zoomed in. "She is holding a blood pack."

"So?" Griffin asked.

"It is sticking out right there. Why would she have that?"

Greta nodded, a flicker of hope crossed her face.

Griffin frowned, disbelieving, "Are you sure?"

"I think so," Alex said and he turned back to the television, "there is more. Alpha, restart it again."

Alex paused it again when Nathan had hit Miranda for the second time.

"Look at Nathan's face," Alex pointed out. "He did not mean to hit her and he only gets back into it when Miranda keeps going."

"No, Alex," Griffin replied, his eyes glistening, "do not make this harder. She is gone."

"There is one more thing," Alex said, desperate for it to be fake. "Alpha, replay the last minute."

They watched as Miranda gave her final plea and Alex paused it again. "Sara?" he repeated to himself, "That is not right. Helen was her best friend's name and Sara was her Earth mother's name." His eyes lit up, "She is lying so that we know this is fake!" Alex pulled the chip out and turned to Evan, "Evan, you have fancy filmmaking applications on your notebook. Take this and analyze every second of it."

Evan took it, hopeful, "I think you are right." He agreed, "I know her best friend's name was Helen. Why would she say Sara?"

Griffin and Greta exchanged hopeful glances.

"But why would they do this?" Evan bit his lip, "Why would they fake it?"

Alex frowned, "They want to hurt us."

Evan's face fell, "It was that rock slide trap they set. I knew we were close."

"Well, that sure sends a message," Griffin said, firmly. "No more looking."

Alex didn't argue, though Evan put up a fight. In the end, he sullenly went to his room to look over the video in private. They had agreed, for now, that Miranda's safety was still a concern and no one was going to threaten that. No one was to go looking for her until they came up with a better plan.

"So what do we do now?" Alex asked no one in particular.

"I think it is time to go public," Griffin answered after a minute. "We need to pretend we believe this video."

Alex started pacing, mumbling to himself.

Griffin and Greta watched him in silence, each with their own thoughts.

Alex sighed in frustration, "I wish I knew what she was thinking." He ran a hand through his hair.

Greta put a hand on his shoulder. "You have seen her, Alex. You know that she is safe and we will bring her home soon."

Alex nodded, "I am trying to stay positive."

Evan returned twenty minutes later with the verdict. "It is definitely a fake." He plugged the chip back into the television and showed them several mistakes, pausing at the right moment to show that Miranda's face was red and bloodied before the first punch. He stopped again on Nathan's face, when he actually hit her by accident and again on the blood packet sticking out of her hand when she wiped her face.

"She left it sticking out so we would notice it," Evan commented with a hint of pride in his voice. Finally he showed the end, just before it cut to black, where all of their attacks miss her by a fraction and she sets off the blood splash.

Griffin let out a sigh of relief and stood up, "Evan, we have to pretend she died. What can we do now?"

Evan shrugged and frowned.

Alex stopped pacing, "Give it one day," he said as he moved to the door. He slipped on his shoes and turned to them before he left, "I have to do something first."

Evan stood up, "I am going with you."

Griffin's face went red, "Neither of you are going anywhere. We talked about this, and know she is still alive. If they want us to think she is dead, then we cannot keep looking. We have to pretend we think she is gone! It is safest to just let it calm down a few days. We tell... Alex!"

Alex wasn't listening. He left the apartment and pushed the elevator button. Evan tried to follow, but Alex lifted him in the air and threw him into Griffin, who was a few steps behind. He caught Greta's eye and she mouthed the words 'Be safe'. Alex nodded and stepped onto the elevator. Evan and Griffin, after disentangling themselves, tried to reach it, but he was gone.

Nathan gloated when he returned from the East apartment. "Alex looks terrible," he chuckled, "The whole family is a mess."

You killed our father, Miranda thought darkly, sure to keep her thoughts from the others, *of course they look terrible*. She quickly turned the glare she had sent at Nathan into a smile before he turned to her.

"I heard they stopped filming the show," Felix added, "several days ago."

"No matter now," Seth cut in, "now they will know for sure she is dead and they can eventually get back to their lives."

"So, where will we go?" Miranda asked, turning to Seth.

Seth frowned, "We have to go to the cave tomorrow and change Rob before he angers me again. Then we must move our whole operation to the alternative location. That means moving the altar as well."

Felix groaned and Miranda looked at him questioningly.

"We have moved the altar before. It is very heavy and takes the powers of several of us," Felix explained. "When Seth became the chief, we moved it here. The last chief lived in the north."

"We have caves all over Utopia," Nathan added, and smiled proudly. "I have studied our culture since I was small."

Miranda turned a look of admiration towards him, "Maybe you can teach me."

Nathan nodded, excitedly.

"Where would you like to go?" Seth asked, touching her face lightly and turning it towards his own.

"Is there a place by the water? I do like water," Miranda answered, smiling sweetly up at him.

Seth nodded and let go of her face. He turned to Felix, "Spread the word, we are heading for City 92986. Let everyone know to meet at the cave at 10 hour tomorrow."

Felix nodded and left.

Miranda looked between Nathan and his father and felt the tension rise in the room. She stood up, "I am going to the pool." Neither answered her so she went to her bedroom, got her bathing suit and headed downstairs.

The morning came and Miranda knew she needed a better plan. She had tried to think of something all day but no good ideas came. She was still torn. She either needed to escape now or leave some kind of message that she had moved. That is, if they got her clues from the video and knew she was alive. She didn't want to think how awful it would be if they believed she had actually been killed but it was better than if someone had actually been killed.

Miranda had a couple ideas but it would probably be best to wait it out, go with them and continue to cause a rift between father and son. How long did she have before one of them demanded more than just kissing from her? Perhaps she should escape today.

At 9:25, Nathan, Seth and Miranda headed towards the cave. They parked in a lot with several other cars and walked up the path to the cave, which was open and ready for them.

Miranda took a few deep breaths to remain calm. She couldn't show how anxious she was or else they might suspect her. Rob already did, and he eyed her when she walked in. Of course, he was there early.

"Now," Rob said, striding up to Seth, "we need to change me now."

Seth sighed angrily. "You will respect me," he demanded. "There is a process," and with a sneer, he turned to the others.

Miranda counted 22 people and wondered how many others would come to this meeting. It might be easier if there were more people and she could get lost in the crowd, but it would also mean more people who would attack her if they saw her sneaking away.

Seth moved around the room, greeting everyone as they arrived. He kept Miranda on his arm, close to him. Miranda took in everything, plotted escape routes and went through various scenarios. She didn't have much time. Soon everyone would be here and they would perform the ceremony, and then leave for City 92986. That was the plan.

Another 50 people arrived before 10 hour and Seth left her side to stand in front of them all. Miranda took an unnoticeable step towards the back of the room. After making the rounds to greet everyone, Seth had left her near the hallway that led to her prison and she wasn't sure if there was a way out. The only way out she knew of was at the back of the room.

"Good morning everyone," Seth said, looking down at everyone from the altar. "Welcome. Today begins a new era for evil and you are all here to bear witness." Seth waited for the applause to die down. "Miranda and I," Seth paused and looked at her. Miranda stopped her slow move towards the back and smiled around at everyone. She tried not to look guilty. "We are going to take our evil way to a whole new level. We are going to take over Utopia and corrupt its way. We are going to fix this disturbing peace, this supposed perfect way. The Utopians do not understand that a civilization cannot be purely good."

Agreement echoed through the room. Miranda tried not to roll her eyes. It had to be one of the worst speeches she had ever heard. She took another step back, but she worried Seth would look at her again. She couldn't be hasty. There were people behind her so she had to make it look like she was just shifting from foot to foot. It was going to take forever. She needed a distraction. Seth was still talking about her so she stood still.

"Miranda has not even begun to use her powers to their fullest potential. I will help her unlock these and she will stand by my side."

Miranda managed a revering smile at him. She frowned when he moved his eyes away. Did he know something that she didn't about her powers? This was it then. She needed to stay and figure this out.

"Without evil," Seth continued, "there would be no balance. We must do more. Small sporadic attacks are not effective and so I have come up with a plan. We need to attack daily and in larger numbers. Fear will feed our evil. It is my plan to rule this planet!"

Everyone erupted in applause and Seth opened his arms wide, soaking it all in. Miranda was forced to join in or look suspicious. She definitely needed to get away. Or did she? She had infiltrated them. She needed to find out what Seth knew about her powers. Should she sacrifice herself to infiltrate them further? Isn't that what a hero did? She felt faint and put her hand up against the wall right beside the entrance of the hallway to her prison cell. She took a few deep breaths trying to calm herself. She needed to think. Should she stay or go? How far was she willing to go to save the planet?

Her internal dilemma was cut short when a hand touched hers. She gasped and whipped her head around.

Relief flooded through her. Alex had found her, finally. She looked back towards the crowd. They were starting the ceremony for Rob, so she took a chance and stepped around the corner out of sight where Alex engulfed her in his arms.

"Let me make your decision simple," he whispered, "you are coming with me."

"How can you hear my thoughts?" Miranda whispered back, refusing to let go of him. Relief flooded her.

"I can always hear you," Alex said, bringing a hand up to her face.

Miranda looked up at him, questioningly.

He gave her a half smile, "OK, not all the time, but I could now."

Miranda smiled and squeezed him tighter.

"Come with me," Alex said, pulling away, "I found a back way out but first, we should put this back on." Alex pulled out her necklace which brightened her smile more. He leaned forward and tied it around her neck.

"Thank you," Miranda said, looking down at it as it fell onto her chest. It felt alive against her skin. She looked back up at Alex. He looked about ready to pour out his heart again so she put a hand up. "We will talk soon. We have to go now before they notice."

Alex nodded. As he reached for her hand again, chaos erupted. Loud bangs and screams rang throughout the hall and one familiar voice was heard above the screams.

"You fool," Rob shouted. "You and your son are not worthy to hold the power. You were tricked by the third child, and I will end you now." The ground started to shake violently.

Miranda's eyes widened and she chanced a peek into the hall. She watched as more than half the room turned on Seth, their chief. Nathan tried to get to him but he died first from the deluge of red beams. They sliced through him like he was invisible. Seth was in shock, but he quickly went on the attack.

Alex tried to pull Miranda away, but she refused.

"We have to know, Alex," Miranda whispered, "We have to know what we are up against."

"Once they kill Seth or Rob, they will look for you," Alex pleaded. "We need to go now, please. I am not ready. I need time to learn."

Miranda looked at Alex's face. It didn't take any more convincing. By staying, she would put him in danger. She nodded, "Let's go."

Alex ran, pulling her along without a look back. Miranda struggled to keep up and as she raced away, her mind raced. This wasn't a good idea. They were bound to come after her right away. What would they do? Kill the remaining family she had? All her friends?

They had to crouch down as they made their way out what must have been an emergency exit. As they reached the outside, the fresh air, Miranda asked for Alex's phone. She, at least, had to warn everyone. Miranda pushed Alicia's name first. It was going to be difficult to hold the phone straight and talk, but neither of them would risk slowing down.

Alicia answered.

"Miranda?"

"Alicia, are you home right now?"

"Yes?"

"You have to get out. Please. They are after me," Miranda said. "Take your parents and go somewhere."

Alicia didn't need convincing. She looked determined and nodded.

"Call as many people from the building as you can and get them out," Miranda said before she hung up.

She dialled Rebecca next and went through the same conversation. Rebecca also needed no convincing. She would get her friends and get out.

Finally, she called Evan and before Evan even said a word, Miranda was shouting, "Evan, get Greta and Griffin and meet us on the roof in 5 minutes."

"Are you alright?" Evan asked.

"They are going to come after us, Evan," Miranda said, scared. "We have to go. I have already warned Alicia and Rebecca. Call the studio and suspend the show. Tell everyone you know to leave, as many people as you can in the next 5 minutes."

"What?"

"I have a plan, just do as I say."

Evan nodded, "See you soon."

Alex took his phone back and called his mother, as they continued to run. He told her to get his grandfather and go. She also did not need any convincing. He assured her that he would call her in a couple days and not to leave wherever they were hiding until his call.

They reached Alex's car and he raced around to the driver's side, tossing his phone in first. Miranda jumped into the passenger seat.

Without setting the destination, Alex started off, driving manually and as quickly as possible. He stayed close to the buildings, making a direct line to their apartment.

Miranda could see the building emptying as they pulled up. Several cars were leaving the parking garage. As told, Evan, Griffin and Greta were waiting on the roof.

"Where are we going?" Alex asked as he made a hasty descent to the roof of their building.

"To the space centre, we're getting out," Miranda said, and nothing more.

As soon as the car touched down, Miranda got out. Evan threw his arms around her, hugging her tight. Greta put her arms around the both of them and Griffin joined.

Miranda held back her emotions, there was no time. She demanded everyone get in the car and they were up in the air again in minutes.

Griffin leaned forward from the backseat and put a hand on Alex's shoulder, "Thank you for bringing her home safe."

Alex forced a smile, "I did not have to do much. She was on her way home already."

Miranda caught his glance and smiled slightly.

"What happened?" Greta asked.

"I have a feeling there is a new chief," Miranda frowned. "There was a fight and Alex and I were able to sneak away without notice, but I am sure they know now. There's no telling how many people they will kill to find me again."

"How did you find her, Alex?" Evan asked, curious and a little disappointed that Alex had not taken him along.

Alex looked out the window, thinking about the day of the rockslide when he went back and found the cave opening. He spent the night in the cave last night alone, studying it and looking for ways out.

"You lied?" Evan asked.

"Avoided the truth, as you both would put it," Alex said and frowned. "I could not risk you all knowing and wanting to come with me. It was better this way."

"So last night when you agreed with Griffin that we should stop looking, you already knew you would not follow that plan," Evan stated.

Alex nodded.

Evan made a face of disapproval. He did not like that his best friend put himself in danger alone, but it had brought his sister back. He sighed, "So where are we going?"

"Away," Miranda answered.

"But..." Evan started to say, but Miranda silenced him with a look back.

They reached the space centre as the ground started to shake. Miranda whipped her head around looking for any sign of danger, but nothing was attacking them. She looked out over the city.

It started out as a dark fog in the distance, but grew darker and thicker until the thick, black smoke was pouring out. Something was on fire.

"The building!" Greta cried, "Our apartment building is on fire!"

Miranda knew it to be true. They had reached her building and would soon find out that no one was in it. Or she hoped everyone had gotten out on time. They had to move. "Go inside the building and get Earth money now!" Miranda crouched to the ground, placing her palms on the grass in front of her. She let her power fill her and sent it into the ground. That should slow them down, she thought as she took some deep breaths. She didn't have time to lose consciousness. Alex bent down beside her to help her up. "You do not have to do this alone," he said, "I can help you now."

Miranda let him help her up. She closed her eyes. She wanted his help, and she didn't. She wanted to keep him safe. She wanted him to keep her safe. It was so confusing. She needed to think.

Griffin and Greta turned for the building. Evan paused, "Earth?"

"Just until I decide what to do," Miranda explained quickly, as she swayed a little on her feet. "I just want to feel safe somewhere for just a day or two."

Evan nodded and followed the others into the building.

Alex held her upright, worried that she might fall over, but Miranda took a step away and turned to him. "I have to find Tim," she said and looked past him towards the parked space shuttles. She thought she saw him. "I hope he is working."

Alex nodded and followed her towards the shuttles. Luckily, Tim was, in fact, exiting a shuttle. He took a fearful look around and saw Miranda heading towards him.

"Hello, Miranda," Tim said as she approached, "The ground was shaking so badly. The attack must be very close."

Miranda forgot any pleasantries and got right to it, "Tim, we need to get away fast. I need to get to Earth. Do you think you can fly us?"

Tim shook his head, "I have just returned from Monrovia. I am not allowed to fly again for several days."

Miranda threw a frustrated look at Alex and turned back to Tim, pleading, "They are after me. Please, how much will it cost? I need to get my family off the planet."

"After you?" Tim asked, taken aback, "Why? How?"

"We do not know," Alex cut in. "We just got her back. They took her."

"They killed my father," Miranda said, her eyes filling with tears.

"Ed is dead?" Tim asked, incredulously. He leaned back against the shuttle to hold himself up. It was a lot for him to take in at once. He frowned and put a hand on Miranda's shoulder, "I am sorry to hear that, Miranda. I hope you find comfort."

Miranda nodded her thanks. She was starting to lose hope. She had no idea how much longer she had before they found her. Would they check the space centre knowing she would be trying to get away?

"OK," Tim said, resolutely, "I will take you, but only if my daughter can come too."

Miranda sighed with relief, "How long will it take her to get here?"

"She will likely be here soon. She was going to pick me up," Tim said, "She will be happy to travel."

"Only your daughter?" Miranda asked.

Tim bit his lip, "My wife and son were killed many years ago by the evil ones. I know what you are going through."

Miranda's eyes softened. She had no idea Tim had lost his family. Their conversations had always been typical small talk, but had never been involved enough to talk about family. "I am so sorry," Miranda said sympathetically.

"It was a very long time ago," Tim said, "Katrina was only six. She is 20 now. I will go call her and see where she is." Tim took out his notebook and pushed a few buttons. "Get in this shuttle here. I will radio into the control tower that the occupants forgot something on Monrovia and we have to go back immediately," he said, then broke off when his daughter answered. He stepped away to talk to her.

Miranda led the way into the shuttle. Once inside, they sat in silence across the table from each other. The silence was only interrupted when the door opened and Evan, Griffin and Greta came in.

"We saw Tim inside," Griffin explained, "He will be here shortly." He turned to Alex and told him how much money they had exchanged. Miranda wasn't listening.

Greta took a seat beside Miranda and put an arm around her, "We will have to get that beautiful hair back."

Miranda took a second to realize that she meant her brown hair. She had almost forgotten she was a blond now. "It isn't important," Miranda mumbled.

"Is everything alright?" Greta asked. Everyone went quiet.

Miranda glanced around hesitantly, "Yes."

Greta shared a look of doubt with Griffin.

"I'm fine, really," Miranda insisted. She tried not to think at all. If she did, she might have a breakdown again. She had been fighting it for so long, but now wasn't the time. She needed to wait for a good time to cry. She didn't want Alex near her because that wouldn't help her resolve. She needed to be strong until she was back on Earth, locked in her old bedroom.

Silence ensued. All of them were trying to decide how best to talk to Miranda or if they should even talk to her about the past week. Did she need time?

Miranda ignored all their thoughts and stared out the window. She knew no one would be able to see inside but she still worried they would be caught before they could leave. She saw Tim leave the building with a young woman in tow and watched as they made their way towards the shuttle. It wasn't until they were 50 feet away that Miranda sensed something. It seemed Alex had sensed it too. He looked up at the same time.

Miranda didn't wait. She jumped up on the bench she was sat on and over the table, out the door. Alex was right behind her.

"Tim! Get down!" Miranda yelled as the wind picked up. "Oh no," she swore under her breath.

Tim ducked and brought his daughter to the ground as a red beam sliced through the air where her head had been. Miranda didn't stop running. She headed straight for the evil person, putting her hands out in front of her. A feeble white light sprung from her palms. She still hadn't recovered from earlier and the evil person easily dodged the slow moving beam. She recognized the person but didn't know his name.

"Can you feel it, chosen one?" he laughed at her. "Rob is the new chief and we are more powerful than ever!" To demonstrate he seemed to draw in a deep breath and put his palms out towards the nearest shuttle. That shuttle burst into flames.

Miranda gasped and jumped back from the flames into Alex's arms.

"You have me," he whispered to her, hoping it would calm the fear written all over her face.

Miranda's face fell. She couldn't risk losing him. Before he could react she picked Alex up and threw him as far as she knew that she could handle and set him down. It wouldn't take him long to get back to her, but at least he was safe for now. She turned back to her opponent who laughed even more.

"I suppose that will make it easier to kill you," he said and shot the flames toward her.

She allowed her shield to protect her. The dazzling mist surrounded her in full force. The flames seemed to hit it like a wall and they spread around, but couldn't penetrate it. She felt no heat from them. Without waiting, she attacked him. The faster she could dispose of this one, the better. She had no idea if there were others nearby. Her white beam shot out faster and stronger this time. The man was struck in mid-cackle and thrown backwards. He didn't move after that and the ground stopped. Miranda glanced around quickly, making sure there was no one else around before she took her shield down. As it was disappearing she felt the evil around her again. They're hiding, she thought as she turned in a semi-circle trying to see something. She couldn't sense anyone when her shield was up. She had no idea how many there were.

The ground started to shake again, this time even harder. The wind whipped through the surrounding trees causing them to bend at unnatural angles. Miranda expected the sky to darken but it didn't. It was the only stable thing in the chaos around her. The ground shook roughly, she could barely keep her balance. Thirteen people, both men and women emerged from the trees in a semi-circle around her. Rob was not amongst them.

"Were you going somewhere, Miranda?" Felix asked.

"No," she shrugged, "Did you betray your chief?"

"Seth was a fool. Everyone but him and his stupid son could see that you were playing them both," Felix answered with a smirk. "We planned to overthrow his leadership and kill the three of you but it seems you slipped away."

"Well, sorry I ruined your descent to the bottom," Miranda said sarcastically, "If you thought I was a fool, you were wrong."

"Ah but you came here, just as we expected when the others found your building empty. Trying to get your family and friends away from us?" Felix laughed. He threw out his arms and another shuttle burst into flames. "Where are they though? Are they in that one?" He set another one in the second row into flames.

"Just stop," Miranda said, "They aren't here. I was leaving by myself."

"Just you?" another woman said, "I do not think so. Alex was here, and you sent him flying away." She laughed and set another shuttle on fire, closer to the one her family were hiding in. Tim and Katrina must have slipped inside as well. Miranda couldn't see them.

Miranda silently hoped they would stay where they were. She would never let anything happen to them. "So, new powers?"

Miranda asked, nonchalantly, trying to steer the conversation away from a hidden family.

Felix chuckled again, "You have not even begun to unlock the powers you could possess. We will defeat you."

Miranda continued to look determined. "You are wrong," she summoned all her energy causing her shield to brighten around her, "I do know what I can do."

"Oh?" Felix asked. He raised an eyebrow and shared a smile with the man on his right, "We shall see about that." And they all attacked her at once.

Miranda's mist cracked and shattered but she continued to glow. She sent out a wave a white energy like a bomb erupting outwards just as the fire overtook her body.

Seventeen

★ ★ ★ ★

Alex hit the ground and fell backwards, his ankle protested the harsh landing. *What just happened?* he thought to himself as he slowly rose to his feet. The ground stopped shaking and he looked towards where Miranda should be. He sighed in anger. Of course she would do that. She did not think of anyone but herself. Alex took a few steps in Miranda's direction, limping slightly, and that was when the ground started to shake violently. He tried to manoeuvre as fast as he could through the parked space shuttles, and he watched as a few of them in the distance caught on fire. Suddenly, he had a sharp pain in his chest.

Moments after, a shockwave pulsed through the air and he was knocked off his feet. He got up quickly and ran, ignoring the pain. When he came to the front of the shuttles, he saw her lying on the ground. He saw everyone lying there on the ground. He yelled her name and dropped down beside her.

"No," he cried as he knelt over her. She looked unharmed but was unresponsive. He looked up at the sky, hoping a medical team would get here soon, and then he grabbed her wrist, searching for a pulse.

Evan appeared on Miranda's other side, his face aghast. He watched as Alex search for a pulse. Griffin closed his eyes, wishing this was all just a bad dream and that he had never actually gotten out of bed yet. Greta turned her face and buried it in his chest. He absentmindedly hugged her tightly.

"No, Miranda," Alex said, taking her face. "You are not going anywhere."

"No Miranda, you are not going anywhere," someone else called to her from a short distance away. The voice echoed, changing. The second voice sounded like Alex, as well.

Miranda could hear but she couldn't open her eyes.

"You have got to stay, Miranda," the voice said and again Alex's voice echoed.

Miranda felt someone take her hand and hold it tightly. She was standing. She could feel the ground beneath her, but she felt like she was floating as well. She slowly opened her eyes and gasped.

Alex stood beside her dressed in a robe of shimmering white like her shield. He glowed like he was filled with power, and Miranda realized it wasn't actually him. The person beside her was too perfect, too silvery. He wasn't looking at her, he was staring down at the scene in front of him.

Miranda followed his gaze and gasped. She could see herself on the ground, wrapped in Alex's arms as he sobbed into her hair. Evan was on the ground beside him, a look of horror and disbelief on his face. Greta was in Griffin's arms, her face buried in her own hands on his chest. She was crying as well and Griffin was grief-stricken as if he couldn't take any more of it. The scene froze.

Miranda tried to let go of the hand that held her. "What is going on?" she demanded. She looked down at the frozen scene again, "Am I dead?" she cried to the silver Alex, "I can't be dead!"

He looked down at her frowned, "No. You are not dead."

Miranda tried to let go again, but he held tight. She wanted to cover her face and cry. She had no idea that fighting them all would kill her. She felt nothing, how could she be dead? Her eyes filled with tears and she looked at Alex on the ground in front of her.

"Stop struggling," Alex, beside her, said. "You are not dead. I needed to speak with you."

Miranda looked up at his face, hopeful, "You can put me back?"

He nodded.

"But," Miranda paused, "Who are you?"

"I am the power of good," he said. "Or your own personal idea of good? Alex?" He smiled at his own joke.

Miranda stared at him blankly, wondering if this was a dream.

"Not quite a dream," he said, and shrugged a little, "but not quite reality. I need you to live. I need you to bring peace to this planet and drive out evil for eternity."

Miranda couldn't believe what she was hearing. "I don't understand," Miranda said, "I am trying but how?"

"Miranda, you are so close," he said earnestly. "So close that evil has exhausted all the elements. They are at their last."

Miranda shook her head, not understanding.

"You must learn on your own but you are missing the whole story. You must unlock your full powers," he continued, ignoring her question. "I daresay you have only just touched on them with this last attack."

Miranda looked down at Alex cradling her body on the ground. She didn't want to unlock her full power. Her full power meant that she would need Alex.

"You will have power without him, but you will be more powerful with him," he said, answering her thoughts. He looked down at her fondly, "I know you will make the right choices. You always do."

Miranda nodded.

"This is very important. You must go to City 1 and find the rest of the story."

"What story?"

Silver Alex smiled, "Why yours, of course. The Legend. It is missing."

"Missing? No, I have read it."

"Go to City 1 and look in the archives," Silver Alex insisted, "I must put you back now. Are you ready? I am sorry to say this does hurt a little."

Miranda took a second and a deep breath, though it felt like she didn't even need to breathe. Was there anything else she should ask before she was sent back? She looked at her silvery Alex again and knew that he would give nothing else away, so she nodded.

"Evil will not like my interfering, but seeing that evil cheated, it is only right that I make this fair."

Miranda stared at the Silver Alex again, not understanding. She wondered what evil did to cheat.

"Close your eyes," Silver Alex said.

Miranda's eyes closed and it felt like she was moving at light speed, circling the planet. She fell forward and hit the ground, falling back into her body. The pain gripped her suddenly. It hurt everywhere and she stifled a scream. She felt the arms that surrounded her stiffen as Alex realized that she was conscious.

"Miranda?" he whispered, pulling back.

Miranda's face scrunched in pain. She burned all over. A coolness started to expand, deep in her core, which made her cringe even more, but then she felt it slowly dissipating.

Everyone grew quiet. They watched her gasping breaths slow until she grew quiet and still. Miranda opened her eyes and locked them onto Alex's. She studied his face for a moment before she felt the blackness move in again as she lost consciousness.

"Miranda?" Alex said again. He felt for her pulse and found it easily this time. It had been so faint when he found it before. He looked up at her family. "She is alive," he said, in disbelief as he pulled one arm away and wiped his face.

Evan needed to check for himself and found her strong beating pulse before letting out a sigh of relief.

Alex gathered her in his arms and carried her quickly to the shuttle.

"Shouldn't we stay and wait for the medical team?" Greta protested as they all followed Alex, "She might still need care."

Alex shook his head and turned back to them slightly, calling over his shoulder, "I cannot risk another minute. More evil could be coming and she needs to heal. If she does not wake, we can take her to an Earth hospital. It is better than nothing."

Tim and Katrina saw them coming and opened the door for Alex and the family.

"What happened?" Tim asked as Alex passed him and headed towards the back, "We could hardly move the ground was shaking terribly. We hid in another shuttle after the evil showed. I was just about to come find you all."

"We have to leave, now," Alex said to them, as he laid Miranda down on the bed, "Before any others arrive."

"Is she alive?" Tim asked. His daughter was quiet, tears streamed down her face.

Alex nodded

Tim sighed with relief and headed for the front. His daughter followed him closely. Soon after, the shuttle was rising quickly, vertically into the sky.

Evan sat down on the other side of the bed, "Alex, what happened?"

Alex ran both hands through his head in frustration, "I do not want to talk about it." He stood. He was angry, relieved, frustrated and happy. He couldn't decide.

Evan tried to listen to his thoughts, but Alex gave nothing away. "Are you sure we should be leaving?"

Alex shook his head, "Your sister..." he said, running his hands through his hair again. He stopped pacing. "We shall just do what she wants this time, for once. I am sure it will not be for long."

Evan nodded and watched Alex start pacing again. Finally, Alex let out a frustrated noise and left the room to join Griffin and Greta.

Evan stayed with Miranda. He didn't want her to wake alone and he still worried that she wasn't completely fine. He took her hands into his, gingerly and let a few tears fall, happy she was back with them.

Griffin looked over when Alex entered. He was seated with Greta on the same side of the booth-style table, his arm over her shoulders. Greta rested her head on him and she sat up, seeing Alex.

"Is she awake?" Greta asked.

Alex shook his head and started pacing again. He didn't know what to do. Should he be angry with her? She had just saved them all again, but she had thrown him away!

"Alex," Greta said, "tell us what happened. Why are you pacing?"

Alex turned his eyes to Griffin, "Your sister threw me."

"What?" Griffin asked.

"She thought I would be in danger and she just threw me so that I would not be," Alex explained, his tone frustrated. "If she had not thrown me, we could have handled this together. She still does not trust me."

"Oh Alex," Greta said, "of course she does."

Alex snorted in disbelief.

"Think about it," Greta said, calmly. She reached out and took Alex's hand. "She was so upset when she lost Jackson, to lose you would just kill her."

Alex's face fell in defeat.

"She loves you more than herself," Greta continued.

Alex squeezed her hand a little. "More than I deserve," he muttered.

"We have to set things right with her," Griffin said. "All this fighting and nonsense. It was all my fault. I am going to make it right. Trust should go both ways. We have to trust her."

Alex nodded at Griffin.

"So, Earth," Greta said, as Alex took a seat across from them, "I have never been there."

Griffin made a face, "I did not think I would ever get back."

Alex sighed and dropped his face into his hands. He had wanted to go to Earth with Miranda when she was well, not like this, not into hiding.

"You will get to bring her back," Greta said, encouragingly.

Miranda was unconscious the whole trip. Griffin went to the front to help Tim navigate the Earth roads when he let them know that they had arrived on December 21 in the late evening. It had been a few months but Griffin remembered a little bit. The Utopians gazed out the windows as they rolled into town. All were in awe. The town was lit up with brightly coloured lights.

"What is going on?" Katrina asked. She smiled at the lights. It was the first smile since they left Utopia no matter how hard her father tried to comfort her. She had been desperately worried about the loved ones they had left behind.

When they turned onto Miranda's Earth street and pulled up to the house, they could see a tree in the front window, decorated with the same lights. The house was completely glowing with lights. A fat man in a red suit sat in a sleigh being pulled by some sort of animal with sticks on their head.

Evan, who had come out from the bedroom when they said they would be landing on Earth, chuckled. "What are these Earth people into?"

Even Alex managed to smile out at the cheery scene.

"It's Christmas," a voice came from behind them.

All turned to Miranda in surprise. Evan scooped her up in his arms, "I am sorry. I wanted to be there when you woke."

"It's fine," Miranda said, a little shortly.

Griffin stepped closer, "Miranda, I am so sorry. I was wrong. Everything I have done was wrong. I hope you will forgive me." He stepped in close to give her a hug, which she returned.

Greta hugged her as well, squeezing her tight, "What is Christmas?"

"A holiday," Miranda replied. Her eyes met Alex's. "We need to talk."

"Yes, we do," he agreed.

"But not now," Miranda sighed and looked out the window at her childhood home. Her eyes welled with tears. She completely forgotten the time of year. She had loved Christmas. It had always seemed so magical and that feeling seemed so foreign now. She regretted coming to Earth but could not turn back now. "We will only stay here for a couple days."

-End of Book Two-